THE INCUBUS
AND THE OTHERS

TRENT ST. GERMAIN

BLACK ROSE
writing™

The final approval for this literary material is granted by the author.

First printing

This is a work of fiction. Names, characters, businesses, places, events and incidents are either the products of the author's imagination or used in a fictitious manner. Any resemblance to actual persons, living or dead, or actual events is purely coincidental.

ISBN: 978-1-61296-735-6
PUBLISHED BY BLACK ROSE WRITING
www.blackrosewriting.com

Printed in the United States of America
Suggested retail price $17.95

The Incubus and the Others is printed in Constantia

For all of you who need a place to escape away to
when it gets to be too much sometimes.

Turn the page, and let's go on a journey…

THE INCUBUS
AND THE OTHERS

PROLOGUE

North of Monroe, Louisiana – 1872

"There must be something that can be done to save his life," implored the man with the dark blond hair and tired blue eyes.

He sat in a wooden chair, illuminated only by the glow of a kerosene lamp on the bedside table, as he looked pitifully upon the sick man lying in the bed only a few feet away. "First my wife, then my children. And now him? He's all I have left."

"I'm sorry, Mr. Ogden. I've done all I can for Adam," Doctor Lewis said. "There's nothing more I can do."

The labored breathing of the young man in the bed and the rainfall outside almost drowned out the conversation between the two. Teddy Ogden stood from the chair and went over and knelt beside the bed.

"Don't leave me," he pleaded in a whisper, reaching across the quilt cover and stroking Adam's sandy blond hair. It was soaked with sweat and tangled in a thick mess from his days-long battle with influenza. "I need you, Adam. You're all that I have left," he cried, burying his head in his frail brother-in-law's shoulder. *"Adam, don't leave me like this. Dear God . . . Not you too..."*

"T—Teddy...*Teddy?*" Adam stammered and gasped. His hazel eyes opened wide and then fell halfway shut. Adam turned his head toward Teddy, his eyes dimmed and darkened, and he suddenly fell still.

"No, come back to me!" Teddy cried. He felt Adam's passing without looking up. He lifted his head from Adam's shoulder, wailed and shook him desperately, though he knew it would yield no result.

Teddy finally surrendered to the truth, pulled himself away from Adam, and stumbled back to the wooden chair where he collapsed with heaving sobs. A moment passed, and Doctor Lewis calmly reached out and closed Adam's lifeless, half-open eyes.

Doctor Lewis wore a charcoal-colored suit, his hair and whiskers silver beyond their years. He had seen more death during his time as a physician than any man rightfully should, but he had seen nothing so deadly as this particular strain of influenza during this brutal north Louisiana winter.

"My children...my wife...Adam. *All gone*," Teddy lamented again. The flicker of light from the kerosene lamp cast his shadow on the white wall behind him. "Why? What is it that *I* have done?"

"You must hold strong to your faith during this time. I have no other answer for this," Doctor Lewis said to the slightly younger, grief-stricken man. "Only the Great Physician Himself knows the answers to these things."

Teddy scowled at the doctor and stood from the chair. He wore a button-up shirt, dingy from days of wear. His own dark blond hair was uncombed, unwashed, and oily. His sharp jawline remained prominent, despite nearly two weeks without a shave. His blue eyes were weary from the dismal plight cast upon the household during that time. In just a few days he had grown to look disheveled and much older than his thirty-eight years.

"*The Great Physician?*" Teddy asked angrily, his tired eyes growing larger. "I think he's a *horrible* physician to let this happen to innocent people!"

"Please, Mr. Ogden," Doctor Lewis protested, walking over to him. "You mustn't say such things."

"I can't say these things?" he asked, his right brow visibly twitching by the firelight. "The hell I can't. This God of yours steals my family away from me, and I can't say these things? Why couldn't He take *me* instead of them?"

"You're suffering a terrible blow, Mr. Ogden. Please, let me give you a sedative to calm you. You need rest," the doctor said, going back over to his bag near the bed. Days of little sleep were wearing Doctor Lewis down as well, and the winter rendered him pale and gaunt.

Teddy backed away. "*No, no, no.* I don't want to be sedated. I must face this. I give to the church, to my community. Why must I be punished this way? Is it because we've continued to prosper after the war? I have to lose the people around me instead? *Tell me, Doctor!* Is that it?"

Before Doctor Lewis answered, Teddy bolted from the room and ran down the long hallway of the second floor. Before he reached the stairs, he heard the doctor call for him to come back.

"Leave me alone! *I must be alone!*" Teddy yelled out, as he descended the winding, wooden staircase. Flickering candles mounted on the wall guided him down to the foyer, where he turned down another darkened hallway. He heard a crash of thunder outside.

Teddy swept into the study and closed the door, took a skeleton key from a nearby shelf and locked the door from the inside. He moved swiftly to an antique wooden desk, took a seat, lit a candle, and took a deep breath as he considered what to do next. He opened the desk drawer and looked into it. Teddy began to sob loudly again and buried his head in his hands.

He paused, took his hands away from his face, and stared back into the open drawer below him, as a bolt of lightning outside briefly illuminated the rest of the dark room.

"I mustn't be alone," Teddy said to himself, as he pulled out a Colt Dragoon revolver that had once belonged to his father. He stared at the barrel and the glint of the steel by the candlelight as he kept a grasp around the wooden stock. The only sounds were his breath and the patter of heavy raindrops splashing against the thinly-draped window behind him.

"We shall be together again," Teddy said, as he calmly looked forward.

Without further hesitation Teddy pulled back the hammer, hearing one of the six chambers click into place. He pressed the cold, metal barrel into his mouth and, with a sigh of relief and expectation, squeezed the trigger until he could not. The round exploded through Teddy's skull, and blood spattered the drape as the bullet passed through the window behind him.

Teddy fell lifelessly over the desk, all at once alone and together with those who departed before him.

1

San Diego, California – 2015

You belong to me, a faceless voice whispered into his ear.

"Belong to you *how?* Who are you?" he asked through the fog yet again, though the answer never came.

Marcus Lanehart's iPhone alarm woke him with a start, and he quickly reached over and hit snooze. Half conscious, he instinctively moved his hand to the other side of the bed and realized no one was there. No one had been there for over a year now, and the person he longed to feel there again was never coming back.

The dream had come and gone in a flash, as it had over the past few weeks. He did not recognize the voice. It never had a face, only a gender. And it always said the same thing. *You belong to me.* Marcus belonged to *whom?* It almost felt nice to belong to someone again, no matter how fleeting or contrived it was.

Marcus rolled out of bed the second time the alarm sounded. He walked into the kitchen of his small, modest apartment to start the coffee. For the past year, a strong cup of dark roast had been his only motivation for starting the day. However, Marcus knew that the world continued outside, and his responsibilities would not pause to accommodate the problems his life presented.

"I wish you were still here," he heard himself say. He dumped a scoop of rolled oats into water as he shook his head disapprovingly. When will all of this stop?

Marcus recognized that it was easier to still talk to him, even though he was not there anymore. As the oatmeal cooked in the microwave, he walked over to the far wall and glanced at a photo of happier times. No more. Those times were just a memory now and would never be real again.

Why won't you come home if you're still out there somewhere? he thought, as he stared at the other man in the photo. Like Marcus, the man had dark blond hair, but his brown eyes were a contrast to Marcus' hazel ones in the photo taken by the sea in La Jolla Cove, just a few years earlier.

"Landon, where are you?" Marcus heard himself say to the photo. Then he realized that no answer would come, and he walked back into the kitchen.

Landon had been gone for more than a year. The past few months of hopelessness finally began to convince Marcus that Landon would never return. He slowly began to accept it, but some days were still more difficult than others.

Marcus finished breakfast, showered, and then dressed in jeans, a light blue button-up shirt and a navy blue blazer. Casual Friday at work, sure to be followed by another weekend of wine, Netflix, and not much else. He grabbed his keys from the coffee table in the living room on his way out and glanced once more inside the empty apartment as he turned to leave.

Nearly twenty minutes later, Marcus parked his maroon Toyota Corolla in a multi-level garage downtown, a rented space paid for by his employer, the San Diego Sun-Times. It was a three block walk from the office, and about three hundred days of the year, the weather was ideal for the trek. He spent that time each day trying to make a reality out of the usual happy front that he put on for everyone else since Landon vanished. Marcus knew, however, the face he wore in public meant nothing anywhere else. Anywhere that mattered.

Marcus was enveloped by the light ocean breeze that drifted downtown, as he thought more about the strange, recurring dream and the voice in his ear. It was not Landon's voice, and there was never a face to go with it. He wondered if it was all somehow connected.

You belong to me.

Eight and a half hours later, in the middle of his telephone conversation with a confidential source about a developing scandal, Marcus received word of his father's death in an e-mail from his Aunt

Hattie. He quickly discarded everything else that had been on his mind that day. The chatter on the other end of the line became grey noise. The computer monitor in front of him and the notes he had typed blurred as his mind raced about what he must do next. He never went to or thought about home anymore, for good reason.

He knew he needed to check the airlines. Airfare would be expensive on such short notice, and he had to leave immediately.

It had been five years. Marcus almost called at Christmas last year but could not make himself pick up the phone. The lines went both ways, and his father could have reached out to him. However, true to his typical domineering form, Maximilian Lanehart had the last word the final time the two had spoken. Marcus' father always enjoyed being the one to put the proverbial period on things. And now, he had managed to do so in the ultimate fashion.

Marcus tried not to think about that final conversation with his father. He was still on the phone with his source, who he referred to in mixed company as "John X." "John" was actually a Jane, and it was all a play on words. Jane Waldenson, a city hall employee, was the one on the other end of the phone feeding Marcus what she had gathered from her own snooping.

"Maybe to keep it more accurate, you should just refer to me as 'JX,'" she told him humorously. "It's very neutral. I don't know if I like being a dude or not."

"That sounds like an energy drink instead of a person," he replied, but the laugh that would usually follow died on his lips. He kept the conversation going, but he wasn't there.

His father was dead, and he wasn't sure how he felt about it. A normal person wouldn't still be sitting at work after such a blow, but he tried not to think about what a normal person would do. Staying on the fringe and keeping himself on guard had been the only ways he made it through the last year

Jane was his friend, but for whatever reason he couldn't share the news about his father with her. There wasn't anyone else he wanted to lean on either.

"Well, Marky Mark, I guess we will have to get together and come up with a clever new name for me," she suggested. "Deep Throat is already taken, you know."

"I would suggest doing it over coffee, but we can't really be seen together..." His voice trailed off as he looked over internet airfares. Everything in the next 24 hours was in the thousand dollar range—or higher. He didn't travel by air often enough to collect frequent flyer miles, so it was the credit card or bust.

"People might talk," she said. "But not for the usual reasons." She laughed. "Or hell, maybe they would. How *out* are you? Does everybody know?"

Marcus was an average height with an athletic build. Jane was strawberry blond, a bit dumpy, and carried faded freckles that irritated her since childhood, for the usual reasons. In her mind, and perhaps even in his, they would be a mismatched couple in any universe—even if the circumstances were different.

A short laugh finally escaped Marcus but only as a cover for what else was on his mind. "Enough people know." *Especially when your live-in boyfriend disappears, and it becomes front page news at your workplace.*

He couldn't dwell on that. "The two of us having coffee wouldn't have any tongues wagging. Anyone we know who saw us would think we were friends... then they would put two and two together... and buh-bye, JX."

"Marcus, what's wrong?" Jane asked, her playful tone switching to that of concern. "You sound kind of like—should I have asked a private question like that? I'm sorry."

"No, no, it isn't you," he said, feeling numb—but not sad.

"I wasn't even thinking about Landon when I said that. I'm such an asshole. I'm sorry," she apologized.

"Don't worry about it. We're good, but I have to go," he told Jane.

His father's death was too much of a distraction. Everything was suddenly about his Dad. The man he hadn't spoken to in years—because of his relationship with Landon. "I have to talk to Peter," he continued. "I'm not sure if this will make it online within a few hours. Peter will want to go through legal and all that. He's scared shitless every time a politician threatens to sue us. One day he's going to drag and hold off on something big like this, and everybody in town is going to take it away and own it."

"Well, if you see some TV reporter doing a live shot in front of city hall with this later, just know it did *not* come from me," Jane assured him.

"Of course not," Marcus replied. He knew he wouldn't be watching TV later, unless it was from an airport.

"You're the only man for me. At least when it comes to city dirt," she said, in an overly exaggerated, flirtatious tone as she hung up the phone.

Marcus suddenly didn't care about exclusives or San Diego City Hall anymore as he set the phone down. He quickly booked the first flight he could find to Monroe, Louisiana.

The entire piece could easily bring down a city councilman and send him to prison for money laundering, but what would normally be an adrenaline rush of exposing a crook never came as his father's death and returning "home" took precedence.

For years he had had no desire to return to Louisiana, but it was now paramount to get there as quickly as possible. That numb feeling continued to sweep over him. He stared at the phone but did not consider the option of calling any family members. That could wait. That *must* wait.

Marcus submitted the story to Peter, his editor, and then walked out of the building without explanation. The biggest story of the last six months, but he wasn't mentally present for it anymore. His mind, his body... so *numb*. During the passing minutes, he wasn't sure what he should think or how he should feel. The news of what happened back home filled his mind as he stepped out onto the street.

A deafening blare of a car horn caught him off guard and brought him somewhat back to life at Front and Broadway, where he absent-mindedly went against a crosswalk signal. He shook his head and stepped back to the curb, attracting a few stares from a few other people who were waiting to cross.

"Hey man, you okay?" some guy in gray slacks and a silk shirt asked. No jacket or tie. He was apparently noncommittal on taking it all the way for casual Friday at his office.

Marcus nodded and didn't offer an answer.

He moved with the rest of the group when the white pedestrian light flashed on the crosswalk sign. His thoughts now narrowed only to getting to the parking garage, getting inside his car, and getting home. This was how he felt after Landon went away. On the verge of an anxiety attack, he knew that he must get away from people and just get home.

He would drive away, go home, pack, and then head to the airport. Anything else beyond that didn't register.

A homeless woman pushed a shopping cart, wearing a bundle of scrappy old clothes and a scarf over her gray hair, as she moved past the group.

"I'll be glad when I'm dead!" she yelled, at nobody in particular.

Marcus ignored her, walked faster and finally reached the parking garage. He got to his car and pulled away from the rented parking space. He eased the Corolla out of the exit of the multi-level garage, a little more mindful this time as he turned on to the street and careful not to pull into traffic the same way he almost stepped into it minutes earlier.

His iPhone vibrated for what must have been sixth or seventh time as he left downtown and headed up Fifth Avenue toward Hillcrest. Peter was desperately trying to reach him, but Marcus was so focused on leaving the city that he ignored the phone. *Just as he had during all those concerned phone calls from friends after Landon went missing.* He drove north from downtown, but he was oblivious to what was going on around him. He instinctively obeyed traffic signals and was subconsciously mindful of the other cars on the street around him.

Without any sense of the time that had passed, Marcus was soon back at his apartment on the western end of Hillcrest, near Mission Hills, packing his things. His phone buzzed once again, and some sense of the moment returned. He realized he needed to answer it. Peter was calling again, but he wasn't sure what he would even say when he answered.

Peter didn't give him the chance to speak first. "For Christ's sake, I've been calling you for the last thirty minutes," he shouted, as soon as Marcus took the call. "Why the hell haven't you answered the phone? I've got questions. John X says—"

"Everything's there," Marcus cut in. "Just like before."

"Well, *before* I wasn't worried about us getting our asses sued. This is a little deeper and more convoluted than before. Where are you? Why did you take off so suddenly?"

"My father died. I have to leave town. *Now.* I'm packing and heading to the airport in a few minutes."

"Marcus, I'm sorry, truly sorry about your father, but what about—?"

"I can't talk now," he said. He used his left index and middle fingers to lightly massage his temple. He felt a headache coming on but wasn't sure if it was because of Peter or the events of the past hour.

Marcus knew that even though his father died, his callous and cavalier attitude about leaving work with the story breaking jeopardized his job, perhaps even his career. But he couldn't think about it anymore now. It was the same as when he shut the world out a year ago. He would weigh the consequences of his actions later.

His United Airlines flight departed Lindbergh Field at 5:45 that evening and took him to Dallas, where the late-spring temperatures projected an unpleasant humidity from which he was protected in southern California. Marcus could almost feel the muggy air that awaited him as he stared out of his window during the descent into Dallas/Fort Worth International Airport. The lush, flat landscape at the end of the flight presented a stark contrast to the tan, sandy appearance of the mountains and deserts after takeoff. He felt oppressive humidity when the short layover ended, and he walked onto the tarmac to board the small express jet to Monroe.

Thankfully none of the airports seemed very crowded, even for a Friday. If they were, his continuous zone-out helped him ignore the other people. He only spoke to ticket agents, employees and flight attendants. Other than nods of acknowledgement or a brief hello he didn't bother to make small talk with anyone seated around him in coach on the first flight, or on the cramped express flight.

Once he landed at Monroe Regional Airport, he realized that he neglected to turn on his iPhone during several hours of travel. It was just before 10 p.m. in Monroe. The lights were still on for at least one rental car agency inside the small airport. Some sense of reality returned, and a partial fog lifted as he realized his options for leaving the airport were limited. Monroe was a small town compared to major cities with airport shuttles and around-the-clock rental car service.

The smartphone came back to life, and after a moment exploded with text messages, missed calls, and a couple of voicemails. Marcus was still out of sorts and unsure of which order to respond. There were three texts from Peter, the last of which read, *WHERE THE HELL ARE YOU??!! PICK UP YOUR GODDAMN PHONE!* Marcus assumed Peter was also one of the two voicemails. Another was from Jane, just as concerned but less abrasive. *Marcus, what is the deal? Please call me! I never heard back, and I'm worried about u!!!*

Marcus was worried, too, but it wasn't about satisfying Peter's and Jane's curiosities. The airport was about to close for the evening, and it was late. If he didn't hurry and find a rental car he wasn't sure how he would be able to leave. He was walking toward the Hertz counter to inquire about a car when a man's voice called out to him from behind.

"Mr. Lanehart?"

Marcus turned and faced an older gray-haired gentleman wearing a designer suit. A silver handkerchief dangling from his front pocket matched his hair and his thin moustache. Marcus had never seen him before and wasn't sure how the other man knew who he was.

"Yes?" he asked.

"Your brother sent me for you. I'm here to take you to Ten Points."

Ten Points. *Home.* The name of the generations-old family property had never entered his mind once during the trip. But the large house and its grounds, a former nineteenth and early twentieth century cotton plantation, had been there the entire time. Marcus hadn't been there in five years. It was now his time to return.

"I had been planning to get a rental, and was—"

"There's no need for that," the strange man protested, holding up a hand. He was about five-eight, a few inches shorter than Marcus, and very slim, but his voice was baritone and strong. "There are extra cars at the house you can use."

"If you insist," Marcus said.

The man who still hadn't introduced himself gave a short, icy smile.

"I *do* insist," he said. "Now come with me."

2

Tilda Lanehart poured her third Scotch of the evening. After she set down the decanter, she promptly lit her fourth cigarette of the hour. She took the glass in her right hand and clutched the long, skinny cigarette between her index and middle fingers. She casually stepped over to where the portrait of Maximilian Lanehart hung on the mahogany wall above the fireplace. In the great room of the Ten Points plantation home, Tilda's violet eyes met the painted, piercing blue ones of her recently deceased father-in-law. She took a sip of her drink and then a quick drag from her cigarette, not once averting her eyes from the large wooden frame. She had been fixated on the portrait for a great deal of the evening.

After a moment, she sauntered back to the other side of the room, put out the cigarette in a glass ashtray, and gulped down the rest of the drink. She contemplated another Scotch and another cigarette but decided against it. She was already forty, and drinking and smoking hadn't helped fight off the effects of time. The Scotch made her feel a little light headed, though her tolerance for it, good bourbon, and premium vodka had developed immensely during her years at Ten Points. No one ever nagged her about quitting smoking anymore, nor did they suggest she take it outside—as most people who still smoked were forced to do.

Tilda was a different kind of beautiful than she was in her mid-twenties when she met Geoffrey Lanehart. She often had to stare into the boudoir mirror and tell herself that—to look past the hardness that hadn't been there in her younger years. A few wrinkles had formed here and there, but makeup still concealed most of what concerned her. She meticulously kept the grays out of her long auburn hair, which she usually pulled back in a clip. She watched her figure and was careful with her diet, even though Geoffrey hadn't paid attention to her body or enjoyed it for quite some time. She was no one's fool and remained well aware of his other women.

On most days she had little to keep her company. The family belonged to the country club, where there was a gym and a tennis court, but her current participation in those things was casual at best. There were horses and a stable at Ten Points, but riding was more of an interest of the children and not a hobby of hers.

There was her husband, Geoffrey Lanehart, the oldest of Maximilian's three children. There were her own three children. Her oldest son, Travis, was seventeen. He was already born when Tilda met Geoffrey, who promptly adopted the boy after their marriage. She and Geoffrey also had another boy and a girl, Bobby and Maxine, who were ten-year-old fraternal twins. The children had their own interests and between household staff, teachers, and tutors, had less and less interaction with their mother. Tilda's relationship with Travis had grown especially distant over the past few years. Both mother and son appeared to relish the space that had crept between them over time. She blamed the deterioration on typical teenage angst, but it wasn't clear what he thought caused the divide.

Tilda's husband returned to Ten Points just before ten o'clock on the night of Maximilian Lanehart's death. At forty-one, Geoffrey Lanehart had preserved most of his looks, despite his occasional fondness for hard alcohol and a line of cocaine. He never did drugs in front of Tilda, but with the other women it was never a problem. Unlike his younger brother Marcus, Geoffrey's sandy blond hair was seeing hints of gray. Tilda resented the fact that men could sport a bit of gray and be even more charming and handsome. Her husband was aging well on the outside. He stood at about six feet, with the same slim and muscular build that had made him a star athlete on the football field during his teen years. He still enjoyed a good game of tennis at the country club. If the alcohol and occasional drug use were doing any damage to the inside of his body, it hadn't yet reached the outside. Geoffrey still had the same seductive smile and sexiness that won her over years ago. But the finesse that at one time caused her to fall in love was now one of the sources of their discord.

Sometimes Tilda wondered if their life together would continue to be cliché enough to end in a divorce once the twins were grown. She was prepared to take what she felt was hers.

She would put animosity aside while Geoffrey mourned his father's passing. Only he didn't seem sad. He looked to be deep in thought, a common occurrence for him. Tilda considered the possibility that he could also be in shock.

"Are you okay?" she asked, when he entered the room. She couldn't think of anything else to say to him.

He nodded without saying anything and poured a Scotch. She stood and stared at him, unsure of what else to do. The way he slowly sipped on the Scotch and rolled the glass in his hand as he thought to himself persuaded her to go ahead and pour herself another.

She walked over and put her hand on his arm. It was the first time she had touched him in a long time.

"Have all the details been worked out?" she finally asked, as she poured the drink.

"Yes," he said, moving away from her. "Did you talk to Bobby and Maxine?" Geoffrey never bothered to ask about his stepson anymore. Tilda couldn't fault him for that.

"I did," she answered. She then arched a brow and looked in his direction. "Have you spoken to your brother and sister?"

"No," he quickly replied. "Aunt Hattie took care of that. Thank God."

"I told D'Lynn they would both be staying here," Tilda said, and then took a gulp of her drink.

She pulled out another cigarette and lit it. Geoffrey never kissed her anymore, so she had no reservations about smoking in front of him. The thought of getting a facelift ten years down the road—after a divorce—entered her mind and then quickly escaped. In spite of what she told herself, the drinks and the cigarettes would continue and would age her soon. She wondered to herself what Geoffrey said about her to other women, then turned her attention back to the matter at hand.

"Everything's ready for when they arrive," Tilda continued, the disdainful look on his face causing her voice to trail off.

"That's fine," Geoffrey said quickly, taking another sip of his drink, in no mood to discuss either of his siblings.

His brother was an unapologetic faggot and his sister was a shameless whore—among other things they never discussed aloud. No matter what the circumstances were, Geoffrey would begrudgingly welcome his brother and sister back into the family home.

"It's been a long time since—"

She immediately stopped when she saw his jaw clench as he clutched the glass of whiskey. As if he needed reminding of how long it had been since he had spoken to his brother. Tilda wasn't sure how long it had been since he had spoken to his sister.

"He should be here...*soon*," Geoffrey finally said, walking over and setting the empty glass down on the oak bar in the corner of the living room.

The interior of the house had gone through various renovations over the generations. The bar had been added for entertaining back in the 60's. Tilda thought it looked like something from another era. She had been toying with the notion of having it removed. A grand piano, or frankly anything else, could better occupy the space. Again, anything to help her cut back. She wished she could age as gracefully as her husband.

Her legion of scattered thoughts went from decorating and bounced back to the situation at hand. "If you don't want to stay up, I can greet him," she said. "*When* is...?"

"I don't know when *she* will arrive," Geoffrey said, finishing the thought for his wife. Despite the divide, they occasionally still found themselves synced in thought. "Tomorrow maybe. Who knows."

"I'm here *now*," a husky feminine voice cut in from the doorway of the living room.

Geoffrey almost lost his usually solid composure, as he turned to face his estranged sister. "*Flannery?*" he said, in a near gasp. The tall, raven-haired woman stood at the doorway with her arms crossed.

D'Lynn, a short, silver-haired woman who had been the live-in housekeeper at Ten Points since Geoffrey, Marcus, and Flannery were children stood nervously at Flannery's side. "*Sh—she* just walked in," D'Lynn stammered nervously. She appeared to be intimidated as she stood beside the younger woman, who towered over her by at least six inches.

Geoffrey was stabbed by the fixed glare of Flannery's bright eyes. She had piercing emerald green eyes, and on this evening there seemed to be a fire behind them.

"You're very quick getting here," Geoffrey said, stumbling for words. "It's, um, good to see—"

"Bullshit," she said, wearing a sardonic grin and keeping her arms crossed at her voluptuous chest and shaking her head. Her full lips were painted a bright red, and her ivory skin looked more pale than the last time he had seen her. "You're no more glad to see me than I am to see you."

Tilda shot her sister-in-law a look but didn't say anything. She quickly put out her cigarette and walked over to another corner of the room and sipped her Scotch quietly, keeping her back to Flannery.

"Is everything taken care of?" Flannery asked her brother.

"The wake is tomorrow evening, and the funeral is—"

"Not *that*. You know what I'm talking about."

Geoffrey grew pale. Tilda turned to look at him was alarmed at how quickly the color had drained from his face. She tried to hide her unease from Flannery as best she could.

"Yes," he said, in a near whisper.

"Good," she said, unaffected by his reaction. "Is Marcus here?"

"Not yet," Geoffrey said. He realized his hand was trembling a bit as he went over to the bar to pour himself another drink. "So how long will you be staying?"

"Well, I'm not sure," she said, directing her eyes toward Tilda, who quickly looked away. "I suppose it all depends upon how gracious my hosts are."

3

Marcus was driven to Ten Points by the stranger at the airport, who finally introduced himself as Ruffin. It wasn't clear if that was his first name or his last name. It also wasn't clear to whom the car belonged he was driving. Ruffin acted as if the Lanehart family employed him, so the silver Bentley could have been one of the luxury cars from Ten Points.

The plantation home and its dozens of acres were situated on the northern outskirts of Monroe. Cotton brought wealth to the ancestors of the modern-day Lanehart family, and Ten Points had remained within the extended family tree since the original house was built in 1817. The first family home burned, and the mansion had been constructed in its place during the 1820's.

Building the large house had been no small task. Even at the age of thirty-six, Marcus still marveled at the white, castle-like structure. Its lights shone from beneath the signature oak trees as Ruffin sped the Bentley up the winding main driveway. The white house was a three story mix of Greek revival and Italianate architecture. Treated cypress logs were used in the construction of the mansion and its Corinthian columns. The original owner and builder, Theodore Ogden, Sr., the great-great-great grandfather of Maximilian Lanehart, spared no expense when it came to the best architects and carpenters of the time. There was slave labor involved, down to the handmade bricks. The house boasted fifty-seven rooms, and required a constant staff over the centuries to keep it running. The Civil War and Reconstruction, which brought down so many other southern empires in the 1860's barely left a dent in the Ogdens' wealth. The Ogden name at Ten Points was lost when Theodore Ogden, Jr.'s children died and his estate went to an orphaned niece, who eventually married a Lanehart.

The cotton fields were long gone, and much of the surrounding property had been sold over the years to other landowners. Even so, business holdings, a grain mill, a construction company, and other investments had escalated the Lanehart family's wealth. Particularly, Maximilian Lanehart's keen business sense and investment in a number of successful restaurants, hotels, an occasional nightclub and even a chain of supermarkets led to contemporary success. In turn, Maximilian's children were born into a life of wealth and esteem, and they never wanted for anything material. Much more of what they longed for never came.

Marcus tried to put the past out of his mind, at least momentarily, as Ruffin parked the Bentley outside the house. He tried not to think about his father and the last conversation they ever had, though Maximilian Lanehart was the reason he was there.

No one was at the door to greet Marcus, and he did not expect them to be. His relationship with Geoffrey was as strained as the one with his father. Tilda usually stood with her husband, despite any personal feelings she might have. Ruffin led him up the curved granite steps that led to the front porch of the mansion.

"So, Ruffin, what exactly is your role here at Ten Points?" Marcus finally asked. The car ride was mostly silent, and there hadn't been much small talk.

"I'm your brother's attorney," Ruffin said, pulling out a business card and flashing another short, cool smile. It quickly faded as Marcus took the card from him. *James Ruffin, III, Esquire,* it read, with an office address and telephone number listed below the calligraphy type.

"Oh, I see," Marcus said, sticking the card inside the front pocket of his light blue button-up shirt.

"Shall we go inside?" Ruffin asked, opening the front door as if he walked into the house unannounced on a regular basis. "Put your bags down. Someone will take them upstairs for you."

Marcus stood in the foyer of the great house, where the shiny marble floor and mahogany wall looked as if they hadn't been touched by time since he was last there. The same center table with the same lamp was off near the right wall. A huge crystal chandelier hung from the elevated ceiling, and a grand, winding wooden staircase began its ascent at the left corner of the room. A doorway in the center of the room between the staircase and the right wall led into the living room where Marcus could hear voices. He also detected cigarette smoke.

His first inclination had been to show himself upstairs, even though it would be presumptuous to think his bedroom from childhood was still available to him. There were plenty of upstairs bedrooms, but there was always the chance one of Geoffrey's three children may have taken up residence in Marcus' old room. Now a guest in his former home, Marcus decided it would be best to check in with his hosts.

He could hear Geoffrey's voice before he entered the living room. When he arrived at the doorway he recognized Flannery, though her back was turned to him.

Geoffrey saw him before he could get any words out. He put on a smile that didn't seem completely genuine or sincere.

"Marcus, you made it," he said, his voice smooth as silk.

Geoffrey inherited the business sense of the three, but he had a greasy, salesman quality that made Marcus uneasy. As a child, Geoffrey could turn it on and off more quickly. He spent years sharpening those skills, something their father had appreciated.

Flannery turned and gave him a friendlier acknowledgement—but it wasn't exactly the warm smile he was hoping to see. The last time Marcus and Flannery had been inside the house together was when Maximilian sat them both down and disowned them. The sting still resonated. Marcus and his sister did not remain close since that night five years ago, but there was no discord between them. Outcasts that they were, they stayed in touch with one another infrequently but more than with the rest of the family.

Flannery's overly pale complexion struck Marcus. Just as beautiful as ever, her life in New Orleans apparently kept her indoors. It surprised and concerned him that she kept him at a distance when his first inclination was to embrace her.

"You look good, Marcus," Flannery said, with a nod.

Tilda gave a nod but nothing else. "Glad you made it safely, Marcus," she said, holding a burning cigarette between fingers on one hand and clutching what appeared to be a glass of whiskey with the other hand.

Tilda still looked the same—pretty, but sharp and stoic and less glamorous and worldly than Flannery.

Geoffrey never changed. There was a bit more age on him, but his looks, which Marcus always envied, remained intact. Unlike many of his contemporaries, he still looked as virile and energetic as in his younger years. Geoffrey had no pot belly or receding hairline.

Marcus thought to himself, as he glanced at all of them and wore a superficial expression of congeniality, *none of these people ever called to check on me or tell me they were sorry for what I was going through when I was worried sick about Landon. He's probably dead, and they don't even care.* He tried to put it out of his mind for now.

Tilda looked tense as she walked over and stubbed out her cigarette. "Marcus, I had D'Lynn make up your old room earlier. It's still empty, and none of the kids have taken it."

"Probably still has all your old things inside," Geoffrey said, with a short grin and nod. He still clutched a glass of Scotch and wasn't making eye contact with anyone.

Flannery kept her eyes narrowed on Geoffrey and Tilda, and Marcus wondered if he had walked in on some kind of confrontation.

"Had ... *He* been ill?" Marcus finally asked.

Tilda darted her eyes away and waited for Geoffrey to answer. Flannery continued to stand with her arms folded across her chest and her feet at a hip-width distance apart.

"Not really," Geoffrey said, running an index finger along the rim of his glass. "It was a heart attack. Quick. Out behind the house. He never would have made it the hospital. At least that's what the paramedics said. I spoke with Doctor Rogers, Dad's physician. He says Dad didn't check out too well at his last physical. He never bothered to tell me though."

Maximilian Lanehart was seventy-two when he died. His own father suffered a fatal heart attack at seventy-one, so it made some sense. If he told anyone in the family about an illness, it would have been "Geoff," his golden child.

"Services?" Marcus replied quietly.

"A wake tomorrow evening, here at the house. The funeral will also be held Sunday evening. Here at the house," Geoffrey said.

"Why a funeral in the evening?" It was a curious thing to hear, and Marcus' reaction slipped out before he thought about it.

"You're in no position to walk in and start asking questions about arrangements," Geoffrey retorted, a cocky smile appearing. The gloves were about to come off.

Fuck you, you smug son of a bitch, Marcus wanted to say.

Flannery quickly interceded. "Daddy's favorite time of the day was twilight," she said, batting her eyes toward Geoffrey. "It's all to do with that. At least I assume so."

"Of course. I'm sorry, I didn't mean to—" Marcus wasn't sure why he was apologizing but felt he must to keep the peace.

All three of them stood in silence for a moment.

"The kids must be a lot bigger by now," Marcus said, since he couldn't think of anything else to say.

"Bobby and Maxine are ten," Tilda said, finally warming up a bit. She gave him a smile. "They're growing up so fast."

The fraternal twins were toddlers the last time Marcus had spent any sort of quality time with them.

"And Travis," she continued, her face growing glum. "He's ...well, he's a teenager."

Geoffrey sighed and poured himself another drink. "So, how is California?" he asked, with an insincere look of interest. Marcus sensed he didn't really care about details.

How do you think? Instead Marcus said, "It's been a rough year, but I've managed." He put on a fake grin of his own and hoped the conversation would end soon.

"I'm glad to hear it," Geoffrey said, setting his empty glass down on the bar where Tilda left hers. "I have some business matters to attend to in the study. That's where I'll be if anybody needs me."

He gave Tilda a brief kiss on the cheek and pat on the arm on his way past her. Her slight recoil told Marcus it was for show and any real affection between the two of them ceased some time ago. Flannery seemed to observe that, as well, and had an amused look. Marcus saw no reason to be humored about anything. Their father was dead, and Marcus and Flannery's presence there only reminded them of how unwanted they were by Maximilian in his final years.

"I hope you'll both be comfortable with the arrangements," Tilda said, keeping her eyes mostly on Marcus. He noticed that Flannery, or something about her, made his sister-in-law uneasy.

"Well, as tired as I am after my trip, I'm not in a choosy mood,"

Marcus said, offering her a friendly smile. "Give my thanks to D'Lynn for preparing the room. I hate that I missed her tonight. Did she turn in already?"

"Yes, she was quite upset about Mr. Lanehart, and I sent her to bed after she showed Flannery in earlier."

"She didn't show me in. She charged after me like a mother hen when I showed myself in, and she didn't seem *that* upset to me," Flannery said.

"She indeed *was*," Tilda tersely replied, keeping her gaze directed at Marcus. Flannery rolled her green eyes.

Marcus decided he would speak to Flannery later about her demeanor. After riling Geoffrey earlier, the last thing he needed was another heated exchange. But Marcus knew that Flannery was likely his only ally for the next few days, so he wasn't prepared to do anything that would pit her against him.

"Well, I hate to be so brief, but I think if you'll both excuse me, I'll turn in," he said. I left my bags in the foyer, so I think I'll get them and—"

"There's no need," Ruffin said. He had quietly appeared at the doorway of the living room. "I already took your bags upstairs to your room."

"Oh ... That wasn't necessary." Marcus was confused why his family's attorney was performing household servant duties. "But thank you."

"Did Geoff go to the study?" Ruffin asked Tilda. She gave a nod, and he quickly exited.

"If you'll excuse me. Goodnight," Marcus said to the women and left.

Once he was gone and out of earshot, Flannery finally uncrossed her arms and turned toward Tilda.

After a few awkward seconds, Tilda gave in first, broke the mutual stare and looked away, as though she felt defeated.

"What?" Tilda demanded. "What now?"

"You know as well as I do I could walk right into that other room and find out what my brother and that rat lawyer are in there talking about," Flannery said, keeping her voice low.

"It has nothing to do with you," Tilda said, walking over to a bureau where her cigarettes were stashed away inside a drawer. She pulled one out and stuck it in her mouth. She fumbled around for a lighter.

"That is a nasty habit. You should quit. Before you're the next one to die."

"What a terrible thing to say!" Tilda gasped, putting down the unlit cigarette.

"Are you afraid to die, Tilda?" Flannery asked. The smirk was gone, and her tone was serious.

"What kind of question is that?" Tilda replied, as she placed her hand on her chest in exaggerated shock. "Have you lost your senses? Your father is lying dead in a morgue tonight, and you're saying these morbid things."

"It's not a morbid thing to say. I think it's an interesting question to ask anyone."

"I don't agree. I really hope you don't talk this way in front of Bobby and Maxine. Please don't!"

"You need to lighten up," Flannery said, as she used her pinky finger to caress the petal of a flower in the vase beside her. "Look at this beautiful white rose."

Tilda squinted and shook her head. "What about it?"

"It's going to die soon," Flannery looked at the rose, as she continued stroking it with her finger. "It was plucked from somewhere, put in a vase with some water for people to admire its beauty. Fading beauty. But it will wither and die soon and be ugly."

"How poetic," Tilda said. "Or is philosophical more appropriate?"

"Wouldn't it be marvelous if there was a way to stop death in its tracks, to freeze the flower in time, but keep it here as it is, forever?"

"I didn't realize you had taken such an interest in horticulture," Tilda said, as she felt a sudden tremble spread over her.

"I haven't." Flannery's tone was sharp, and she was no longer entranced by the white rose. She looked away from it and stepped back. "Just an observation, that's all."

Tilda put the cigarette away without ever lighting it and closed the drawer. "How long are you planning to stay?" she asked. The look on her face said she hoped Flannery's visit would be as brief as possible.

"I'll be staying a little longer than last time," Flannery replied, only to irritate her.

4

The next morning, Marcus was startled awake at the shrill shriek of a young girl, which sounded as if it came from the yard. He sat up in the double bed. It was the same mattress he slept on as a teenager, some twenty years prior, and he had forgotten how comfortable it was.

Marcus got out of bed, took a pair of white shorts and a red t-shirt from his bag and got dressed. He walked downstairs in his bare feet. The wooden stairs felt warm and almost wet under his feet, as the ever-present mugginess of north Louisiana permeated the home, something he never felt in southern California. He stepped down and went through the foyer to the open front door. Tilda and D'Lynn stood in the yard and tried to comfort young Maxine, who erupted in tears as she pointed at something in the grass he could not see from the doorway.

Marcus cautiously stepped to the edge of the porch for a closer look and saw what caused commotion.

"I just don't understand. I've never in my life ever. *Ever!*" D'Lynn spoke slowly and dramatically, her thick north Louisiana accent like molasses.

The housekeeper had withered a bit in her older age since rearing the Lanehart children for the better part of two decades after their mother's death. Her olive complexion knew many more wrinkles than it had in years past. From this distance, she looked shrunken to Marcus, as well.

Marcus observed the carcasses of two ducks and a raccoon laid out neatly on the lawn. The ducks were obviously from the nearby pond on the property, and the raccoon had apparently come from the wild during the night. Except for their immobility, nothing appeared abnormal about the animals. In fact, they looked almost like they were napping.

"This is horrible," Tilda said, holding her daughter close to her. It was a little past eight o'clock in the morning, but she was already impeccably dressed in a dark gray wool cashmere pantsuit, with a purple button-up dress shirt underneath. Her hair was pulled back just as it was the night before but held by a different clip.

Marcus walked down the granite steps and joined the three in the yard. The cool morning dew on the well-manicured St. Augustine grass gave a comforting sensation between his toes he had forgotten since moving away.

"What happened?" he asked. "How did these animals get here? What caused this?"

D'Lynn's look of worry turned to relief and warmth when she saw him. "Oh Marcus, I'm so sorry I didn't see you last night," she said, rushing to him and taking his face into her small, gentle hands. "Let me look at you. So handsome. My boy, I've missed you so much." She kissed him on the cheek and hugged him tightly. Then she turned back to the dead animals with a look of concern. She kept a hand firmly on his arm. "Maxine started screamin' and we ran out. We just found 'em here like this."

"Daffy and Dewey!" Maxine cried loudly. She clutched her mother tightly. The little girl wore braids, thick eyeglasses, and was a bit chubby. Tilda stroked the back of her daughter's head and tried to console her.

"That poor child loves animals," D'Lynn told Marcus. "She has names for all them ducks down at the pond. I can't tell any of 'em apart, but she can."

"Do the ducks normally wander up here?" Marcus asked.

"I ain't never seen the ducks come up here," D'Lynn said.

"Somebody did this intentionally," Tilda said quietly.

"Who killed Daffy and Dewey?" Maxine asked, sniffling and knocking the red-rimmed glasses around on her face as she wiped away tears. "Who, Mommy?"

D'Lynn looked away and shook her head. Marcus sensed she had a particular suspect in mind.

Tilda let go of Maxine, took her cellphone from her pocket and made a call. "Geoffrey, I need you to come back to the house. There are two dead ducks and a raccoon out on the front lawn."

"What can Geoff do about it?" Marcus asked D'Lynn, who shrugged.

"No, it wasn't a dog or a coyote," Tilda said into the phone. "They're not ... they're *not*..." she stared warily at Maxine, then lowered her voice a bit though the girl could clearly still hear her. "They're not torn apart or anything..."

The thought of that caused Maxine to cry again. Tilda looked at her helplessly and stepped away. D'Lynn went over and put her arms around the child. Marcus walked closer to the carcasses but did not find any indication of what happened to them. He knelt down to the ground for a closer inspection and he noticed a tiny protrusion of bone from the raccoon's neck. From that vantage point, the necks of the ducks appeared wrung.

Tilda ended the call and slid the phone back into her jacket pocket. "It looks like somebody broke their necks," Marcus told her quietly. D'Lynn had moved a short distance away with Maxine. She walked through the yard as she spoke gently to the girl, and the two were unable to hear.

"Damn it," Tilda said, shaking her head. "Travis. He's killing animals now. What am I going to do with him? He's out of control."

"Do you really think Travis did this?" Marcus asked. "How did he manage to catch a wild raccoon and snap its neck?"

"How does a rebellious teenager manage to do anything? He could have used a sling shot to stun it first. Who the hell knows. It's just sick. Isn't this how serial killers start? What am I going to do about it?"

"Maybe it wasn't him," Marcus said, although Tilda's theory made perfect sense. "Maybe there's another explanation."

"I should probably call Geoff back. He's worried about rabies, and he's calling our vet right now to come have a look. If their necks are broken, then we at least know they probably weren't sick. No need to have a vet drive out here."

"Maybe it wouldn't hurt to have the vet still come and check everything out," Marcus told her.

"Maybe you're right," she agreed. Tilda looked at Marcus and mustered a short smile. "You're a good man, Marcus. I'm sorry you and Geoff don't see eye to eye and things have been so strained between you."

Marcus nodded and looked away. He had never seen things as *strained* with his brother. He had only seen Geoffrey acting as

Maximilian's puppet most of their lives.

"I mean it," she said. "And your father didn't hate you either."

"No?" he said, looking back at her. The new topic was making him uncomfortable. "I'm not so sure about that."

"He hated what you ... *what you were,*" she said, unsteady with her words. "Love the sinner, hate the sin."

Marcus felt the heat grow inside him. "Oh, I see," he replied. "He thought I was going to Hell for being a big ol' faggot? Is that why he felt the need to cut me off and not speak to me for the last five years?" He was growing angrier and louder. "Or in the past year, when I was worried sick out of my mind when my partner of six years vanished into thin air and he never called or wrote or did anything to see if I was okay? Actually, not a damn one of you did!"

"Marcus, keep your voice down," Tilda said, growing nervous. "Maxine might hear you."

"What if she does?" Marcus asked, his voice reaching a crescendo. "You mean the twins don't know that Uncle Marcus is a flaming homo? You and Geoff haven't told them the big ugly family secret?"

"No, we haven't," she said tersely, regretting she had complimented him just a moment ago. "And you're making a bigger deal out of it right now than we *ever* have. We may not agree with your lifestyle, but we never—"

"*A lifestyle?*" Marcus asked furiously. "A lifestyle is what kind of fucking car you drive or how many times a week you go to the gym! This is my *life!*"

"Watch your language!" Tilda snapped at him. "My daughter is only thirty feet away!"

D'Lynn left Maxine and quickly came over. "Marcus, Tilda, what's goin' on over here?" she asked.

"Sorry, I was raised with the Bible, and I believe every word it says. Geoff does, too," Tilda continued, as Marcus' eyes widened with fury. "Leviticus, Romans...go read the verses. It's all there. You're going against God with the way you live."

"Let's not get into this," D'Lynn said, moving between them. "This ain't the time."

"Well, Tilda, if you take the Bible that literally, I hope you haven't eaten seafood recently. You may also be in danger of going to Hell if you're the one who braided Maxine's hair today," Marcus told her.

D'Lynn snorted as she stifled a giggle.

"How dare you!" Tilda exclaimed.

"I'm not allowed to defend myself?" he retorted. "Where were any of you when Landon went missing last year? I could've used my family then."

"D'Lynn, do you hear this?" Tilda asked. "Can you believe what he's saying?"

"Marcus, Geoff, and Flannery are like my own children. I love them no matter how God made them," D'Lynn said.

"What?" she spat, looking down at the older woman. "You honestly think God made him gay?"

"Probably," D'Lynn shrugged. "I doubt Marcus wanted anything that would cause all this hostility between y'all."

"It is blasphemous to say such things!" Tilda continued. "The Lord is *not* responsible for any of that!"

"How do you know? Did *He* tell you?" Marcus asked. Tilda shot him a look, but an interruption from the front porch diverted everyone's attention.

"Holy shit! What the hell happened?"

A scrawny young man with dyed black hair and a streak of blue down one side stood at the top of the front steps. He dressed in a black T-shirt and black shorts. He wore a large, wide grin, and his skinny, pale legs were a stark contrast to the dark shorts. The grin grew even wider as he stood there and nodded and chuckled quietly to himself.

"Oh, as if you don't know!" Tilda yelled at the teenager, directing her anger elsewhere.

"Is that *Travis?*" Marcus asked.

His memory of his step-nephew was a quiet, precocious twelve-year-old boy who was neatly dressed and had perfectly-combed brown hair. He was not familiar with the swearing, black-clad figure that stood before him now.

"That is so frickin' cool," Travis said, walking down the steps and toward them. When he came closer, Marcus saw a small studded nose ring in Travis' nose and multiple piercings in one of his ears. "Did somebody shoot 'em and leave 'em there for us to eat later?" The boy's southern accent was badly misaligned with his pale, underworld appearance.

"Don't play games with us," Tilda said to her son. "We all know you did it, Travis. Don't even try to lie about it."

"Shit, Mom, I already said I didn't do it. Jesus, what the fuck—"

"You watch your dirty mouth!" Tilda scolded. "I didn't raise you to talk like street trash. I'll slap the tongue right out of your head."

Travis paid no attention to his mother's threat. "Uncle Marcus, how are you?" he smiled. Marcus wondered if the boy was stoned. "I don't care if you like dick or not. I think it's cool to have a gay uncle."

"Travis!" The tendons stood out on Tilda's neck.

"I have a black girlfriend, so I know what it's like to be an outcast in this family, too," Travis added.

"We are *not* racist," Tilda said, rolling her eyes. For whatever reason she was feeling the need to explain herself to Marcus. "I just think it's important to—to not *mix the soup.*"

"Oh for Christ's sake," Travis said, laughing loudly. *"The soup?* Really, Mom? It's not like I knocked her up yet or anything."

"Stop swearing!" she yelled at him again.

"I think it's time to go inside for some breakfast. Tarva is helpin' me in the kitchen this mornin', and I think blueberry pancakes may be on the menu," D'Lynn told Maxine, putting a short arm around the chubby girl. "Ain't those your favorite?"

Maxine was still sniffling but managed a nod.

"Travis, you're skinny as a broomstick. Come inside. You need to eat, too," D'Lynn told him.

"In a minute," Travis said, his grin gone. He stood with skinny ivory arms folded, staring down at the three carcasses. "So how do you think they died?" he asked, not taking his eyes off the dead animals.

"Travis, *please,*" Tilda said, shaking her head.

"Mom, I swear, I didn't do this!" he said, sounding more serious.

"Looks like their necks were wrung. All of them," Marcus said.

"He knows how they died," muttered Tilda. The sound of a truck coming up the driveway caused her to turn. "Well, that was quick," she said.

"Is that Doctor Colson?" Travis asked.

"Yes," Tilda said, her tone short and aggravated. "I should make *you* pay whatever he charges us for this little visit."

34

"*Colson?*" Marcus asked, a wave of familiarity coming over him.

The driver of the blue Ford F-250 parked and stepped out. Marcus saw the leather cowboy boots first, then the jeans, then the man himself step out from behind the driver's side door. Zeke Colson also wore a denim shirt with rolled-up sleeves and a baseball cap. Nothing about him except the bag he carried made him look like a professional. Still strapping and as good-looking as when they were in college, he was tanned and his face bore a few more wrinkles, but the age he had acquired in the years since Marcus had seen him made him more attractive.

Tilda immediately stood with better posture and thawed, as she offered him a welcoming smile. "Hello, Zeke," she said.

"Hey there, Tilda," he said, then looked over to Marcus. "Wow, I wasn't expecting to run into you this morning," he said, seeming a little caught off guard. He offered a shy smile. "It's been a long time." His look grew more serious. "I'm sorry to hear about your Dad's passing."

"Thanks," Marcus said. "You're right. It's been a long time."

He and Zeke stood and held eye contact for a moment without saying anything. Tilda noticed and grew visibly uncomfortable. Travis took note as well, and when he realized he and his mother were sharing a thought, his grin returned—this time over seeing her displeasure.

"Anyway, we have three dead animals here," Tilda said, growing frosty again. She stared disdainfully at her son. "Marcus seems to think their necks were broken. I'm not—well, if we had figured this out sooner there would've been no need to call you out here." She shot a glare over at Marcus, who was still exchanging occasional glances with Zeke.

"Well, I can look at them and tell their necks are broken, but I'll check them out." He pulled latex gloves from his bag.

"Travis, why don't you go in the house and eat breakfast," Tilda suggested. "You've done enough out here."

"I kinda wanna watch this," he said, as Zeke kneeled down and began picking up and examining the carcasses with gloved hands.

"Like the arsonist who goes back to the scene of the fire," she said quietly. "I went so wrong somewhere."

"Well, I'll be damned," Zeke said, after a few minutes had passed. He set down the dead raccoon, removed one of the gloves, and began digging around in his bag.

35

"What's the matter?" Tilda asked.

"I'm not sure yet, but..."

"But what?" Travis asked.

"Will you shut up and go inside?" Tilda told her son, through clenched teeth.

Zeke pulled out what appeared to be a scalpel, turned the raccoon on its left side, and sliced it open with one swift slash. Tilda let out a scream and Travis a "Whoa!" Marcus stood silently and tried to figure out what he was doing.

"I don't believe this," the veterinarian said, looking up at the three in confusion. "This raccoon's blood has been drained. I don't know for sure yet, but I think it may be the same with the ducks."

"How is that possible?" Marcus asked.

"See, Mom. Now how the hell would I get the blood out of them? Believe me now?" Travis asked, shaking his head and relieved that he was vindicated.

All of the color left Tilda's face, and she looked appalled. But she did not direct her disdain at her son or the other two men.

"Oh my God," she said quietly and turned away.

"Tilda, are you okay?" Zeke asked. "I can still look at the ducks. I found puncture wounds. I can't tell if some other animal did this. I don't know of one that could. And it still doesn't explain the broken necks."

"I'm not feeling well. I need to go inside and really don't think I need to know anymore," Tilda gave a slight wave to Zeke and walked away without saying anything more.

"So do you believe me now?" Travis called after her, eager for acquittal. She walked up the steps and into the house without a response. He looked at Marcus and Zeke. "I think she still thinks I did this shit," he said, looking glum. "I was up in my room chillin' all night last night."

"Did you hear anything strange out here?" Marcus asked.

"No, I mean I had my earbuds in, my music cranked up. I keep the outside out."

Zeke was back down on the ground examining the dead ducks. "I just don't understand. The damndest thing I've ever seen."

Zeke stood up and took off the latex gloves a final time. "I don't know of any animal that would drain another animal's blood. At least not in a way as neat as this. A dog or coyote or wolf wouldn't be after blood. It would've ripped all three of them apart and strewn the carcasses around everywhere."

"That sounds really cool!" Travis exclaimed, the big grin returning. The small stud in the right side of his nose twinkled in the sunlight. "Do you think maybe there was some Satan sacrifice, like, right here in our own front yard?"

"I wouldn't go that far," Zeke said, holding up a hand to slow down Travis' imagination. He looked over at Marcus. "I'm taking the ducks and the raccoon to my office. For my own curiosity. I'll do a necropsy to get a better idea of what could have happened. I can't conclude anything right here."

"Holy shit, can I watch?" Travis asked.

"I'll let Tilda and D'Lynn know," Marcus said. "And Geoff..." he continued, remembering his brother.

"How is it being home?" Zeke asked, offering a smile and changing the subject.

Marcus gave him a look and then a grin. "How do you think?" he asked.

"How long will you be here?" Zeke asked him.

"I'm not sure. At least two or three days. Maybe longer. I'm just not sure yet."

Marcus hadn't even thought of work that day or anything back in San Diego. Maxine's screams had stirred him right out of bed. He realized he hadn't even brushed his teeth yet and was thankful he was several feet away from Zeke.

The night sixteen years before when the two childhood and college friends gave in to their desires resonated strongly for both of them. It happened after a night of drinking at a popular college nightclub long since closed. Marcus often reflected on it, but the remembrance never lingered for long, especially as more time passed. The two of them began kissing in Marcus' dorm room, and before they realized it, were almost ripping the other's clothes off and rolling around on the bed. After giving in to their pent-up urges, the two 20 year olds spent the night in each other's arms. Zeke awoke the next morning, quickly darted out of the bed they had shared, put his clothes on and left. He returned to his girlfriend, didn't speak to Marcus for almost three days, and when he did, he pretended as if nothing had happened.

"Well, let's do something while you're here. Maybe catch a movie, a game on TV ... go grab a beer or something," Zeke suggested, fumbling around nervously with his words and darting off in different directions with his eyes.

It was the first time in those sixteen years Zeke had suggested they do something. They had never been alone again since that night, and they had never spoken to one another at length after their sexual encounter. Marcus was closeted back in those days, unsuccessfully dating a series of young women. It pleased his father—and his friends. Zeke had a steady girlfriend since high school Marcus later heard he married.

"That would be okay," Marcus said, noticing Zeke wasn't wearing a wedding band.

The two of them seemed to share a thought. "I moved into my parents' old house," Zeke said, referring to the Colson family homestead two miles away. "I live there alone."

He and Marcus continued staring at one another. Apparently Zeke was no longer married and was now living the truth ... or testing the waters. Marcus was curious to know more, but there were other matters of concern at the moment. His father's wake would take place in a few hours, and he still had to get through the day and keep the peace with Tilda and Geoffrey.

Travis broke the silence. "So can I watch you do the autopsy or not?"

"It's a necropsy, and do you have an interest in becoming a veterinarian?" Zeke asked him.

"Um, not really," Travis answered, turning up his nose as if he were offended at the thought.

"Then the answer is *no,*" Zeke said. He turned to Marcus. "Let Tilda know I bagged and took the animals. There won't be any charge for my services today. I'm going to...well, this is going to be a kind of independent project to satisfy my own curiosity."

"Someone must have snapped the necks," Marcus said.

"Yes, but why would anyone drain their blood?" Zeke asked. "It makes absolutely no sense."

5

"Where is Flannery?" Marcus asked. "I haven't seen her all day."

"Tilda said Ruffin took her to a hotel last night," D'Lynn said. "She didn't want to stay at the house. She'll be here in a little while."

It was early evening, and Marcus was dressed in a pair of gray slacks, a jacket and a tie for the wake. He walked into the living room where Tilda, the twins, and D'Lynn were. Tilda wore a different pant suit that evening, this time something darker and more somber. D'Lynn donned a matronly black dress, and the twins looked as if they were going to church. Maxine's hair was brushed out with brown curls. She wore a dark-colored dress. Bobby, shorter and slimmer, had on a black suit and shiny black dress shoes. He stood and stared at Marcus and said nothing. Maxine was talkative but still eulogizing the two dead ducks from that morning.

"Mommy, do you think Daffy and Dewey are in heaven with Grandpaw?" Maxine asked, fidgeting and looking uncomfortable in the dress.

Tilda turned and gave the wall a blank stare as she thought about what to say. Marcus could tell that she wanted to tell the girl no. Instead, she turned back toward her daughter with a half-hearted smile. "Of course they are, sweetheart. There's probably a big pond up there that they're all standing beside."

D'Lynn looked at Marcus and rolled her eyes. Then the mention of Maximilian Lanehart suddenly made her sadder than Marcus had seen her since his arrival home. "I can't believe he's gone," she said.

"Neither can I," Tilda said. She rolled a silver ink pen around her fingers, craving a cigarette but not wanting to smoke in front of the children. "What a wonderful, godly man," Tilda sighed.

Marcus found it all hard to stomach and turned his gaze out of the window. Out past a large oak tree adorned with Spanish moss, and beyond the west edge of the property near the duck pond, the sun began its descent behind the woods in the distance. Darkness began to fall over Ten Points. Marcus noticed heavy, dark storm clouds rolling in, and he knew the rain would come.

Through the doorway of the living room and into the foyer, Geoffrey cast a shadow on the wall as he quickly came down the stairs, dressed in a dark designer suit. It was made of exquisite, expensive fabric Marcus could never afford.

"The hearse is pulling up the driveway," Geoffrey announced, walking into the room. "We must go out and greet Daddy. Tilda, where's Travis? Why isn't he down here with everybody?"

Flannery appeared behind Geoffrey in the doorway. "I didn't hear you come in," Marcus told her. He smiled and was happy to see his sister, especially after a tense day with Tilda following the morning's confrontation.

Flannery offered a short smile. She looked exactly the same as last night, only she now had on a short black dress. Her pale, yet ample, cleavage protruded from the top.

"I just got here," she said.

Geoffrey turned and looked surprised to see her as well. He then looked back at Tilda in an agitated manner. "Where the hell is your son?" he said angrily, in a near whisper.

"He's your son, too," Tilda snapped back quietly.

Tilda looked relieved when they walked into the foyer, and Travis came down the stairs. He was wearing the same black T-shirt from the morning but had put on black slacks and black shoes. His dyed black hair was neatly combed, the blue streak going in a perfect line down the left side of his head.

"I know you have more than one suit," Geoffrey said, looking at the boy disapprovingly. "Your clothes are entirely unacceptable. Don't even get me started on the rest of you. You're *such* an embarrassment! As soon as they bring Daddy in here, I want you to go back upstairs and change before the guests arrive."

Marcus felt a chill go through his body. In that moment, Geoffrey's voice and mannerisms were a carbon copy of Maximilian Lanehart. The angry tone, the belittling. Marcus knew Geoffrey would have also liked to berate Flannery for her choice of clothes. But she wasn't his child—not by blood or by adoption.

The family walked outside to the porch. Night had fallen, and crickets were already chirping an uneven melody across the span of the large front yard. A group of men, presumably from the funeral home, rolled the silver casket from the back of the hearse and carried it, pallbearer-style, slowly up the steps and past the seven Laneharts and D'Lynn. The faithful housekeeper cried a bit and dabbed tears with a handkerchief. The rest of them stood reverently in silence.

The Bentley from the night before pulled up and parked beside the hearse. Ruffin stepped out of the driver's side, wearing a dark, pin-striped suit. Half of a black handkerchief dangled from his front jacket pocket.

Another chill struck Marcus and lasted longer as the passenger door of the Bentley opened. The tinted windows made it impossible to see another person was inside. A sudden wave of nausea made Marcus feel unsteady on his feet. He reached over and clutched the bannister at the edge of the porch, as the coffin was carried into the house. He felt dizzy, and his temples began to throb.

"Are you okay?" Tilda asked, reaching over and touching his arm. Flannery also looked over at him but said nothing.

A man, about six feet tall and very muscular, stepped from the passenger side of the Bentley and closed the door. He was tan, with slicked back medium-length dark brown hair, and firm European features. His face was perfectly chiseled, from the cheeks to the strong jawline, and the cleft in his chin was visible from fifty feet away. Tilda stared a few seconds longer than she should have and quickly looked back toward the doorway.

Marcus regained his composure, but he still felt a light throbbing in his head as Ruffin and the other man approached. The stranger looked out of place in north Louisiana, wearing a tight gray T-shirt, with a black blazer. The shirt clung tightly to an obviously beefy but slim frame underneath. He looked as if he had stepped out of a Calvin Klein ad. His dark brown eyes made contact with Marcus' as he and Ruffin ascended the steps.

"Ruffin, I'm glad you're here," Geoffrey said, shaking his attorney's hand. "Conrad," he continued, next shaking hands with the stranger. "Thank you so much for coming."

"As I told you last night, you have my deepest condolences," Conrad said. His accent was neutral and middle American. He looked to be in his late twenties, but he spoke and carried himself with the demeanor of someone much older.

Marcus' headache disappeared as quickly as it had begun. He massaged his temples and realized it was no more. He caught Flannery staring at him.

"I guess we should go inside," she said.

"I hope you're getting accustomed to being back home," Ruffin said to Marcus, as he walked past with his sister toward the front door.

"As best as I can," Marcus replied. He stopped, but Flannery went inside.

Conrad quickly turned away from Geoffrey and looked directly at Marcus without any expression. He finally managed a friendly grin, but Marcus felt like a hostage with the direct stare the other man was giving him.

"I'm Conrad," he said. "You must be Marcus."

"That's right," Marcus replied. "And how did you know that?"

"Simple deduction," Conrad said, with a bigger smile that showed perfect, bright white teeth. "Geoffrey has told me everything about his family. I couldn't think of anyone else you could be."

"Oh I see," Marcus said.

"My condolences on the loss of your father," he said.

"Thank you," Marcus replied. There was something behind the extremely handsome man's eyes that put up a wall when it came to any perception Marcus wanted to draw. Who he was, his relationship with Geoffrey, and why he was traveling with Ruffin were things for which Marcus would later seek answers.

The extravagant sapphire, stainless steel casket of Maximilian Lanehart was set up in the foyer of Ten Points, just over from the doorway into the parlor. Marcus thought putting the coffin in the parlor would have been more pragmatic and less gaudy, but he wasn't the one making the decisions. Apparently the living room area was being used for hors d'oeuvres and mourner mingling.

Marcus waited to see if the casket would be opened, but it was not. He had forgotten to ask if it would be an open or closed casket funeral. In the South, an open casket was customary, but most wakes and funerals took place inside churches or funeral homes.

Flannery was standing over at the casket, casually running her hand over the polished silver. Marcus went over to her, and placed a hand on her shoulder, which felt ice cold, even through the fabric of the dress she was wearing. She immediately gasped and pulled away from his touch.

He recoiled, his feelings hurt. First she had rebuffed his attempt to hug her the night before and now this. He was confused over why she was behaving so strangely toward him. He would understand if it were Geoffrey or Tilda.

"Flannery," he said. "I was just seeing if you were okay."

She smiled nervously but kept a space between them. "I know. I'm sorry. You startled me."

"You didn't let me hug you last night, and you acted like a leper touched you just now," he said to her in a low whisper so no one else would hear. "Are you angry with me about something?"

She rolled her eyes and shook her head. "No, of course I'm not. You just scared me, like I said. I feel like I'm maybe...*maybe* catching a cold. I don't want to give you my cold germs."

She looked less pale than last night, but there were still signs of dark circles under her eyes makeup couldn't quite conceal. Marcus wondered if Flannery was abusing drugs. She had always behaved rebelliously. It would explain her absence from Ten Points during the day, up until that evening. Marcus had never judged his sister about anything in her past and hoped she would come to him if she were in some kind of trouble. He decided to keep a closer watch on her during the rest of the trip.

"Oh, I see," he said, straining a short smile to cover his thoughts. It was hard to tell what she was thinking by looking at her. She had shown little emotion both times he had seen her.

Flannery walked away and left Marcus at the casket. For Marcus, it was nothing more than a shiny case that held a man who he would never see again. He turned toward the living room and nearly ran into Conrad, who had been standing behind him.

"My condolences on the loss of your father," he said, the dark brown eyes piercing Marcus again.

"You already said that," Marcus said, wanting to get away from him.

Conrad gave an apologetic grin and a slight shake of the head at his own mistake. "You're right, forgive me. But I really am sorry. I know what it's like to lose someone close to you unexpectedly."

"We weren't really that close," Marcus said, turning to walk away. He wished there was someone there whom he trusted enough to inquire about this Conrad fellow.

Guests began pouring in during the next half hour, including Aunt Hattie, the flamboyant younger sister of Maximilian Lanehart. She strolled in with a large white smile, wavy dyed-yellow hair cut into a bob, and a low-cut sparkling black dress with more cleavage poking out than Flannery ever dreamed of putting on display. It looked to Marcus as if her face was a little stiffer and tighter than the last time he had seen her.

Aunt Hattie had grown up at Ten Points, like all the other Laneharts. At the age of eighteen, she dropped out of college and married her first husband, the wealthy attorney son of another prominent north Monroe family. She was now sixty-eight, but she only let the official records and a Google search tell the world that fact. She didn't discuss how old she was with anyone, and tried to pass herself off as forty-eight to strangers.

"Oh, you look wonderful," she said, holding Marcus' face with well-manicured fingernails and soft, tiny hands.

"Well, so do you," Marcus said, trying to avert his eyes from her manufactured bosom. "You never change."

She smiled and waved away the compliment. Her bright red fingernails were long and lethal, and he hoped she had them under control. "It's the diet and exercise. It's what keeps you young."

He doubted that was all but smiled in agreement with her. "How is...?" he struggled for the name of her latest husband but couldn't recall what it was.

She looked confused. "How is *who*, sugar?"

"Raymond?"

"Oh, no, you're thinkin' about Derrick. Raymond was before that. But Derrick and I are divorced now, too." She picked up an hors d'oeuvre from a platter and nibbled at it. "Oh my word. Who is that hot, tall drink of water over there?" she asked, in a near swoon, as she spied Conrad across the room. He was in a conversation with Geoffrey and Ruffin.

"I'm not sure," Marcus said, keeping a neutral tone. "He arrived with that lawyer Ruffin who works for Geoff."

"Well, honey, you have to find out," Aunt Hattie said, nudging him with an elbow. "Do you think he plays for your team or mine? Wanna see which one of us can *find out?*"

"I don't think—"

"Oh, what a hunk of man. Such a young buck. I bet he could do things—"

"He's all yours," Marcus said, using that as his exit and escape from the conversation. Part of him had hoped Aunt Hattie could explain to him who Conrad was. She obviously didn't know anything about him, except that he ignited her cougar instincts.

Conrad looked directly at Marcus from across the room. He gave a smile and a nod as he continued his conversation with Geoffrey and Ruffin. Marcus quickly looked away and nervously went over to the bar, where a hired bartender in a white dress shirt, dark vest and bow tie was serving drinks.

"May I please have a Stoli neat?" Marcus asked. The bartender looked confused. Marcus had forgotten where he was. "Never mind, just a vodka tonic," he said.

Marcus took his drink and found Flannery alone over near a corner. "You should eat something," he told her.

She snapped out of an apparent daze. "Wh—what?"

"Food," Marcus said, smiling at her. "It will maybe help your cold and keep you from getting sick."

"Oh," she said, nodding. "I'm not that hungry."

He noticed she too seemed captivated with Conrad after seemingly not noticing him on the porch earlier. Now she couldn't take her eyes off him. The man was extremely good-looking, but Marcus didn't understand why Tilda, Aunt Hattie, and now, Flannery, were all so enamored by him.

"Do you know him?" Marcus asked.

"Do I know *who?*" she asked, appearing confused and shaking her head. She was in a fog, and the thought of drugs crept back into Marcus' mind.

"Conrad, the guy who came here with Ruffin," Marcus said, keeping his eyes intently on her. Her actions and behavior were too aloof for his liking. "Do you know him?"

Flannery made a face and shook her head. She snapped out of whatever consumed her and looked at Marcus. "Never seen him before in my life," she said and walked away.

Marcus stood alone with his drink and scanned the crowd filling up the living room. Travis was back, now wearing a suit, grinning and with his arms around a pretty girl with long, curly hair as dark as his, but naturally so. She was African-American, almost as thin as Travis, and acted in a timid manner, as he paraded her around the room. Marcus assumed she was the girlfriend Travis had spoken of earlier. Tilda's disapproving stare at her son told him as much. It amused Marcus how some people claimed segregation no longer existed in the South when it clearly did.

The crowd inside the house was mostly white. *Mostly.* Marcus glanced over to a far corner of the room and saw an older black woman with salt-and-pepper hair staring at him with wide eyes. She had an anxious look about her. She wore a black dress and white pearls and on an ordinary day would have looked like someone on her way to church on a Sunday. She clutched a white handkerchief and was almost wringing it with her hands as she absent-mindedly played with it. She continued to stare at Marcus. Her eyes were sad, and it looked as if her chin was starting to tremble.

Marcus set down his drink at the bar, but when he turned back to walk toward the woman on the other side of the room, she was gone. Marcus glanced around the room, and quickly scanned sections of the crowd for her, but he could not find her. He walked out to the foyer, but no one was there, only the closed casket that held the body of his father.

He stared at the coffin, roped off and alone at the back of the room, just a fancy box that would hold his father's lifeless remains for all eternity. He walked over and put his hand on the lid, running his palm across the hard, cold surface. He felt an overwhelming desire to lift the lid and look inside at Maximilian one final time. No one was in the foyer. If he did it quickly, there was only a small chance someone would walk out from the parlor and catch him. Didn't he have a valid excuse for wanting to see his father's face? It had been five years since he last looked upon it.

"Would you like to open it?" a voice interrupted, causing him to jump. He turned to find Conrad standing there.

"How long have you been there?" Marcus was still unclear and curious about this guy's presence and interest in the family.

"Long enough," Conrad said, walking closer. "I think if you want to see your father one more time, then you should."

Marcus gave Conrad a smile. "Who exactly are you?" he asked.

"A friend of your brother's," Conrad answered, giving him the stare again.

He seemed to read Marcus, but Marcus was unable to tell what he thought. His job had taught him how to read facial expressions and body language, but Conrad and his dark eyes weren't giving away any secrets or motives.

"Did he send you out here to check on me?" Marcus asked. He didn't understand why, but he felt defensive all of a sudden. "I don't need any friends of Geoff's keeping tabs on me, okay?"

"You don't like me very much, do you?" Conrad said, starting to smile.

"I don't even know you," Marcus said, stepping away from him and walking upstairs.

6

"Oh my God!" Tilda moaned, bent over the antique oak desk in the Ten Points study, as thunder struck and rain fell outside. A naked Conrad took her doggie style from behind.

Her small breasts jiggled back and forth as he thrust hard and deep, making low grunts. She found herself getting carried away and then a sense of reality set in, an inner voice telling her to keep her volume down—as difficult as it might be. Conrad kept both his strong hands on her narrow hips as he moved back and forth. Part of her wished he would put one of those firm hands over her mouth because her faith in herself to keep quiet dissipated each time he went in and out of her.

His large, masculine hands moved up to both her breasts, squeezing them harshly. He pulled her closer, and pressed his body more against hers. She could feel his large biceps flex against her shoulder blades, and the hardness of his muscular chest against her upper back.

"Oh God, oh God … I can't take it anymore …" she moaned.

"Oh yes you can," he whispered in her ear, as he wore a smirk and nothing else. "And you *will*, damn it. You won't stop until I tell you to stop," he ordered, going faster and harder and causing her eyes to roll into the back of her head.

All of the guests from the wake had been gone at least an hour. The twins were upstairs asleep, and Travis had taken off somewhere unknown with his girlfriend. Marcus hadn't been seen by anyone in some time and was presumably asleep in his room. The thought of her brother-in-law then sent a shudder through her that was not orgasmic. She prayed he was in a deep slumber and the storm outside and what was going on in the study wouldn't stir him or the kids. Geoffrey had assured her the downstairs walls were soundproof following the last renovation of the house.

Without warning the door to the study swung open, and Tilda found herself face-to-face with a wild-eyed Flannery.

She gasped in embarrassment at having been caught but was stuck as Conrad clutched tightly, stopped the thrusting, and let his fully erect penis rest inside her. It was then Tilda realized he and Flannery were deadlocked in a stare over her head.

"You have got to be fucking kidding me," Flannery spat, looking at him angrily. "First, I have to watch you show up here and schmooze with my brother and his lawyer all night, and then *this!*"

Flannery broke eye contact with him and glanced down at Tilda, who wanted to get out from under Conrad but couldn't remove herself from his grasp.

"A means to an end, my dear," Conrad said, caressing Tilda's left breast more gently with his left hand. He began rolling his thumb over the nipple.

Tilda looked confused and grew even more uncomfortable. She tried again to squirm out of his hold but he was too strong with his right hand and slowly began thrusting his hips back and forth again, penetrating her, as he looked at Flannery and started to smile. "She loves it so much," he said. "Isn't that right, Tilda?"

The brightness of a lightning flash through the study's drapes went unnoticed.

"I don't think—" Tilda shook her head and was about to turn combative.

"Why *her?*" Flannery asked, as if her sister-in-law wasn't naked and only ten feet away. She grew angrier and disgusted, as her eyes ping-ponged between the two of them.

"Well, I'm not in love with her," Conrad said, making a few hard thrusts to get rises out of both of the women. He looked down at a petrified Tilda and grinned and then up at Flannery with a mischievous sneer. "Don't worry, my sweet. You know how I am. No matter how much I play around, I'm always still here for you when you need me."

"I don't care whether you're ever anywhere for me ever again!" Flannery screamed at him. "I don't give a shit about you and her. I want to know what you were doing with my brother and Ruffin."

"Well, ask Geoffrey," Conrad said, still moving back and forth like a stud horse.

"I don't know where Geoff is. I assumed he was in here with you and Ruffin, talking more about whatever the three of you were conspiring over in the living room earlier."

"Look behind you," Conrad said, his smile growing larger.

Flannery turned. Over in a dark corner of the room, Geoffrey sat in an armchair, his arms crossed over his lap and a blank stare on his face. He seemed in another world and unaware of her presence.

Flannery turned back to Tilda and Conrad. "How long has this little arrangement been going on?" she asked, her anger starting to frighten Tilda.

"Long enough for Tilda to know that not even her husband can make her come as good and hard as I can," Conrad said. "But then again, nobody's really been trying." He finally pulled out and stood there fully erect and on display for all three of them.

"Do you two know each other?" Tilda finally asked Conrad and Flannery. She stood to her feet and ashamedly cupped and covered her bare breasts with her hands.

"Get dressed," Conrad ordered Tilda dismissively, as he stood there naked with his raging hard-on.

Tilda quickly grabbed her clothes from a pile on the floor and began putting them on. A loud clap of thunder outside didn't faze her as she pulled her panties and pants back on and buttoned her blouse.

"Neither one of you is going to tell me about this little friendship you've developed?" Flannery asked. Her back-and-forth glances were now directed at Conrad and Geoffrey. "When did this happen? *How* did this happen?"

"Do the two of you know one another?" Geoffrey asked, finally breaking his silence by repeating Tilda's question, and acknowledging his sister's presence. His tone was sober as he straightened his arms and sat up more properly in the chair. He acted as if his concentration on a baseball game was broken.

Flannery laughed, but it was mostly to herself. She grew more infuriated with the lack of answers. "Do we know one another, Conrad?" she asked, looking back over to him. "Tell me what the *fuck is going on!*" she screamed at him.

Tilda was so caught off guard by the outburst she backed herself against a wall as she pulled her pants up to her hips.

In a flash, Conrad was behind Flannery, with a handful of her wavy black hair. He yanked her head back harshly, causing her to wince and gasp. "Have you forgotten *to whom* you are speaking, bitch?" he snapped, as the grin turned to a sneer. His brow was furrowed, and his carotid artery was throbbing at the side of his neck. His penis had gone flaccid, but that wasn't where anyone was looking.

A blinding bright white light pierced through his eyes and then they turned a solid black. Pupils, irises, eyeballs, and all morphed into two dark shiny pools. Geoffrey stood frozen in horror. Tilda was against the wall, her blouse still half-unbuttoned, too scared to let a sound escape.

A bright lightning flash through the drapes and another boom of thunder outside wasn't seen nor heard.

"All this for you, and this is the *thanks* I get, you ungrateful bitch," he spat in Flannery's ear, pulling her hair harder. The voice was different and lower, down an octave in a guttural tone. "I should snap your fucking head off right now."

"*Do it!*" she dared him, her eyes wide. If she was frightened of him she was doing her best not to show it. "Because I don't believe you're doing a goddamn thing for *me.*"

Conrad released her and disgustedly shoved her away. His eyes swiftly returned to their normal state, and he breathed heavily as he regained his composure. His angry expression faded, and after a moment, he looked back and forth at Geoffrey and Tilda and smiled. He pulled on a pair of briefs and his slacks as Flannery rubbed the back of her head and angrily sulked. He buttoned the pants and stood shirtless, a light coat of sweat still glistening on his well-defined torso from the sex earlier.

"Don't ever test me like that again," Conrad said to Flannery. His voice was his again. "You've developed quite a mouth, and if you keep it up I won't stop with threats next time."

He turned and gave another apologetic grin to Geoffrey and Tilda. "I'm really sorry you both had to witness that," Conrad said. "Most of the time I try to do a better job of controlling my emotions, and Flannery seems to forget her manners at times. Geoff, my friend, I would go as far as to say your sister has forgotten her place with me."

"Her *place?*" Geoffrey finally asked, dumbstruck. Tilda slid a few feet away from them but kept her back against the wall. She still looked as if she wanted to scream but couldn't make the sound.

"Well, since she burst in here like a woman scorned, I guess it's time to tell you the truth. I met your sister a while back in New Orleans. Back when she was—"

"We've known each other a while," Flannery quickly cut in before he could finish. "But the question is, Geoff, how long have you and Conrad known one another?"

"How exactly ... are the two of you involved?" Geoffrey asked Flannery, looking alarmed. "Does he have anything to do with—?"

"*No,*" she answered before he could get the words out.

"You lied to me," Geoffrey said to Conrad. "I thought that—"

"Geoffrey, what is going on? What are you all talking about?" Tilda asked, finding words but staying on the other side of the room.

"Geoff, you're a fool if you trusted *him,*" Flannery said. She shook her head at her brother. "And to think Daddy always said you were the smart one."

Conrad kept a smile and turned in Flannery's direction. "What did I say to you about that mouth? That will be enough from you."

"I did trust you," Geoffrey said to Conrad. The look of betrayal on his face drew disbelief from his sister, who walked over and stood between the two men.

"Let me guess," she said to her brother. "He promised you something? But there was a price." Flannery looked over at Tilda. "How many times a week do you loan her out to him?"

"Now Flannery dear, I never promised you monogamy. Tsk tsk," Conrad's tone turned mocking. "But as my wife, I suppose you have the right to know. Tilda knows my cock quite well."

"*Flannery is your wife?*" Tilda finally pulled away from the wall and walked closer to the three of them. "You son of a bitch!" she gasped at Conrad. "Geoff, did you know this?"

Geoffrey turned and slowly walked back over to the corner and stood beside the chair he had been sitting in earlier. "He's not even human, and I let him in," he groaned in despair. "What damned difference does it make. Oh my God," he cried out. "What's happened? To me ... to this family? *What in God's name have I done?*"

"That's what I've been asking since I walked in here!" Flannery exclaimed. "*What* did you do, Geoff? Why are you friends with Conrad, and *why* are you letting him have sex with your wife? And why the hell do you sit off in the corner and watch them while they do it? I want to know the answer, damn it!"

Instead of chastising and holding Flannery back, Conrad stood back and gave her leeway, crossing his arms over his chest and watching with amusement.

Tilda walked closer to him. "I think this has gone far enough," she said, her voice flat and a bit shaky. "I think there's a way we can end this. I'm not sure what my husband promised you or said you could have, but—"

Flannery looked over at Tilda with disgust. "You've been putting out for him, and you don't even know why? And you dared to call *me* a whore all those years ago."

Tilda stood up straight and walked over to Flannery. "I'm not a whore," she said. "I can still say that."

"Can you?" Flannery asked her. "You still think you're better than me? You've got some nerve—"

"Unlike *you*, I've never taken money for sex," Tilda said. Her anxiety over Conrad was fading, and a smarmy look developed as she stared down her sister-in-law. "After all, isn't that the textbook definition of what a whore is?"

Geoffrey sat in the chair and crumpled over, his head in his hands. Conrad remained closer to where the women were, his arms still crossed as he watched their exchange.

"You're obviously being used as a piece-of-ass barter in some shady deal between our husbands," Flannery told Tilda. "That makes you a whore, darling. And there must be one hell of a payoff I don't know about because I can't imagine why else Conrad would stick his dick inside some frigid bitch like you."

"Well, no matter what happens, at least I can sleep at night knowing my Daddy didn't disinherit me for humiliating the family," Tilda said, a small smile escaping. "Maybe I just like the way your husband feels inside me. And do you have any room to call somebody frigid? At least Conrad isn't having sex with a corpse when he's with me."

Flannery's green eyes flared as she finally lost her temper and attacked. Geoffrey saw the fangs before he could react, and by the time he ran over and tried to stop her, Flannery had already torn into Tilda's neck and pierced her carotid artery.

"No!" Geoffrey yelled, trying to pull his sister back.

When he tore Flannery loose, Tilda swayed back against the desk. Blood shot across on the wall and then the ceiling, as she stumbled and fell across the top of the desk where Conrad had mounted her earlier. Every accelerated heartbeat sent a projectile of blood from the gaping hole in her throat. Geoffrey's pull on Flannery had ripped the puncture wounds further open. Flannery finally wriggled out of her brother's grasp with a growl and was back on Tilda's neck sucking hungrily and rapidly. Heavy blood spatter was on several spots of the wall, and it was starting to drip from one area of the ceiling. Tilda's blouse was soaked and dark at the collar, her own blood was smeared across her jaw and covering her neck. Her look of paralyzed shock gave way to surrender. Her arms stopped writhing, and her eyes began to flutter and roll into the back of her head as Flannery continued slurping life away from her.

"Oh my God!" Geoffrey screamed, backing over closer to the wall. "Conrad, it's gone too far. You have to make her stop!"

"It's too late," he said calmly. "I can't control her when she's like this."

A mixture of suckling and crude animal sounds came from the old desk where Flannery remained hunched over Tilda. Another moment passed, and she looked up, blood streaming out of her open mouth and coating her chin. Her razor-sharp cuspids were on display and were twice their normal size.

Geoffrey bellowed loudly. He had known for more than two years what his sister had become. This was the first time he had ever seen the fangs out—or witnessed them in lethal use.

"That was so much more delicious than a goddamned raccoon," Flannery said as she licked her lips.

"No!" Geoffrey screamed, crying aloud. "Oh God. No ... no ... *no!*"

Conrad turned and tried to calm him, but Geoffrey became sick and ran over to another corner of the study and began to vomit on the floor.

"Is she dead?" Conrad asked, walking over and shoving Flannery out of the way.

Some blood still trickled out of the large gash in Tilda's neck, but it looked as though she was drained. He shook his head and quickly opened one of the desk drawers and began digging around.

"What is your problem?" Flannery asked, still licking blood from her lips. Her canine teeth started to shrink back to their normal size. It was impossible for her to pay full attention to a sick and weeping Geoffrey until her blood lust subsided. It would take at least ten or fifteen more minutes before it was completely gone and her immortal body and mind adapted to the swift and fierce feast she had just provided them.

"She's dead," Conrad said, feeling around for a pulse. "Get over here. *Now!* You know what you must do."

"The hell I will," Flannery spat. "I absolutely will not, and you can't make me."

"Please! *Please! You must!*" Geoffrey pleaded through tears. He stumbled back over to them, wiping vomit from the corner of his mouth with a sleeve. "Bobby and Maxine need their mother," he cried, starting to hyperventilate. "Oh God, please, Flannery. Please, I'm begging you..."

"Get the fuck over here!" Conrad ordered her, louder, his eyes angry again.

Flannery stood defiantly, staring back at him and refusing to move.

In a flash, he was at her side, roughly grabbing her arm with a yank that might have dislocated the shoulder of a mortal. Another flash and millisecond later, they were back at the desk over Tilda's body, his grasp on her arm still strong.

"Do it," he said, in no mood to play games.

"Oh Conrad," she sighed. "I never even liked her before any of this. Even before she took their side against me. I don't see why—"

Without any further word, he reached into the desk drawer and pulled out a letter opener. He let go of her arm, grabbed her wrist, and sliced it open with the letter opener before she could move away from him. Dark blood oozed out of the cut.

"You bastard!" she screamed in pain. "You didn't have to do that!"

"Feed her," he demanded. "Do it now."

"Flannery ... you *have* to!" Geoffrey continued sobbing. "What will I tell my kids? Oh God, don't let her be dead. Conrad, can't *you* do it?"

"You *know* I'm not one of them," he said, pulling Flannery by the wrist.

"No, you're worse," she spat.

Conrad turned and slapped her hard across the face. "This may be the last thing you ever do," he said to her, parting Tilda's lips and picking up Flannery's bleeding wrist again. He stuck it over Tilda's mouth and squeezed. Blood began dripping into her gaping mouth, but nothing happened.

Flannery stood speechless and in a state of surprise as Conrad guided her sliced wrist over Tilda's lips. It was the first time he had ever struck her. Yes, he had pulled her hair and manhandled her a number of times, but he had never hit her before. It made her wonder what he might do next.

Forcing blood from Flannery's undead wrist was a chore for Conrad. He squeezed and she grimaced as more drops of blood fell into Tilda's mouth. Whatever Flannery had feasted on the night before was likely digested. The fervor with which she had attacked Tilda said as much.

"I can't believe you hit me," she finally said, as Conrad released her.

"That's not all you have coming. I might stake you through the heart while you sleep tomorrow."

"You wouldn't. What would *your* Master say?"

Conrad went defeated and quiet as he realized she had him.

There was another bright flash of lightning visible through the drapes followed a few seconds later by the low rumbling of thunder. The pitter patter of light rain could still be heard outside, as well as Geoffrey's heavy breathing over by the wall as he tried to calm himself and regain his composure.

Tilda's lifeless eyes sprung open, and a horrible moaning sound gurgled from her throat. Geoffrey gasped, and Conrad rushed back over to the desk.

"It worked," Conrad said, like a half-naked, mad scientist in a dungeon laboratory. "She's coming back."

Conrad reached back into the desk drawer and pulled out a handkerchief to cover the nasty wound on her neck.

He turned to Flannery. "Go get a bandage and something to clean her up with. I don't have the authority to fix anything that ails her."

"I'm not a nurse," Flannery said.

"I'm tired of repeating myself with you tonight," he growled, looking over at her. "Do what I say!"

Flannery walked over to the desk. "Move out of my way," she told Conrad. He obeyed and stepped aside as she held an index and middle finger to Tilda's torn neck, where meaty flesh and tendons were exposed. A bright yellow light suddenly protruded from underneath Flannery's pale fingers, illuminating Tilda's entire neck and moving upward across her face. The sensation caused Tilda to make more uncomfortable moans and breathe heavily as she came back to life. Her body squirmed uncomfortably and her arms shook, as the reanimation process took hold.

Geoffrey looked as if he might start crying again. "What are you doing?" he asked, in a near scream.

Flannery lifted her fingers. A red mark that looked more like a hickey remained on Tilda's neck, but the large gash was gone.

"There," Flannery said. "Good as new. The red will be gone in a couple of days, and she won't even have a scar."

Tilda choked as she tried to get words out. She coughed and sat up on the desk, nearly falling back over as she tried to find her balance and move her feet to the floor.

"What the *fuck* did she do to me?" she finally asked, her voice hoarse. Tilda clutched her throat where she had been bitten but hardly any evidence remained. She appeared scattered and confused. "Did I go to sleep? I think I had a dream that I died."

"It wasn't a dream," Flannery replied. "You're dead. Welcome to Hell."

"*What?*" Tilda asked. "I don't understand."

"But you will," Flannery answered. She turned to Geoffrey and Conrad. "She's still in a daze right now. The blood I gave her wasn't enough. Not nearly enough. When she comes to her senses she'll want to feed."

"Oh my God," Geoffrey said, the silent sobs coming again as he hunched over and his shoulders began heaving.

Flannery took no pity on him since he was the one who had begged for his wife's reanimation. "You better hurry. Maybe a duck from the pond. If you're lucky maybe you'll see a squirrel or a raccoon when you go out for the duck. It isn't human blood, but it sustains for a while. She won't be choosy in the beginning, so I would keep her away from people for at least tonight. D'Lynn, Marcus, *the kids.* And *you,* Geoffrey. Be careful and get Conrad to protect you. *She won't be choosy.* Don't forget you're the one who begged and cried for this.

"One of you needs to clean up all the blood and puke. It's a real mess in here! Oh, and boys?"

Geoffrey and Conrad stared at her.

"I will be waiting to find out exactly what it is the two of you and Ruffin were all cozy about earlier tonight—and what exactly is going on that you're keeping secret from me."

With that, Flannery walked out of the room leaving the three of them on their own.

7

Zeke's business card listed his home address, but Marcus could still clearly remember the way as he held the card in hand and looked at the gold type that read *Ezekiel Colson, DVM*. In his other hand were the keys to one of the other Lanehart cars, another Bentley that was gray and darker than the one Ruffin had at his disposal. He made his escape from Ten Points that evening before all the guests at the wake were gone from the house. The strange headache and nausea he experienced earlier in the evening...the strange man Conrad...the strange black woman in the church dress and white pearls who seemed to vanish...and the strange behavior of Flannery's were all enough to drive him away for a few hours. He considered his options and decided to first see if Zeke was at home.

Rain pelted down on the windshield as he drove two miles to Zeke's place. He was relieved to see a black umbrella on the floor board of the passenger's side of the car when he glanced over.

Zeke had grown up in a smaller, more middle-class rural setting. He lived in a modest house that he had moved into after his parents passed away. The house had undergone a renovation since Marcus had last seen it. Additional space at the east end of the one-story brick home contained a separate entrance and was used for Zeke's veterinary practice.

He answered the door, holding a beer and wearing a gray tank top. Since he was no longer married, he appeared to be spending more time at the gym. Marcus was impressed by his old friend's well-defined arms, but decided to play it as if Zeke was standing there in a baggy sweater. It wasn't clear to him yet what Zeke's story was—and the years that had passed with almost no communication made them virtual strangers.

There was no doubt of this in Marcus' mind since he suddenly felt shy, and he detected the same from the other man.

"Well, I wasn't expecting to see you tonight," Zeke said, with a grin. "I see you remembered how to find the house."

Marcus stood outside the door holding with an umbrella and smiled back at him. Zeke was wearing a Texas Rangers baseball cap this time, and Marcus was starting to wonder if he covered up a receding hairline. "It's been a while. The house looks different."

Zeke nodded. "Daddy went first, and then Mama. After she passed it was too sad to leave it the same. So I moved in and made some changes. I wanted my practice closer to home, so I built more space." He smiled bigger and motioned Marcus forward. "Don't keep standing around outside. Come in. I'll show you my clinic space. You probably saw the add-on from outside."

"So, how long ago did you move back in?" Marcus asked, following him through the living room and down a hallway. A doorway at the end of the hall that wasn't there years ago was clearly Zeke's own private entrance into his veterinary clinic.

"About three-and-a-half years ago. After Mary Ann and I—well, you know..."

"I'm sorry to hear it didn't work out."

Zeke shook his head as if he didn't want to elaborate and then looked at Marcus. "So, anybody in your life these days?"

Marcus' face fell. "Um, no, no. Not anymore. There was, but—"

"It didn't work out?" Zeke asked.

"No," Marcus said. "He left one day and never came home. He went missing. He's presumed dead. Nobody knows for sure."

Zeke reached out and touched his arm. "That's terrible. I'm sorry, Marcus. I had no idea. Nobody ever said anything."

"Nobody here?" he said, with a half-smile. "Of course they wouldn't. My family acted like Landon never existed."

"I'm sorry for your loss—I mean, I should say..."

"It's okay," Marcus replied. "If he was still alive I would have heard something by now. It's been more than a year."

Zeke nodded and managed a smile. "Let me show you my home away from home that's *in* my home."

A few minutes later, after the tour of the veterinary clinic ended, the two walked back down the hallway to the den of the house. "Would you like a beer or a drink?" Zeke asked. "I'm not sure where my manners are. I should have asked you when you came in."

"A beer is fine," Marcus said.

"The ducks and the raccoon were completely drained of blood, as I thought," Zeke said, walking into the kitchen that adjoined the den. He reached into the refrigerator and pulled out a bottle, twisted the cap, and then handed it to Marcus. "I had to report it to the sheriff's office. Whoever did it could face animal cruelty charges. I'm sorry to put this on your family right now, with your Dad and all. But it was my duty to report it."

"Who would snap their necks and drain their blood? That is just a little ... morbid," Marcus said. He took a sip of beer. "What do you think the sheriff's office will do? Question Geoff or Tilda—or Travis?"

"The kid is a little strange to say the least. He's my prime suspect, but it's out of my hands now."

"He's going through a stage, trying to find himself. I think Geoff and Tilda are too hard on him. Despite the Marilyn Manson thing he has going on, I don't think he could've done such a thing."

Zeke laughed. "Does he even know who Marilyn Manson *is?* Isn't that our generation?"

They sat a cushion-space apart on the couch in the den. "Oh yeah, I forgot how much time passed. The kids probably don't know who was around during our time."

Zeke held up his bottle. "Here's to getting old," he said, and they toasted with a chuckle.

"Seasoned, not old," Marcus corrected with a smile. Their eyes locked, and then Zeke looked away nervously.

"You know, sometimes—" he began, and then shook his head and stopped talking. "Never mind."

"Sometimes *what?*" Marcus asked. After the morning and evening at Ten Points—and why he was there to begin with—the day couldn't get any worse. "Tell me what's on your mind."

"*You,*" Zeke said, unable to look at him and staring off across the room. He looked as if he was struggling with what to say. "You went away, and you changed. You're not quiet about things anymore. I mean, I don't know how to talk about it..."

"Talk about what?" Marcus asked. "Zeke, we used to be able to talk to each other about anything. I know it's been a long time, and we've gone off and lived our lives and lost touch, but you used to be my best friend."

"The night we—*you know,*" he said, still looking away from Marcus. "I'm sorry I ran out on you. I ran out on our friendship after that. I didn't know how to handle it. For years I said it was the fact we were both drinking that night. I was a chickenshit, and it wasn't fair to you, and I'm sorry."

"Don't worry about it," Marcus said. He was astonished the topic had come up so suddenly and early during the visit. That and what had happened with Landon. He hadn't expected to talk about any of it when he arrived. "You had Mary Ann, and I wasn't out then either..." He paused mid-sentence. "I mean, I'm not saying you were *like me.* Oh shit, I'm sorry. That came out wrong."

"No, it came out right," Zeke replied. "When I went to vet school, I had this lab partner," he continued. "He and I studied together a lot and became close. Well, I'm sure you can figure out the rest. I broke it off after one of the semesters ended. I *did* love Mary Ann, and I knew I was supposed to marry her because that was what everybody expected me to do. That was what *she* expected me to do."

Zeke stood from the couch and began pacing around. His failure as a husband clearly struck a nerve and still appeared difficult for him to discuss with anyone.

The sounds of rainfall and the rumbles of thunder outside broke the silence between them.

"Okay, so you felt obligated because of your family or whatever," Marcus finally said. "That happens sometimes. Especially in places like this."

Zeke looked at him. "Marcus, stop rationalizing for me. This is hard. I would be with her, and then I would have all these other thoughts about what I really wanted. It was horrible. As silly as it sounds, I would watch shows like *Will and Grace* and be jealous because those guys got to live their lives on their terms."

Marcus set his beer down on a coaster, stood up, and put his hand on Zeke's arm. "It's okay. It was years ago. You're in a better place with

62

yourself now. We both moved on. You don't have to explain yourself to me. You did what you had to do. I did what I had to do and got the hell away from my father. He always favored Geoff anyway. He hit the roof when he found out I was gay and told me I was nothing to him."

"What?" Zeke asked.

"Five years ago," Marcus said. "I finally told him. Someone had taken photos of Landon and me at a gay pride parade. He was apparently having me spied on in California from here. He told me I was on my own and no longer his son. We never spoke again after that. We hardly ever spoke before that, so it wasn't that much difference."

"I'm sorry to hear that," Zeke said. "My mother told me she was proud of me and said she still loved me when I told her I was. I didn't see that coming."

Marcus looked at him with a half-smile. "I didn't see any of this coming," he said. "I didn't come over here on a fishing expedition."

"Well, now you know," Zeke said. "I was in love with you, Marcus. That's why I pushed you away after what happened. I wanted to be with you, but I wanted to be with Mary Ann, too, at the time. And I didn't want to be gay. It was confusing. It took years for me to figure out what I really wanted. It was unfair to her, too, but she forgave me. She even has a new husband, and he's a good guy who treats her like she deserves to be treated."

"*I* was in love with *you*," Marcus said. "That's why it hurt so much when you put the space between us."

Zeke looked at him for a moment. "Wow, so it went both ways? We were both too scared to say anything."

"I guess it took all this time to quit acting like a couple of macho rednecks and lay the cards out."

"That sounds like an accurate statement."

"We were too young and too unsure of ourselves. Even in the best of circumstances, it would've never worked out. There were too many barriers back then. Real ones and the ones we invented."

Zeke smiled. "Are you a psychologist now, too?"

Marcus returned the smile and shrugged. "I may need a new job after this trip is over. I kind of left things hanging in San Diego."

Zeke put his hand on Marcus' cheek and leaned in and kissed him softly on the lips. Before Marcus processed what was happening, he instinctively kissed back. It had been more than a year since anyone had done that. They slowly pulled away from one another and opened their eyes.

"Maybe you should leave them hanging there permanently," Zeke said quietly. He smiled again and his hand was still on Marcus. It had moved from his cheek to the top of his shoulder.

"I don't know," Marcus said, not wanting Zeke to release his grip. The touch of an old friend and the storm outside were inviting him to stay longer.

8

Flannery cleaned the blood from her face and hands and body and changed into a casual blouse and pair of jeans. The cut on her wrist had healed almost immediately after Tilda finished feeding.

Drinking from her sister-in-law, feeling the loathed woman's fading heartbeat, and experiencing her ultimate death brought an unspeakable pleasure Flannery had never felt in this new existence, an existence that had begun more than five years ago when another life she believed to be uncertain faded forever. On nights such as this, when the feeding was over and her blood lust was satisfied, she realized maybe her prior life had not been such a failed one.

The ecstasy of killing Tilda—the rush and excitement of exerting such control. The feeling of the drink and the kill was overwhelming every time and gave her a high as it was happening. When it ended, there was always a bit of guilt and shame. That was usually the only time Flannery still felt remotely human.

As Conrad and Geoffrey cleaned up the bloody mess in the study, she walked out barefoot on to the front porch of Ten Points. The bricks beneath her feet were still damp from the spring storm as it finally tapered off. The rain stopped, and a soft breeze cooled the muggy air from earlier. Spanish moss swayed in one of the nearby oak trees. If Flannery sat on the steps and closed her eyes, she could go back to a time when she was a little girl, and she still believed there was more good than evil in the world. That people grew old—and they died.

The remainder of her time on earth, whether it was one year or thousands of them, would be as her twenty-nine-year-old self. The memories of the woman she once was took her back several years to a balmier August night in New Orleans, at the French Quarter apartment rented for her by her lover, Senator Frank Castille. Despite having a wife and a very public profile, he became enamored by Flannery when she worked for him as a campaign volunteer. He pursued her relentlessly, and after first resisting, she finally gave in to his charms.

Castille was only forty-one years old, a rising star in his party, and still an attractive man. His once-black hair was turning salt-and-pepper, but that was the only real sign of age. He rarely overdrank and stayed in shape by working out and playing racquetball several times a week. He was well-favored by his constituents and had been elected to the U.S. Senate in a landslide, after serving as a state representative.

Castille showered Flannery with lavish gifts. Jewelry, a sports car, vacations to Jamaica and Europe, and he took her to the finest restaurants in New Orleans and along the Gulf Coast. Despite his career and having a wife, he seemed not to mind the potential scandal he courted by being seen in public with her. He always traveled in a group, back and forth to Washington, D.C., and she was referred to as "an aide" or "the secretary."

About a year into their arrangement, Castille decided to let Flannery in on a secret he was keeping. He had discovered and secured an avenue for wealth and a path to the U.S. presidency. It was all as good as his, and he was also working on a way the two of them could be together publicly without causing a scandal. A promising and fruitful future was within their grasp.

"You know what they say," Flannery told him. "If it sounds too good to be true then it probably is."

"It's already guaranteed," Castille told her, as they cuddled in bed at her apartment that particular August night. An evening of dinner and an extra glass of wine made him more talkative. She had suspected for about three months he was keeping something from her. She feared it was someone new and was relieved it wasn't the case.

"I'm afraid I don't understand," she said. "You'll have to explain."

"What if I show you?" he asked, a sparkle in his baby blue eyes. There was something more he wasn't telling her that seemed to make him excited—and aroused underneath the covers. He pulled her close to him, and they made love one more time before drifting off to sleep.

The following evening, Flannery returned home to find Castille and a stunningly handsome younger man in the living room of her apartment. The tanned stranger wore gray slacks, and a lighter and much tighter short-sleeved shirt that looked almost painted on to a very muscular body. She couldn't help but notice his appeal and immediately tried to make it look as if she wasn't mentally undressing him when he locked his dark brown eyes on her.

"Flannery, my dear," Castille said, standing and greeting her at the doorway. "I would like you to meet Conrad."

"Hello," she said, offering a short smile but nothing overly friendly. She was wondering why he had brought this strange but incredibly sexy man into her home.

Conrad stood from the sofa. "I'm very pleased to meet you, Flannery," he said. The accent gave away no particular region, but he clearly wasn't from the South. His features looked European, but he sounded American-born and reared. "What a charming southern name you have. Frank has told me a great deal about you."

"Has he?" she asked. She looked over at her lover. "All good, I hope."

Conrad smiled at her. She felt entranced and couldn't look away from him. "Of course he has told me all good things. Why wouldn't he?"

"I don't know," she said. She was still holding two bags from a shopping excursion.

"You've been to Louis Vuitton," Conrad noted, still smiling at her. "Did you bring me anything?" he asked, with a flirtatious wink.

She slowly shook her head and appeared to be going into a haze.

"Tsk tsk," he said mockingly and waved an index finger at her. He smiled brightly again and placed his hands on his lap as he sat at the edge of the luxury red burgundy leather sofa. "Then I guess you should at least tell me what you got for yourself."

"Shoes," she said. "I like shoes," she added, childlike.

"Flannery?" His dark eyes burned into her, and she dared not look away.

"Yes?"

"What if I told you I had something better to offer you than shoes?"

"You do?"

Conrad extended an arm toward a velvet maroon armchair only inches away from where he sat on the edge of the couch. "Come, have a seat," he instructed, as if it were his living room and not hers. Castille kept a pleased grin as his eyes darted back and forth between the two of them.

"Yes," Flannery said. She dropped her things on the floor and slowly made her way over to the chair. Conrad continued to look deeply into her eyes and reached out and took her hand as they sat across from one another. Flannery had forgotten Castille was in the room with them.

The Senator sat back on the opposite end of the couch away from Conrad and watched intently, as the other man's hypnotic effect over his mistress grew stronger.

"Your family doesn't understand you," Conrad said softly, the dark eyes burning into her. "They've never understood you."

"No, they haven't," she said. She held his hand more tightly as she spoke. Her voice fell monotone. "Not at all."

"Maximilian Lanehart wanted three sons. Instead he received a daughter in the mix. He made you feel inferior at every turn when you were growing up, didn't he?"

"*Yes*," she said, in a near whisper. "I never felt like Daddy loved me. Not the way he loved Geoff. Or even Marcus."

"Most of the time you wish you would have been born into another family. A family that appreciated your potential ... gave you more opportunities. Is that not true?"

"*Yes*," she said softly.

"What if I told you I could make you even better than all of them?" he asked, moving closer to her.

Their faces were only inches apart. Her eyes widened and she finally went from a blank stare to a smile.

"You can?" she asked.

"I can," he replied, his own smile growing larger.

"*Flannery Lanehart, is that you?*" Another man's voice pulled her out of the past. Flannery looked up from where she sat on the edge of the porch. A sheriff's deputy stood before her. His patrol car was parked about fifty feet away in the driveway. She had been so lost in her reminiscence she failed to notice the car come up the driveway. She also hadn't noticed the man she suddenly recognized step out and walk up to where she sat.

She gave him a smile. "Wes Washer, well, look at you," she said. He was in a deputy's uniform and looked much like he had when they were in high school together, minus some pimples and a few extra pounds.

He returned the smile and gave her a nod. "You're more beautiful than ever," Wes said, then looked embarrassed. The compliment slipped out before he had time to choose his words more carefully.

"Why thank you," she said. She could tell he was still a bit on the shy and bumbling side, as he had been when they were teenagers.

"I was terribly sorry to hear about your Daddy," he said, his north Louisiana accent thick and his face growing grimmer. "My daddy's preachin' the funeral tomorrow." Wes' father was a Baptist minister who officiated at one of the larger north Monroe congregations the Laneharts belonged to but irregularly attended.

She nodded. "Yes, it was a bit unexpected." It then occurred to her his visit might not be a social or sympathy call. "So, what brings you by?" she asked, her eyes moving away from him and toward the patrol car he had arrived in.

"Oh, I just need to ask your brother some questions about somethin' that was reported to us," he said.

Her emerald eyes moved back to him. "Oh?" she replied. "Nothing serious, I hope."

"It's not anything you have to worry about," Wes said, walking up to the top of the white granite steps. "Is Geoff at home?"

Flannery stood to greet him at the top of the steps. "It's been a long day. I think he's probably already gone to bed for the night."

"It's not even ten o'clock yet," he said, keeping a grin. "Are you sure he's not still up?"

"Why don't you come back tomorrow? There won't be any question about it then."

In high school, Wes had always been a dorky, gawky boy with a crush on Flannery. She was popular and on the drill team back in those days. He was in the band. She always rebuffed any attempt he made to get closer to her and had never given him the time of day. He had been a sweet boy but not her type. Flannery always enjoyed the jocks or the bad boys with more of an edge to them. Wes did not fall anywhere close to that category. She was a little surprised he was able to have a job where he carried a gun.

"Well, is there any way you can go inside to see if he's still awake?" Wes asked, in a sweet and coaxing manner.

She saw through the attempt and decided to play it to her advantage. "Okay, okay," she smiled. "Why don't you come inside," she suggested, opening the front door and leading him into the large house. She was a step ahead of him and anxiously glanced around the foyer for anything amiss. She led him to the living room. "Here, have a seat. I'll go look around and see if I can find Geoff anywhere. Would you like something to drink while you wait? I bet you have a long night ahead of you. I could always go out to the kitchen and get some coffee."

"Oh, does D'Lynn still work here?" he asked, looking around the room in wonderment. He acted as if he had fond memories of Ten Points, but Flannery couldn't recall any time Wes had ever spent there.

"She does, but she goes to bed with the chickens, so there's no doubt she's asleep. Would you like me to make you a cup of coffee?"

"Oh no, that's okay. I probably won't be here long."

She nodded and hoped he was correct. "Let me go see if Geoffrey is awake anywhere in the house. I'll be right back."

His smile widened, and she could feel his eyes following her as she left the living room. When they were teenagers such a leer would have creeped her out, but now she looked at it as something she could use for her own benefit. She knew she would somehow have to charm Wes into leaving the house if Geoffrey was still a disheveled emotional heap whenever she found him.

She walked across the foyer and down the hallway to the study where she had earlier left Geoffrey and Conrad to clean up the mess she created. If only Tilda had held back, bitten her tongue, and watched her words—she would not have ended up the one bitten.

Conrad sometimes warned Flannery about impulse control, but she wondered if that was something better left for humans. Maybe if she had better practiced *impulse control* in her previous life, she wouldn't be damned to the existence she now led.

She walked into the study. Geoffrey scrubbed a spot on one of the oak walls, and there was a mop and a bucket over in the corner of the room where he had vomited. The floor was now clean. The desk was back in order and from across the room showed no signs of any attack. Flannery glanced upward and saw a streak of blood on the ceiling that had not yet been cleaned away. A small part of her greedily considered cleaning it herself, just so she could find out if there was still any taste to it. She quickly put the thought out of her mind.

"Geoff, are you—are you *better* now?" she asked, not sure how else to phrase it. He slowly turned and looked away from the wall toward her but didn't answer. "There's a sheriff's deputy in the living room waiting to see you," she continued. "It's only Wes Washer, so don't be, um, don't be too alarmed."

"What?" he asked. He was clearly still numb from everything earlier. "What does he want with me?"

"He says he needs to ask you some questions about something. He didn't tell me what it was."

"Well, you should have asked him before you came in here and concerned your brother with it," Conrad said, sitting over on a black leather sofa adjacent to the desk. He was still shirtless, wearing only his pants. He seemed so proud and boastful of his flawless body. At that moment, Flannery hated him intensely and wondered what his physique would look like pale and horizontal, cooling inside a morgue refrigerator. If only it were that easy to accomplish.

"Where is Tilda?" she asked, noticing someone was missing from the room.

"Is she *not* with you?" Conrad asked, sitting up straighter and looking concerned.

"Of course she's not with me!" Flannery told him. "Did you not see me walk out of here alone earlier?"

"Oh my God," Geoffrey gasped, dropping the sponge he had been scrubbing the wall with.

"Fools!" she shouted at them. "I told you to keep an eye on her for the rest of the night."

"*The children!*" Geoffrey said, his eyes bulging with new fear. "Oh God!" He ran from the room.

Flannery and Conrad chased after him, and it was when all three of them arrived in the foyer they heard a thud and a crash of something falling over in the living room.

"Oh God, *no!*" Geoffrey screamed, as he rushed into the living room and saw what was happening.

A lamp and side table beside the sofa were knocked over on to the floor, apparently by Wes, who was pinned down on the sofa by Tilda. She was straddled on top of him, her mouth to his throat. He was turning pale and appeared to be in shock, and his attempts to struggle wasted away as he lost his strength.

Tilda pulled away and looked back at them with a feline-like hiss, her long fangs out. Blood ran down her chin, and the three could see puncture wounds in Wes' neck from the doorway of the living room. "Get out!" Tilda ordered. "Get out of here!"

Flannery walked over, grabbed Tilda by the hair, and pulled her off Wes and dragged her a few feet away. "Stop!" she ordered. "You must stop before you kill him."

"You did this to me," Tilda snarled at Flannery. She was still wearing the same bloody clothes she had been killed in an hour before. "You bitch. Why didn't you just leave me dead?"

Conrad and Geoffrey ran over to assist Wes, who was still conscious but weak, hazy, and unsure of what had just happened to him. Conrad grabbed tissues from a dispenser on a coffee table and dabbed at the puncture wounds, where blood continued to ooze.

Flannery released Tilda and walked over to Wes. "Let me do it," she told Conrad, and he moved aside. She applied her index and middle fingers to the wound on Wes' neck and a bright light emanated. Geoffrey's eyes widened. His emotions were too scattered and he hadn't paid full attention earlier, when she had performed the trick on his wife.

"That will stop the bleeding," Flannery said, "but the puncture wounds aren't going to fully fade away for a few days."

"Oh God, did she just turn him into—" Geoffrey asked, looking as if he might start crying again.

"No," Flannery said. "He's alive. He's weak, but he'll be okay."

"I'm still *hungry*," Tilda said quietly and angrily, like a toddler whose ice cream had been taken away. Conrad stepped over to her side, in case she decided to lunge for Wes or Geoffrey without warning.

"Why don't I pour you a Scotch or bourbon," Geoffrey nervously suggested, walking toward the bar. "A cigarette might help. I can bring you one. You keep those over here in the bureau, right?"

"No. I want more from *him*," Tilda said, the bright violet eyes on Wes.

"She won't be needing or wanting booze and cigarettes any longer," Flannery said. "Addictions cease after death. *Human* addictions anyway..."

"We must kill him," Conrad said, looking squarely at Wes. "He can't leave this house with the knowledge he now has."

"May I finish then?" Tilda asked hopefully. Her fangs were still out and grew even larger.

Still unable to speak, Wes gasped and used his frightened eyes to plead for mercy.

Flannery stepped between Conrad and Wes. "No!" she exclaimed. "There's been enough death tonight. We're not killing him."

"You don't have the authority to make such a decision," Conrad told her.

"I have more to lose than you do by Wes knowing what he knows," Flannery pointed out. "He doesn't know what *you* are. You're still only a bystander."

"You've just implied in his presence I'm something that is also inhuman," Conrad said. "That's a label I don't mind wearing, but right now he's a threat to that. And getting you to obey me has been too much of a chore tonight. Maybe I don't feel as though I should do you any favors, my dear."

"Oh my lord," Wes muttered, finding words. He clutched his neck where he was bitten trembled with fright. "What's goin' on here? What are you people?"

"We are the last people you will ever see," Conrad said, looking directly at him. "Before I do what must be done, I need you to tell me why you came here tonight."

Wes looked down and realized his gun was missing. He fumbled around the holster with his hand and looked back up helplessly at Conrad and Flannery. He looked as if he were about to cry. "Please," he begged Flannery. "Don't let him do this."

"There has to be another way," she told Conrad. "Don't do this. He's harmless."

Conrad calmly shifted his eyes back and forth between the frightened deputy and his undead wife. He crossed his arms over his chest and turned to Wes. "Tell me why you came here tonight," he said. "Look at me, and don't lie to me. I'll be able to tell if you're lying to me."

"I—um, I was sent to check about the two dead ducks and the raccoon. We were told that their necks were broke. And all the blood was drained but there—there wasn't no signs of no other animal

73

attackin' 'em."

Conrad laughed. "Oh, of all the things to come ask about at this hour of the night." He squatted down so he was face to face with Wes, who was seated and to the very back of the couch. Conrad glanced up at Flannery. "Why were you so sloppy? Why did you kill and leave dead animals out where they would be found and cause suspicion? Are you now a cat?"

"I—I was," Flannery glanced over at Tilda with a furtive smirk. "I knew it would piss her off, so I left the animals out on the front lawn. I had no idea she would get Zeke Colson to come over here and snoop around."

"Who is this Zeke Colson?" Conrad asked. He was speaking to Flannery, but he began staring at and studying a quivering Wes with the morbid fascination of a child holding a magnifying glass over an ant.

"He's a veterinarian. And an old school friend of my brother's," Flannery said. "I don't think there's any need to—"

"So, Geoffrey, tell me about your old school friend," Conrad said, his stare staying on Wes. He slowly moved his face closer to that of Wes', who was starting to sweat. Beads of perspiration were visible on the petrified deputy's upper lip.

"He was Marcus' friend, not mine," Geoffrey said quietly. He poured himself a drink over at the bar and resigned himself to anything else about to happen. He had seen his wife attacked and transformed into one of the living dead. He then saw her attack and drink the blood of another person. In his mind nothing else tonight could be any worse.

"Marcus..." Conrad replied. "Marcus ... yes."

Conrad took Wes' face in both his hands, causing the other man to let out a loud gasp. "So, Deputy Wes, do you know I once held somebody's face just like this, one hand on each side, and snapped their neck?" he asked, giving him a big grin. "It was over so quickly. But I gave her the best orgasm of her life right before that, so she at least died with a smile on her face. But, she was a succubus who was out of control. I was under orders to send her back *home*. You, on the other hand, I might do it to you just for my own amusement."

"Oh my God," Geoffrey muttered, clutching his glass of bourbon and turning to face the corner. If it was about to happen he didn't want to see it. Maybe not seeing it could somehow make it not real for the moment.

"Conrad, *don't*," Flannery said quietly. "Please don't kill him. There's got to be another way to handle this."

"This ain't Christian, none of it," Wes cried, his chin trembling. "I try to live a good life. I shouldn't be treated and punished this way."

"Look deeply into my eyes, Wes," Conrad said. His expression turned solemn, and he continued holding the other man's face in his palms. There were now only about two inches between the two of them. "You came here tonight, and young Travis admitted to you he killed the animals and took their blood. He saw it in some movie or comic book. You know how those Goth kids can be. Travis' parents told you they would decide a suitable punishment for him. *That's* what happened."

Wes stopped shaking, and his face relaxed as he stared back into Conrad's eyes. He began to smile at Conrad. The paleness from Tilda's attack made brown freckles on his cheeks and nose stand out even more. "Travis could still face animal cruelty charges. Ain't that what I should take him in for?"

"If he were just anyone, yes," Conrad said. His hands slid off Wes' face and down to his shoulders. "He's a Lanehart. I think you can help *us* by making this go away. Right, Wes?"

Flannery felt some relief, but she didn't trust Conrad enough to feel completely confident yet.

"I could make it go away," Wes repeated, nodding dumbly and smiling even bigger. "Geoff and Tilda said they would punish Travis. I trust they'll see to what happens."

"I still say you should kill him," Tilda said. Her metamorphosis from dead to undead was still incomplete, and she stood frozen for stretches between words and reactions. The quick meal she had made of Wes also seemed to have a woozy effect on her.

"No, he will not be killed," Conrad said. He gave Wes a final pat on the shoulders with both hands and stood to his feet. "I've decided he's more useful to us alive than dead."

"I'm more useful to you alive than I am dead," Wes parroted, with a simple grin and a nod. His eyes were no longer locked with Conrad's, but he still appeared to be in some kind of hypnotic state.

"What did you do to him?" Flannery asked, observing his childlike mannerisms and behavior. "He acts like he's retarded now."

"I think the appropriate term these days is *mentally challenged*,"

Conrad corrected, waving a finger at her.

"You were about to twist his head behind him, and you're calling me out for not being politically correct?" Flannery scowled at him.

"Well, my dear, your untidiness is to blame for everything terrible that's happened here tonight. The dead animals you displayed in the yard indirectly led to your friend here almost meeting two possible deaths. You killed Tilda over there just about an hour ago. I don't even think all the blood is going to come out of the wood in the study. Geoffrey will probably need to have the wall re-varnished. We're still about an hour and a half away from midnight. Should I expect more careless behavior from you before then?"

"I thought you enjoyed *bad?*" she asked. For the second time that night, she wished to see his death. She hoped on all still in her favor he had no way of reading her thoughts. It was an ability he bore with some.

"I enjoy bad when it doesn't interfere with my plans," Conrad said.

"You still haven't told me *what* those plans are," Flannery replied.

"In due time. We must bury your father, so let's focus on that," he told her. He turned back to Wes. "Wes, after you leave Ten Points, I want you to radio your dispatcher and say you're getting food. Go to a nearby diner, order a meal and a glass of orange juice to regain some of your strength. Oh, and Wes, if anyone asks ... those marks on your neck were some kind of accident. Maybe you did something to yourself in your sleep." Conrad then snapped his fingers.

Wes sprung awake, as if he had been sleeping. His green eyes widened, and he sat up straighter on the sofa, looking all around him. Flannery noticed his firearm had also materialized and was back in its holster.

"So, I see you found Geoffrey," Wes said to Flannery, with a bashful smile. "And you brought out everybody," he noted, looking over at Tilda and growing alarmed at the sight of her bloody blouse. "Oh my lord, Mrs. Lanehart! Are you okay?"

"She's fine," Flannery said. "She had an accident with, um, with some *paint* earlier. We were trying to spray paint a mural for Daddy's service tomorrow, and she forgot to change into her casual clothes before the can exploded," she lied. "It got everywhere. I just got out of the shower myself."

"It looks almost like blood, and it freaked me out," Wes said, appearing to buy the ludicrous story. He stared warily at Conrad, who had yet to put on a shirt. "Do I know you, man?" he asked.

Conrad reached out for an introductory handshake.

"I don't think we've met. I'm Conrad, a friend of the family. Pardon my half-dressed appearance. I was about to get into the shower and heard there was law enforcement downstairs. I wanted to make sure everyone was okay. The Laneharts have been so kind and generous to me."

Flannery finally felt confident to wear the look of relief she felt, and Geoffrey was once again turned and facing them. Tilda stood off to the side, motionless and quiet again.

"Well, my dear, a simple 'thank you' would suffice," Conrad said to Flannery, as Wes Washer stood and prepared to leave the house alive.

9

A sense of quiet and stillness gave no hint of the chaos earlier in the night when Marcus arrived home from his visit to Zeke Colson. If anyone was still awake they had retired or weren't heard about downstairs as he came in through the front door. There facing him was the silver casket, roped off near the far wall of the lighted foyer. The sight of the casket brought unease and reverence Marcus wouldn't have been able to explain to anyone.

When he was younger, he might have come home to find Maximilian Lanehart in his study, or in the living room, having a drink, talking with an associate on the phone. Or even simply watching a ballgame on television. There was no echo of activity in the study from the down the hallway and no hum of a TV coming from the living room.

Marcus walked past his father's casket to the living room, which was dimly lit. He turned on a lamp. He sat down on the dark green antique sofa where, unbeknownst to him, Wes Washer had been attacked and bitten by Tilda only about an hour earlier. Much of the furniture was back in place after being cleared out earlier for the wake. He reached for the remote control and turned on the television, which was on Fox News. He turned off the TV, decided to let the room stay quiet, and sat in silence a few minutes, thinking over the events earlier at Zeke's house—things he hadn't expected.

After the kiss, he and Zeke pulled away and took a seat back on the couch. They sat in silence a few minutes, glanced over at one another, and then were back on one another—kissing, attacking, touching, and repeating the same moves from that night sixteen years earlier. The fire and fervor from before was still there. This time they weren't drunk, but

Marcus still couldn't clearly remember at which point they went from the couch to Zeke's bed. After it was over, they lay together under the covers, holding one another and talking for at least an hour. Marcus finally realized the time and knew he needed to return home.

Zeke's hand affectionately brushed Marcus' bare back as he sat up on the edge of the bed and began putting his clothes back on. "Why don't you stay?" he said.

"They will wonder where I'm at," Marcus said, looking back at him with a smile.

"You can stay here tonight, but I meant stay for good," Zeke said, his head still on the pillow. The Texas Rangers ball cap was gone, and his closely-cropped brown hair wasn't receding as Marcus had wondered about earlier.

"I don't have a life here anymore," he replied. "It's all back there now. There's still a lot to deal with there."

"Make a new life here," Zeke said. "With me. You still have to live, Marcus."

Marcus looked at him. "Don't you think this is kind of sudden? We only just—"

"We did what we should've done all those years ago," he said. "We found our way back to each other."

"Zeke, I don't know—"

"Just *think* about it," he said. "I know, it's sudden and I don't mean to pressure you. But if I don't say it, I'll wish I had later when you're gone. I don't want to be like I was before, when I—when I shut you out. When I didn't say how I really felt."

"A lot has happened since then," Marcus said. "We're different people now."

Marcus left it at that. Part of him knew Zeke's idea was pure romantic fantasy and not very pragmatic. Marcus couldn't just fly back to San Diego and pack up his things and come back to Monroe so he could be in a relationship with somebody from long ago.

He also had those text messages from Peter and Jane he had never returned. His complete blow-off of his job—for reasons even he still couldn't understand—made him wonder if there was anything left to go back to in San Diego, except maybe bagging groceries at Trader Joe's. And going home every night to an empty apartment, living a lonely existence and waiting for someone who was never coming home.

Marcus slumped down on the sofa in the living room at Ten Points and let his head rest over the back. It was two hours earlier in California, and his body and mind still hadn't adjusted to the time zone change. He wondered to himself why Maximilian Lanehart couldn't be given a normal service, during the late morning or afternoon, in a church or funeral home. Why was he so relaxed and nonchalant, when the corpse of a man he was so estranged and removed from was lying right in the next room?

Marcus stood from the couch and went to the foyer. Without hesitation, he stepped behind the maroon velvet rope that kept his father's encased body in its own private little world. He put his hand on the lid of the casket. He ran his fingers along the top, to the edge, and then the side, where he reached underneath for the groove. He felt the lid start to rise, when a hand reached from behind and fiercely shoved him away.

"What the hell do you think you're doing?"

It was Geoffrey. His sandy blond wavy hair was a mess, his nose was red, his eyes glassy, and Marcus could smell bourbon on his breath. "I said, what do you think you're doing down here?" he repeated almost immediately, before Marcus had time to respond.

"I was just—"

"Just *what?*" Geoffrey asked, his left eye starting to twitch. "Just hoping for a last look before he's in the ground? If he had even wanted that, his final wishes with Ruffin wouldn't have been for a closed casket."

Marcus stepped back over to the other side of the velvet ropes where Geoffrey stood. "So Ruffin was Dad's lawyer? I thought he was yours?"

"He's one of the family attorneys. *And* the executor of the will. What difference does it make?"

Things started to make a little more sense. At least in some ways. "Dad made these final demands? You told me he hadn't been sick. He apparently still thought he might die at any time?"

"I told you what Doctor Rogers told me after Dad died. I don't feel like getting into all of this with you. I need to leave this house for a little while."

"Ruffin is the family attorney *and* the executor?" Marcus asked. "Isn't that a little ... odd?"

"He's just one of our attorneys. He's not *the* attorney." Geoffrey grew aggravated. "Do we really have to get into this? I really need to go."

"It's getting close to midnight. Where are you going this late?" Marcus also wondered if Geoffrey was in any shape to drive.

Geoffrey stared suspiciously at his brother. "Why do you want to know? And *where* did you come from? I thought you were upstairs asleep a long time ago. Exactly *when* did you come back inside the house?"

"Just a few minutes ago. I was out," Marcus said. "I was with a friend."

Geoffrey gave him a derisive grin. "Yeah, please spare me the details. I'm sure it was more than that."

"What is that supposed to mean?" Marcus asked him.

"Never mind," Geoffrey said. "You should go to bed and get some rest. It's late."

"You're right. It's getting late. Maybe I will do that."

Geoffrey fumbled in his pockets for his keys. "Good. And stay away from that casket. Don't touch it again."

"Are you sure you need to be driving anywhere?"

"Of course I am. And what the hell business is it of yours what I do?"

"You've done a good job of asking me about my schedule tonight. I thought I would return the favor."

"Well, it's *my* house! I don't even know why you bothered coming back here," Geoffrey said. His eyes grew larger and appeared more bloodshot. "There is nothing for you here anymore. Everything is mine now. Not yours, and not Flannery's. *Mine!* You got that?"

"Don't worry, I can leave after the funeral. I can be gone the minute it's over. There is nothing here for me here anymore anyway. You and Dad saw to that." Marcus felt the anger rising. *Who the fuck did Geoff think he was?* Why did he have to take the golden boy title and run with it the way he did? His red nose and twitchiness were a dead giveaway he had been off somewhere else in the house snorting coke before he walked in on Marcus in the foyer.

"Good, go back to California and be with all your little faggot friends, and be—"

The right hook of Marcus' fist caught Geoffrey in the jaw without any warning and knocked him into the wall over by the casket. He fell over on to the floor on his behind and looked up stunned at Marcus.

"Would you like to get dragged outside and have your ass kicked by a faggot?" Marcus asked. He felt like somebody else had just struck Geoffrey, and that the words coming out of his mouth weren't his.

"What the hell," Geoffrey muttered, rubbing his jaw, which was already turning red. "Did you really just do that?"

"You son of a bitch," Marcus said, as he stood over him. "You were fucking *nowhere* at the lowest point of my life when I needed my family! Where were you? Huh? Landon went missing, and not one of you could pick up a goddamn phone and check on me. So *you* don't get to talk about my life, you bastard."

"I've been busy, and I didn't really know Landon—"

"Fuck you, asshole," Marcus cut in, continuing to stare down at him on the floor. "We'll see what all your boot-wearing, duck hunting, Fox News-watching friends have to say when I'm done kicking your golden boy ass around the front yard and sell the video online."

Geoffrey tried to chuckle, but his jaw was starting to hurt. *"Really,* Marcus?" He put his hand on the wall and pushed himself off the floor to his feet. He looked warily at Marcus. "You better never do that again," he said, stumbling back toward the front door. "I'll be glad when the funeral's over. That means I never have to see you or that whore sister of ours ever again. You can both rot in hell for all I care."

"Is everything okay down here?" Conrad came down the stairs. He had changed into gray jogging pants and a white tank top.

"Everything will be fine as soon as this house gets a little emptier," Geoffrey said, looking directly at Marcus. He dug his car keys out of his pocket. "I'll be back later."

"Where are you going?" Conrad asked. "Are you okay?"

"Who the hell are you?" Marcus asked Conrad, still angry. "Are you some long-lost member of the family? You show up with Ruffin, and now you're suddenly moved in and spending the night? I'm really confused."

"Conrad is a business associate and *my* guest," Geoffrey said. "He doesn't need your permission to stay in this house. It's my prerogative to move anybody in that I see fit."

"Or tell anyone else to leave," Marcus said, staring at Conrad. The way he looked in the tank top would have made Marcus glance twice in any other situation, but the strange man had been under his skin too

82

much throughout the evening.

Conrad gave Marcus a friendly smile. "I'm sorry if my presence here offends you so much."

"Offended isn't the word I would use," Marcus told him. The smile and calm demeanor of this man during all their exchanges was getting old. It also made him more suspicious in Marcus' eyes. "I just don't understand what your purpose is for being here."

"I just told you why he's here," Geoffrey said. "I'm leaving. Don't wait up. *Either* of you."

Marcus wasn't satisfied with his brother's explanation, but he had already stirred the pot enough with him for one night. He was cooling down and glad the slug hadn't escalated into a fight in the foyer. The echoes of such a commotion in the high-vaulted room would have likely awakened other people inside the house.

"Do you think maybe you should stay and put some ice on that jaw?" Conrad asked.

Geoffrey waved him off and walked out the front door. Conrad turned to Marcus. "I heard voices and came to the top of the stairs. That's when I saw you hit him. I was worried there might be a fight. I kept an eye on you two and then came down after that."

"So you're a referee, too?" Marcus asked, gazing at him suspiciously. "Nice to know."

"You're not making this easy, Marcus," Conrad said, following him into the living room. "I feel like you haven't given me a chance since I arrived. You clearly don't like me, and I'm not sure exactly what it is I've done to you."

Marcus turned and faced him. "You showed up and started insinuating yourself into the circle. There's just something about you that seems..." He kept looking at Conrad as he tried to find the word.

Conrad smiled again. "Do you always treat strangers this way?"

"Of course not."

He walked over to the bar and looked back at Marcus. "Could I fix you a drink? You also look as though you may need some ice for that hand."

Marcus hadn't noticed his hand. He took a look and realized it was red, just as his brother's jaw had been when he left the house. Conrad had shown up just as his anger started subsiding over Geoffrey's hateful words, so he hadn't taken the time to process any physical pain or discomfort.

"Vodka neat," Marcus said. "Stoli, if there's any over there."

"Well, there is!" Conrad replied in an exaggerated and dramatic manner, holding up a bottle with a wider smile. He was clearly trying to jest and make nice. "Do you mind if I join you?"

"No, be my guest."

Marcus decided this could be a way to get some answers about who this man was. And perhaps why he was so put off—and maybe even threatened—by his appearance at the house. Conrad did have a point. He had done nothing *to* Marcus. Why the rush to judgment? But Marcus' intuitive study of the man set his radar off, and it couldn't be helped.

"There isn't a trace of the South in your voice," Marcus said, when Conrad returned to the sofa with their drinks. "Where are you from?"

"There isn't much in yours either," Conrad said. "Have you been away long, Marcus?"

"But this isn't about me. I asked you the question."

"I'm from Chicago. Now, let's look at your hand."

"It's fine," Marcus said, as Conrad presented ice cubes wrapped in a cloth napkin. "I never hit. I *don't* hit. I don't know why I did that to him."

Despite a slight protest from Marcus, Conrad took his right hand and held the wrapped ice over his knuckles. He held Marcus' hand in his and stared directly into his eyes as he massaged the wrapped ice over the swollen knuckles. "Maybe you had finally had enough. Geoff isn't the most open-minded person in the world, is he?"

Marcus felt a bit uneasy but resisted the urge to pull away from him. "No, not at all. He's a younger version of our Dad."

"It must be difficult coming here and not being accepted by anyone."

"That's not true. Flannery is okay, even though she seems to be wrapped up in her own problems. There's D'Lynn, who's never judged me. And my Aunt Hattie..."

"Is she the older blonde lady with all the makeup and perfume who walked up to me and slid her phone number into my jacket pocket this evening?" Conrad asked.

Marcus shook his head and rolled his eyes. "Yes, that sounds about like my Aunt."

"I was flattered, but I guess I will have to find a way to avoid her at the funeral tomorrow."

"Good luck with that. Many men tried to run away from the charms of Aunt Hattie but still ended up married to her."

"I'm not most men," Conrad said quietly, the brown eyes fixed on Marcus again.

"Neither am I," Marcus said, as their eyes locked.

"You look like you're sad about something. Or *someone*," Conrad said.

"My Dad is lying dead in a casket in the next room. What do you think?"

"It isn't that. Something else is troubling you."

"Well, I just punched my brother, and I don't agree with violence. So that troubles me."

Marcus refused to discuss anything about Landon with Conrad. He wouldn't allow himself to be that deeply vulnerable before someone he distrusted and couldn't see himself ever liking.

"People often don't want to accept what they cannot understand," Conrad said, still looking at him and continuing to lightly rub the icy napkin across Marcus' hand. "I accept, and I understand, Marcus."

Conrad then leaned in and gave Marcus a soft kiss on the lips.

Marcus recoiled as if he had been shot and leapt from the sofa. *"What the hell?!"* he exclaimed, caught off guard and furious again. The napkin fell on to the floor and ice cubes spilled out on to the navy blue and green Persian rug. "Did I say you could do that?"

Conrad smiled demurely. "You never said I couldn't."

"What is your *deal?* I don't understand you."

"Maybe I find you interesting. You intrigue me, and there is a part of me that does enjoy your attitude."

"I need sleep," Marcus said, exiting the room. "It's been a long day."

"Goodnight," Conrad called after him. Marcus was already gone.

Conrad sat back comfortably on the sofa and finished his drink in silence.

10

Marcus stepped out of the hot shower, toweled off, and slid into a T-shirt and shorts. The steam followed him and dissipated into the cooler air as he walked out of the bathroom and into his old bedroom. The blue and gray comforter was pulled back and the fresh sheets welcomed him into the queen-size bed from his youth. Once he settled in he reached over to the nightstand and turned off the lamp. He lay in the dark, staring at the white of the ceiling as it came into focus, and thinking about the events of the past day.

Besides all of the chaos and clashes at Ten Points over the past twenty-four hours, there was Peter to deal with back in San Diego. Marcus had gone the entire day without returning any texts or phone calls. He hadn't given much thought to work or the *Sun-Times* since his hasty exit from California. Despite what he had said to Geoffrey downstairs earlier, he wasn't sure if he was ready to go back. The same gravitational pull that had detached him from his life and dragged him back to Louisiana kept nagging at him. He knew he should care about his career—it was likely all he had left after tomorrow—but something inside was telling him he *must* stay.

Zeke wanted him to stay. But it was all said after a close moment between the two of them. Marcus couldn't put any stock in it.

Zeke. The last thing Marcus had expected was what had happened between them earlier. The conversation between them about the past, and then what followed afterward. Something had reignited on Zeke's end, but Marcus wondered if they were too different now for it to go any further. Strangely enough, he hadn't felt as if he were betraying Landon in any way by being with Zeke. But any possibilities with Zeke weren't what was making Marcus feel he should stay at Ten Points. He still couldn't give himself a clear answer on what the pull was.

And then there was whatever the hell Conrad had been thinking downstairs. The kiss caught Marcus off guard. He was already infuriated by Geoffrey, and then the unexpected move by Conrad set him off again as he had started to calm down. It felt calculated and not genuine. It felt almost as if Conrad was teasing him, and perhaps that was what made him angry about the whole thing. But the idea of Conrad being attracted to him wasn't an idea he welcomed either.

A mishmash of other things and people and places from the present and the past wandered into and out of his thoughts, as he felt himself start to drift off. Such a long day, and sleep would put it to an end. Some rest, and maybe he could better deal with some of today's problems tomorrow when he was recharged.

He felt himself nod off and drift away into a sea of black. After what could have been a few minutes, Marcus felt himself rattled awake. "Who's there?" he asked, unable to see anyone in the darkness of the bedroom.

Chills ran through him and he felt a cold sweat break out on his body as he realized someone was holding his hand. It was too dark, and he couldn't see who it was. He wanted to reach for the lamp but somehow couldn't make himself do it. It felt like the hand of a child—not that of an adult.

"Who is it? What do you want?" There was no answer. Only a tug. Marcus felt frightened—more than he had in a long time.

His whole childhood had been filled with a fear of the dark and paranormal legends, much of it fueled by ghost stories about Ten Points. When he wasn't much older than the twins, one of the housekeeping staff had quit without any notice, saying she kept seeing a man in nineteenth century garb in one of the bedrooms. Then there were claims over the years by staff and visitors alike they had seen the three children of Theodore Ogden, Junior. And, of course, other tales of apparitions and strange noises and occurrences.

Now after all these years and nights spent inside the house throughout his life, Marcus wondered if it could finally be his turn.

Whoever was grabbing his hand kept tugging and wanted him to get out of the bed and come with them. Marcus suddenly felt less fearful and more obligated to do so.

Once he left the bed and was outside the bedroom door in the dimly-lit hallway, Marcus couldn't see anyone holding his hand, nor could he feel the other person's hand in his any longer. He still felt something call to him from the other end of the hallway, near the stairs. There wasn't any sound, it was all something...subconscious. Marcus walked barefoot down the carpeted hallway toward the foot of the stairs wanting to turn and go back to his room but unable to resist the call. The urge to keep going didn't end once he reached the stairway.

The large antique crystal chandelier that hung over the foyer was lit after hours, so he could see the room down below. The shiny marble of the cream-colored floor and the glint of the steel from his father's casket over by the wall, behind the velvet ropes, were all caught underneath the low light. Marcus felt his feet move down the stairs though he felt as if he wasn't the one taking the steps.

Before he realized he had reached the bottom of the staircase, it felt as though he was already over at the casket. Between the ropes and where his father's body lay. Geoffrey was nowhere around to stop him this time. There was nobody else anywhere. He looked around to the side and behind him. The room was darker than in the daytime, but there was enough light to tell him no one was nearby.

Marcus ran his hand along the lid of the casket again. This time, he decided not to waste any time. He reached under and pulled up the lid. It came up fairly easily, and there in front of him was the body of Maximilian Lanehart.

An older man who had been handsome and dashing in his day. Now gray and wrinkled, but still not unattractive. During Marcus' later childhood and teenage years, after his mother died, he remembered his father dating a bevy of women of all ages but never settling down with any of them. There was no doubt quite a few of them longed for the prestige and financial comfort of being the next Mrs. Maximilian Lanehart--something the children were thankful never happened. By the time they were older they had settled on D'Lynn being the closest thing to a maternal figure they wanted or needed.

As Marcus stared into the opened casket, it was almost like looking at an older version of a sleeping Geoffrey--but with angrier, furrowed, and grayer brows. Maximilian Lanehart wore a charcoal gray suit and light-colored shirt with a dark tie. Even in the dim lights, Marcus could see the funeral home's powder makeup job. Why, he had no idea, since the casket was ordered closed.

Maximilian Lanehart's hands were rested at his middle, one on top of the other. They looked puffier than the last time Marcus had seen him. Maybe it was from a weight gain before his death or the embalming afterward—there was no way to be sure.

He looked away from his father and toward the living room doorway. Their last conversation still ran through his mind. Part of him always hoped they could find a way to reconcile. His father had never shown him any kind of love or affection, so he wasn't even sure why he longed for it or had any desire for it. But he had, and now, for the first time since learning of his father's death he felt a sadness and a deep regret for the way things had turned out for them. He started to wonder what would have happened if he had picked up the phone after two, three, or four years and called his father. Maybe Maximilian was being stubborn. *Maybe* he was waiting on his son to make the first move.

Marcus felt a tear fall down his cheek. He wiped it away and gasped as he looked back down and met the steely blue eyes of his father staring back at him.

Maximilian turned his head on the pillow, "Why are you crying?" he asked, his expression turning to a scowl through the make-up.

"Oh my God," Marcus wailed, stepping back. "It can't be..."

Maximilian raised a hand and summoned him back over. "Come here, Marcus."

"You're dead!" Marcus said, his voice rising. "This *can't* be happening."

The hand was relentless and kept waving him back over to the casket. *"Come here, Marcus!"*

Marcus slowly tiptoed back over but with his eyes closed. *If I don't look, then it can't be real. None of this can be real,* he told himself. Without looking, he sensed he was back over at the edge of the casket. But his kept his eyes tightly sealed.

"Open your eyes," his father ordered.

"I can't..."

"Be a man, goddamn it. I said *open your eyes and look at me!*"

Marcus slowly opened his eyes. Maximilian was still awake and staring at him. "I don't understand," Marcus said in a whisper, his voice shaky. "I don't understand any of this."

"No, you don't. Not at the moment, but you will. I need you to listen to me," Maximilian said. His lips were moving and he was making slight tilts with his head as he spoke. The rest of his body was lying stiffly inside the casket.

"Listen to you?"

"Yes, there isn't much time. You can't leave after they bury me. You must stay. Your brother...oh, *your brother.*" Maximilian shook his head as much as he could in the limited confines of his eternal bed. "May God help him. It's all up to you now, Marcus."

"What's up to me? I don't understand!"

But it was too late. Maximilian's eyes were closed, and his head and face were back as fixed and positioned as they were when Marcus first lifted the lid.

He instinctively closed the casket. Without anyone telling him, he knew Maximilian was finished speaking. It was all too surreal...the dim lights, the glistening silver casket, a talking corpse. Marcus wondered if it was his imagination. There was no sensible explanation for any of this.

He turned and saw Bobby standing at the foot of the stairs. His nephew who was still very small to already be ten years old. As at the wake, the dark-haired boy only stood and stared but didn't say anything. He was shorter and much slimmer than his chubby fraternal twin sister.

"Bobby? What are you doing out of bed?" Marcus asked, walking toward him.

The boy stood expressionless and stared at him, and then turned and began walking up the winding staircase as Marcus approached.

"Aren't you going to answer me?" Marcus asked, following after him. Whether he had seen what transpired at the casket wasn't clear. The boy could have been sleepwalking. Marcus reached the top of the stairs and stood and watched, as Bobby casually walked down to the end of the hallway toward his bedroom. He reached for the doorknob and went inside but not before turning back to give his uncle another blank stare until he finally went inside and closed the door.

There was a chance he had seen and heard the casket conversation and was frightened—or he had witnessed a one-sided conversation on Marcus' end and was confused. Was he the one who had come into

Marcus' room and pulled him out of bed? If so, there had to be a reason. Did Bobby know what would happen if Marcus went downstairs, and did he intentionally lead him down there? He would have to try and talk to the boy tomorrow and get answers.

He closed his own bedroom door and slid back into bed beneath the covers. It took time for his eyes to adjust to the pitch black again, to make out walls and the ceiling. He felt himself drifting off, and this time a fluorescent blue that appeared as ocean waves began to wash over him. The colors went from dark to light, and then crashed together to make a myriad of shapes and glowing designs before Marcus' eyes. He felt his eyelids flutter and knew in his subconscious only the remnants of awareness eroded as he floated back into sleep.

He then felt someone there again, and this time Zeke appeared out of the kaleidoscope of blue and smiled at him. Marcus smiled back, and they took each other's hands. "I couldn't leave you alone," Zeke told him. "I had to sneak in. I want to stay with you tonight. Let me be with you." They began kissing and soon they were holding on to one another tightly beneath the covers of the bed. Zeke was already naked, and began pulling Marcus' T-shirt and shorts off. "I want to feel you," he said. "Let me feel you against me."

"How did you get in here?" Marcus whispered, getting lost in the feeling of warmth against him.

"I remembered where you always slept," he whispered back in Marcus' ear, giving him a soft peck on the neck.

"I can't believe you sneaked in here," Marcus said, realizing he was fine with all of it. "But I'm glad you're here. I'll sneak you back out later. *Much* later..."

Marcus was out of his clothes, and they were skin on skin. They were kissing more, and soon Marcus was underneath Zeke. He ran his hands up Zeke's back, across his broad shoulders, and finally up to his hair, when he realized Zeke's closely-cropped short hair was now longer and more lush and thick. His body and his touch felt more strong and muscular, and the lips were different when they kissed. Marcus opened his eyes, and saw Conrad on top of him.

"What? I don't understand what—"

"Shhh," Conrad gently caressed Marcus' cheek with the back of a hand and gave him another light kiss on the lips.. He then kissed again a trifle more aggressively, and his tongue slid into Marcus' mouth and then quickly went back out. "Just let it be. Just let yourself be mine."

"I don't—Stop!" Marcus protested and tried to wrestle his way from underneath him, but Conrad was bigger and stronger and held him in place.

"Look at me," he ordered, his expression going from tender to controlling. A soft glow of moonlight through the bedroom window made Conrad and those eyes of his come into better focus. His smooth muscular shoulders and traps tensed as his grip tightened on Marcus' arms, pinning him uncomfortably. "Don't take your eyes off me."

"But, we can't—"

"You are mine, damn it," he said, giving Marcus another kiss. "Now do as I say and look at me."

You belong to me. The voice. It finally had a face. But *how?*

"Where is Zeke? Zeke was here just a minute ago. *How did--?"*

"Don't say his name. Don't dare say his name in front of me again. Only say *my* name," Conrad said, brushing his lips against Marcus' chin. He thrust his hips upward, and Marcus could feel the erection pressing against him.

"We can't do this," he said. "This isn't—"

"I want to be with you right here, tonight," Conrad said, his warm breath against Marcus' face. He gave him yet another kiss. "Don't resist me, Marcus. Deep down you are attracted to me. You want this as much as I do."

"Conrad, please—"

"It is impossible to fool me, Marcus. I can see inside you."

He continued to thrust back and forth against Marcus. "I want to be with you tonight," he repeated. "Let it be."

"No! Please!"

"But if it were Zeke you wouldn't resist."

"I don't know. That's different. This isn't something I want to talk about with—"

"Where were you earlier tonight?" he interrupted. "Were you with him? Look into my eyes. Don't lie to me. I'll be able to tell if you're lying to me."

"Conrad, *no—"*

Marcus woke up in a loud wail and sat up in the bed. Breathing heavily and feeling another cold sweat, this one genuine, he reached over to the nightstand and turned on the lamp. The bed was empty, and there was no one else in the room.

He laid his head back on the pillow, and his breathing began to slow down and calm. He left the light on and stared at the ceiling, going over the events that had just happened in his mind. He was only half-awake and still feeling drowsy, but he could remember everything clearly.

The small, childlike hand holding his in the dark. His opening of the casket downstairs. His father opening his eyes and speaking to him. Bobby's appearance at the foot of the stairs in the foyer. And then Zeke sneaking into his bed and transforming into Conrad.

You belong to me. It finally had a face. Or did Marcus subconsciously want that to be the case? It was all too much to consider.

He realized how nonsensical it all was, as he groggily went back over all the details.

Then the realization struck him.

Marcus was naked, and as he looked down at himself he noticed a red mark that looked almost like a handprint on each one of this upper arms.

11

"Flannery, you don't have to watch me so closely every second. I feel like you're some big cat, and I'm a vulnerable little mouse you're waiting to pounce on. Oh wait, never mind, you already did that tonight. Too late."

Tilda paced back and forth in a long-abandoned room on the third floor of Ten Points. It had once been a bedroom during the nineteenth century but had been used for storage over the past few decades and was filled with old boxes and crates covered with dust and cobwebs. Still, the fact there was also an old bed stored in the room, and any windows once there were shuttered long ago, made it an ideal spot for her during daylight hours. For now, it was still dark outside and she was only getting acquainted with the space where she would soon spend her sleeping hours.

"I must say my plans for tonight didn't involve babysitting, so you're no more miserable than I am right now," Flannery said. She sat on an old wooden bench and flipped through a *LIFE* magazine from another era she had pulled from one of the dusty boxes. "There are so many cigarette ads in this magazine. Wouldn't you love a big long one right now?" She gave a fake laugh. "Oh never mind, you can't do that anymore."

"What I want right now is more of what I got from Deputy Wes," Tilda said. She had cleaned up from earlier and changed into a more casual ensemble complete with black yoga pants and tennis shoes she had rarely worn in her previous life. Despite her attire, she had the mannerisms of a twitchy addict awaiting her next fix. "Where did Conrad send Wes? We should go find him."

"Forget it," Flannery told her. "Wes should be left alone. You weren't supposed to be wandering the house by yourself. That was a mistake."

"This whole thing is a mistake!" Tilda said. "How am I supposed to stay in here, Flannery? That mattress probably has mold, and there could be spiders and rats in this room!"

"Well, rats are a good blood source when there aren't any humans around."

"I can't sleep on that thing," Tilda said, turning her pale nose up at the single bed over in the corner. The steel frame was from the 1950's, and the blanket appeared as though it hadn't been washed in almost that long. "Shouldn't I be sleeping in a coffin if I'm dead?"

"Not unless you want to be buried," Flannery said. "You find a nice sealed room away from sunlight and you can still have a bed. Those are the daytime rules you must abide by."

"Then Geoffrey will have to move my real bed in here," Tilda said. "This is a huge inconvenience. You were right earlier. I *am* in hell! Why did you have to do this to me?"

"I didn't *have* to," Flannery told her. She became bored with the magazine and tossed it back into the box. "You worked my last nerve, and I lost my temper."

"Well, Conrad is good at what he does," Tilda said. She took a seat in an old armchair covered by a sheet and cocked a wary eye in her sister-in-law's direction.

"That's not what made me upset. You can do whatever you want with that son of a bitch. But I have to warn you, he prefers the living, so your days of getting it over a desk have likely ended. Our marriage hasn't exactly been ... *affectionate.*"

"Will I still be able to—*you know?* Can I even still have sex?"

"I—I don't know," Flannery said nervously. "I honestly don't have an answer for that."

"You mean, you and Conrad never...?"

"No."

"But you're his wife?"

"That's just his way of trying to own me like a piece of property."

"You haven't been with anybody at all in all these years since...?"

"No."

"Well, I'm done with Conrad. After tonight, Geoff has to find a new way to—" Tilda abruptly stopped mid-sentence as Flannery stood and walked closer.

"Go on," Flannery said, crossing her arms and standing before Tilda. "Geoff has to find a new way to please Conrad? Is that where you were going?"

Tilda looked away, defeated, and realized she had said too much. "Something like that."

"And you don't know why any of this is taking place? You didn't know what Conrad *was* when you started this little sexual arrangement?"

"Of course not, Flannery. What the hell *is* he? He transformed into some kind of monster in the study. His eyes turned black. His voice changed. Is he the devil?"

"No, not the devil. Just one of the servants," Flannery said. "I met him several years ago in New Orleans."

"Is he the one who turned you into a—?"

"*No,*" Flannery quickly cut in. "Conrad wasn't the one responsible for that."

"Then how did you get mixed up with him? Was Senator Castille involved with him somehow?"

Flannery winced at the mention of Castille's name and turned away. The thought of Senator Frank Castille always took her back to another time. It had only been five years, but at the same time, it was another lifetime ago. If only she could have physically gone back, she would have changed so many things.

During their relationship, it was impossible to ignore the fact Castille had a wife. She often wondered why his wife Katarina, a blonde Swedish former model, never traveled with them. Other than glimpses of Mrs. Castille in recent newspaper and older magazine photos, she had never seen nor met the other woman.

Not until one night when Katarina Castille began banging incessantly on the door of Flannery's apartment—the one Senator Frank Castille paid for. Even though the French Quarter was no stranger to rowdy behavior, Flannery quickly went to the door before there was a scene.

"Where is he?" Katarina demanded, pushing her way inside. She spoke English well and fluently but still sported a heavy Scandinavian accent. "I've been sitting outside for an hour since I followed him here. I know he is in here somewhere. Get the fuck out of my way, whore."

"Hey, you can't just barge in here!" Flannery said, following after her.

She was wearing a lacy, cream-colored nightgown that compromised any legitimate excuses about why a married man was inside her apartment after dark. "What the hell is the matter with you?"

Katarina Castille turned on her stiletto heels to face Flannery. She was even more beautiful in person than in the photos, where she often looked glacial in mannequin poses at charity events and other gatherings. According to the math, she had to be at least ten years older than Flannery but barely looked a day older. Her lips were large and pouty; her cheekbones high and refined. Her hair was long, blonde, and naturally straight. She was thin but not in an emaciated way.

"Seriously?" Katarina asked, arching a brow. "My husband's whore tells me what I can or cannot do in the apartment *we* pay for?"

Flannery realized the other woman had her. "That *you* pay for?" she finally managed to ask.

Katarina nodded and appeared to calm a little, but she kept an icy gaze on the other woman. "He is my husband. What is his is mine. I'm no fool. I know what the two of you are doing here. I don't often protest to him, but it doesn't mean I condone anything."

Flannery returned the nod. "Well, my intention was never to hurt you. I'm sorry if—"

Katarina waved away the words with her hand. "I do not need apologies from the whore," she said.

"Is it necessary to keep calling me that?" Flannery asked.

"Go collect my husband from your bed and tell him it is time to leave."

"Isn't it presumptuous to assume that he's in my bed?"

"It is a shame. I have seen you and I have watched you. You are young, you are very pretty, and you seem like an intelligent woman. Why degrade yourself this way?" Katarina asked, still staring down her nose.

Flannery put on a bitchy smile. "I'm not degrading myself. I think you're mistaken. Why don't you just do what you came here to do and then leave?"

"You come from a very prominent family in north Louisiana," Katarina continued. "You have so much potential. Why are you wasting it as my husband's mistress?"

"Who told you about my family? What do you know about me?"

Katarina continued to look at her with a frozen expression that divulged nothing.

Senator Frank Castille appeared in the living room of the apartment still fastening the top button of a long-sleeved dress shirt. He was neatly dressed, shirt tucked in, belt tightly fastened around khaki pants. "Katarina, I wasn't expecting to see you here," he said.

"The car is waiting outside," Katarina told her husband. "Come."

"But I came in mine. I can go—" he began, with a slight protest.

"Go to my car and wait with the driver. *Now*, Frank," she ordered, looking directly at him with cold blue eyes. He cowered underneath the forcefulness of her voice. "I will be there in just a moment. I wish to have a word with Miss Lanehart."

Castille gave Flannery a sheepish, apologetic glance and then obeyed his wife, making a quick exit out of the apartment.

Katarina looked pleased with herself. She closed the door behind Castille and turned to face Flannery once more. She gave an uncomfortable, icy stare for a full ten seconds before she began speaking. "The time has come for you to stay the fuck away from my husband," she said calmly, looking down her nose at Flannery. Flannery was tall at five-foot-eight, but Katarina stood even taller in her stiletto heels.

"I can't control what Frank does," Flannery replied. "If he wants to see me, then I can't stop him. After all, I am on his staff."

"You are on his staff in name only," Katarina said, her heavily accented tone growing more condescending. "The only dictation you take from him is on your back. Not everyone is as dumb as you apparently think. If you must submit a letter of resignation to make this all look more official, then do so. But you will do as I tell you."

"And if I *don't?*"

Katarina gave a short smile and shook her head. "Then you are a fool. I will drag you through the mud and cause such a stink that even people as far north as say, *Monroe*, will smell it. Including Maximilian Lanehart."

The thought of her father finding out about her affair with Castille sent a jolt of fear through Flannery, but she was determined not to allow Katarina to see her rattled.

"How would you do that without also tarnishing your husband's name?" Flannery was doing her best to put up a strong and confident front but felt the inside of her mouth going dry.

"You do not understand who you are dealing with."

Flannery thought of Conrad. *He* could help her with this problem. "I'm not afraid of you," she told Katarina.

The other woman moved closer to her face, and Katarina's visage went expressionless. "You should be very afraid of me," she said. "I can wreck your reputation and then do so *much* more. And I will, if you don't follow my orders..."

"So, Flannery, how did you get involved with Conrad?" Tilda's voice brought her back to the present.

"I'm not going into all of that right now."

Flannery worked to put Castille and Katarina out of her mind. She took a seat on one of the musty crates where she faced Tilda. "The question is how did Geoff get involved with Conrad? That's what *I* want to know."

"I honestly don't know all the details. At this point, I would probably tell you if I did."

"That's good to hear because I hope you're not holding back on me, Tilda. It would be quite unfortunate for you."

Tilda slanted her eyes defensively. "Is that some kind of threat? Just what is that supposed to mean? You've already killed me tonight! What more do you think you can do?"

"You need me now. Your survival in this new existence depends greatly on my guidance. I hate being a teacher, but that's the penance I must now pay for losing my temper and attacking you. You'll need to know more than how to avoid sunlight. And find blood..."

The mention of blood caused Tilda to sit up a little straighter. "Flannery, I need more. Wes Washer wasn't enough. You pulled me off him too soon."

"You have to try to be neat about it. If I hadn't pulled you off him when I did you would've killed him."

"But Flannery...I need *more*..."

Conrad walked into the room and quickly closed the door behind him. "Well, if it isn't my two favorite night crawlers," he said, with his usual sardonic grin. "Tilda, I know these are not the accommodations you're used to, but given your history with Flannery I thought it wiser to keep you hidden away up here on the third floor, since she's stashed away in the basement during the day. I have to keep you girls separated so you don't try and hurt one another."

"I think until Tilda gets adjusted it would be a better idea to keep us closer together," Flannery said, standing from her seat on the crate.

He ignored Flannery and stared down at Tilda where she sat. "We still have a few hours before daylight," he said, with a smile and gleam in his eyes. "Would you like to go on a little road trip?"

Tilda shrugged. "If that's the only other choice I have besides sitting in this God forsaken room the rest of the night, then I guess that'll be okay."

"Good," Conrad said. "I have to go pay someone a visit, and I think, Tilda, you could be very useful to me when I do this. *Very useful.* I hope you're hungry."

Tilda's violet eyes widened and a big smile showed half-sprouted cuspids. "Yes, please, take me with you," she told Conrad.

"Let's go," he said, opening the door and allowing Tilda to pass through first. He then turned to Flannery. "You stay here at the house," he told her. "This won't take very long."

12

"Oh, baby, you're so tense," Rochelle Dubois cooed into Geoffrey's ear as she massaged his shoulders. "What has you so wound up? You seem so upset tonight."

"I can't talk about it," he said in a near whisper, as she continued digging her hands in. He sat on the edge of the couch at Rochelle's apartment, shirtless but still wearing dress pants from earlier. She worked fervently around his shoulders and then down between his shoulder blades, where she found knots in his muscles. He wore anxiety on his face, and she could feel the tension in his body.

Rochelle was black, with long, dark hair, and large breasts Geoffrey fancied. She also carried a few extra pounds on her short, five-foot-two frame. The other women he played around with enjoyed running and the gym, but Rochelle enjoyed food. Fried meats, syrupy waffles, and late-night fast-food were her attraction. She was moving into the chubby zone, but at age twenty-six she was still firm enough.

Geoffrey enjoyed the variety she added into the mix of the other women. Of course, his affairs were an open secret, but he kept his arrangement with Rochelle completely hidden. Maximilian would have probably died much sooner had he known his son was having a sexual relationship with a black woman. It also did no good to scorn Travis for his black girlfriend if Geoffrey was doing the same. But Rochelle was only a plaything to him, even if he did occasionally buy her expensive gifts and tell her how much he loved certain attributes she possessed.

Her dark hands and brightly painted purple nails provided a stark contrast to the paleness of his back and shoulders. It was only spring, and Geoffrey always lost his healthy summer tan during the fall and winter.

Rochelle wore a purple negligee that matched her painted nails, and Geoffrey began to relax a bit as he felt the fabric and the large breasts against his back as she continued to give the massage. Given her short stature, she was propped up on her knees behind him on the couch as he sat in front of her.

"I wish I could just stay here a few days. A few weeks. God, if only..." he sighed.

"Then pack your bags and come over," she said, concerned over the sadness in his voice.

"If only I could," he said, his voice staying low. "There's so much to do. The funeral is tomorrow. My wife. *My wife...*" He trailed off. Much of what had happened with Tilda that night was still a blur.

"Let's don't talk about her," Rochelle said, rolling her dark brown eyes.

She worked as an analyst at a major telecommunications company in the area, and was far removed from the world of Geoffrey Lanehart and his family. But Rochelle had heard all about the family through office gossip and others about town. It wasn't until a chance meeting with Geoffrey out at a bar several months before that she had ever met any of the Laneharts. What she had gathered from Geoffrey was that Tilda was a steely, cold-hearted bitch. Then again, she never had any contact with the woman and only heard his side of things.

"I can't *not* talk about it," he said. "Everything has changed." He pulled away from her, stood and began pacing the carpeted living room of the apartment. "It won't be the same again. I asked for something, and I shouldn't have ... Oh God, I must be having second thoughts, and it's too late for that..."

Rochelle stood and quickly went over and stopped him in his tracks. "Oh baby, it'll be okay."

"Got anything to drink?" he said, reaching into his pocket and going back over the couch.

"Yeah, and you want some ice for your jaw?"

His jaw was red and slightly swollen from where Marcus had punched him, but it wasn't terribly noticeable. "No, I'm fine."

She nodded and went off into the kitchen. When she returned, he had produced a small vial of cocaine and was using a credit card from his wallet to chop out lines on the coffee table. "Oh well, I wondered if you were holdin' tonight," she smiled eagerly. "I didn't want to ask, but *okay!*"

"Yeah, one for each of us," he said, carving out two parallel white lines. The coke on top of the booze always made for an edgier buzz.

Rochelle set down a pint-sized bottle of Jack Daniels and two glasses on the other side of the coffee table. She poured a little whiskey into each glass and watched intently as he finished with the lines and pulled out a twenty-dollar bill and rolled it.

"You always have the good stuff," she said, going down for her cut when he handed her the twenty. After she was finished, she raised her head, held a finger to one side of her nose and gave another loud snort to drive the powder home.

"Oh hell to the yes," she smiled, picking up her glass of whiskey and taking a sip. "Thank you, baby."

Geoffrey took the twenty-dollar bill back and quickly snorted the remaining line on the table. He sat up, pinched both his nostrils and snorted again, and he felt the coke burn into his sinuses. Despite having had some earlier at Ten Points and a night of drinking, he suddenly felt a little more alert and in control of things. He thought about his queer brother punching him in the foyer at Ten Points and laughed aloud, catching Rochelle off guard.

"That son of a bitch," he said. "I ought to kick his ass."

"Who are you talking about?" Rochelle asked. "Have your drink and let's go get in bed and have some fun, baby."

Geoffrey reached over, pulled down the negligee, and began caressing one of Rochelle's fully exposed cantaloupe-sized breasts. He gave her a kiss on the lips and then started unbuttoning his pants.

"Who says we have to go to the bedroom?" he said.

"Ain't nobody," she giggled, giving him another kiss and rubbing his bulging crotch with the palm of her hand. "Oooh, somebody got themselves in a better mood," she said, giggling even more.

A knock at the door broke the moment of play between them.

"It's nearly two in the morning," she said. "Who could it be?"

"Don't answer it," Geoffrey said, pulling her closer to him. "Maybe they'll go away."

She smiled in agreement, and they began to kiss again. There was another knock, and whoever it was outside the door rapped away, more loudly and incessantly.

"For Christ's sake," Geoffrey said, pulling away from Rochelle and giving an annoyed glare at the door. "I guess you should answer it. The goddamn complex better be on fire."

"Geoff, I'm half naked. I can't go to the door like this," she said modestly, pulling the negligee back up to cover her bare breasts.

"Okay, I'll answer it," he said, getting off the couch and going to the door. "Who's there?" he called. There was no answer, just another loud knock.

Rochelle quickly reached over to the coffee table and put the vial of cocaine out of sight as Geoffrey unlatched the lock.

"What the hell," Geoffrey muttered, as he opened the door.

There stood Tilda in her gym wear, and Conrad in his jogging pants and tank top. They looked like a health-conscious couple on their way to a twenty-four-hour workout facility.

"Well hello there," Conrad said, with a smile. He and Tilda entered without an invitation.

"Oh my God," Rochelle exclaimed, both scared and embarrassed. She tried to cover herself with a pillow from the sofa. "Is that...?"

"Why yes it is," Tilda said, walking over for a closer look at the other woman. "Geoffrey, a black woman? Really? How can we scold Travis for *mixing the soup* when you're doing the same thing?"

"Mixing the *what?*" Rochelle asked, confused.

"I'm sorry," Tilda said, with a smile and a shake of the head. "I meant to say *fuck a nigger.*"

An angry Rochelle sprang from the couch. "Why, you skinny white bitch! How dare you come in my place and say—"

Tilda's violet eyes flared, and she pointed her finger at Rochelle, causing her to back off one step. "Lower your voice and calm down," she warned.

"Why are you here?" Rochelle asked warily. She was scared again. "How did you even know where I live?"

"I know lots of things," Conrad said to her with one of his bright smiles. He looked over at Geoffrey. "I keep a close watch on my friends."

Geoffrey grew more uncomfortable. "I think I'll get dressed and leave," he said, looking to a corner of the room. "My shirt is right over there on the chair. Tilda, Conrad, let's go back to the house."

"I want all y'all out of here," Rochelle said, feeling more unsafe as the burn of Conrad's and Tilda's eyes seared into her.

"Not yet," Conrad said, crossing his bare arms, as he watched Rochelle squirm. Tilda stood even closer to the other woman, and her eyes looked even brighter than when she first arrived.

"Let's just—" Geoffrey felt a knot form in his stomach.

Conrad uncrossed an arm and held out a hand to silence him. "Go lock the door," he ordered Geoffrey.

"Conrad, look—"

"Goddamn you," Conrad said, turning and looking angrily at Geoffrey. "Go lock the door as I say. After all that's happened tonight, I'm going to teach both you and that stubborn sister of yours obedience. It looks like it will have to be the hard way. You get to go first."

Geoffrey slowly went over to the door, and had to use both his hands to latch it when he realized the right one quivered out of his control. "But Conrad, I was willing to leave and go—"

Rochelle looked as if she were about to start crying. Tilda kept a firm stance near her, as if to keep her from moving and trying to run away.

"What you were about to do *here* is not the point, Geoffrey," Conrad said. His tone had shifted to that of a parent scolding a young unruly child. "Dismissing me the way you did when you walked out of Ten Points and ordering me not to wait up for you...*well,* that is not the way you are to handle me. Since when do you lay out the rules for me?"

"But I—"

"You know the rules, Geoff. Tilda now knows the rules, too. I explained them to her on the drive over here."

"What's going on here?" Rochelle demanded, her voice shaky. "Can't y'all discuss this somewhere else? I don't want any part of this."

"Too late," Tilda told her quietly but authoritatively, as she watched her with a catlike stare. "That time has passed."

"What are you going to do?" Rochelle asked with a whimper, backing toward the sofa.

"Why tell you?" Tilda said, moving even closer. "Surprises are so much more fun."

Rochelle fell on to the sofa with a gasp and started to cry. "Please don't hurt me. I promise, I'll—"

Before she could get the rest of the sentence out, Tilda was on her, sucking like a leech. Rochelle screamed and tried to fight her off, unsuccessfully. Tilda overpowered her and was latched on to her throat too quickly.

"Oh my God, what is she doing?" Geoffrey exclaimed, beginning to turn hysterical as he had in the study earlier. He tried to go after Tilda, but Conrad grabbed him by the arms and held him back.

"No," he told Geoffrey, forcefully restraining him. "This is *part* of your lesson. Obey me. Do what I say."

"Geoff, help me..." Rochelle gasped, still jerking and moving about and trying to get out from under Tilda.

It was no use. Rochelle's body soon went limp and her eyes fluttered shut.

"This was never part of our agreement. She can't go around killing people!" Geoffrey cried. Conrad still had a firm grip on his arms so that he couldn't move.

Tilda continued making suckling sounds at Rochelle's throat causing Geoffrey to go back just a few hours when it was Flannery doing the same to Tilda. All the events of the last five or so hours made him crazy. All of the liquor and coke in the world wouldn't make it go away. He wanted to wake up from this hell and have everything be normal again. For his father to be alive again; for *Tilda* to be alive again.

But it was too late.

Tilda arose from the couch over Rochelle's lifeless body, licking her bloody lips. She had somehow managed not to get any of the blood on her clothing, while Rochelle's purple negligee was soaked at the top. A small amount of blood still oozed from the puncture wounds on her neck.

Tilda looked pleased with herself. "Thanks for the invitation, Conrad," she said.

"Oh no. No, no, no..." Geoffrey moaned, turning his head and closing his eyes. Conrad finally released him.

"You know what you must do now," Conrad said to Tilda. "We have to finish teaching Geoff his lesson, now don't we?"

"Yes, dead girlfriend. Throat wound. His fingerprints everywhere. Drugs and alcohol. This isn't going to be good for you, Geoff, when the police arrive," Tilda said coldly. Some of Rochelle's blood was still on her lips and the corners of her mouth.

Geoffrey looked up in a panic. "Oh my God, *what!*"

"I'm afraid she has you there, Geoff. Creatures like Flannery and Tilda have the ability and power of never leaving DNA evidence behind. Yours is all the police will ever find."

"Oh God, why are you doing this to me?" he yelled, walking off to the corner of the room and starting to cry. "Conrad, this goes against everything we agreed on. I can't take any of this anymore!"

"Should I call the police?" Tilda asked.

Conrad crossed his arms and looked over at Geoffrey. "Not if Geoffrey gets back on track and also agrees to do something for me."

Geoffrey turned and looked at him. "What? I'll do anything. Please. Just tell me!"

Conrad smiled. "That's my boy. I want you to convince your brother to stay after the funeral and not go back to San Diego."

"I don't want him in *my* house, and I can't make him stay if he wants to leave!"

"Tilda, I guess perhaps you *should* call the police..."

"Okay, okay, please don't! Okay, I'll do whatever you say. But what if he doesn't want to stay?"

"Then I strongly suggest you do whatever you can to make sure that doesn't happen."

Tilda's canine teeth were still elongated, and she savagely bit into her own wrist as if it were an apple.

"Oh dear God!" Geoffrey wailed. *"Why are you doing that?"*

She placed her bleeding wrist over Rochelle's open lips and began squeezing it with her other hand.

"I'm completing your punishment. I'm adding to the family," Tilda said, looking back at him with a wide, toothy smile.

She then glanced over to Conrad who granted her a nod of approval.

13

The long, antique wooden table in the formal dining room at Ten Oaks seated a dozen, but the next morning only Marcus, D'Lynn, and Aunt Hattie sat at one end of it. They enjoyed a spread of hot chicory coffee, scrambled eggs, sausage, bacon, hash browns that had been fried in the bacon grease, and homemade biscuits with honey—all prepared by D'Lynn and her assistant Tarva. The two women had brought out enough to feed the entire family and then some, but the tantalizing aromas from all of the food set out at the center of the table were so far not attracting anyone else into the dining room that morning.

"I had no idea you were staying here at the house and not at a hotel," Marcus said to Aunt Hattie, who was seated across from him. She already had on a yellow sundress with ample cleavage exposed, full makeup, and a lush, blonde wig with hair that fell to her shoulders and covered the natural bob she wore the evening before.

"Oh, sugar, I just love an excuse to stay in the house I grew up in," she replied cheerfully, as if her brother's corpse wasn't in the next room. "I have so many stories I could tell you about when I was a little girl here."

"I know plenty of 'em from when you were an adult," D'Lynn pointed out, from her seat next to Marcus.

The two women then laughed loudly. "Oh, D'Lynn, I was a wild lil' thang when I was younger. Of that there ain't no doubt," Aunt Hattie said, waving a hand around and showing off the long red fingernails. "All this food you and Tarva made sure is good. If I ate like this every day I would lose my figure."

"Thank the Good Lord for Tarva. I'm gettin' old and need help in the kitchen," D'Lynn said, talking slowly in her thick country accent. "The arthritis. My back, my knees. I need a young 'un in there with me to help do all the bendin' and liftin' I can't do much of no more."

If the truth were to be told, D'Lynn was about the same age as Aunt Hattie, but the women had led much different lives with D'Lynn coming from much less privilege and clearly having the harder lot of the two.

"Honey, don't think about it like that. Age is just a number. Focus on all you can still do. It's a darn shame nobody else is here to eat any of this food after you went to all that work. Marcus, where's your brother? And where are the kids?"

"I have no idea where anyone is," Marcus said, distracted as he sipped his coffee. The last time he had seen his brother was when he had punched him in the jaw the night before in the foyer.

"They must be sleepin' in," Aunt Hattie said. "I heard some racket downstairs last night, but after I put in my earplugs I was able to get to sleep okay. Sugar, you look like you were off in another world just now."

"What did you hear?" Marcus asked, wondering if she had heard any of the commotion after Geoffrey sneaked up behind him at the coffin. And Aunt Hattie was correct. He was in another place this morning.

That damn dream. Marcus still couldn't figure out what had really happened and what had not. The mysterious child's hand grabbing his, the experience at the casket he couldn't bear to think about anymore, young Bobby appearing in the foyer, and then whatever the hell that was in his bedroom afterward.

You belong to me.

He had awoken with those red marks on his arms, almost like...handprints. He kept trying to tell himself he had somehow done it to himself in his sleep. That was the only plausible explanation. That could be the *only* explanation. None of it could have really happened, and it must have been entirely his imagination on overdrive.

"It sounded like somebody yellin'. In the study," Aunt Hattie said. "You know, my room is right above there. Geoffrey gets all worked up with his business deals. I figured he was chewin' somebody out on the phone, so I put my earplugs in and rolled over and don't remember nothin' after that."

"Who knows," Marcus said. "Geoff can be temperamental."

He made a face as he looked away and took another sip of coffee.

"Are y'all gettin' along okay?" Aunt Hattie asked, concerned. "He ain't givin' you a hard time because of all that stuff between you and your Daddy, is he?"

"It'll be fine," Marcus said. "I'm leaving after the funeral this evening."

"Sugar, I'm sorry he's bein' the way he is. You know, the gays are some of my best friends and hired help. There's my hair guy, and that other guy who helped me decorate my house for Christmas that one year, and..." Aunt Hattie's eyes fluttered back and forth as she tried to count out gay men on her fingers. She didn't make it to the end of her hand. "Well, I just know I could think of some more if I tried..."

Marcus was amused at her effort and appreciated it but would have been offended by those stereotypical examples from anyone else. "Geoff is a younger version of Dad. That's how it's always been, and I never expect anything to be different," he said.

"I love all y'all like you was my own. I hate that you don't love each other," D'Lynn said, looking glum.

Marcus realized everything that had happened at bedtime the night before had diverted his attention from another peculiarity earlier in the evening. "D'Lynn and Aunt Hattie, *who* was the woman at the wake last night in pearls and a black dress?" Marcus asked.

"Honey, it was a wake. A woman in a black dress don't narrow it down too much," D'Lynn said.

"The African-American woman," Marcus said.

The women looked puzzled. "I never seen anybody like that," D'Lynn said, looking over to Aunt Hattie. "Did you?"

"I wasn't payin' attention and didn't see any colored woman, other than that little girlfriend of Travis'," Aunt Hattie said, nibbling on a piece of bacon. Her archaic choice of words made Marcus cringe. "I was too busy checkin' out that hunk of a man talkin' to Geoff and that weasel-lookin' lawyer guy."

You belong to me.

The mention of Conrad made Marcus uneasy. He still wasn't completely convinced their encounter had been only a dream. It seemed ridiculous to think it wasn't, but none of it seemed like any other dream Marcus had ever experienced.

"That young man could be your grandson," D'Lynn said, shaking her head. "You are just somethin' else, Hattie."

"Oh, hogwash," Aunt Hattie said. "I could *probably* be his mother, I'm *sure*, but there's no way I'm old enough to be his grandmaw."

D'Lynn looked as if she wanted to dispute that but left it alone. "Anyway, he's stayin' here at the house. I had to fix a room for him after the wake ended last night."

Aunt Hattie gave a big smile and sat up in her chair. "*Oooh?* That beefcake was upstairs with me the whole time last night? He must not've known where my room was if he didn't come and see me. Too bad I have to go back home after the funeral later. Is he stayin' again tonight?"

D'Lynn rolled her eyes and shook her head again. "I have no idea. I reckon Geoff will tell me later what to do about the room."

"Well, speak of the devil," Aunt Hattie said, looking over as Geoffrey entered the dining room. "Good mornin', sugar."

Geoffrey smiled and looked more refreshed than he had while intoxicated the night before. Freshly shaven, he wore a striped dark dress shirt, with a tie and gray slacks. There was no sign of redness or puffiness around his eyes. But there was still a red mark on his left jaw.

"Good morning, everybody," he said, pulling up a chair beside Aunt Hattie and across from his brother. Geoffrey's ability to always put himself back together on the surface so quickly never failed to amaze Marcus.

"Honey, what happened to your jaw?" D'Lynn asked, reaching out and touching his shoulder like a concerned mama bear. "It looks red, like you almost have a bruise."

"Oh, clumsy me, I banged it on the medicine cabinet," he said, with a grin. His smooth, salesman voice was out and working. He looked over at Marcus and narrowed his eyes. "Before I fix a plate, may I have a word with you in private?"

Marcus decided to keep a cool demeanor. "Sure, let's go in the other room," he said, as he stood from the table.

Geoffrey also stood and led him out of the dining room and down a hallway out of the earshot of the ladies. Once they were a safe distance away he turned and faced him. "I want to talk to you about what happened last night," he said.

"What about it?" Marcus asked, keeping a poker face.

Geoffrey gently placed his hands on Marcus' shoulders, catching him off guard and making him wince a bit. Geoffrey nodded, as if he understood the reaction. "I had no right to say those things to you last night," he told Marcus. "That was unforgivable. You had every right to hit me."

"*What?*" Marcus said. Was he in a dream again?

"I was wrong, Marcus," Geoffrey continued, looking down at his feet like a naughty child. He then looked back up at Marcus. "This place is always your home. I don't want you to feel like you have to leave after the funeral is over. Not right away, anyway. Would you please stay at least a few more days? There are estate things to go over, and no matter what happened between you and Dad, you're a part of this family."

Marcus tried to hold back a scoff. "Well, last night you couldn't wait for your faggot brother and whore sister to be out of your sight. And then there was that thing about hoping we both rotted in hell. This is quite a change in just a few hours, Geoff."

"Marcus, oh Marcus! My little brother!" Geoffrey pulled his brother to him for a hug. He gritted his teeth in a grimace as he embraced him. *Why do you have to be so stubborn? Just forgive me, and let me get this over with. Conrad, I fucking hate you,* he thought to himself. "I wish there was some way I could take back those terrible, awful words," he said instead. "I had a bit to drink. Still, I know that's no excuse. I hope you will find a way to forgive me, Marcus."

Once they pulled apart, Marcus' look of surprise told Geoffrey he had made a dent in the armor. He even looked as if his eyes were about to tear up. "I never thought I would ever hear you say anything like that," he said. "Do you really mean that?"

Maximilian's words in the dream. Maybe his brother did need him. Maybe it was some kind of strange prophecy, though Marcus wasn't sure he believed in such things. It had all seemed so dark and ominous in the dream, but maybe it was a sign of some kind of breakthrough for the two of them.

Geoffrey put on a smile. "Of course I do. No matter what's happened, deep down I've always loved you. Maybe part of me even admires or envies you sometimes." He leaned in and gave Marcus a kiss on the cheek. "Let's start over. Let's be a family again." *Goddamn you, Conrad. I deserve an Academy Award for this.*

"I haven't called and made any arrangements yet." Marcus was thinking more about work than airline reservations. "I could probably stay a while longer if you need me to stay."

"That would be wonderful," Geoffrey said, putting his arms around his brother as they walked back to the dining room. "I'm so glad we were able to talk this out. Let's always try to talk to each other from now on before things get messy again. Does that sound like something we can work on together?"

"That sounds reasonable to me. Geoff, can I ask you something?"

Geoffrey patted him affectionately and turned to him with a look of concern. "Yes?"

"Who was the older black woman in the black dress at the wake last night?"

Geoffrey looked away and shook his head. He looked back at Marcus. "I'm not sure I follow you."

"She was in the parlor with the other guests," Marcus said. "She looked to be about middle age. There was some gray in her hair. She seemed sad and kept looking across the room at me. When I went to find her later she was gone."

"Marcus, a lot of people are sad about Dad, but I never saw anybody like that inside the house," Geoffrey said as they reached the dining room.

Aunt Hattie looked up with a smile. "Well, look at you two," she said. "You're both as handsome as your Daddy was at your age."

"Well, thank you, beautiful aunt," Geoffrey said suavely, giving her a peck on the cheek as he retook his seat beside her.

"Speaking of handsome," Aunt Hattie said, with a mischievous expression. "Where is that stallion of a friend of yours?"

"I'm afraid I don't know who—" Geoffrey began.

"She's talking about Conrad," Marcus said, taking a sip of coffee and looking away.

"He will be at the funeral later," Geoffrey said. He and his brother finally had something in common when it came to wanting to drop the subject of Conrad at the breakfast table.

All of the tap dancing was starting to wear on him. It was taking all he had to put on a happy front for the rest of the family and not crack. *What Flannery did to Tilda. What Tilda did to Rochelle.* All the things he didn't want to do that Conrad was making him do. The endgame that was a secret to everyone but Ruffin, Conrad, and him. It was all starting to eat away inside of him, but he couldn't let anyone see it.

"And where are Tilda and Flannery this morning?" Aunt Hattie asked.

"Flannery is back at her hotel until later," Geoffrey lied. She was dead to the world inside a storage closet in the basement for the next nine or so hours. "And Tilda isn't feeling well and is resting," he said.

Geoffrey hadn't decided yet how to cover Tilda's absence during daylight hours from then on. He knew it would soon be a problem. He had been so panicked the night before he had never taken the time to thoroughly go over tedious details that would come up later.

"Oh maybe I should take her breakfast up to her?" D'Lynn suggested, setting down her napkin and about to rise from the table.

"No, there's no need for that," he quickly intervened. "She told me she didn't want to be disturbed before I came down."

"Well, I hope she's feelin' better later. It's probably just those spring allergies," Aunt Hattie said, taking another bite of bacon.

14

"Travis, put that thing away. It scares me."

Travis Lanehart slid the sword from its steel scabbard and playfully swung it around his bedroom. It was given to him when he was a boy by Maximilian, who told him it was pulled off a Union soldier who was shot and killed on Ten Points property during the Civil War. When he was sixteen, Travis decided to take it to a pawn shop to find out its worth. He had never had the courage to tell his grandfather that he knew the sword was only a twentieth century replica and not the real thing. It made him wonder what else the old man had lied to him about during his childhood in the house.

Despite its lack of authenticity, the long weapon still sported a sharp, curved blade with elaborate lettering, and it made Travis' girlfriend Regan anxious when he took it from where it hung on the wall. Between his dark clothing, pitch-black hair with the blue streak, and his pale hand around the black leather-wrapped sword handle, the skinny teenager looked more like a character from a Goth-themed anime than anyone trying to re-enact a battle from the War Between the States.

Regan was also nervous about being found inside her boyfriend's darkly decorated bedroom at the end of the second floor hallway of the house. She sneaked in and spent the night after lying to her parents about staying with a girlfriend on a Saturday night. Instead, she stowed away in Travis' private den, which included windows shuttered with dark black curtains, a black light, a life-size replica of a human skull on top of his dresser, posters from several Rob Zombie horror movies, and last but not least—a pet tarantula named Harry, which lived on crickets.

Thankfully, the arachnid was secured in an aquarium. Regan wasn't so sure about staying safe from anyone else who lurked about the house now that morning had arrived. Unlike her boyfriend, she dressed casually, and often wore bright colors, jeans, normal makeup, and keeping her naturally curly black hair fastened in a ponytail.

"I still say I could take this thing to school and make people think it's the real deal. I would be the shit," he said, swinging and making jabs against an invisible enemy.

"You'd probably get arrested and expelled for taking that to school," Regan said. "They don't play around. Don't even try that."

"Not if it's 'show and tell' for history class," he teased, then gave her a look that made her giggle.

Travis slid the sword into its sheath and hung it back on the wall. He gave Regan a big smile as he kneeled down and kissed her where she sat on the edge of his unmade bed. "What do you wanna do today?" he asked.

"I have to try to figure out how to sneak out of this house without anybody seein' me," she said. "And I already texted Marcie to make sure my Mama didn't call her house lookin' for me."

"Let's sneak out of here together," he said. "It's too damn depressing around here."

"We can't go to my house. My Mama's way less thrilled than your Mama is about the two of us."

It wasn't only the interracial part of their relationship that made Regan's mother uneasy. Travis' appearance convinced her he was probably some kind of devil worshipper out to convert her baby girl to the dark side.

"Who says we have to go to your house? Let's go out to Pecanland Mall, or maybe over to West Monroe. We could go to Tinseltown and see a movie?"

"You've got to stay here with your family. Y'all are havin' a funeral downstairs. I've still never seen a casket inside somebody's house before. At least not until now. Kinda creeps me out."

There was a sudden knock at the door. "Travis?"

"Holy shit, it's D'Lynn," he whispered to Regan, as his blue eyes grew wide. He motioned for her to go hide in the closet. He prayed D'Lynn wasn't bringing in any laundry she would insist on hanging for him. He opened the bedroom door a crack once he was certain Regan was safely tucked away. "Yes ma'am?" he asked, with an innocent smile.

"I got breakfast downstairs," she said, trying to look past him into the room. He always had the feeling D'Lynn suspected he was up to no good when he was in his room with the door closed. Sometimes she was correct in her assumptions.

"Thanks, but I'm just not very hungry this mornin' and all, so—"

"Not hungry, my foot!" she said, reaching in and grabbing him by the sleeve of his black T-shirt and pulling him into the hallway. "You are way too skinny, and I will fatten you up if it's the last thing I ever do."

"But D'Lynn, I can't go downstairs right now," he said, then realized he would have to quickly come up with an excuse.

"Well, why not?" she asked. "There's a ton of food down there, and I'll have to start puttin' it away soon and get ready for lunch."

He gave her a look. "Well, you know ..."

"No, I don't know nothin'," she said with a frown, getting impatient. "Why can't you come downstairs with me, boy?"

"It's kind of embarrassin'," he said, looking away.

"*What* is?"

"Nature's about to call," he finally said, raising a dark eyebrow.

"What is so embarrassin' about that?" she asked, with a frown and a shrug. "Everybody that's alive's got to go to the pot. Go do your business and then come on downstairs, okay?"

He nodded as she walked off down the hallway and then quickly darted back inside his bedroom and closed the door. "Oh shit, D'Lynn is trying to get me to go downstairs and eat breakfast with the family," he said to Regan, as he opened the closet door. "This is gonna be tough to get out of."

"I've got an idea," Regan said, with a sly smile. "Let's be real quiet and sneak downstairs. You can go eat, and I'll slip out the front. After that, I can ring the doorbell and pretend like I'm just gettin' here."

"Do you think anybody saw your car outside today?" he asked.

She shrugged. "If anybody says anything I'll just say I had car trouble and you had to take me home last night."

"What if they ask who brought you here today?"

"I won't worry about that unless somebody asks me."

"Okay," he nodded, as they went to the bedroom door. Travis cracked it open again and peeked down the long hallway. "I think the coast is clear," he said and motioned her to follow after him.

They tiptoed quietly down the carpeted hallway, with Regan closely behind Travis. Wooden doors up and down the hall led to bedrooms. Many of them were the original oak ones with skeleton key locks from the nineteenth century when the house was built. So many damn rooms in the house, Travis often thought, and nobody uses or ever goes inside most of them. He sometimes wished he could live in a smaller, contemporary home like the other kids at school. But being the nonconformist he was, he usually tried not to compare himself to his classmates.

One of the rustic doors creaked open unexpectedly, and Conrad stepped out into the hallway. He was wearing a tan blazer, white dress shirt, with jeans, and looked as if he were off to some kind of casual business meeting.

Travis smiled nervously as their eyes met. "Oh, shit, hey man..." he muttered and looked away, realizing he had just been caught by one of his Dad's friends. He didn't know this man well enough to know what to expect.

Conrad turned away from the bedroom door and looked squarely at both of them. "You two look as though you're trying not to get caught doing something," he said.

"What makes you say that?" Travis asked, putting on another smile as an attempted cover.

"The 'oh shit' and the fact you're both practically walking on your tiptoes kind of gives it away," he said, looking down at both of them. He kept a neutral expression that failed to tell them whether he was amused and would let them pass—or if he would turn them over to the adults for disciplinary action.

"Um, oh..." Travis said, not sure what else to say. He looked back at Regan, who appeared frightened by Conrad.

"Let me guess," Conrad said, thoughtfully tapping the cleft in his chin with an index finger. "Travis, is it? So Travis, it appears to me you and your girlfriend most likely spent the night together, and now you're trying to sneak her out of the house before anybody finds out. Is that a correct assumption?"

"Oh please don't tell on us," Regan pleaded, walking around to Travis' side. "We were watchin' a movie late and fell asleep. I didn't mean to stay all night."

"What movie did you watch?" Conrad asked, a grin forming.

"Um," Travis looked over to Regan. *"House of 1000 Corpses."*

"You're lying," Conrad said, the grin gone.

"Who the hell are you anyway, man?" Travis asked, turning angry. "Are you suddenly my Dad or somethin'?"

Marcus appeared at the top of the stairs on the other end of the hallway. "What's going on up here?" he asked, walking closer to where the three of them stood.

Conrad turned to Marcus and smiled. "Well, good morning."

Marcus kept a solid expression. "Are you bothering my nephew and his friend?" he asked.

"Yeah, he's a fuckin' creep," Travis snarled, walking on past. "Come on, Regan, let's go."

"Wait a minute, you two," Marcus said, turning to them. "Keep your voices down when you go down the stairs. Geoff is right around the corner in the dining room."

"Thanks, Uncle Marcus," Travis said. He spun back around and gave the middle finger to Conrad once Conrad's back was turned and he faced Marcus again. Travis and Regan then went downstairs.

Conrad nodded and continued to smile at Marcus. "You're such a cool uncle," he said. "So when you were that age, did you sneak girls—or I guess in your case, *boys*—into the house?"

Marcus shook his head. "No, but he gets enough of a hard time from his parents. I'm not going to get him into more trouble."

"Well, you should give your little nephew of the night some advice and suggestions on a cleaner mouth and how to show more respect toward adults," Conrad said. "He's got quite a tongue on him."

"I don't think he's a bad kid," Marcus said. "If he spoke unkindly to you then I'm sure he had his reasons."

"How does your hand feel today?" Conrad asked, changing the subject.

You belong to me.

The eyes were burning into Marcus, just as they had in the dream when he was only able to see them by moonlight. Had it been real or not? He stared at Conrad's full lips just then and remembered how they had felt on him. "Is it still swollen?"

"It's fine," Marcus replied.

"What were you thinking just now?" Conrad asked, looking at him. "You seemed lost in your thoughts for a moment."

"Not at all," Marcus lied. "I think I have a clear mind today."

"I thought we were getting along better last night, but I suppose I took it backwards with that little thing in the living room. I should apologize for anything I did that was inappropriate."

"That little thing?" Marcus asked. "You mean, the kiss? Yeah, that came out of left field. I just think it's kind of funny, and maybe even a bit ironic, that my homophobic brother is hanging out with a gay guy."

Conrad gave a short laugh. "I'm not gay."

Marcus was confused. "Straight men don't normally stare deeply into the eyes of other men and then try to make out with them."

"I didn't say I was straight either," Conrad said, with an amused expression. "I'm a sexual being. If I'm attracted to someone, I'm attracted to them. Gender isn't an issue."

"Then you're bisexual," Marcus said. "I get it. Well, good for you."

He was ready to end the conversation and move on. The only reason he had come upstairs was to unpack a bag, since he clearly wouldn't be going to the airport later.

"I don't like bisexual either," Conrad said, shaking his head. "I don't like labels. Why must we all have to wear labels? Why can't we all just ... *be.*"

"Good luck with all of that," Marcus said. "Please excuse me."

"Marcus, wait..." Conrad reached out and placed his hand on Marcus' arm. On the sleeve—in the exact area of one of the red marks from the night before. The touch brought back a familiarity. A feeling Marcus knew wouldn't have been there if it had never happened before. "Let's get back on track with one another and not have any hostile feelings," Conrad suggested.

You belong to me.

"Oh my God," Marcus said, pulling his arm away from Conrad's touch. "You *were* in my room last night. I thought it was a dream, but somehow it was ... it was *real.*"

"I'm afraid you've lost me," Conrad said, narrowing his dark eyes. "I was in your room last night?"

"Yes. At first it was...*how were you able to do that?*" First it was Zeke, and then Zeke had transformed into Conrad. The dream, or what he thought was a dream, was still crystal clear. "Even before I met you, *you were there all these past weeks...*" he continued. No, no, no, it couldn't be real. Such things weren't possible.

"Marcus, I must say I really don't know what you're talking about. Maybe you should explain."

He realized he had confused himself. "It was like déjà vu just now, when you put your hand..." He stepped away. "But it couldn't have been real. I don't know..."

Conrad smiled. "Some people say déjà vu is a sign of a past life. Maybe we knew one another in another time, as other people."

Marcus shook his head. The dream, or what he thought was a dream, had taken place in *this* life. "I don't believe in reincarnation," he said. "We didn't know one another in some past life."

Conrad kept the smile. "Are you so sure about that?"

"I'm not sure about anything, except that I have to go unpack a bag. So, please pardon me..."

"Unpack a bag? So you're not leaving after the funeral?"

"No, I'll stay a little longer. I'm not sure how long, but I won't be leaving today after all."

Conrad nodded. "I'm glad to hear that."

"Why?" Marcus asked. Why did this man want to be so close to him?

"Because I would like to get to know you better, Marcus. Is that so terrible?"

You belong to me. Damn it, stop thinking it. Get it out of your head, Marcus thought.

Marcus gave Conrad a noncommittal smile that was neither warm nor cold. "You should head downstairs," he said. "D'Lynn has quite a spread of food out for breakfast. Probably the kind they don't serve where you come from."

"I'm sure that's an understatement," Conrad said, his smile fading as he watched Marcus walk away to his bedroom.

15

Marcus' iPhone vibrated on the end of the bed as he unpacked the suitcase he had packed early that morning. He had laid out all the clothes from dressy to casual along the side of the bed and prepared to put them back in drawers and the closet when the call came. He picked up the phone, saw the name, took a deep breath, and then answered it.

"Peter," he said.

"Look, I know your father passed away, and I'm sorry, but you have to answer your damn phone sometimes and give me a status on things sometimes," his superior began. His tone was abrasive as always when he was stressed out over his staff. "They just arrested Turner, and it's looking like bribery, extortion, and maybe even obstruction of justice. He may not be the only city council member involved in this—"

"Oh, I see," Marcus said. "Well, we knew the Turner part was coming."

"Did 'John X' tell you anything else about anyone else?"

"No, just Turner. That's all my source had access to."

"When can you be back here? Can you get a red eye out of there tonight? I need you back here ASAP."

"That won't be possible," Marcus said, his tone flat. Why was he even talking to Peter? He somehow didn't care anymore.

"Tomorrow then?"

"I'll be staying here for a little while. My family needs me to stay a little longer than expected."

"How long is a little longer? I need you to get your ass back here!"

"I just told you that's not possible. At least a few days."

"Then give me access to this 'John' guy."

"They won't talk to anybody but me."

"Then get the fuck back here!"

"Why don't you take it down a notch?" Marcus asked, his voice rising. "Has it ever occurred to you that some things are more important than a goddamn story?" To hell with the *Sun-Times*. And to hell with this prick who only cared about outscooping everyone else and had no concept of family time.

"Did you really just say that?" Peter asked more quietly. "You used to be my number-one, most reliable guy. Knocking down doors, demanding answers, a bulldog. What the hell happened to you? You've been on another planet lately, and I know you've had a tough year before all this stuff with your father, but really? Life goes on, Marcus. Now after your father's funeral, I want you to—"

"Listen," Marcus said, irritated at Peter's mention of Landon and his nonchalance about what was developing at Ten Points. *"I can't come back right now.* How many more times do I have to repeat this?"

"Well, hurry back, before you don't have a job to come back to," Peter said. "I guess I will have to hand this over to somebody who's competent."

Marcus was suddenly angry. "Competent? I'm incompetent now? How dare you bring up my personal problems and harass me on the day my Dad is buried. You son of a bitch. I quit!"

"I'm sorry, what did—"

"Go fuck yourself, Peter! I'll send my forwarding address for my *final* paycheck. And if my overtime isn't there you'll be hearing from me!" Marcus ended the call and threw the phone down on to the bed.

"Goddamn it to hell!" he shouted, and then kicked the other empty suitcase on the floor so hard it went halfway across the spacious bedroom.

"Whoa, holy shit, Uncle Marcus. I've never seen you act like that before!" Travis stood behind him at the open doorway with a big smile. He walked into the bedroom. "That was, like, totally sick. You told that guy real good."

Marcus nodded, and began putting clothes back in a dresser drawer. "He's a jerk. It was a long time coming."

"Was he, like, your lover or something?"

Marcus frowned at the boy. "No. Weren't you listening? Didn't you hear the part about my final paycheck? That was my boss. I just quit my job."

"Oh wow, Uncle Marcus. What do you think you'll do now?" Travis took a seat on the end of the bed and made himself at home, not taking the hint Marcus wasn't in a sociable mood at the moment.

"I don't know," he said. "I don't know anything right now."

"You should go get a job at KNOE," Travis said, referring to one of the local television stations. "You could probably even be on TV and stuff."

"I don't like being in front of a camera," Marcus said, shaking his head. "I'll figure something out."

"Well, the reason I came in here was to say thanks for helping me out earlier," Travis said, and handed Marcus the rest of his stuff from the bed. "That guy Conrad is a fuckin' tool. Why does he hang around here all the time?"

"You live here," Marcus replied, as he put the rest of the clothes away and closed the drawer. "I figured you would know the answer to that before I would. And you're welcome."

"I don't know what Geoff, um, I mean, Dad, does with anybody. We aren't that close. Me and Mom don't really talk anymore either. The twins aren't close enough to my age to hang with. Plus, Bobby's the way he is, you know. I do what I can to entertain him sometimes, but it's a challenge. I stay in my room most of the time when I'm not at school or with Regan."

Marcus was on his way to the closet to hang clothes when turned back to Travis.

"Bobby's the way he is *how?*" Marcus asked. No one in the family had ever discussed anything about Bobby with him. Marcus only knew him as one of Geoffrey's children.

"Uncle Marcus..." Travis gave a light laugh. *"Come on.* You don't know?"

"No," Marcus said, walking over to him. "Tell me."

"Bobby's not all there. Kind of slow. He looks normal for the most part, but he's a lot smaller than Maxine and almost never talks. They said Maxine took all the oxygen away from him when they were still inside Mom. At least that's the excuse, I guess. Nobody figured it out until he got up a little older and wasn't acting like other kids his age. Of course, Dad and Mom won't 'fess up to there being a retard in the family, so nobody ever talks about it."

"Don't say that about your brother," Marcus gently scolded. "That's not a nice word to use. He can't help the way he is."

"I guess not," Travis said. "But that's the story. He doesn't even go to a real school. Mom and Geoff, I mean, *Dad,* are too embarrassed to have him go to a real school and be in special ed classes. He has a tutor that comes to the house during the week. I wish I could have one of those. I fuckin' hate school like a motherfucker."

"Travis, may I make a suggestion?" Marcus said, with a wary smile.

"Sure, Uncle Marcus," Travis grinned.

"All the profanity," Marcus said. "You drop the F-bomb way too much. I don't have any room to talk right now, but it's one of those words... *well ...*"

"I fuckin' love that word!" Travis exclaimed enthusiastically.

"You need to cut back," Marcus told him. "Try to use it only when you really need to emphasize something. Like, when you called Conrad 'a fucking creep' earlier. That was—that was perfect."

"Oh okay. Well, I guess I could try to do better."

Marcus finished hanging the rest of his clothes and closed the closet door. "Come on, let's go downstairs," he told Travis.

When they reached the bottom of the stairs, they heard the panicked voice of D'Lynn from the living room. They rushed into the room as she hung up the landline phone. She wrung her hands, and the deep wrinkles stood out on her forehead as she raised her brows and shook her head. She began to pace.

"D'Lynn, what's the matter?" Marcus asked.

"It's one of the horses down at the stable," she said. "Geoff's on his way down there. I just called Zeke Colson. One of our guys called up and said it's on its side and seems like it might be sick."

"Oh that's terrible," Marcus said. "We should go down there."

"Maxine," D'Lynn said, continuing to shake her head. "She's still upset about the ducks. I don't know what I'm gonna tell her."

"Let's go see what's going on before we tell her anything," Marcus suggested. "Maybe there's a misunderstanding, and it won't turn out to be as serious as it sounds."

The three of them left the house and walked down to the stables along a dirt road at the far northwest end of the main house. It was barely ten o'clock, but the sun was shining down brightly after the storm of the night before. The spring grass along the road was dotted with blooming Black-Eyed Susans. It was already starting to feel a little humid for April, but a gentle breeze kept things pleasant and not uncomfortable.

After about five minutes, Marcus, D'Lynn, and Travis reached the long row of stables where Geoffrey stood outside a stall with Buddy, a stocky, bearded groundskeeper at Ten Points.

On the other side of the two men, a beautiful, thoroughbred mare that would have normally been the picture of health was lying on her side, making horrible gasping sounds and then taking shallow breaths. Her long, thick black tail thrashed back and forth every so often, but the animal appeared to be almost out of strength. In the other stalls a short distance away, some of the other horses neighed mournfully, as if they sensed one of their own suffered.

"That horse is about to die," Geoffrey said, walking over to where the others stood. He appeared distracted and more disoriented than he had at breakfast earlier.

"Angel's Glory!" D'Lynn gasped, recognizing the horse and looking as if she were about to cry. The pitiful sight instantly affected her. "Do you have any idea what happened? Zeke should be on his way."

"Zeke?" Geoffrey said, his eyes growing larger. "Why did you call him? We don't need him here!"

"Well, the horse is sick. I thought you'd want him to take a look," D'Lynn said, taken aback.

"What do you think is the matter with her?" Marcus asked. "I think Zeke should probably come and have a look."

"I brought Maxine down here a few days ago. The horse was fine. Buddy checked on everything yesterday evening and fed and watered them, and they were all fine. This one somehow got out of her stall, and Buddy found her like this a little while ago." Geoffrey appeared to Marcus as though he had something else on his mind.

"Oh, Maxine," D'Lynn said. "She's up at the house with Hattie right now havin' her breakfast. Angel's Glory is her favorite horse. I just don't know how I'm gonna tell her about this."

Geoffrey pulled out his smartphone.

"Who are you callin'?" D'Lynn asked.

"I'm calling Zeke and telling him not to come," Geoffrey said. "We don't need him. I'll just shoot the horse and we can bury her and be done."

"No!" D'Lynn protested. "That child will never forgive you!"

"Then we won't tell her what really happened," he said, looking pointedly at each of the others. *"Right?* Let's just agree right now to keep this to ourselves. I'll figure out a way to tell Maxine when she notices the horse is gone."

"Where is Tilda?" D'Lynn said, stepping toward Geoffrey. "She needs to be here to have a say in this."

He shook his head and looked as if he were about to lose his temper. "I already told you. She's not feeling well. And she's not to be disturbed. She will understand when I explain it to her later."

Buddy spit tobacco juice off into the dirt and walked over closer to them. "Those marks ain't like anything I ever seen."

Geoffrey motioned for Buddy to be quiet, as he put the phone back into his pocket. "Zeke went straight to voicemail. Shit, I guess he'll pull up any second."

"What marks?" Marcus asked Buddy.

"That horse has puncture marks on its—"

"Buddy, can you go check the other horses?" Geoffrey quickly cut in. "We should check and make sure they're okay and not sick."

"Little tiny holes in her neck. Kinda like—" Buddy continued.

"For God's sake, Buddy! The other horses!" Geoffrey shouted, turning and pointing to the corridor of stalls a dozen yards away.

The groundskeeper nodded and lumbered away toward the other horses. Geoffrey turned back toward the others and then away again, putting his head in his hands.

"Geoff." Marcus went over and tried to console him, but his brother pulled away. "Can't I do something to help you?"

"No," Geoffrey said. "It's too late. Nobody can help me now."

Marcus squinted his eyes and shook his head. "Nobody can help you? I don't understand."

Before Geoffrey could respond, Zeke Colson's blue Ford F-250 pickup pulled up at the stable near where they stood. He shut off the hum of the truck's engine and quickly stepped out carrying his bag and wearing a casual white T-shirt, jeans, and boots but no ball cap. He gave Marcus a short smile and a nod as he walked past. Zeke reached into his bag and pulled on latex gloves before he reached the animal.

"How long has the horse been like this?" Zeke asked kneeling down and starting to examine her.

"Buddy found her about thirty minutes ago," Geoffrey said. "Somehow she was outside her stall. We're not sure how long she's been like this."

"Looks like it's been a while," Zeke said.

Marcus watched him as he examined Angel's Glory. His thoughts went back to the previous night. The dream. First it had been Zeke, and then Zeke transformed into ... *Conrad.*

The two men had no connection to one another, except they had both kissed Marcus at some point during the evening. Then there were all the other things Zeke had said when they were at his house.

"I'll be damned. It's the same damn thing as yesterday," Zeke said, backing away. He had more instruments out, including a stethoscope. "Only this one's neck isn't broken. I don't get it. What the hell is going on around here?"

"The horse lost blood?" Marcus asked, walking closer.

"She's showing signs of tremendous blood loss, even though there's no evidence around that she bled out anywhere. The puncture wounds. The lack of strength. The breathing. The pulse. Her heart is struggling to pump what little blood could be left. Unless we could give her some kind of transfusion. Well, it's hopeless," Zeke said, defeated. "I don't know what else to do."

"I agree," Geoffrey said, coming back from his distracted state. "I was just about to shoot the horse before you drove up."

"I can euthanize her in a quieter, more humane way if you like," Zeke said, frowning and shaking his head. "Such a beautiful animal. I don't understand what or who is doing this!"

"Doctor Colson, why do you think they didn't break the horse's neck?" Travis asked.

Geoffrey went over to the boy and grabbed him by the shirt collar. "You little bastard," he growled.

"Geoff, no don't!" Marcus tried to intervene, but Geoffrey used a free hand to push his brother away from them.

"Get back to the house. Now!" he said through clenched teeth, shoving Travis away. "Get the hell out of my sight, you freak."

"Fuck you! *I hate you!*" Travis yelled, looking as if he were about to start crying. He then ran away back toward the house, his thin, black-clad frame quickly disappearing down the dirt road behind them.

"Why did you do that?" Marcus said to his brother, with a petrified look. "He only asked a simple question."

"He probably did this!" Geoffrey said, knowing to himself it was a lie, but waving it away. The fact he was distraught over something besides the horse and taking it out on everyone around him was apparent. "I'll deal with him later."

"We don't know that he did anything," D'Lynn said, also alarmed at what she had seen. "I need to go back to the house and check and make sure he's okay. Geoff, he's just a boy."

"A boy who dresses like a goddamn freak and has a smart mouth," Geoffrey said, all his composure gone. "He needs a belt across his ass. Maybe it'll straighten him out and make him start acting and dressing normal and quit wearing black eyeliner like a little *fa—*" Geoffrey quickly paused, as he realized the company he kept at the moment. And he caught the sharp glances of Marcus and Zeke.

"I could've tried to answer the boy's question without all of that," Zeke said, looking annoyed.

"All three of you need to mind your own goddamn business. I don't need you all telling me how to discipline any of my children!" Geoffrey gave Marcus, D'Lynn, and Zeke a one-two-three cock of his head.

Zeke let Geoffrey's anger roll off his back. "Then let's get back to something that *is* my business," he said. "I can put Angel's Glory down for you if you like. She won't feel any pain and it'll be relatively quick. You also won't have to worry about your daughter hearing a gunshot."

"Fine," Geoffrey said, ready to walk away from the three of them. "Do it and bill me."

16

Travis ran into the house and quickly wiped away tears when he closed the front door. He didn't want anyone to see he had been crying, especially Regan, since she had come back into the house as if she arrived there today and had eaten breakfast with Aunt Hattie and the twins. He assumed she had gone back upstairs to his room after she was finished, since the two of them had become separated during his chat with Marcus. And after that, there had been the ordeal with Angel's Glory down at the stables.

He climbed the stairs, and glanced down at the roped-off casket in the foyer, wishing it was Geoffrey inside.

Sometimes Travis fantasized that his biological father—whoever it might be, for he had never known—would swoop in and carry him off to a new life. He often entertained the notion Tilda had a secret past life as a groupie and his father was some famous rock star or a 1990's grunge band frontman. Then there were times like now where the fantasy wasn't as elaborate and romantic and it was just anyone but Geoffrey who claimed him as theirs and came to his rescue.

Ever since he was a child, and his mother had met Geoffrey and married into a life of privilege, he had been treated like the bastard he was. The only reason Geoffrey had adopted him and given him the Lanehart name was because Maximilian insisted on it to avoid any potential embarrassment. All these fucking people cared about was putting on a good front for outsiders. He couldn't wait to turn eighteen, graduate high school, and move somewhere cool, where nobody would tell him what to wear, no kids would make fun of him, and he could be himself.

That's what would have to happen. He would have to move on when it was time and find his own way because deep down part of him was resigned to the fact he would never learn the identity of his biological father. Tilda would likely never tell him, and despite the seditious show he put on, he had never worked up the courage to ask her.

Travis came to face to face with Conrad when he reached the top of the stairs. It was unexpected and gave him a start. His blue eyes widened when they met the dark ones.

"Well, hello Travis," he said, seeming to block his way down the hall. "Looking for someone?"

"I'm trying to get to my room. In case you forgot, I live here. Can you move out of my way?" Travis said, walking past.

"I haven't forgotten. But you've forgotten how to treat guests in your home. Or did you parents never teach you your manners?"

"I don't know who the hell you are, but I don't have time for some weird musclehead I never saw before to come in here and boss me around. Who are you in your fancy jacket? The new family bodyguard?"

Conrad grabbed him by the arm. "I saw your pretty little girlfriend coming up here earlier when you left the house with D'Lynn and Marcus," he said, keeping his voice low and his mouth close to Travis' pierced ear. Travis tried to pull away, but Conrad held on to him tighter. "I told her she didn't need to be sneaking around the house and sent her home. I think your parents would agree with my decision."

"Man, stop. You're hurtin' my arm," Travis said, still trying to tug loose. But Conrad was much too strong and powerful for the small, skinny boy.

"I ought to break your fucking arm, you little punk," Conrad hissed, his dark brown eyes starting to glow yellow. Travis' face turned even paler, and he let out a gasp. "You've got such a mouth on you. Maybe you need to be taught a lesson."

"Oh Jesus, what *are* you?" he said, shaking and starting to break out in a clammy sweat.

"Am I scaring you, Travis?" Conrad smiled, as his eyes slowly turned back to their normal color. "You look like you're about to piss your pants."

"Make it stop," Travis cried, his voice starting to shake. "Oh dear God, your eyes are *hurting* me!"

"Yes," Conrad said, staring at him more intently. "But you can't stop looking into them, can you, Travis?"

He trembled with fear, and his disquietude amused Conrad. "What—Why are you doing this to me?"

"You were so rude to me earlier. I didn't like it. Maybe I just don't like *you.*"

"Oh God, I'm sorry. Please make it stop!"

Conrad laughed but kept it at a reasonable volume so it didn't travel downstairs within the earshot of anyone else. "You are going to be a fun one."

"Wh—what? *Fun?*"

"I'm not done with you yet. This is only the beginning of your servitude to me," he said, staring deeply into Travis' eyes and moving his face closer to that of the boy's. "Look into my eyes, Travis. Look deeply. When I snap my fingers, you won't remember anything about this conversation or that I scared the living shit out of you. But you'll know in your subconscious to neither disobey nor disrespect me. You'll know there are dire and very unpleasant consequences for doing so. Do you understand, Travis?"

Travis was shaking violently but managed a nod. "Yes, I understand," he muttered in a whisper, unable to look away from Conrad.

"You won't remember this encounter, but you *will* know to serve me. You'll do whatever I tell you to do," he said, pulling Travis so close that their noses almost touched.

Conrad then smiled, released the boy's arm, and snapped the fingers on his other hand. Travis went limp and appeared disoriented for a full two seconds before regaining his composure. He then turned and continued to walk past Conrad as before.

"Going somewhere, Travis?" Conrad asked.

"Oh yeah, just to my room," he said, looking down at the floor.

"Is something wrong, Travis?"

Travis looked up at him sadly. "Just something at the stables. Geoff's an asshole. I don't feel like talkin' about it."

Conrad nodded. "Okay, well, I saw your girlfriend. Regan...isn't that her name?"

"Yeah, that's right," Travis said, finally offering a small smile. "Did she come up here?"

"She did, but I told her you had to go to the stables with your uncle and D'Lynn for an emergency with one of the horses. She left and said she would be back later for the funeral."

"Oh okay, well, thank you for letting me know, man." He started to walk off and then turned back. "Are you into anime? Nobody else in the house is. I have some cool graphic novels in my room if you ever want to come check them out. Some are even steampunk gothic. Ever heard of that?"

Conrad gave a dismissive grin. "That sounds interesting but not right now. I have other things to do. Maybe some other time. I'll catch you later, Travis."

"Oh okay, man, later on then."

Conrad watched as Travis walked down the hallway to his room and then turned and descended the stairs. As he reached the foyer, he gave a brief stare toward the casket.

It would soon be out of the house and in the ground underneath the dirt—where it belonged, he thought to himself.

People from the funeral home had begun arriving at the house by late morning, bringing in floral arrangements from far and wide. The entire downstairs had gone from smelling like a down-home Southern diner to a funeral parlor in a matter of an hour or so.

As Conrad turned to go into the dining room from the foyer, D'Lynn came through the front door. She looked distressed and shook her head. Her eyes met his, and she gave a sheepish expression.

"Oh, hello there," she said. "If you're hungry, there should still be food out in the dinin' room. We have plenty to eat. Take a plate and make yourself at home," she nodded and then tried to walk away.

"Just a moment, please," he said. She paused and looked back. Conrad could tell something about his presence stirred the older woman's subconscious in an unpleasant way.

"Yes, what can I help you with?" D'Lynn asked, looking at him uneasily and with a hint of distrust.

"Do you know where Marcus went, by chance?" he asked, as he locked eyes with her.

She melted into a warm , relaxed smile. "Why yes, young man, he's down yonder at the stables with the vet."

"The vet?" Conrad asked, raising a brow.

"Why yes, Ezekiel Colson. He goes by Zeke. They're old school friends."

"Ah, so I've been told," he said. "I should go meet this Doctor Colson and find out what's going on. It all sounds so terrible."

"Oh, it is," D'Lynn said, as she warmed to him and placed her hand on the sleeve of his tan blazer. "I bet you're hungry. Why don't I give you one of my homemade biscuits to take with you? It'll take a few minutes to walk down there. You can eat it on the way."

"That sounds delightful," he said and gave her a bigger smile.

"Oh!" she cooed. "Let me go get it for you. Stay right here. I'll put some honey on it. I'll give you extra napkins so it don't make a mess!" She giggled as she trotted off to the dining room.

But by the time D'Lynn returned with the homemade biscuit, the front door was ajar and Conrad was gone.

17

After Zeke performed the unpleasant task of euthanizing Angel's Glory, Buddy and Geoffrey had two other Ten Points groundskeepers help them load the carcass and take it away to be buried off at the edge of the property near the woods. Zeke was saddened by what he had to do and suggested a necropsy like the one performed on the ducks and raccoon, but Geoffrey adamantly refused. He grew increasingly distracted, and the smooth-talking and apologetic demeanor Marcus had seen at the breakfast table earlier that morning dissipated.

"I'll see you back at the house later," he told Marcus, as he rode off in a pickup truck with the other men to go bury the horse.

Marcus watched the older model Chevrolet disappear down the dirt road and off toward the woods further north of the property. Geoffrey's mood and temperament changed too much in the past two hours for his liking. His brother had been pleasant and cordial at the breakfast table. The sudden erratic and angry turn could be attributed to the tragedy with the horse, yes, but there seemed to be more to it. The way he lit into Travis for asking a simple question, and the manner in which he snapped at the rest of them. Something else ate at his brother and caused him to lose his resolve.

In their years of growing up, Geoffrey had always done an exemplary job of holding it together under pressure. That was one of several things that had made him Maximilian's favorite. Marcus could be moody and sometimes let his emotions dictate things. Flannery was the stubborn one. Geoffrey, however, could handle himself under stress and not show his hand too early. Something had changed, and Marcus wanted to believe maybe it was only their father's death that caused his brother to come apart.

He *wanted* to believe that's all it was.

"Your brother's a jerk, but I've always thought so," Zeke said, after Geoffrey was gone. "He probably would have beat the shit out of Travis if none of us had been standing here. Your Dad's death seems to be affecting him pretty bad."

"Well, the jerk apologized to me this morning for the way he's treated me and said he wanted to start over," Marcus said, as they walked toward the stalls where the other horses were finally calmed down.

"Oh wow," Zeke said. "How do you feel about that?"

Marcus reached up and gently stroked the long, beautiful face of another thoroughbred that stuck its head out and lovingly nipped at him. "I accepted his apology, and I guess we'll see what happens from here. Geoff asked me to stay and not go back to San Diego right away."

Zeke's face brightened for the first time since his arrival. "So you're not going back?" he asked.

"Not for at least a few days," Marcus said. "I don't know what will happen after that."

"Yeah," Zeke said, looking away. "I guess you have your job to think about. "

"No, not anymore. I quit this morning. I had it out with my boss when he called. I think I quit before he could fire me."

Zeke moved closer and put his hand on Marcus' shoulder. "Marcus, I meant everything I said last night. Who says you have to go back at all?"

"Last night was nice, but I don't think we should rush into anything, and you shouldn't get your hopes too high. I haven't agreed to anything permanent. I do have a life back there."

Marcus said one thing, but he hadn't moved away from Zeke and allowed his hand to stay where it was.

"I know that, but you could have one here," he said. He moved in and gave Marcus a light kiss. Before he could resist and pull away, Marcus found himself kissing back even harder. They wrapped their arms around one another, and after the kiss ended they hugged and held each other tightly. Marcus closed his eyes as he took in the light detergent scent and the cotton fabric feel of Zeke's white T-shirt against his face. Zeke's arms were snugly around him; his were firmly around Zeke. He suddenly never wanted to let go.

"Damn it, Zeke," Marcus laughed. "You aren't going to make this easy, are you?"

"In all the years since we were kids have I ever done anything the easy way?" he asked, reaching up and stroking the back of Marcus' head and running his fingers through his thick, dark blond hair.

Marcus pulled his head from Zeke's shoulder and looked at him. "Part of me really does want to go along with this," he said. "Part of me really does want it to be as easy as you make it sound."

"Then listen to that part, and let the rest of you catch up later. You know, the part of you *scared* to say yes."

"You're right," he admitted. "I am scared. I waited more than a year. He's never coming back. I know I have to move on," Marcus pulled away and became agitated. "But I need answers about what happened, too."

"I understand," Zeke said, pulling him back close. "I waited sixteen years to be with you. I can wait a little longer if I have to. I'll spend time showing you that you don't have to be scared of anything."

"You know, we're not exactly in the most free-thinking part of the country," Marcus said. "Coming back here is like reverse culture shock for me."

"Yeah, you're right, but it's home to me," Zeke said. He put his head on Marcus' shoulder and they held each other. "I always figured I would never get to do this again."

"We wasted a lot of time, didn't we?" Marcus asked. "If only you hadn't been a macho asshole and walked out that morning and pretended like you didn't know me for the next three months."

Zeke playfully whacked him on the other shoulder. "Stop it," he said, as they both laughed. "I already told you what an idiot I was for doing that."

Marcus pulled away and looked at him. "I had to get out of here. It wasn't just you. I tried to present myself as one way in college, and then I finally had to admit to myself that it was all a lie. Do you know I once wrote an editorial criticizing a gay student group for defiling the moral fiber of the campus? I mean, that was a big deal for them. They were breaking new ground for the time. I deserved all the bad karma in the world after that."

"I remember," he said. "We were kids. I did something worse. I strung Mary Ann along and even married her. I forced her to live my lie with me for years. Gosh, she is one hell of a woman for putting up with me and then forgiving me when it was all over."

"Who was the girl I was with when we went on the double date that time?" Marcus asked, as they continued to hold one another close. "Jolene? Maureen? Well, she must be a trivia question now if I can't even remember her name."

Zeke took his head off Marcus' shoulder and looked back at him. "Well, all these years later, here we are. The two of us. Still here..." They smiled at one another and began to kiss again, and soon wrapped themselves tightly back together.

"For the love of God, Marcus. Stay and don't ever leave again," Zeke whispered in his ear, sounding as if he were about to cry. "I'll make up for everything from all those years ago. I promise."

Marcus looked into his eyes and felt the same emotion sweeping over him. "Oh Zeke," he said quietly, as they continued to kiss.

"Oh my ... you two are going to cause the horses to blush if you don't cool it down ..."

Marcus and Zeke quickly pulled apart and saw Conrad standing at the end of the corridor, propped against the door of an empty stable stall. His dark eyes were narrowed and he wore a mischievous smirk. He was clad in a tight white button-down dress shirt, with the tan blazer in his hand and slung over his shoulder. He had apparently strolled down the dirt road in Prada dress shoes and had one foot casually propped on the stall gate.

"Do you always sneak up on people like that?" Zeke snapped, back to his senses. "Who the hell are you?"

Conrad laughed and stepped away from where he stood and walked over. "Everybody keeps asking me the same old question. I'm Conrad," he said, coming closer and extending his hand.

Zeke stood frozen and didn't accept the handshake. "We were having a private moment. Do you mind?"

"I don't doubt it," Conrad said to Zeke as he stared at Marcus. "I wondered where you were when I didn't see you at the house. I guess this answers that."

Marcus was noticeably uncomfortable. "What brings you down here, Conrad?"

Conrad smiled but didn't reveal what he was really thinking. "I was actually looking for Geoff. I heard what happened with the horse, and I wanted to make sure everything was okay."

"Oh yeah, well, Geoff's gone now to bury the horse," Marcus said. "So I guess that answers that question."

"So, you're a guest at Ten Points?" Zeke asked, studying Conrad cautiously.

Conrad returned the stare and appeared to take notes as well. "Yes," he said. "I'm a business associate of Geoff's. It's very tragic about Mr. Lanehart's sudden passing," he said, a sympathetic dart of the eyes toward Marcus. "I arrived yesterday evening. And, I'm sorry, I never caught your name?"

"Zeke Colson," he said and extended his hand, as he looked warily at Conrad. "I'm a veterinarian and came out to see about the horse."

Conrad gave a chuckle. "Well, not to discount the tragedy with the poor animal, I must say from the looks of what I just walked up on, you make one hell of a house call, doctor."

Zeke looked squarely at him with a solid face. Conrad's small grin faded as he realized the challenge he faced in swaying the other man to his merriment—however false it was.

"I'm sorry, I didn't mean to joke or offend. Do you think Geoff will be back soon?"

Marcus shrugged. "It could be a while. They have to dig the hole. I assume he's trying to keep this from Maxine since she does have Dad's funeral to deal with today."

"That poor child. I'm sure she will be devastated when she hears about this," Conrad said.

"So you didn't arrive until yesterday *evening?*" Zeke asked Conrad.

He nodded. "Yes, I arrived with Ruffin right behind the hearse. Why do you ask?"

Zeke shook his head and kept an advertent expression. "No reason. I was just curious is all."

"Hmm, I see."

"So, Geoff has a lot of business associates, from what I've gathered. Are you the only one staying at the house?"

"So far it appears that way," Conrad replied, as a cocky grin formed again.

Zeke's face never changed, and the two of them continued to stare at one another. It wasn't difficult for Marcus to see Zeke deeply disliked and distrusted the other man. Conrad obviously sensed this, too, and appeared ready for anything Zeke might volley next.

"There's nothing else you would like to know?" he finally asked after a moment's silence.

"No, not for now," Zeke said. He went over near where Angel's Glory had lain and collected his bag. He came back and gave Marcus a full kiss on the lips. "I need to go back to my clinic for a while," he said, and then glanced over at Conrad. He turned back to Marcus. "I'll be back for the funeral later," he said.

Marcus nodded and smiled at him. "Okay."

"It was ... *interesting* to meet you, Conrad," Zeke said, as he walked to the Ford pickup. He climbed in, the engine roared to life, and he gave Marcus a final wave. He backed the truck around and then drove away down the dirt road.

"Well, D'Lynn said he was an old school friend of yours, but apparently your housekeeper has a gift for understating things," Conrad said, turning to Marcus after the blue pickup was out of sight.

"How long were you standing there?" Marcus asked.

He secretly hoped after that unsolicited move by Conrad in the living room the evening before he had taken in as much of the scene with Zeke as possible. But he also chided himself for his attempt to ruffle Conrad. Why did it matter? *Did* it matter? It dawned on him that Zeke was off in the distance, gone, and now it was only Conrad and him. It was almost like the dream. The dream that began with Zeke and ended with Conrad invading like an incubus. *An incubus.* That was what it had felt like—someone else had walked into his imagination and rearranged the order of events to their own liking.

But it still didn't explain the marks on his arms. *Maybe* he did it to himself in his sleep, during the dream. *Maybe.*

"I have a better question," Conrad said, walking closer to him.

You belong to me.

Marcus felt a touch of unease come over him. A slight throbbing of his head, almost like the evening before when the door of the Bentley had opened in the driveway outside the house. But it suddenly disappeared before an ache set in and wasn't as intense as the day before.

"What would that be?" Marcus asked, looking directly at him.

"Is he a better kisser than I am?" Conrad asked, with a smile.

Marcus returned a sardonic grin. "I know what you're up to. You aren't fooling anybody."

Conrad pointed a finger at him mockingly. "Tsk tsk, here we are getting off on the wrong foot again."

"I'm not interested in playing footsy with you," Marcus replied. "You can wait here for Geoff," he said, as he walked away back toward the house.

"I'll wait here for Geoff," Conrad said to himself, when Marcus was out of earshot. He watched him walk off into the distance. "But I'll be seeing much more of you later."

18

Maximilian Lanehart's funeral took place after sunset, off another dirt road that led to the family burial plot on the southeastern edge of Ten Points, near some woods. Fortunately, the weather was more cooperative than it had been the night before. Dozens of fold-out metal chairs with covers had been placed out for mourners, with the front two rows reserved for the family.

A black tent had been set up over the gravesite. Six pallbearers, all Lanehart employees from various business holdings, carried the casket from the hearse and set it on the lowering device where the grave had been dug. A dark drape that matched the tent kept the grave concealed beneath where the casket was now perched. A green mound cover just outside the back corner of the tent obscured the earth that was dug up for Maximilian Lanehart's final resting place. An overhead outdoor light illuminated what would have otherwise been a crowd of people sitting in the dark. Mosquitoes and other bugs swarmed around the bright light, but it was high enough so that they weren't a menace to funeral goers.

The crowd stood and then took their seats after the casket was set in place. The Lanehart family sat on the front row. Geoffrey, Tilda, Flannery, Marcus, Aunt Hattie—in that order. Travis, Bobby, and Maxine sat behind Geoffrey and Tilda, next to D'Lynn and a few extended family members they usually never saw. Marcus couldn't help but wonder why Tilda was wearing sunglasses when it was dark outside. Flannery looked paler than she had the night before but wore a black dress tonight that covered her more. On the other side of him, Aunt Hattie had changed into yet another wig, this one still yellow-blonde but shorter and more conservative than the one she had worn at breakfast. Some of her lush, false locks were obscured by a dark veil she wore over her heavily made-up face.

Geoffrey showed more composure than at the stable, where he came apart in front of everyone. He wore a black designer suit and made no eye contact with anyone. Tilda sat completely still, made no sounds and seemed to look straight ahead, though the sunglasses hid her eyes.

Flannery fidgeted and glanced back and caught the eyes of Wes Washer on another row. He looked at her with a small smile, and she returned the expression. She also caught the unexpected gaze of Clementine LeMonde, who gave her a loathsome stare from where she sat—a few rows back, adjacent to Wes. All three of them had gone to high school together. Clementine longed for Wes' attention in those days, but he had been too infatuated with Flannery to pay her any mind.

Flannery turned forward and faced Reverend Wilkins Washer, Wes' father, who tossed her a look of disdain almost equal to that of Clementine's as he began to speak. His pudgy face relaxed, as his eyes moved over the rest of the mourners. The short, plump, gray-haired man broke a sweat through his frock as he stood before the casket. Crickets chirped loudly across the burial ground as he started to speak.

"We are gathered here today, to say our final goodbyes to Maximilian Lanehart, as he's welcomed into the arms of our Savior..." The Reverend began.

Bullshit. Flannery and Marcus shared a thought. They were both convinced *if* there was an afterlife, their father wasn't in the nice place.

Marcus barely listened to any of the words coming from the minister's mouth. All he heard was noise in the form of an authoritative tone as he slowly turned his head and quickly scanned attendees a couple of rows back. Zeke, dressed in a black suit, offered him a look of warmth. Marcus smiled at him and then slowly looked behind him in the other direction and received the wide blue-eyed stare of young Bobby, from the seat behind Tilda. He looked at Marcus, expressionless without blinking. It was impossible to tell what was on his mind. After what Travis had told him, Marcus wondered if the boy was thinking about anything at all. Marcus quickly turned back around.

A few seats away, Conrad had taken note of the exchange between Marcus and Zeke. He casually looked down at his wristwatch as the Reverend continued on. He decided he would bear this farce for however long it took. The bigger picture was worth all of it.

What began as a minor disturbance on one of the back rows caused a domino effect of head turns. An uninvited guest three of the funeral goers had gone to lengths to keep tucked away made her entrance, stepping through the back row for an empty seat she spotted.

"Excuse me, *excuse me* ... oh Lord, it's crowded up in here..." Rochelle squeezed her way past half a dozen people before taking her seat. She had somehow managed to go to her apartment, change into a black dress, and make it back to Ten Points, where she had been stashed with Tilda the entire day. "Thank you, baby!" she said, rather loudly, to the last person who let her slide past.

Tilda and Flannery gave one another a curious stare and then glanced back at Conrad who replied with an amused shrug. Geoffrey shook his head and buried his face in one of his hands.

"How the hell did she get loose?" Flannery whispered to Tilda. "She was supposed to be locked upstairs."

"She was. I don't know," Tilda hissed back quietly, looking straight ahead. The large sunglasses under the cover of night obscured any facial expressions.

"We have got to get her out of here the minute this is over," Flannery said, keeping her voice down.

Marcus glanced over at the two women, but their exchange was too low for him to hear anything. The increasingly loud chirp of crickets, the buzzes and nocturnal noises of other nighttime north Louisiana insects, and a loud, lonely bullfrog off in the distance made it difficult to focus on what Reverend Washer was saying. Marcus realized most of the people there must have thought it excessively eccentric of Maximilian to request his funeral be held at night. He *assumed* this was his father's wish. He had never gotten a clear answer and only offended his brother when he had inquired about the odd hour on the night of his arrival.

Reverend Wilkins Washer continued on with the service after he offered a disapproving arch of the brow to the commotion. He closed the service with a reading of the twenty-third Psalm. The pallbearers removed the white roses pinned to the jackets of their suits and placed them on the casket. Marcus and Geoffrey followed.

Marcus took one long final look at the closed casket. He would be relieved to see it gone when he walked back into the foyer at the house.

He saw Tilda and his sister off by themselves in a conversation but instead of going over he decided to walk back to the house, where most of the guests were now going for food and drinks.

"I know babysitting is new for you, but you should have kept a closer eye on her," Flannery said to Tilda fifty feet away, once the crowd dispersed and she could speak louder. "She very well could've attacked someone. She's probably here to hunt."

"She's not the only one," Tilda said, eyeing Wes a dozen or so yards away. He was in a conversation with Clementine LeMonde. "He doesn't remember anything from last night and has no reason to be afraid of me."

"Wes is *off limits,* and even if he weren't, we have to think less about ourselves and keep Rochelle in line," Flannery said.

"I'm so hungry I could eat a ... *horse,*" Rochelle said, as she walked up to the other two women with a smug exterior. "Hello bitches."

"Do *not* go near those stables again," Tilda said tersely. "Of all the choices you had down there, you had to pick my daughter's favorite riding horse?"

Rochelle nodded and narrowed her eyes, which reflected dark and shiny from the overhead light near the funeral tent. "You bet your skinny ass I did. Tit for tat, Tilda. You took something away from me, and I returned the favor. I think *one* horse is a very small price to pay for my *life,* you sanctimonious rich white bitch."

Tilda flashed a grin. "Let's not bring race and status into this. One I can't help ... the other I worked my ass off to land. If you hadn't been sticking your hand in my cookie jar, then you wouldn't be as dead as my father-in-law over there."

"Well, I've always had a giant fucking appetite, so you better round me up something real good to eat tonight if you don't want another one of your beloved farm animals keeled over in the dust come sunrise."

Flannery cut in. "You should look to us more as your mentors and go easy on the threats. We're here to help you." She managed a smile, but Rochelle scoffed and rolled her eyes.

"I had a job I liked, a decent apartment, and friends. I'm not that close to my family, but I had them sometimes. Now I have nothing. You two owe me more than just a *little* help."

Tilda shook her head. "Well, you *were* messing around with my husband..."

Flannery gave her a light elbow jab to be quiet and not rile Rochelle. She then put another false smile and went over to her. "Look, it's never easy at first," she said, maternally placing an arm around Rochelle. "But look on the bright side. You'll never get old." She let her eyes wander up and down the other woman's body. "You'll never get any fatter..."

Rochelle broke away from her. "Are you calling me fat now? I'm big boned, and thanks to that bloodsucking bitch over there I'll never be able to enjoy a Whopper ever again."

Tilda let go of her melancholy expression of the evening long enough to present a short laugh. "I wouldn't call Geoffrey a *whopp*—" Then she stopped and realized what Rochelle meant. "Oh never mind ... Look, thanks to Flannery over here I can't even take pleasure in a drag off a cigarette anymore. I feel your pain, Rochelle."

"I doubt that," she replied. "You seemed awfully intent on inflictin' it last night!"

"We take care of our own," Flannery said, placing her hands on Rochelle's shoulders and trying to reassure her. "Tilda and I will help you adjust to this new existence."

"I still need you to help *me* adjust. It's only been twenty-four hours," Tilda said, scowling at Flannery.

Flannery waved her sister-in-law's comment away. "Rochelle, I need you to tell us everything you did after you woke up and left the house this evening."

"I took one of those fancy-ass Bentleys in the driveway that had the keys in it, I went to my apartment, put on this black dress and my heels, and then I came back here to crash this funeral. I needed to find you two. And maybe do a little scouting..."

"That's all? You didn't run into anyone? You didn't *attack* anyone?"

"Not yet," Rochelle said, her eyes scanning the leftover people standing around. A great number of those who attended the service had already left, but others who stayed behind had broken into smaller groups and chatted amongst themselves.

Geoffrey stood off by himself near his seat from the service and anxiously watched the three women. He felt as though his heart had almost stopped when Rochelle arrived at the funeral. More like *crashed* the service, he thought to himself. It made him sick to his stomach every time he thought about what he had seen Tilda do to her the night before. And what Flannery had done to Tilda before that. To make it even worse, there was his dead but not-so-dead wife who looked ridiculous attending a nighttime funeral service with sunglasses on. The sight of her as she entered the living room earlier that evening after a day of slumber on the third floor gave him a dull ache in his stomach and made him queasy and unsteady.

D'Lynn could detect a speck of dust from across the room and had an inquiring mind. Geoffrey knew it wouldn't be long before she grew suspicious and began to question Tilda's daytime whereabouts. Before she began to question *everything*.

Just as he couldn't bear to watch his undead wife, detestable sister, and chubby lover in their private conversation any longer, he turned and nearly walked right into Ruffin who had come up behind him.

"For God's sake, don't sneak up like that," he said, rattled and clearly annoyed. "What is it now?"

"Conrad requests your presence in the study back at the house. He wants to speak with both of us," the shorter man said. Even though it was growing darker, Geoffrey could tell Ruffin too was at unease, and his gray moustache appeared to quiver a bit.

"There are funeral guests all heading back to the house. I have to be present. I can't be off in the study stuck in some meeting when there's a houseful of people. I don't even know if I ever want to go back in that room anyway."

"Why do you say that?" Ruffin asked, as the thought of Conrad shook him.

"I don't feel like talking about it," he replied.

"Is he starting to scare you, too?" Ruffin asked, in a low voice.

Geoffrey grew more irritated. "Of course not! Why the hell would you ask me a question like that?"

Ruffin was indeed nervous. "I've never seen you act like this. I'm always the one who does the stressing out for you. He's doing a number on you, too, isn't he...?"

Geoffrey moved in closer so no one could hear and lowered his voice. "I need *you* to stay calm and go along with what we agreed on. This will all be over soon."

"Can you be so sure about that?" Ruffin asked, blinking his small, beady eyes unsteadily. "He's made all these promises, and I don't see anything so far..."

"Just be patient," Geoffrey said, anxiously chewing the inside of his lip.

"Can you really take his word for anything?"

"You mustn't say such things," Geoffrey warned him. "Please don't talk like that."

"Why the hell not?" Ruffin spat. "He's something not of this world."

"He's no longer the only one who isn't."

"*What?*"

"Nothing. Just try to stay calm because he knows what you're thinking."

19

Marcus walked up the curved granite steps to the front porch of the house when he saw her again from behind. She wore the same black dress, pearls, and carried a black leather purse across her left arm that he hadn't noticed the night before. Underneath the bright light of the porch, he recognized the middle-aged black woman he had seen across the room in the parlor. Tonight, she was back at the house and about to walk inside as he found his way to the steps.

"Wait a minute," he said, calling out to her.

She turned away from the door with a startled look and clutched her hand to her chest.

"Who are you?" he asked. "I saw you here last night and then I couldn't find you later."

She stood and stared back at him without a word and appeared to catch her breath. She had a pretty face that was aging gracefully, and there were patches of gray blended into her ebony hair. But her countenance was sad and downtrodden, as it had been the evening before. She glanced down at the ground and then back up at Marcus again.

"I was beginning to wonder if you were a real person," Marcus said. "Aren't you going to answer me?"

"I—I shouldn't have come here," she finally managed, her voice soft. "I stopped in last night, but I left before anybody saw me. I saw D'Lynn, but she didn't see me. I had to leave."

"*I* saw you," Marcus said. "Why were you afraid to be seen?"

She shook her head and looked away. When she turned, Marcus could see she still clutched the white handkerchief from the night before in her right hand.

"I can't go into all that," she said. "You're Marcus?"

"Yes," he said, and she then nodded. "What is it you're so afraid of?" he asked. "You looked frightened and sad last night, and you seem the same way tonight."

Her chin trembled a bit, as if she might cry at any moment. She faced him. "There is great danger here. Your brother. *Your sister... oh your sister,*" She began to sob. "Oh, I think it's too late. You're the only one who maybe has a chance."

Marcus went over and tried to console her. "I'm afraid I don't know what you're talking about," he said. "Who are you, and how do you know my family?"

She shook her head. "You must be careful!" she hissed, with a hard, direct look at him. She placed her hand on his forearm and gripped tightly. "I see things. I've always seen things in this house."

"*Always* seen things? So you've been here before?"

"Let's not talk about that. There is evil in this house. It's been here before, and now it has come home again. You must either do something about it, or leave before it consumes you, too."

"If you feel determined to warn me about this, then why are you so scared? Are you afraid some harm will come to you for being here?"

"The harm that once came to me in this house is no more," she said, as she looked up and down and lightly brushed a hand against one of the porch's white Corinthian columns. "So long ago." She turned for the steps. "I must go. You were the only person I wanted to have a word with."

"Is that why you were here last night? To talk to me?"

She nodded and wiped her nose with the handkerchief before she finally managed a small smile for him. "Yes. That and to see if I had the courage to ever walk through those doors again. Of course, in those days here, I rarely ever went in or out the *front* door. It was already the 1970's and past Dr. King, but your father ... oh *hmmm.*" She shook her head and walked toward the steps.

"So you worked here back then? Is that how you know this place?"

"Let's not get into all of that," she said, shaking her head as she walked down the steps.

"Wait a minute, don't leave yet," Marcus said, following after her. "I don't even know your name. Who are you?"

She stopped on one of the curved steps and turned back to him. "Do you have your phone on you?"

He took it out of his jacket pocket. "Yes."

"Can you keep a secret?" she asked and darted her eyes around. She seemed afraid someone might be eavesdropping somewhere.

"Yes," he said.

"I'm Izzy," she said, and gave him her phone number and address. He added them into his contacts on his phone. "You don't remember me?"

Marcus was confused and shook his head.

She managed a quiet laugh. "I used to read you *Goldilocks and The Three Bears* and *The Billy Goats Gruff.* You were maybe two years old. No, I guess you wouldn't be able to remember that."

"What brings you back here after all this time? Why did you leave in the first place?"

"Not right now," Izzy said. "None of it matters right now. You have to be aware of the evil here."

"But what evil? *Who* should I be aware of?" he asked.

Who did she mean? Geoffrey? Flannery? Izzy acted as if all hope was lost for both of them and even cried for a bit after mentioning Flannery. Her dire warning seemed almost comparable to the one Maximilian had given Marcus from his casket in the dream. What was he supposed to think? Where and what was he supposed to be searching for?

"Am I supposed to call you?" he asked, as she reached the bottom of the steps. "Tell me what to do."

She looked back at him once more. "I can't tell you what to do," she said. "But I can tell you there's a devil inside that house, and he's raisin' an army. And some of them can't be saved any longer. That much I can tell you."

"Who? *What devil?*" he asked. *"Conrad?"* he heard himself suddenly say.

She clutched her chest again, as if her breath had been stolen from her. After a moment, she released her hand and walked away without an answer.

It was unclear where she parked. Marcus saw her disappear into the darkness. Cars were lined a quarter mile down the long driveway leading up to the house. Marcus felt a sense of relief that he now knew the woman was real, and he hadn't imagined her as he was concerned he had. Somehow, she had slipped into the house unnoticed by the one person who should have seen and recognized her from years ago. D'Lynn had apparently been too busy tending to the other guests.

What Izzy had said about evil at Ten Points left Marcus with more questions. Now he wondered what kind of business Geoffrey, Conrad, and Ruffin had discussed over in the corner at the wake. And what was *Flannery's* involvement in all of this? Marcus had found her intently watching them, acting shell-shocked when he broke her concentration. He assumed she was eyeing Conrad in the same manner as some of the other women who were present, but she claimed she had never seen him before. Was she lying? Did she know what was going on, and if so, was she somehow involved?

Then there were Izzy's hints about having worked at Ten Points in the past. She made it sound as though some of her duties even included babysitting. He wanted to go ask D'Lynn about Izzy, but it would now feel like he compromised a secret if he did so. Geoffrey was five years older than Marcus. Maybe he had a more vivid recollection of who she was. But based on the way she had acted, Geoffrey could be the wrong person to consult. He would have to think of a hypothetical way to ask about the woman without disclosing that he held a conversation with her on the front porch.

Marcus went inside the house, where he immediately spotted Flannery with Tilda and a slightly chunky black woman he had never seen before. The three were off in their own circle away from the rest of the crowd, in a private conversation. For whatever reason, Tilda wore dark sunglasses and appeared pale, as if she felt ill. Marcus wondered if she was drunk but put the thought out of his mind when he also noticed how pale Flannery was under the bright lights of the foyer's chandelier. She wore makeup and looked lovely underneath the moonlight at the graveside service. Indoors, Marcus could clearly make out the dark circles underneath her eyes from across the room.

Nearly everyone in the foyer and those who spilled over into the living room held a drink or a small hors d'oeuvre napkin or a miniature paper plate. But the three women were neither drinking nor eating, Marcus noted. He hadn't seen Flannery eat or drink either time he had been around her since their arrival home. He found it odd.

"I was wondering where you were," Zeke said from behind him, gently touching him on the arm. "God, if it wouldn't piss off all these old rich, white Republicans I would kiss you right here and right now," he whispered, as he moved closer to Marcus.

"That actually sounds like a good reason to do it," Marcus half-joked, with a smile at him.

"I'll make up for it later," he said. "Let's go into the living room and get a drink at the bar."

Marcus caught the eyes of Conrad watching as they passed by on their way to the living room. He was with Geoffrey and Ruffin over near the doorway, and the three were in what appeared to be yet another private discussion.

"I see Mr. Pretty has us in his crosshairs," Zeke said, once they were at the bar. "Is he *family*? He certainly can't take his eyes off you, I've noticed. And it doesn't take a rocket scientist to figure out he doesn't like me."

"He claims he's flexible. So basically he's bi. Oh yeah, and he did kiss me right here in the living room last night," Marcus said, as he leaned against the bar and surveyed the rest of the crowd inside the house.

"He *kissed* you?" Zeke asked, with raised brows. It amused Marcus to see he was a bit miffed and maybe even a little jealous. "What the hell made him do that?"

"It came out of nowhere. I think I did a good job letting him know it wasn't okay and that he shouldn't do it again."

Marcus realized telling Zeke about the dream would be a mistake. And part of him still wasn't convinced it hadn't really happened. There was no need to rile Zeke further, when the mention of a kiss ruffled him as it did.

"You seem to think this is funny, but it pisses me off," Zeke said, turning toward the bar. "I ought to go knock the teeth out of his pretty little head."

"Oh geez, that would be just a bit much," Marcus said, as he ordered a couple of beers from the hired bartender. He handed one to Zeke. "But speaking of people getting punched, I laid one on Geoff in the foyer last night."

"Whoa, you didn't tell me about that part earlier. You must've knocked some sense into him if he came apologizing and asking for forgiveness today."

"Things seemed okay at breakfast but sure turned ugly again at the stables later. I guess we'll see how it goes from here on."

Zeke took a swig from his longneck. "The question is should I expect to get another call out here tomorrow about another mysteriously bled-out animal. I still for the life of me can't figure out what the hell is going on."

The thought of Izzy's words on the porch went through Marcus' mind, as well as her mention of Geoffrey.

"You know, you saw the worst of it when he went after Travis, but Geoff started flying off the handle when D'Lynn said she had called you," Marcus heard himself say. He hadn't given it much thought earlier. "He was adamant about shooting the horse and leaving you out of it."

Zeke looked over skittishly. "Are you saying you think Geoff might have something to do with this?"

"Why would Geoff be draining the blood out of ducks and raccoons and horses? It makes absolutely no sense."

"Marcus, it doesn't make any sense for *anybody* to do that," Zeke pointed out.

"No, it doesn't, but I ran into somebody on the porch on my way in here. This mysterious older woman I saw in here last night," he said.

"That sounds weird. And kinda spooky."

"I know it'll sound crazy, but part of me almost thought I had seen a ghost last night until I ran into her tonight on my way back into the house. She's a real flesh-and-blood person. She wouldn't come right out and say it, but she said other things that indicated she used to work here when I was little. She started to come in, but I think she was too spooked to follow through with it and stay."

"Why did she even go the trouble of coming to the house in the first place then?"

"She said she needed to talk to me. She was here last night during the wake, standing right over there across the room. She was acting all nervous and left really fast because I couldn't find her later. Nobody I asked today had seen her. I thought I was losing it and had only imagined her."

"What did she want to talk to you about?" Zeke asked.

"She said there was evil inside this house," Marcus said.

Zeke laughed out loud. "What? That's silly. What makes her think that?"

"She wouldn't go into the details. Something about how it was too late for Geoff and Flannery, but I still had a chance to either defeat or get away from whatever the evil is."

Zeke continued to chuckle and shook his head. "Oh my gosh. It's all so 'Tangina from *Poltergeist*'. I love it!"

Marcus finally laughed along with him. "Okay, okay. It does sound crazy. But she was dead serious. I want to ask D'Lynn about her, but I'm trying to figure out a way to do it without making her suspicious."

"Well, if she worked here when you were little then D'Lynn should remember who she is. Maybe she can help confirm for us whether this woman is a nut job or not."

"Who's a nut job, sugar?" Aunt Hattie slid up to the bar, patting Marcus on the arm and unabashedly looking Zeke up and down with her big blue eyes. Her veil from the funeral was long gone. "Well, hello there," she said, batting her eyes dramatically. "Marcus, who is this?"

"This is Zeke," Marcus said. "Zeke, you never met my Aunt Hattie?"

Zeke smiled at her. "Why yes, Marcus, I met your Aunt Hattie many years ago when you and I were teenagers."

"Well, shoot," she sighed, disappointed with herself and shaking her head. "Honey, I like to think I never forget a face. I hate I don't recall one as handsome as yours."

"Me too," he said, putting his arm around her. "You were the 'cougar MILF' that Marcus' friends all drooled over back then, you know?"

"Now sugar, I wasn't old enough yet to be a cougar *or* a MILF back then!" she chided, playfully elbowing him in the ribs. "That's what I am *now*," she said. She turned and wrapped her arms around him, and looked up seductively from where she stood at only five-foot-three. "So, are you single?"

"Actually, whether I'm single is a little disputable," Zeke said, looking over at Marcus. "For much longer anyway."

"Oh?" Her tone was challenging, and she put her hands on her hips and continued to look up at him.

Zeke put his arm around Marcus and kissed him on the cheek. "Yep," he said.

Aunt Hattie raised a brow and smiled. "Well, in that case, you better treat my nephew right," she said and lightly wagged a finger at him as she walked away.

"That was good," Marcus laughed, once Aunt Hattie was gone.

"I have to say she's still got it going on for her age," Zeke said with a smile and shook his head.

"Excuse me," Reverend Wilkins Washer appeared at the bar. "Could you two at least have *some* kind of decency?"

Marcus turned to face the minister. "I'm sorry. *Decency?*"

"I saw your friend put his arm around you and give you a kiss. That's not acceptable, and I really don't think it's the time or the place for that kind of behavior," the portly Reverend said, his jowls shaking as he spoke.

"Now, just a minute..." Zeke began. Marcus could feel the heat come off him. He quickly put his hand up, to calm Zeke down.

"He only did it to tease and get a rise out of my aunt," Marcus said. "He wasn't trying to offend anybody."

"Get a *rise* out of your aunt?" the Reverend said, with a frown.

"Yes, and apparently she wasn't the only one," Zeke cut in, stepping in front of Marcus.

Reverend Washer was mortified. "Excuse me, son?"

"I'm not your son," Zeke replied angrily.

"Is there a problem over here?" Flannery seemed to come out of nowhere and was at Marcus' side. Her emerald eyes locked on the Reverend. "Why Reverend Washer, I would like to thank you for the lovely service for our father," she said, with a slow smile that made him cringe.

The room had quietened, and the group at the bar quickly gathered an audience.

"Your father prayed for your soul all the time," he said. He glanced over at Marcus. "Both of you. We both prayed together that you would get off your sinful paths and come to Christ."

"You know, Reverend," Flannery said, her smile still large as she visually surveyed his girth, "gluttony is a sin, and you look like you eat a lot."

A sound of someone stifling a giggle came from somewhere over near the sofa. A few beads of sweat had appeared on the Reverend's heated and trembling upper lip.

"One day it will be too late, and there will be no mercy for you!" he bellowed, his eyes growing wide. "None for *either* one of you!"

Geoffrey was soon in the middle of them with his car salesman smile. "Reverend Washer, my brother and sister are extremely upset about our father. Please excuse—"

"Don't you *dare* speak for me," Flannery said, her velvety voice so strong it caused Geoffrey to back off a step.

"Nor for me," Marcus said, walking away. Zeke followed him out of the room. Conrad watched from over in the corner with his arms crossed and an index finger on his chin.

Geoffrey gave a fake laugh and shook his head about. He forced another smile for the Reverend and put a hand on his shoulder to steer him away from the bar and back toward the other side of the room. "Please, please forgive them. They just simply don't know what they're saying with all that's happened."

"God, if only I could still drink," Flannery muttered to herself with an eye roll, once they were gone.

"Flannery, I'm so sorry about what Daddy said," Wes Washer was over at her side, once he was certain he was out of his father's line of sight. "He just don't know you the way I do."

She looked over to Wes with a grin. "That is a sweet thing to say. Thank you, Wes."

Over in another corner of the room, Clementine LeMonde's frosty glare caught Flannery's attention. She was in a black dress, without much makeup and had long, straight blonde hair that reminded Flannery of Katarina Castille's blonde locks. The hair was the only thing the two women had in common as far as appearance went. Clementine was plain, not very attractive, and not putting much effort into trying to do better. If she couldn't charm Wes after all these years then it wasn't Flannery's fault.

Feeling Clementine's hatred from yards away, Flannery put on a smile as manufactured as Geoffrey's with the Reverend and turned to Wes. She placed a hand on his sleeve for effect.

"You are always so considerate," Flannery told him. "Would you like to walk with me for a tour of the house? There have been renovations over the years. I bet you've never even been upstairs."

"That would be great!" he said with a wide grin. He looked around the room nervously, to make sure his father couldn't see him. "I think I'm gonna get a bottle of beer and pour some in a cup to take with me. You want the other half?"

She rubbed his arm affectionately and peered out of the corner of one eye to make sure Clementine was watching. "Oh none for me, thanks, but you go right ahead."

20

Once they were some distance away from the others in one of the downstairs hallways and out of sight, Flannery pulled Wes into a bathroom. His face went almost as white as it had the night before as Conrad threatened to kill him, when Flannery closed and locked the door behind them. Wes began to blush as she put her arms around him and pressed her generous breasts against his body through the fabric of their clothing. She gently and affectionately brushed his cheek with her hand and locked her emerald eyes with his, which were another shade of green.

She was hungry. *For several things.*

"Can I?" she said with uncertainty, mostly to herself instead of him.

Wes' back was against the bathroom wall, and he gave a wary grin. "Oh my gosh, I wasn't expectin' this."

His face went completely red, and she could smell the beer on his breath. He wasn't completely unattractive, but slightly pudgy and not the type of man she would have ever gone for in her previous life. But for now he was a man, and he would do.

"Maybe not, but you always wanted me to do this when we were younger," she said to him. "Isn't it about time your fantasy came true?"

He squirmed nervously and seemed afraid to reciprocate her gesture. "I just don't understand why you're doin' it now," he said, as his voice quivered.

The truth was his self-righteous father and Clementine LeMonde's invidious stares had her in a spiteful mood, but she couldn't tell him that. She was also determined to prove something else to herself that she couldn't share with him.

"Maybe you shouldn't think about it so much," she said. "Kiss me, Wes."

"*Wh—what?*" He seemed frightened.

It took everything in her not to be impatient with him. But he was the only easy target at the moment. She needed to know if she could still be a woman with a human. She had had no sexual encounters in the past five years, not since everything changed so drastically for her. She wasn't even convinced she could still make love with the living, since she was not.

"You heard me," she said, keeping him against her and moving her lips closer to his. She took one of his hands and put it on her breast.

She heard an anxious gulp come from him. "Your hands are so cold, Flannery," he said. "Are you feelin' alright?"

"Damn it, Wes," she whispered. "Do what I say and *kiss* me!"

What the hell was the matter with him? She might be dead, but he didn't know it. And she was still just as beautiful as she had been in life—as well as the days when he likely had his horny teenage boy dreams about her.

"Um...okay," he said sheepishly and gave her a light smooch on the lips. "Your mouth feels cold, too."

"Then make me warm," she said, grabbing him by the back of the head and kissing him back harder. The motion still felt natural, but she wasn't sure how much further than this someone like her could go with a human. She was eager to find out, but something else struck her before she could hike up her dress.

When she pulled back and gave him a peck on the cheek, all while moving his hand inside her hemline and up her thigh, she noticed the throbbing carotid artery poking out of his neck. Her sensations shifted, and a sudden salivation from hunger began inside her mouth. She had had nothing to drink since feeding on Tilda the night before and needed blood. But she also needed to know if she could still have intercourse with a man.

"Oh Flannery. Daddy would have a heart attack if he knew what I was in here doin'," Wes said, starting to caress her right breast where she had placed his hand. His other hand was underneath the bottom of her dress and on her behind. Her chin was on his shoulder.

Flannery realized her cuspids had sprouted. *Damn it.*

"Your Daddy would have a heart attack if he knew what I was in here doing," she said, at first hesitating and then biting into his neck without further thought. She instantly received a mouthful of blood and swallowed it.

"Ah," he gagged lightly, as he felt her teeth sink in. His grasp on her breast loosened, and she pulled him more tightly to her. *"Flannery, wh— what?"*

She was too preoccupied to pay attention to him, much less explain to him what was happening. She had given in to that *other* desire. The one she felt she had no control over. Her mind went blank as she did what became natural for her. She could feel and taste the warmth of him as it flooded her mouth. She drank and suckled, feeling it all flow into her.

She came to her senses and knew he was probably still weak from the night before, and she knew she must tell herself *when* to stop.

Her eyes closed as she fed on him, and she went back to another time.

The memory of that rainy New Orleans night five years ago still haunted her. "You have ignored my orders. Why are you so stubborn when it comes to my husband?" Katarina Castille asked her.

Katarina had walked into Senator Frank Castille's downtown office after hours, catching her husband and Flannery fully clothed but in an embrace. They quickly pulled apart when the door burst open and she entered just as lightning flashed outside. Katarina looked stunning as always, with full makeup, a blue pantsuit, and the perfect long, blonde hair.

"I'm in love with him," Flannery said. The other woman gave her a look of disgust.

"Katarina, go home. I'll be there later. We can talk then," Castille said, as he turned away from the women and walked over to a window.

"We will talk about it *now!*" she demanded, with such ferocity that Flannery was jarred for a moment.

"Go away, Katarina," he said. "I'm not in the mood."

Her blue eyes radiated furor over his dismissal. *"You* are not the one who calls the shots here! Do not forget what I can do to you, Frank."

"I wouldn't be so sure about that anymore," Castille said, peering outside. The sounds of rain outside the window and the ping-pang of drops that hit the glass broke the silence during the pauses between them.

"We will see about that," she said. "Come home with me this instant."

He turned back to face her. "I won't do this anymore. I'll see you at home later. Now leave us alone!"

"She says she loves you. Are you in love with this whore?" Katarina asked in her thick accent, pointing at Flannery.

Flannery walked over and slapped Katarina so hard across the face that her head swirled around. "I have had *e-fucking-nough* of you calling me a whore!" she said, standing firmly in place as she braced for whatever happened next.

Katarina regained her composure, tossed her hair back into place and appeared unaffected by the loud strike.

"If the shoe fits," she said to Flannery. "You will regret doing that." She looked to her husband. "And Frank, you will regret doing this to me."

She walked out and slammed the door.

Flannery turned to Castille in fear. "She's already threatened to drag us through the mud. Do you think she will? God, I wish I wouldn't have hit her, I don't even know why I did it, but—"

He sat down at his desk and shook his head. "I wish I could say she wouldn't retaliate, but I think she might try. But we have an ace in the hole. Conrad can stop her."

"Conrad can stop her *how?*" Flannery asked. "Who is this guy? He shows up, we start talking and then it's two hours later, and I can't remember anything. If I weren't with you, I would suspect he's drugging me or something."

"Well, of course he isn't," Castille said, looking insulted. "I'm here. You know I would never let him do something to harm you."

"Then what is he doing to me? It's starting to creep me out, Frank."

"Well, I can let you in on one thing. And I did tell him *not* to do this. But Conrad doesn't take orders well. The last time he was over he hypnotized you and ordered you to stand up to Katarina the next time she attacked you. It apparently worked."

"What else has he hypnotized me to do?" she asked, angry at the idea of someone messing with her mind. Sure, she had a mouth on her, but actually striking somebody was out of her character.

"That I can't tell you right now," he said, turning his swivel chair back toward the window.

"Well, you better tell me!" she exclaimed, walking over to face him. "Who the hell is this guy? Why does he feel the need to *hypnotize* me? For all I know he could brainwash me into being the next Patty Hearst."

"Don't be ridiculous," Castille told her, staring out the window. It was pitch black outside, and the usual topiary outside his bottom level office window was obscured by nightfall. Drops of rain rolled down the outside of the pane. She wasn't sure what he saw through the glass.

"He isn't going to make you do bad things."

"I hit your wife!" she said. "What if I think *that's* a bad thing? She has every right to call me a whore. Sometimes that's what I feel like, so she could be right!"

Castille stood from his seat and put his arms around her and gave a kiss. "Shhh," he quieted her. "You are not *that*. You are so much more, and one day you will be my wife."

"*How?*" she asked, desperately wanting him to give her a solid answer she could believe. "She will follow through on her threat if you try to divorce her."

"It won't happen," he said and gave her another kiss as he stroked her back with one hand.

"How can you be so sure?" Flannery asked. "My family is very well known up north. Katarina could have hired Conrad to mess with you and could be planning to use him to ruin me somehow."

"Now you're just being paranoid," he said. He unbuttoned the top of her silk blouse. He looked at her and kissed her again. "She has something to lose as well if she exposes us. She's saying these things to try and scare you."

"I still don't understand how you think you can just be rid of her so easily," she said, beginning to get aroused as he had a hand on one of her breasts and another up her skirt. "Oh, Frank, what are you doing? Not here..."

He cleared a spot on the desk. "I love you," he said, setting her on the desk and continuing to kiss her. She sat on the edge of the desk and wrapped her arms around him as he undid more buttons on her blouse. "I want to be with the woman I love. The *only* woman I love..."

"Oh wait a minute," she gasped, pulling away from him and removing herself from her seat on the desk. She started rebuttoning her blouse.

"What are you doing?" he asked, with a disappointed frown.

She smiled and gave him a kiss. "Let me go to the restroom first."

"*What?*" he asked.

"My, um, I need to..." she said, with a cock of her head. Even she didn't understand why it was so difficult and embarrassing to say the word *diaphragm*.

"Ah gotcha," he said with a nod. "It's down the hall. Hurry!" He gave her a smile.

She gave him another kiss and let her hand gently slide across his cheek. "I know the way, and I'll be right back."

She grabbed her purse from a chair and walked out of the office. The lights were out in the rest of the building, and lightning went off like camera bulbs outside the windows as she walked down the darkened, carpeted hallway to the restroom. She had been around Castille's office building enough to know her way around, so there was no need to find a light switch anywhere. The frequent flashes from the storm outside also helped guide her.

She thought she heard a sound behind her and stopped, then only heard the low rumble of some thunder outside. She continued on and went into the restroom but did not hear anything else.

A couple of minutes later she emerged and went back down the hallway. Something felt different, and she wasn't sure what it was. A few feet down the hallway, she could see Castille's office door was ajar, and the light from inside spilled out into the darkened corridor. She wasn't sure if she had closed it completely on her way out, or why she suddenly felt ill. She slowly walked toward the doorway and heard no noise from inside the office.

She reached the door, slowly slid it open, and screamed at what she saw. Senator Frank Castille was back in his swivel chair, his face pale, his blue eyes wide open and staring at her, but his head turned in such a way it appeared his neck had been snapped.

Katarina stood behind the chair with a cruel smile across her face. She held on to the chair with both hands and looked directly at Flannery. "This is the *first* part of what happens when you fuck around with me," she growled with a smile.

"*No, no! Oh my God!* What did you do?" Flannery cried, gasping and putting her hands to her face.

"I wish I could take credit for this, but..." She shrugged and shifted her eyes away from Flannery. Her face fell flat as she barked out a command. "*Boys, grab her!*"

Two large men in dark suits, stepped away from each side of the door and grabbed each of Flannery's arms, causing her to drop her purse as they held her on each side. They appeared rather young, handsome, and could have been old friends from Katarina's modeling days instead of two hoodlums on her payroll.

"I ought to tell them to rip off your fucking arms, bitch," she said, as she stepped from behind the desk and her dead husband. "I watched Bernard here do my dirty work with Frank," she said, glancing at one of the men. She looked back to Flannery. "I think I shall enjoy taking care of you myself."

"No, Katarina, *please,*" Flannery said, mostly crying over the sight of Castille dead in his chair. The men were hurting her arms, but the shock of walking in on the sight of the man she loved dead and staring vacantly back overwhelmed her at the moment.

"Oh, the poor widow," Katarina said quietly and dramatically with a small smile, her accent thick but the words clear. She held her hand to her chest and faked a quick sob. "They will all pity me. But they will especially pity me when news of my husband's whore comes out. Do you want to hit me now—for calling you what you are?"

"Is that what this is about?" Flannery sniffled. "You killed him because I *hit* you?"

"No, no," Katarina shook her head and paced around. After a moment she turned back to face Flannery. "That was already happening tonight. You hitting me just makes all of what's in store for you more delightful and worthwhile. Your punishment will be a little slower and more painful than my husband's was. Oh, how you should have listened to me and heeded my advice. *Whore.*"

Flannery spit in her face. If she was going to die, she wasn't going to die a coward. "Fuck you," she said.

Katarina slapped Flannery, as her two men held her on each side. "This will be so much fun," she said.

"I hate you," Flannery said, starting to cry again. *"Why* did you have to kill him? You would've found another man. One who actually wants you."

"*That* is not the point," she said and stepped even closer. "It was not your decision to make."

"Do what you have to do and get it over with," she said, as she came to terms with her fate. If she had to die she wanted it to be as quickly as possible. The building was empty. There was no way she would leave alive if it was only the four of them there.

"I'm hungry," Katarina said. She glanced over at each of her two friends with a wicked grin.

Flannery was confused. "What?"

Katarina's canine teeth had grown to twice their normal size, and there was a glow in her blue eyes that hadn't been there before. Flannery screamed, but it cut short as the other woman tore into her neck with her teeth and began sucking away.

Flannery fought for as long as she could, but the more she struggled to get her arms away from the two men, the more she felt her strength drain. She felt life slip away from her and everything went bright before her eyes. This must be what it feels like, she thought. It had been so sudden for Castille that she knew he hadn't felt the journey. He had gone from being alive to being dead in an instant. Although she began to lose consciousness, Flannery could still think and reason and knew her journey would be a longer one than that of her lover.

Castille told her Conrad could help them when it came to Katarina. But Conrad was nowhere around tonight. Flannery's last longing was for Conrad; realizing she *needed* Conrad. He was the only person who could save her now.

"Your turn," she heard Katarina say, as she started to float away.

Flannery thought maybe she was on the floor now. She could no longer feel anyone's hold on her arms. It would have been impossible to still stand on her own at this point. The last she could see through the bright light and the fog were the two men, their cuspids also elongated, as they came down on her throat for their turn.

Everything faded to black.

Flannery came to her senses, released her mouth and teeth from Wes, and then put her index and middle fingers to his throat. After a few seconds, she released them. It looked as if she had given him a hickey, but no puncture wounds were apparent.

He was still awake and staring at her strangely. "Oh my gosh, Flannery, what did you do to me?" he said. "That hurt, and I feel funny."

She checked the mirror to make sure there wasn't any blood on her mouth or spattered anywhere else. Five years of practice, and she could do it without leaving evidence if she was not in a frenzy of blood lust. Thankfully no blood had spilled on to Wes' light blue dress shirt. She kept the collar pulled back the entire time. But she knew he was going to be weak.

"Let's go get you something to eat," she said, fastening and fixing his shirt and collar properly for him. The collar covered up the mark on his neck. "Not in the living room. I'll take you to the kitchen."

"I feel kinda dizzy," he said, almost falling over as he tried to step toward the door.

"You need food," she said, hoping anyone else would only think he had had too much beer.

He turned back to her with a lethargic smile. "I'm *yours*," he said.

She returned a quick, noncommittal nod. She would figure out a way to erase his memory of what had happened when they got to the kitchen.

"Let's go," she told him.

21

"You're turning into your sister when it comes to being a stubborn mule," Conrad said to Geoffrey. They had escaped to the study after most of the funeral guests were gone. "Why have you become so difficult since last night?"

Ruffin stood nervously away from them, over near a wall, as if he were afraid to come closer.

"Conrad, I had guests. It wouldn't have looked appropriate to—"

"That's fucking unacceptable!" he shouted, poking Geoffrey harshly in the chest with his index finger. "We have an agreement, and one part of that agreement is *you* take orders from *me*. Not the other way around."

"The last twenty-four hours have been a goddamn rollercoaster," Geoffrey blurted loudly, near tears. "First Tilda, then you both came over and terrorized Rochelle and me...then what you did to Rochelle. Oh my God, and dead horses. *God help me, I can't fucking take it anymore!*"

"Keep your voice down and stop it with the sniveling," Conrad said, as he backed away and looked down on him like a disappointed father. "If only they could see you now."

"What more do you want from me?" he asked.

"You know the answer to that," Conrad said, tapping his chin with his index finger. "I never thought your wife was that hot when she was alive. And she smelled like a booze-soaked ashtray half the time. I wouldn't touch her with a ten-foot pole now. The only reason I ever had sex with her was to show you who the new man of the house was. I think now..." He paced around the room. He stopped in front of Ruffin and looked squarely at him. The attorney quickly shifted his eyes off to the side and began to fidget. "I think I want something more permanent in my life."

"We've already talked about that," Geoffrey said uneasily, looking down at his hands. When he realized they were shaking, he put them into his pockets.

"I'm not talking about our deal. I'm talking about what happens *after* that," Conrad said, taking further note of Geoffrey's shaky demeanor.

"Well, s—*speaking* of our deal," Ruffin began nervously.

"Let's not speak of that right now," Conrad said. "There's something else I want to discuss."

"What now?" Geoffrey said. He desperately wanted a drink. There was no liquor anywhere in the study. He felt he needed it to hear whatever Conrad's next request would be.

"I need a mate. A life partner. When you give me control of Ten Points, and I give you what you want, well, I'll need somebody here beside me," Conrad said. He walked to the window and stared out of it reflectively.

"Well, you claim you're married to my sister. As much as I can't bear her staying around, I guess it would make sense that she does if she's your wife," Geoffrey said.

"Flannery is his wife?" Ruffin asked. He stepped away from the wall. "I had no idea they knew one another."

"Yes," Conrad said. "Even Geoff didn't know until last night."

"I'm still confused about why you never told me, or how you met my sister and became involved with her," Geoffrey said. He still appeared agitated but had calmed somewhat. "After the Frank Castille mess in New Orleans, most men would have stayed far away."

"Well, I helped Flannery out of a little jam, and she's repaid me with servitude," Conrad said. "But our marriage isn't one that's legal or binding. I can release her from our agreement anytime I want. And I'm about ready to do it."

"Then that contradicts what you said about needing someone here beside you at Ten Points," Ruffin said, getting braver.

Conrad smiled. "No, it doesn't. I never said I wanted Flannery here with me."

"What do you plan to do with her once you release her?" Geoffrey asked. "That isn't code for *kill* her, is it?"

"Your sister is already dead," Conrad said. "I can't kill her. I would have to destroy her. And you despise her, so what difference does it make?"

"Flannery is *dead?*" Ruffin gasped. "I've seen her here all evening. She looks alive to me."

"Long story," Conrad said.

"Is there any way when you release her to bring her back—?"

"Back to *life?*" Conrad asked. "No, I'm not responsible for her creation, and even if I were, I don't think her condition is one that can be reversed. I wouldn't have authority anyway."

"Well, can't ... um, *you know* ... Can't h—he do it?" Geoffrey stammered.

Conrad laughed aloud. "Spoken like a true Baptist. No, *he* wouldn't. Just because Flannery is no longer mine doesn't mean she's no longer *his.*"

"Oh dear God," Geoffrey said. He steadied himself against the desk as he put his hand over his mouth.

"I hope you're not backing away from what we've agreed on," Conrad said to him. "*Everything* we've agreed on."

Geoffrey had nothing to say.

But Conrad wasn't finished. "Let's not forget the terms of what we've discussed. I mean, what kind of man sacrifices his own—"

"I get your point," Geoffrey interrupted.

"What exactly is Flannery's condition?" Ruffin finally asked. "You said she's dead, but she appears alive to me, and now you talk like she has some kind of illness? I'm confused."

Conrad placed his fingers on his temples and closed his eyes. After a few seconds, he released his fingers and opened his eyes. "Why don't I let Flannery explain it herself? I just summoned her here. Oh, and I also decided to include Tilda and the obnoxious new one."

"What does Tilda have to do with this?" Ruffin said, as he watched Geoffrey's face grow pale.

"It's time you learned more tonight, Ruffin," Conrad said. Then he smiled. "There are other branches on the tree of darkness besides myself."

The door opened, and Flannery, Tilda, and Rochelle filed into the room. Ruffin was suddenly frightened and backed near the wall. The short man clasped his hands together and quickly looked away when he caught Rochelle staring at him with her dead eyes a little longer than he liked.

"I hoped I would never have to come back here," Tilda said, removing her sunglasses in disgruntlement.

"You summoned us," Flannery said coldly to Conrad, without looking at him.

He stood before her. "Yes, my beloved. I have good news. I'm giving you a divorce."

"How is that even possible?" Flannery asked. "We were never married by law."

"That means it's easy," he said, with an amused expression. "I *don't*. There... now we're no longer married."

Flannery was confused. "So what does that mean? You've kept me close most of the time over the last five years. Where do I go and what do I do now?"

"Frankly my dear, I don't give a damn," he said half-jokingly, giving his best impression of Rhett Butler. "But you can go and you can do it without any concern over me."

"You're up to something," she said. Her tone was less baffled and now sober. "There's something you don't want me to find out about, and that's why you're trying to get rid of me."

Conrad looked at the rest of the group and sighed. "She acts like she's miserable when we're together, and then she gives me grief when I dump her." He turned to Flannery. "Why must you be so pig-headed all the time? This is your chance to get away from me. Why don't you take it and run with it?"

Flannery wasn't moved. "This has something to do with what you three are up to," she said, pointing to Conrad, Geoff, and Ruffin. "I don't feel like granting you your so-called 'divorce' until I find out what you're up to."

Conrad moved closer to her, and his smile was gone. "Last night in here will look like a number from *The Sound of Music* compared to what I do if you don't go along with this," he said.

"What is it you really want, Conrad?" she asked. "After all we've done together, after all that's happened...you won't even let me in on that much?"

"When I decide you need to know, I'll let you know," he said. "Oh, and I'm sorry I had to disturb your little feeding session with our deputy friend, to bring you in here."

"*What?*" Tilda asked, angry as she turned to Flannery. "You told me he was off limits just so you could have him for yourself?"

"Peeking through walls again, Conrad?" Flannery asked. She kept a narrow-eyed, sarcastic glare on him. "That's not very polite."

"Between you and Tilda, that poor 'good ol' boy' is going to need a blood transfusion soon," Conrad said, wagging his finger.

"I'm really confused," Ruffin said, his eyes moving back and forth across the group. "Feeding sessions, blood transfusions? What the hell is going on?"

"Maybe we should show you," Rochelle said, continuing to leer at him.

"Not yet. Back down," Conrad warned her.

Rochelle hissed at him. "But I'm hungry."

In a flash, Conrad was at her side and in her ear. "If you don't want to have a stake driven through you in your sleep tomorrow, you'll learn some decorum and learn it quickly." His voice had dropped to a growl but not as guttural as it had been the night before when he went after Flannery.

Geoffrey and Tilda watched in fear, waiting to see if Conrad's eyes would turn again. Flannery stood nonchalantly, as if she had seen a similar scene play out dozens of times in the past.

Rochelle gave a quick apprehensive grin and a nervous chuckle. "Oops, sorry, baby, I just need some blood."

Ruffin's eyes widened and he shifted anxiously in his stance over at the wall. "*Blood?*"

"Again, a long story," Conrad said. "But that's not the reason I've called this little gathering. The reason we're all here is because some of you need to be reminded *who* is in charge here. *Flannery!*" He suddenly looked over at her.

"But I thought you said I had my freedom," she said quietly, looking over at him out of the corner of an eye.

"Exactly," he replied. "Which means you better go quietly."

"This is my family home," she said. "What if I don't want to go at all?"

"You mean you want to *stay?*" Geoffrey said disgustedly. "It's bad enough he's already making me have Marcus stay."

"What if I do?" she asked, with a shrug.

"If you stay, then you do my bidding," Conrad said.

"Okay," Flannery said. "But I still want to know what you, my brother, and rat-face over there are conspiring about."

"I take offense—" Ruffin began.

"*Silence!*" Conrad ordered loudly, making them all stand up a bit straighter. "Flannery, I'm done going in circles with you all the time. You stay, you're my servant. If that's a problem and you insist on staying anyway, I'll stake you in your sleep."

"I'll *try* to behave," she said, though her tone was noncommittal. She had to find out whatever the hell Conrad was up to. It couldn't be just controlling Geoffrey and the estate. There had to be something more to all of it.

"Jesus, could any of this get any worse," Geoffrey said.

"Actually, when do *I* get to find out what this big secret is between you three?" Tilda asked. "I live in this house and have for many years. I *am* your wife, Geoffrey."

"Well, if anyone has a right to know, then it *is* Tilda," Conrad decided, "because it does concern her."

"Concerns me *how?*" she asked.

"No," Geoffrey said, shaking his head and looking away from them. He walked to the other corner of the room with his head down. He looked as if he might lose it again at any moment. "I can't—I *can't* talk about it yet."

"Fair enough," Conrad said. "We have plenty of time anyway." He chuckled. "Four of us have even more than plenty of time on our hands," he said, smiling at Flannery, Tilda, and Rochelle.

"Eternity with you three," Flannery said, with an eye roll. "How lovely."

"Bitch, you don't even know me," Rochelle said.

"I am very confused," Ruffin said.

"Apparently, Rochelle over here is too, if she thinks her mouth is going to do her any favors with us," Flannery said. Her patience was wearing thin, and her willingness to guide the woman in her new existence was withering away as well.

"You don't have any room to criticize anybody for unruly or

insubordinate behavior," Conrad reminded Flannery.

"What am I? A child?" Flannery replied. "May I suggest somebody keep a closer eye on her tonight before the whole fucking stable turns into a crime scene?"

Conrad closed his eyes and put his fingers to his temples. The room went quiet for a few seconds, as everyone watched.

Tilda finally broke the silence. "What are you doing?"

"Watch," he replied, with a smile.

In a matter of about thirty seconds, the door of the study opened and Travis entered. He was as pale as Tilda and Flannery, but his was by choice. He was still in his black designer suit from the funeral that matched his dyed black hair.

"Travis? What in the hell?" Tilda exclaimed, surprised to see her son.

He looked at no one but Conrad as he walked in. "Yes, what can I do for you?" he asked, as if he were in a trance and taking no notice of anyone else.

"Could you bring me a glass of ice water?" Conrad asked him. "I'm thirsty."

"I'll be right back," Travis said. He turned and left the room looking straight ahead robot-like and not acknowledging anyone else.

"What did you do to my son?" Tilda asked, with a look of horror.

"Oh my God," Geoffrey walked over to the window again and stared outside. *"What have I done ..."*

Flannery shook her head at Conrad. "Turning a teenage boy into your servant is a really low move, Conrad."

He smiled at her. "The kid stays in his room listening to dark music and looking at comic books. It's time to improve his work ethic."

Travis quickly returned with a tall glass of ice water and presented it to Conrad. "Can I please go to my room now?" he asked Conrad, still acting as if they were the only two people in the room.

"May I," Conrad corrected, with a wag of his finger.

"May I please go to my room now? There's a cool download I want to listen to," Travis said, in a more grammatically correct fashion.

Conrad gave a short laugh for the benefit of the others. "Have you done all your homework? Are there any tests coming up at school this week you should study for?"

Travis stared up at the ceiling and slanted his blue eyes as if he were thinking and then looked back at Conrad. "I don't think so," he said, in a monotone voice.

"Very well then. Go listen to whatever music it is you kids enjoy these days. Don't stay up too late!" he smiled, sending Travis off.

"You son of a bitch," Tilda said, once her son was gone and the door was closed. "What did you do to him?"

"Let's not start with the name calling, Tilda," Conrad said. "You've been so obedient and subservient since last night. I'll need you to be Rochelle's teacher, so I hope Flannery's poor influence isn't rubbing off on you."

"But why my son?" Tilda demanded to know.

"I thought with this 'change' of the last twenty-four hours you would care even less about him today," Conrad said. "It's interesting you still feel these maternal urges."

Conrad then took a sip of the cold water and then made an exaggerated sigh of his thirst being quenched. "Okay, now that my mouth is no longer dry, I have some announcements to make," he proclaimed. "The other reason I called you all in here tonight."

Geoffrey turned away from the window and looked at him. "Are you about to tell them—?"

Conrad put a hand up to silence him. "No, I'll leave that up to you when you feel it is the right time. Don't interrupt me again," he scolded. "My announcement tonight is that Ruffin, I want you to draw up papers giving me power of attorney over this household—and naming me executor of Maximilian Lanehart's last will and testament."

Geoffrey's face dropped as he tried to process what he had just heard. It was all too soon. *Much* too soon.

"But *I'm* the executor," Ruffin meekly stated, without any real authority behind his words. "What about me?"

"You will get your reward as soon as the deed is done," Conrad said, nodding his head. "You remember? The reward we discussed?"

Ruffin gave a short, wondrous smile, his small round face and the moustache reminding Flannery of the Cheshire Cat in *Alice in Wonderland*. "So as *soon* as it's done?" he asked.

"What reward?" Flannery asked. "What is he getting? Was this the plan all along?"

"The reward, yes," Conrad said. "The other stuff I just announced is kind of spur of the moment."

"So this isn't what the three of you have been discussing?" Flannery asked, pointing to Ruffin and Geoff.

"Are you serious? Power of attorney *and* executor?" a flabbergasted Geoffrey asked Conrad. "I don't recall agreeing—"

"I don't *recall* asking your permission!" Conrad said, walking closer to him. "Now, Geoffrey, do *not* interrupt me again. This is your last warning." Their eyes were locked and only inches apart. Geoffrey appeared ready to challenge him, but then after a few seconds backed down.

Conrad looked pleased. Then he turned to Ruffin. "Come here," he commanded.

Ruffin looked nervous and took the black handkerchief from the jacket of his dark suit to wipe sweat from his thin moustache and brow. "Why?" he asked.

Conrad smiled but not as a pleasantry. "Come here. Don't make me ask you again."

The attorney hesitantly stepped over. Without warning, Conrad grabbed him by the face and pulled his head to his so that their foreheads touched. "Oh God, no!" Ruffin screamed, as Conrad's grip on his head tightened.

"What is he doing?" Rochelle asked the others.

"Osmosis," Geoffrey said quietly, looking away.

"I've seen him do this to people before," Flannery said in a low tone, to no one in particular. "He's probably taking all of Ruffin's legal expertise for himself. That's my guess."

"This isn't the first time he's done it to him," Geoffrey said, looking down. He started to cry. "Oh for God's sake, I can't do this anymore..."

Tilda looked over at him. "What have you gotten us all into?" she asked. "What have you done to this house and this family?"

Ruffin made gurgling noises, and it appeared as if his eyes were about to pop out of their sockets. A small amount of blood trickled from one of his nostrils and became lost in his gray moustache. From where the others stood, it looked as though Conrad was putting a great amount of pressure on Ruffin's skull with his hands.

"*Make it stop!*" he screamed, as Conrad kept their foreheads pressed together.

Finally, just when the smaller man felt he couldn't take it anymore and might either go into a seizure or die, Conrad released him, causing him to fly back about ten feet. He gasped to catch his breath, and when he had his bearings about him, he pulled the black, silk handkerchief back out and dabbed at the blood coming from his nose. A large, wet spot was on the crotch of his pants where he had urinated on himself.

"I feel so much smarter now," Conrad said, with an impish smile for the others. "Ruffin, soon there will be no more use for you at all. Now, let's get back to my other announcement. *My mate.* The person I want at my side."

"Which won't be me," Flannery said.

"I want Marcus," Conrad said. "He is mine, but he just doesn't know it yet."

"*What?!*" everyone responded in unison.

"I had to go to him in a dream. He's not like any of you. I can't get through to him when we're together in person. Why is he not like either of you?" Conrad asked, looking back and forth at Geoffrey and Flannery. "Why does he make this so difficult for me? I can't get into his head unless he's asleep."

Geoffrey shook his head and looked away. Flannery shook her head and smiled. "Maybe Marcus doesn't let you in because he doesn't like you, and you disgust him."

Conrad was at her side without any warning. Full of rage, he grabbed her by the hair and pulled. "That's it. I'm about to fucking destroy you."

"*No!*" Geoffrey shouted, over at the desk. He opened a drawer and pulled out a .357 Magnum. His face shook, as he held the long-barreled Smith and Wesson Model 19 up and pointed it at Conrad. "Step away from her," he said.

Conrad let go of Flannery and turned to Geoffrey. "Put that down!" he demanded.

"I'm about to blow your fucking head off," Geoffrey said, suddenly calm and cocking back the hammer on one of the chambers.

"No, you won't," Conrad said, moving away from Flannery and walking toward the desk. "You *can't* and you *won't.*"

"I will," Geoffrey said, looking at him. He walked around to the other side of the desk. "I have to take back control while I still can."

"You won't," Conrad insisted, creeping closer to the desk. "Put down the gun, Geoff."

"*No,*" he said, sweat starting to bead on his forehead. "I won't do what you say anymore."

"You can't pull the trigger. You want to. But you can't." Conrad came closer. "Everything's come too far now, and you know we must *finish* this."

"Don't come any closer," Geoffrey warned, breathing heavily, his eyes growing wide. "Stay the fuck back!"

Conrad reached the tip of the barrel and let it poke into his chest. "I told you that you couldn't do it," he said.

Geoffrey started crying again. "I hate you. You've ruined my life," he wailed, lowering the gun.

Conrad quickly reached out and grabbed his throat with both hands. He held Geoff over the desk, strangling him. "You shouldn't have done that Geoff," he said calmly as his grip tightened around the other man's neck.

Geoffrey's eyes grew large and veins bulged from his neck as Conrad showed no mercy. The other four heard coughing, gasping sounds, as his arms and legs flailed.

"*Conrad, no!*" Flannery finally screamed.

Tilda and Ruffin watched in horror. Tilda put her hand over her mouth, and Ruffin only stood there with his mouth wide open.

Rochelle looked on in an aroused fashion, her eyes wide and her cuspids starting to sprout, as Conrad squeezed the life out of Geoffrey. A low growl emerged from her throat as blood lust began to overcome her, and her dead eyes grew fervently as she went in for a closer view.

After a moment, Geoffrey stopped struggling and went limp on top of the desk. Conrad released him and turned to the rest of the group.

"Does anybody else want to try me?" he asked. His tone was flat, and he had no expression. "This is what happens when you keep running your mouth and you try to cross me. *Who's next?*"

Flannery shook her head and was about to cry as she stared at Geoffrey's lifeless body on the desk. "Did you really have to kill him?" she asked. "W—wasn't there another way?"

Conrad looked to her, then to Geoffrey's body, and then back to Flannery.

Rochelle stepped in closer. "May I?" she asked, with longing in her eyes.

Conrad's eyes went from Flannery to Rochelle. "No, you may not," he said.

"Oh my God," Ruffin whimpered. "Geoffrey...and what is wrong with her?" he cried, pointing at Rochelle and her exposed canine teeth.

"I'm as dead as Geoffrey over there, you fool," she said, smiling even more widely and frightening him. When she moved toward him, he screamed and ran from the room. His loafers echoed off down the marble floor of the hallway, as the door to the study hung open behind him.

"Tilda, Rochelle, you know what you have to do," Conrad said. *"Stop him."*

Flannery stood over at the desk near Geoffrey's body. "We always had our issues, and he acted like he hated me. I think deep down he really didn't," she said. She still looked ready to cry.

Conrad turned away from watching Tilda and Rochelle exit the study. "He saved you from being destroyed by me. The gun is right there on the desk," he said. "Why don't you pick it up and finish what your brother started? You have the opportunity."

Flannery turned to face him. "Why kill you?" she asked. "If those two are going off to do what I think they are, then I can't have all three of you dead, now can I? How would I ever find out what you've been hiding from me?"

Conrad looked to her with a smile. She looked away in disgust.

"You may be stubborn and mouthy, Flannery, but I take back any of the times I've ever called you stupid."

22

James Ruffin, III ran out of the mansion as fast as he could, but he feared he wouldn't be quick enough when he heard the sounds of feet scurrying behind him. He went out the front door and down the winding steps of the front porch, caught one step the wrong way, tripped, and nearly twisted his ankle and fell before he got to the bottom. He took off down a sidewalk to the driveway, where the Bentley loaned to him by Geoff was parked.

When he got to the silver car, he realized it was locked and he had left the keys inside the house. Not knowing what to do next, he took off across the grass in the front yard and headed for a cluster of oak trees southeast of the property.

He hid behind one of the larger ones, catching his breath. At fifty-two, he had never been an avid athlete of any sort, and the black loafers he wore also hindered his running ability. He still had a dull headache from Conrad's hold. He tried to quiet his breathing when he heard whispers coming from the yard. The sounds of two women's voices. He tried to hold his breath, but he wasn't successful for long. He was too winded, and had to continue breathing.

He closed his eyes and counted to ten in his head. All he wanted was the nine hundred thousand dollars he had been promised for his participation in this deal and he would be on his way. He never wanted to come near the old plantation home again, he never wanted any association with the Laneharts again, and he would pack his bags and leave the city if only he could get out of this alive. His two children were adults, and his wife had divorced him three years ago after the kids finished college. He had no one to answer to, and he would gladly make himself scarce.

Ruffin realized he no longer heard whispers. Other than the loud chirps of crickets and some of nature's other nighttime dwellers, he could hear no one.

He couldn't stay hidden behind a tree all night. They would soon find him if he didn't make a run for it. He saw a patch of woods off in the distance. Maybe they would have trouble finding him if he could make it there. He exhaled and slowly peeked around the corner of the tree to see if anyone was in sight. The yard was empty, and no one was behind him. Maybe in his fear and paranoia he had only *thought* he heard the whispers earlier? Conrad had done a real number on him in the study.

Either way, he knew it would be impossible to leave the property by car, so he took off on foot again, running as fast and quietly as he could with only moonlight to guide him through the maze of large oak trees. A low-lying piece of Spanish moss came out of nowhere and caught him in the face, causing him to howl out in fright. He quickly brushed the large piece of moss away when he realized what it was, but the distraction caused him to trip over a small hole in the ground.

"Ruuuufffffiiiiinnnn!" a woman's voice echoed from the shadows. He couldn't see where it was coming from, but it sounded like it was from about one hundred feet away.

"Ruuuuuuufffffffffffffiiiiiiiiinnnnn!" This time it was from a different woman. Two of them. He had seen Rochelle's elongated teeth. She was a monster. Like a creature from mythology. Nothing that should be of this world.

He pulled himself to his feet and hobbled off, his right ankle aching and likely sprained, he thought to himself. His hurt ankle and his shoes made it all the more difficult to get to the trees. They were close, but it felt as if they were still too far away with the slower pace he was forced to endure.

Ruffin then screamed loudly as he saw a brightly lit shape fly out from behind a sycamore tree off in the distance. It came for him, and when he tried to turn and run in the other direction he saw another similar figure coming for him on the other side.

As the shapes came closer, he recognized Tilda and Rochelle. Both of the women had extraordinarily long canine teeth showing, and when he tried to run away, they both struck from the air with rapid ferocity, hitting him in the neck teeth first.

The force of their attack knocked Ruffin to the ground. He was a small man and could not put up much of a fight for very long. He quickly fell into unconsciousness. As the two women fed on him, the loud, high pitch of a coyote's howl in the distance went ignored.

23

"You have got to be kidding me," Marcus said, when Rush Limbaugh came on the radio the minute Zeke cranked the Ford pickup.

The two had escaped Ten Points and gone for a bite to eat at a diner off of Highway 165. Zeke kept the radio turned down on the drive over, but when he started the truck, the volume was back up on the conservative talk radio channel.

"You don't approve?" he asked, with a smile.

"You do? The guy has made horrible, bigoted comments about gay people. You're still a fan?" Marcus said in disbelief.

"So let me guess. You also hate Fox News and watch only MSNBC?" Zeke asked him.

"I didn't say that, but one is definitely not as fair and balanced as it claims."

Zeke laughed. "Oh come on! *Neither* of them are. Yeah, it sucks that many conservatives aren't supportive of gay rights, Marcus, but there's the bigger picture to worry about. There's the economy ... border security ... the whole gun debate."

"So that's why you're red? I get it. But you don't have to be a flaming conservative to be concerned about those things, you know." He stared out the truck window into the darkness as Zeke drove down the highway.

Zeke reached over and switched the radio to a top forty pop music station. "There," he said. "I bet we can agree on some things here."

"So I guess living here means you have to put up with a lot of crap from people like Wilkins Washer, huh?" Marcus finally said, looking over at him.

Zeke shook his head. "People are nice for the most part. As long as you don't talk about it. Even the nicest ones get fidgety and uncomfortable if you make mention of it."

"We didn't even do anything bad. I don't know why he got so touchy about it."

"Because he knows he'll have eighty percent of people around here on his side. Your sister put him in his place though."

Marcus nodded. "I'm a little worried about Flannery. She and I have barely had two words in the past two days. She's never around during the daytime. And when she shows up at the house she's always preoccupied and not in a talkative mood. At least not with me."

"She looks awfully pale since the last time I saw her, too. And those raccoon eyes. Damn."

"Yeah, I noticed the dark circles when she was inside under the light. I hope she's not on drugs. She's always been a little too edgy for her own good."

"After all that's happened ... *Well* ..."

"The scandal made its way out west as well. Of course, the internet always helps out with that kind of thing," Marcus said.

"Did they ever find out who leaked those photos?" Zeke asked.

"Nope, and something tells me they'll find Jimmy Hoffa before they ever find Frank Castille," Marcus replied. "The man is obviously buried in concrete somewhere."

"Along with that Swedish model wife of his. They never found any trace of her either. How did Flannery get out of being accused or arrested? Nobody thought she ...? Yikes, sorry Marcus." Zeke looked ahead and kept driving.

"It turned out Castille had too many mob ties. It's always been assumed that he and his wife ... Katarina, I believe her name was ... got offed by the mafia and are probably underneath one of the newer high-rises. Flannery was just an innocent victim in all of this."

"*Innocent?*" Zeke questioned, then looked ahead again. "Sorry ... sorry. I didn't mean for that to slip out. I guess you can't help who you fall in love with," he said, looking back over at Marcus.

"Maybe not, but she certainly could have made better choices," Marcus said. "Dad came down so hard on her. *Both of us.* I could never judge her. We both got it at the same time ..."

"Got *what* at the same time?" Zeke asked.

Marcus shook his head and tried to make the memory go away. He was being taken back to a place where he didn't want to go. That night five years ago when Maximilian had summoned both of them home and to the study at Ten Points, where he made them sit before him as he faced them from behind his desk.

"I'll start with you," he said, with a disgusted look in Marcus' direction that caused the old man's face to wrinkle even more. The prescription eyeglasses he wore while working were down on the edge of his nose, which appeared red. Marcus assumed it was from all the Scotch he drank every evening. His silver hair was perfectly parted, and not a hair was out of place.

"What is this?" Maximilian asked, sliding a pile of photos across the desk toward Marcus.

Marcus picked up the photos. They were eight-by-tens of him at a gay pride parade in San Diego's Balboa Park the summer before. He was shirtless, holding hands with a shirtless Landon. In another photo, Landon had his arm around Marcus. A giant rainbow flag banner was on a float that rolled past them in one of the photos.

He felt his mouth go dry as he set down the photos. *His father knew.* It was about time. He was thirty-one years old, and the secret was getting more and more difficult to keep from him and everyone else in the family. Plus, he had Landon. Geoffrey had Tilda, so why couldn't he share his special someone with the world?

He braced himself for whatever was about to happen. But he also wanted to know—why and *how* did Maximilian have photos of him from his life seventeen hundred miles away? Was he having him watched?

Marcus looked up at his father. "What do you think it is?" he asked. "What do you want me to say?"

"I'm not having a faggot for a son," Maximilian growled, his blue eyes piercing Marcus from over the rims of the glasses. "What made you decide to start doing these kinds of things with other men?"

Marcus could only speak his truth. "Nobody made me decide. That's the way it's always been."

"Lies," Maximilian said. "You had girlfriends when you were younger. You went and lived around all those goddamned liberals on the West

Coast, and they somehow made you think all of this is okay. Well, it's not!"

"It's how it always was. I tried to deny it, but this is who I am. I can't try to change just to please you," Marcus said quietly and meekly, looking down at his hands. He knew none of this would end well.

"I should've known when you weren't as good at sports as your brother that something wasn't *right* about you," Maximilian said, shaking his head. "Always reading, doing those things. I should've figured out a way to straighten you out then."

"Oh for God's sake," Flannery muttered from over in her seat. "Do you really think that would've prevented anything? It's in his wiring. He has no control over it."

"You shut the hell up!" Maximilian yelled at her. "You're a whore who's no better than he is!" She looked down and away from him as well.

"Both of you," he said, his eyes going back and forth. "You both disgust me. You're no longer a part of this family. I'm disinheriting both of you."

"But where's your—" Marcus began. He felt his throat start to close up. Tears began to well up in his eyes.

"Where's my *what?* My mercy, my compassion? You don't get that," Maximilian said. "You're a sodomite, and you're going to Hell, along with that whore in the seat beside you."

"I don't think anybody has ever expected compassion from you at any time," Flannery said, clasping the arm of the wooden antique chair tightly. Marcus thought he heard the crack of wood underneath her grasp. When he looked over, it was almost as if her green eyes had gotten brighter.

Maximilian seemed to notice, too, and there was some alarm on his face. "You just need to settle down," he said. "This is my house, not yours. What *I* say goes. You go to New Orleans and act like a cheap Bourbon Street whore with a married man, and then you are out of my family!"

"Have you even been down Bourbon Street lately?" she asked him, rolling her eyes.

He ignored her, as he continued. "Those photos leaked to magazines. You kissing Frank Castille in his office. The wife must have had some private eye watching. Good for her. God knows you're probably the reason he's missing. I bet you killed that man and his poor pretty wife. Did some other married man you're screwing help you get rid of the bodies?"

"Wouldn't you like to know, old man," she snarled, hatred in her husky voice. If he was going to kick her out, she would make damn sure he knew what was on her mind.

"You're a disgusting jezebel," he said. "I should've smothered you in your crib. Get the hell out of my sight and don't ever show your face in this house again."

"Fuck you, and *fuck this family!*" she growled, as she stood from her seat. Marcus could tell their father's words stirred some pent-up rage that had boiled underneath the surface for some time.

Flannery held her hands on the edge of the desk and bent in closer to Maximilian as she spoke. The petrified look on his face suggested he saw something Marcus could not from where he sat.

"Oh dear God, you have got Satan inside you," he said, his hands beginning to shake. "Get out of my house. Get the hell out of here and never come back! Both of you! You're both no longer my children!"

"I don't want to be your child, you self-righteous son of a bitch," she spat, knocking her chair over as she stormed out of the room.

Marcus started to cry. "Flannery, no, don't leave me here alone!"

"You're pathetic," Maximilian said, going back to his paperwork and business matters now that his hands had stopped trembling. "You're excused. Go. Catch the next flight back to your new and permanent home. Go be with your faggot friends and forget you ever had a family here. Because you no longer do."

"I'm *nobody?*" Marcus wasn't sure what was happening. He started to cry more, and Maximilian worked at the desk and ignored him. It was if he no longer existed.

Marcus wiped away tears and walked out of the study, feeling numb and helpless and unsure of what to do next. He realized all he could do was simply go to the airport and see if he could catch an earlier flight out.

When he walked out the front door and on to the porch, that's when he saw.

That's when he saw ...

He had been so overcome with emotion that evening five years ago. Something he had caught a glimpse of never clicked with him until now.

"Drive faster," he heard himself tell Zeke. "Get to Ten Points. *Hurry.*"

"That's where I'm taking you," Zeke replied. "Why the rush?"

"I think I just figured something out about my sister," he said quietly, not caring to elaborate.

24

Flannery and Conrad sat in the living room, where short bursts of conversation were followed by long silences. Flannery perched on the antique dark green velvet sofa with her hands folded across her lap, while Conrad was over in a leather armchair nursing a glass of bourbon. The hour wasn't terribly late, and both of them were aware being in the living room left them vulnerable to anyone else walking in. But after the events of the past hour, each felt a need to be out of the study—even if it happened to be for completely different reasons between the both of them.

Flannery anxiously played with the black fabric on the sleeve of her dress and couldn't help but notice how pale her hand was next to the fabric. Wes had been a quick fix but not what she needed. She was still hungry, and she wasn't sure what to do about it. After what had happened in the study, she was fearful to go far from the house.

"Considering which duck you'll catch and make a meal of later?" Conrad asked. He knew her well. *Too well,* she realized. He expertly twirled the glass around in his fingers, barely jostling the liquor. "Aren't duck wraps a popular menu item in these parts these days?"

"That's not funny," she said. "After everything you've done tonight in this house, I don't understand how you can sit over there and make jokes."

"It wasn't a joke. It was a legitimate culinary question," he replied. "And for someone who I finally set free you certainly are staying rather close. I had no idea you cared so much. It's all so flattering."

She looked over at him sourly. "I wish he would have shot you."

Conrad laughed aloud. "Now your real feelings come out. Well, I can remember a time when you needed me and wouldn't have said such hurtful things."

"Yes, you're right. There was a time I needed you. *Was.* But that time has passed. Now I just need to know what this agreement is you two made."

"Don't forget Ruffin," Conrad said, waving his index finger as he always did. "He was in on it, too. He was only getting nine hundred thousand dollars for going along with all of this."

"I don't even know what *this* is, but Ruffin was a greedy fool. I can log on to Amazon or eBay and spend nine hundred thousand dollars in an hour's time. He deserves whatever Tilda and Rochelle did to him."

"They are still busy disposing of whatever is left. Nobody will ever find a trace."

"Tilda never liked to get her hands dirty. I would love to be a shadow on one of the trees watching this."

"Tilda is not the woman she was in life, though it disturbs me to see she still seems to feel some attachment to her children. The way she was set off by my enslavement of Travis bothers me."

"It must please you to walk into this house and create your own museum of monsters and servants in only about thirty hours."

Conrad laughed at her again. "Don't forget your part in this. You set the ball rolling when you lost control and attacked Tilda. She needed to feed to survive, and that's how Rochelle came to be. I gave them strict orders *not* to bring Ruffin back, even though I think that was understood without my having to say anything."

"We don't have to worry about another mouth to feed, but he still never got to enjoy his nine hundred grand. What a pity."

"Do you know one of things I *do* like about you, Flannery?"

"I'm not sure I want to know," she said. She stared at the wall and refused to look in his direction.

"Despite how stubborn, insubordinate, and difficult you can be, you rarely ever go all *human* on me. Other than begging me to spare your friend Wes and getting upset over my killing your brother, you've actually done a very good job over the years of not letting your emotions get in the way of what must be done."

"Most of those feelings went away after...*after* Katarina and her goons did what they did," she said. "Most of them."

"Yes, you were all gone by the time I arrived at Frank's office," Conrad said, thinking back. "They took Frank's body with them, and they took you as well. But I had been inside your mind. I knew everything that had happened the minute I walked into that empty office."

"Is there any reason we have to discuss this?" Flannery asked, shifting on the sofa and visibly uncomfortable with him bringing up unpleasant memories. "That was the most frightening moment I ever experienced. The moment I was murdered by three people."

"Yes, but you had your revenge," Conrad said, a glint in his eye. "With my help."

Flannery shook her head and shifted in her seat on the couch. She could still remember those first moments five years ago when she was reawakened, or reanimated, after her death. She came to in a strange place, to find Katarina and her two men standing over her. There was still blood around their mouths, and Katarina had some on her chin. Flannery wasn't sure how long it had been, or if the blood was hers from the attack in the office—or somebody else's.

"Welcome to my lair. *Whore*," Katarina smiled. Her cuspids were still long and spike-like, as if she had just sucked more blood. *What was she? What were they?*

Had it only been a few minutes since they were all in Castille's office?

Flannery felt foggy and numb. And cold. "Where am I? I'm still alive? I don't understand..."

Katarina laughed, and looked over to the blond goon and brunet goon who began laughing alongside her. "She has no idea what we have done to her," she told the men.

"Did what? *What is this?*"

"Killing you, and letting you rot would have been too easy," she told Flannery, kneeling down beside where she lay. She began stroking Flannery's wavy black hair softly, then grabbed a handful and yanked, pulling Flannery's face closer to hers. "I couldn't let it all happen too quickly." She let go of Flannery and moved aside, and Flannery then screamed at what she saw.

Across the room, the body of Frank Castille, which was turning blue, was propped up in an armchair. The dead, blue eyes were shiny in the dim light, and there was still the same look on his face, as if he had been caught by surprise and gasped at the very end, as his neck was broken.

"Why did you do it? And what the hell are you?" Flannery asked, trying to move away from Katarina. She realized she was lying on a brown leather sectional sofa with a blanket underneath her. "Why did you bring him here?"

It looked as if they were all inside the living room of a house or an apartment. The room was dimly lit, and it was either night time or the windows were blacked out. Flannery was too woozy to be certain. It then occurred to her there were candles scattered around and no lights were on.

"It would only be fitting that you keep looking at him," Katarina said. "You wanted to be with him in life so much. You now get to be together in death."

"I—I don't understand...Why do your teeth look like that? Oh my God, what did the three of you do to me?"

Katarina gave another laugh. "It's okay. You will have plenty of time to think about all of it and figure it out," she said. "Bernard ... Oswald. Bring it," she commanded.

The brunet, who was apparently Oswald, dragged out a large wooden trunk, with a closed lid and a sizeable silver lock. It was big enough to ... Flannery finally understood what was going on.

"No!" she protested, as Bernard and Oswald dragged it closer to the couch.

"Yes," Katarina said, stepping back. "Wood doesn't last forever in the grave, but if you ever manage to dig yourself out, after a century or so, I'll figure out how to deal with you then."

Bernard unlocked the trunk and lifted the lid, while Oswald lifted Flannery off the couch. She screamed and tried to fight against him, but the muscular man's strength was much greater than her own. He pinned her down inside the trunk, forcing her to bend her knees so she could fit more securely inside. The wood felt damp and rough against her skin. She continued to struggle, determined not to give up until she absolutely had no other choice.

"It's time to let the whore have my husband. Just as she wanted," she heard Katarina say, somewhere in the room.

"Oh God, no, please!" Flannery screamed, as she saw Bernard dragging the body of Castille over to her and setting it at the edge of the trunk. He positioned himself better, so he could roll the corpse into the trunk on top of her. She continued to beg and plead but knew somewhere in her mind there was no point in doing so. These weren't humans with souls. They were monsters, and the one calling the shots had not one iota of regret or feeling in the matter.

"Together forever," Katarina said, as Bernard rolled the body over into the trunk and on top of Flannery. He then moved aside and Katarina appeared, looking down on her with a smile. "Watch out what you wish for, bitch."

"Katarina, please no, you can't do this!" Flannery implored.

But it was no use. Katarina reached in and bent the legs of Castille's corpse so that it was completely inside and she could close the lid.

"Goodbye. Whore," Katarina said with a smile as the lid crashed down, and everything went to black.

Flannery realized there was nothing else she could do when she heard click of the lock. She had seen their teeth, the blood, and she wondered why she was still alive. What made them drink blood? She didn't understand any of this.

As she realized she would suffocate and die inside the trunk, with Frank's cold, stiff, decomposing body on top of her, she noticed something else peculiar. She could breathe or hold her breath at will and wasn't feeling the loss of any air supply in the cramped space of the trunk. Her position was uncomfortable, but she wasn't in any pain.

"It won't be enough," she heard Katarina tell them. "Get the chains. *Silver.* Use gloves so your hands are not burned."

"Where are we taking it?" she heard one of the men ask. He sounded American but no north or south Louisiana accent.

"There are some woods in St. John Parish," she heard Katarina say. "I'll lead the way. I want the hole deep. More than six feet. No one but the three of us must ever be able to find this."

"We still have to go back and clean up at the office," Flannery heard a third voice. This one with an accent similar to Katarina's. They must have known one another from Europe, Flannery decided. Maybe they were even family.

"The silver burns," she heard the American say. "Even with the gloves."

"Don't be such a pussy," she heard Katarina say. "Shall I do it, so you can protect your delicate little hands?"

"Why do we even need the chains?" the American asked. Flannery wasn't sure by the sound of the voices which one was Bernard and which one was Oswald. She had never heard them speak before they stuffed her into the trunk.

"You fool. How long have you been one of us?" Katarina replied.

"Well, apparently not long enough because I don't know why the chains that go around the trunk have to be silver. If they're not to keep her from escaping, then what else?" he asked.

"The silver chains sustain her without the blood and keep her in a semiconscious state for however long she's buried," she heard the man with the Scandinavian accent explain. *Blood?* Semiconscious state? She hadn't a clue what they were talking about.

"She could be down there for five hundred years and be awake the entire time," Katarina said, with a cackle. "She will feel my husband rot and wither away on top of her."

"Five hundred years?" Flannery said. She didn't understand what it meant. She didn't understand *why* she wasn't suffocating inside the trunk. Her ability to breathe or stop breathing at will was baffling. But the fear of being buried alive gave her little time to think about her breaths.

"Katarina, please! Let me out of here!" she screamed one more time, pounding her hands from the inside, to no avail. They ignored her and continued their conversation amongst themselves.

"Here, let's get this thing to the car," the American said. "I'll get this end, you pick it up down there," she heard him instruct the other one.

Flannery felt the trunk come up off the floor, along with the grunts of the two men—or whatever they were—as they slowly and methodically carried it across the room.

"Damn it, I am so much stronger than I ever was as a human, but this thing is still a bitch to move," the American continued, with more grunts.

As a human? What was he now?

"I am the one who is walking backwards with this thing. Why are you complaining?" she heard the man with the accent say.

"I suppose I will have to listen to this all night long," Katarina grumbled.

Then there was what sounded like a rap at the door. Was someone there? Flannery strained to listen.

"It's midnight. Who the hell is knocking on my door?" she heard Katarina say.

"You don't have friends?" the American asked.

"Shut up, you imbecile," she heard the man with the accent say.

"Are you going to answer it?" the American asked her.

"Shhh, be quiet and make no sound," Katarina said. "Maybe they will go away."

"I'm still hungry," the American said. "Maybe we should open it and invite whoever it is inside."

"That is actually a good idea from you for once," the man with the accent replied in agreement.

"I said be quiet," Katarina hissed, sounding farther away.

From inside the trunk, Flannery heard the door burst open and then a scream from Katarina. The trunk was dropped with a thud and Castille's chin pressed further into her shoulder as the trunk landed on to the floor.

Flannery heard two loud gasps from the two men, only about five seconds apart, and then the trunk rattled violently as one of the chains from outside was ripped off in one swift pull.

"Stop! You can't do this!" she heard Katarina yell. Flannery could hear a loud clinking as the chain was dragged across the living room. "Oh God, no! It burns! *Make it stop!*" Katarina screamed loudly.

A moment later, the trunk was jarred again as Flannery felt a tug from outside. She heard the lock click, and then lid lifted. Conrad stood above her, with a victorious smile. "Well, it looks like I got here just in time," he said.

"Th—they killed him," was all Flannery could say.

Conrad shook his head, as he pulled the corpse off her. "Think about yourself," he said. "They were about to bury you underneath the earth for all eternity."

"But h—he's dead," she said, as he pulled her free.

"So he is," Conrad said, placing Castille's body back inside the trunk once Flannery was out. "What's done is done. Now we must focus on the problem at hand," he said, looking over to Katarina.

She was wrapped into a chair with a silver chain, writhing and moaning in torment. A look of worry also overcame her when she saw

Flannery was free. Her two thugs were lying dead on the floor, one with a hole in his chest; the other with a wooden stake still protruding from his.

"You won't get away with this," Katarina said, trying to wiggle her way out of the chain but then screaming in pain as it burned her. "My husband sold his soul to you, and now you conspire with his whore."

"What is she talking about?" Flannery asked. "What *is* she?"

"The same thing you now are," she spat, looking squarely at Flannery. "You will live only at night, and you will only be able to survive by feeding on blood. You won't be able to face the sunlight without incinerating and melting away. You are *dead*, Flannery Lanehart!"

Flannery looked to Conrad. She clasped her hands together and felt the icy cold of them together. There was something different from before all of this. Her consciousness and the way she felt in general. She couldn't explain it but knew there had to be a reason for all of it. Katarina's explanation began to make sense. "Is it true? Did they kill me? Is this some kind of strange afterlife?"

"Yes, and yes," he said quietly. He then smiled and turned to Katarina. "I think I'll set you out in the sunlight in a few hours and see if that melting thing you claim is really true."

"Be my guest," she said. "I would rather be destroyed than beg for mercy from the two of you."

"Well, you were about to bury my good friend Flannery here with your husband for the rest of time," Conrad pointed out, turning back to Flannery. "I guess whatever we decide to do to you shouldn't be too much of a surprise."

"How did Frank marry a woman that lives only at night?" Flannery said, still getting her bearings and wobbly on her feet. She sat on the sofa where she had awoken earlier. "He's a high-profile person. How can he have a wife who can't go out in the daytime?"

"His inauguration and public events were at night. I was the dutiful wife with a career during the day. *I* made him! He came to me because he wanted it all," Katarina said, still trying to pull free from the chair. "I am three hundred forty-six years old. I've accumulated power over the centuries, even before I came to America, and I let him have some of it. *For a price.*"

"Well, you don't look a day over twenty-nine," Conrad quipped. "You know, under different circumstances, we could've been a great team. I'm sorry we ended up on opposite sides."

She narrowed her eyes on him. "Then there was you," she said. "You promised him more than I could give him."

"My connections are better than yours," he smiled. "I have a direct line."

Flannery looked warily at him. "Frank sold his soul to the Devil?" she asked, then peering into the trunk at her lover's corpse. "All to be President of the United States?"

"Something like that. It was the path he wanted, but unfortunately it will never happen now," Conrad said, as if it were only a friendly wager that was lost. "But I have what he agreed to give to me in return."

"What would that be?" Flannery asked him.

But Katarina cut her off. "Enough with the chit chat. If you're going to destroy me, then do it and get it over with," she snarled, gasping from the burn of the chain and trying one last time to pull herself free.

"Oh, I was joking about setting you out to fry in the sun," Conrad grinned. "I'm not going to destroy you. You weren't going to destroy Flannery here, so I think we should do something similar with you."

"Bury me? How original," she remarked, with a roll of her eyes.

"Not just bury you," he said. "I have something even better in mind."

Two hours later, the trunk with Katarina and Castille was on board the yacht of Trewitt Longhaven IV, as it pulled away from the South Shore Harbor Marina into Lake Pontchartrain. Katarina's screams could no longer be heard, since the trunk had been encased in a cement burial vault above deck on the watercraft. An anchor was attached to the vault. Deep inside, within the wooden trunk, Katarina was entombed, still wrapped in the silver chain with her husband's corpse on top of her.

Flannery wasn't sure how Conrad knew Trewitt Longhaven IV, how he had gotten his hands on a burial vault on such short notice, and she wasn't sure she wanted to know.

Trewitt sat over on a barstool below deck, numb and motionless as Conrad steered the large luxury boat from up above.

"What is he doing down there?" Flannery asked, peeking down.

"He won't remember any of this later," Conrad said. "He's under a deep state of hypnosis right now."

"I know all about how you hypnotized me during those visits to my apartment," Flannery said, as the night breeze from the massive lake swept through her hair. "Not that it probably matters now, but I would still like to know what you did during those times that I can't remember."

Conrad smiled at her. "I didn't violate you, even though you are a very sexy woman," he said.

"I know you didn't," Flannery said. "Frank was there. He never would have allowed that." She was saddened at the thought of him. "He wanted it all, and it ended like this for him."

"Life's a gamble, Flannery," Conrad said. "He could have had what he wanted, died forty or fifty years from now, and then had an even bigger price to pay later. He wasn't the big picture anyway."

"What do you mean?" she asked.

"I only made Frank's acquaintance so I could have access to you," he said, looking over at her. He seemed to be half-joking, but there was something sinister behind the dark eyes.

"I'm afraid I don't understand," she said warily, walking closer to him.

"You will," he said, looking out on to the water ahead. "In time."

"Did you know Katarina would have Frank killed? Could you have prevented it?"

"I suspected she was up to something, and Katarina also has the powers of darkness on her side. Hence the chain I'm keeping around her. I maybe could have tried harder to protect Frank, but she would've continued to try and outwit me."

The talk of dark powers and such things made Flannery uneasy. "How much farther until we get to where we're going?"

"Not far," he said, glancing over at the encased trunk. "I'll just make sure it's really deep. Would you like to do the honors?"

"I can't lift that thing," she said. "It must weigh a ton. How do you plan to ever get it overboard?"

"You're forgetting that I'm not human," he smiled. "And neither are you anymore, my dear."

"Katarina's thugs claimed they weren't either, but they were getting winded moving the trunk before it was ever put inside a vault."

"They were pansies," he smiled. She took note of how dashing and handsome he appeared in the moonlight, with his tan, chiseled face and wavy, thick brown hair. He was dressed in a white button-up dress shirt and slacks as he captained the yacht. If it hadn't been for the grim task at hand, and the fact Flannery was dead and Conrad was a demon, it might have all been somewhat romantic.

"They were too easy to destroy," he continued, "and I don't have to lift a finger to move that thing overboard."

"I guess I should thank you for rescuing me," she said.

"Oh you will," he said, looking at her again with the intense stare and no longer smiling.

She grew uncomfortable and looked away.

Within minutes, Conrad reached a spot on the water he deemed suitable. He took a quick look around to make sure no other boats or eyes were on them.

"Any final words for our lovely Katarina?" he said, pointing toward the concrete vault in which the trunk was encased. "I can even fix it so you get one last look at her inside, if you like."

"No," Flannery said. "Frank is in there, too. It could have been me in there. I can't bear to think about it anymore. Just do it, Conrad. Get rid of it."

"As you wish," he said, snapping his fingers. Flannery watched as the large vault slid across the deck of the yacht, almost seeming to levitate. The vault reached the starboard edge and went over, causing a colossal splash so thunderously loud that Flannery couldn't resist the urge to watch as the anchored, encased trunk submerged and slowly sank out of sight, leaving ripples across the top of the water as it made its way to the bottom of Lake Pontchartrain.

Katarina was left to her watery grave, buried with the husband she had ordered killed—and the silver chain that would keep her semiconscious and never allow her to sleep.

"Oh my God," Flannery muttered softly to herself.

"He had nothing to do with it," Conrad said, with a large smile. "And he's no longer *your* God, my dear."

"Wh—what?" she stammered, looking back at him.

"You must be hungry," Conrad said, looking at her impishly.

She only stared at him but didn't respond. Somewhere in her vernacular, she knew what he meant and slowly nodded her head.

"In just a moment I'll take you below deck and let you become better acquainted with Trewitt. You will take what you must, but be careful and use caution. I will guide you, since you're new at this and have no one like yourself to be your teacher. We can't kill anyone else tonight."

"Yes," she said. Her mouth watered. She realized what she was and what she must do.

"*I wonder what Katarina's doing right now,*" Conrad said, back in the present in the living room at Ten Points, where he finally took a sip of his bourbon. "Ha! Holding her breath, I presume," he added, with a guffaw.

"I don't want to think about it," Flannery said, still seated on the sofa. "We did what we did, and that's it. She was going to do the same thing to me."

"I should take an excursion on Lake Pontchartrain sometime."

"I try to stay away," she said, wanting to change the subject.

"And those photos of you and Castille kissing in his office. They didn't show up in the newspapers and tabloids until *after* Katarina went missing," Conrad pointed out.

"What about them?" she asked. "And after you explain, can we please talk about something else?"

"The private eye she had spying on you and Castille never collected on the last payment Katarina promised him. He sold the photos to media outlets after she went missing and he realized he wouldn't get paid by her."

"It makes sense," Flannery said. "Everybody wants their money at the end of the day."

"Indeed. He needed to finish paying off his yacht Katarina helped him out with," Conrad said, with a grin. "I paid him another visit after we were done that night. They'll never find his yacht *or* him."

"Is that supposed to impress me? The damage was done. What difference did it make by then?" she asked him. "You even said he wouldn't have remembered later."

"I needed to be sure," he replied. Conrad's eyes did a dance, and he gave her another grin she didn't understand. "I'm still not completely confident Katarina can stay trapped in a concrete vault forever. Who knows when or *how* she could escape. I do try to look out for you, Flannery."

"You have a heart?" she said, finally looking over to him with a smile.

"Well, speaking of New Orleans, I think it's time we discussed your future either here or there," Conrad said. "Are you planning to stay here, or go back there?"

"I don't know," she said. "I've already told you I'm not leaving this house without any answers about what you and Geoff and Ruffin have been doing."

"And you think you'll get them out of me?" he asked.

"Maybe she thinks she can get them out of me," Geoffrey said, appearing in the room.

He had grown much paler but a bit more serene since the last time anyone had seen him.

"I see you've cleaned up," Conrad said. "Nobody will ever suspect a thing."

"Until he and Tilda are never seen during the daytime hours anymore," Flannery replied, refusing to look at either of them.

"You were right, Conrad," Geoffrey said. "It hurt for a little while, but it was over, and now I have eternal life," he smiled, and moved as if he might start dancing around the room. "Never ending life, untold wealth, and Ruffin is out of the picture."

"And there's still our deal to discuss," Conrad said. "I have to hold up my end of the bargain, don't I?"

25

U seem moody & different, Regan's text message to Travis read.

I'm ok, he texted back to her, in no mood to further explain himself to anyone.

He was in his bedroom, with his iPod on, earbuds in, and listening to First Wave music. He wanted to be alone and relax after a trying day. Ever since Regan had left an hour earlier, it had been nonstop texts asking him about his behavior toward her that evening. He was seventeen and had an entire future ahead of him that didn't include the Laneharts, Ten Points, or north Louisiana. Maybe it shouldn't include a girlfriend, either.

Then there was Conrad. He had hated the man twelve hours ago, and maybe he still did. But there was also something else about him Travis felt inclined to like—maybe even admire. He wasn't sure how or when it had begun to happen that day. One minute he found himself hating Conrad. The next, he was a cool guy. The mixed feelings were a mystery, and the thin line between like and dislike puzzled him. Maybe Conrad could help him. Conrad could help him escape his hateful stepfather and cold mother, as well as the suffocating atmosphere at Ten Points. He wasn't *that* close to Maxine or Bobby. He would be eighteen in seven months. They wouldn't miss him if he left.

Maybe his Uncle Marcus could even help him find a job in southern California. It was a good place to start. He wanted to end up in Portland or Seattle, so just getting to the West Coast would be ideal and closer to his goal than where he was now. He could worry about the rest later.

Travis shut off the iPod and decided to go downstairs for a snack. He often sneaked into the kitchen after D'Lynn had retired for the evening, and he was craving a piece of cake, or quite frankly, any kind of leftover food from the wake or funeral. It was the Deep South, and wakes and funerals were notorious for well-wishers bringing casseroles and plenty of other delicious items. It was as if mourners were expected to eat their feelings.

He descended the staircase, glancing down at the foyer and noting the empty space where the casket of Maximilian Lanehart had set earlier. The sight of a casket inside Ten Points had freaked out Regan, but Travis thought it was cool. It was the first time he had ever heard of anyone in modern times having a body of a family member on display inside their home. He assumed perhaps Laneharts and Ogdens of generations past had done it, back in the horse and buggy days.

Travis heard voices coming from the living room and quickly crept back to the top of the staircase to listen in on the conversation. He could hear Geoffrey, Flannery, and Conrad discussing something.

"I'm sure you would like to know what we've been talking about, but that's up to Geoffrey here whether to tell you," Travis heard Conrad say.

"Well, Flannery, we may be the same now, but I don't think you can expect it to bring us any closer together," Geoffrey said.

The same? Travis thought to himself. *What does that mean?*

"Then I suppose you'll be in need soon," Flannery said. "Let's hope you make out better than Rochelle did last night."

"No, I need a real live human," Geoffrey said. "Who all is here? Did Aunt Hattie leave?"

What the hell is he talking about? Travis wondered.

"You wouldn't!" Flannery said.

"Don't forget how you've felt at times, my dear," Conrad said.

"Yes, but never—" she began.

"Can we leave and go somewhere?" Geoffrey asked someone. His voice sounded anxious. "After seeing what Flannery and Tilda both did in the space of one night, I don't think I want to stay here."

"Your bitch of a wife set me off," Flannery said.

"I'm flattered you were jealous," Conrad said, causing Travis to shrug and shake his head at the top of the stairs. *Was there something between Flannery and Conrad he didn't know about?*

"Get over yourself. You can screw whoever you want. It was just a surprise to see you pounding that holier-than-thou, Frigidaire sister-in-law of mine," Flannery told him.

Travis held his stomach and felt disgusted. *Conrad and his mom?* He wasn't sure if he wanted to eavesdrop any longer, but something made him stay and listen.

"And Geoff you allowed it to go on," Flannery continued. "I won't even bring up the part about you watching. There has to be a major reason behind all of this."

Travis felt as if he might be ill, but he couldn't force himself away from where he stood.

"Okay, okay," Geoffrey said. "Several of our businesses are in the red. The economy has been fucked the last few years, thanks to who we have in the White House!"

"He inherited that problem from a previous administration, and it's rebounding under his watch," Flannery said. "But we're not having a political debate tonight. Geoff, tell me more about the financial problems the family holdings are having ..."

"Conrad has promised to bail me out, and then some. Unlimited, untapped resources and money," Geoffrey said.

"In exchange for ...?" Flannery replied.

"I—I can't tell you that," Geoffrey said to her.

"Why not? How bad could it be?"

Conrad laughed. "I'll make sure Ruffin's share is deposited into your bank accounts soon, Geoff."

"Did they take care of him?" Geoffrey asked.

"Let's not talk about that right now," Flannery said. Travis wasn't close with his step-aunt but was impressed with her persistence. Her smoky voice was also intimidating from where he stood. "I want to know, Geoff, *what* are you giving Conrad in return? I know there's more to it than Tilda's ass and your soul."

Travis continued to shake his head. *Take care of Ruffin? Geoff's soul? What the living fuck was going on?*

Geoffrey laughed. "My soul? I'm already dead. How can that be?" he said, eliciting a loud gasp from Travis at the top of the stairs.

Travis quickly covered his mouth and prayed no one had heard him. The conversation continued, so it was evident they had not.

"Being one of the living dead is a cruel, solitary existence," Flannery told him. "The thought of eternal life is quite romantic now, but you will soon miss the things you enjoyed and took for granted in life. I know I do. The sunlight. The wonderful food. A glass of wine—or, in your case, Scotch or bourbon. The ability to love people the same way. The connection to your children..."

Travis was trembling, his eyes wide, and he realized he was starting to hyperventilate. *Is this really happening?* he thought to himself. *I can't be hearing this correctly. Living dead? Geoff is dead? Aunt Flannery, too? Geoff mentioned 'what Tilda did in the space of one night...' My mom, too? Is this a dream? It has to be a dream. None of this can be real.*

"I already need blood," Geoffrey said quietly, in a sudden shift of mood. His temperament still changed just as it did in life. His voice was low but still audible enough for Travis to hear. "I need somebody to help me find it. Flannery, I need—I *need*..."

"Were you about to say you needed my help?" Flannery asked. "Well, I'll be damned. I think I'll stand back and let you finish getting the sentence out. Continue on, Geoff."

"Damn it, Flannery!" Geoffrey shouted. *"Please!"*

"If only Daddy could see you now," she said, with a chuckle. "Coming to his whore of a daughter for help. He just now made it into that grave, and I bet he's already rolled over in it."

"Your father knew more than you give him credit for," Conrad said.

"What does *that* mean?" Flannery said. "Oh my God, Conrad, I should have known—"

"Yes, your father probably would have had another good twenty years if it weren't for me," he replied.

Travis was frozen to the wall upstairs, afraid to move. He knew there were plenty of goings-on inside Ten Points he knew nothing about, but what he had overheard was on another level. Where was his mother? Did he overhear everything correctly? Was she one of *them* as well? It made sense. She apparently had some kind of thing with Conrad, which grossed Travis out to even think about, but how could she not know her own husband and sister-in-law were no longer alive and among the living dead? *How could she not?*

Travis heard the front door open downstairs and quickly peeked around the corner to see Marcus enter the house. Did his Uncle Marcus know about any of this? What if his Dad tried to obtain the blood he needed from his Uncle Marcus? Or, what if Marcus was one of them as

THE INCUBUS AND THE OTHERS

well? What would Travis be able to do to protect himself against all of them? Pretend he didn't know? He had questions—many, many questions—and at the moment he knew no one he could trust for answers.

The conversation in the living room quickly shifted upon Marcus' arrival, which led Travis to believe his uncle knew nothing of what was going on.

"Well, where have you been?" he heard Conrad ask Marcus.

"I was out," Marcus said, somewhat coldly. He sounded in no mood to explain himself or his whereabouts. Travis knew his Uncle Marcus wasn't a big fan of Conrad's.

"Zeke Colson, huh?" Flannery asked. "I always wondered but wasn't absolutely sure."

"He dropped me off," Marcus replied. "It's getting late, and he wanted to go home."

"Let's discuss other things," Geoffrey said, apparently still homophobic in death. "Marcus, I meant what I said this morning. I do hope you consider staying longer."

"I'm willing to stay at least a few more days, like we agreed on," Marcus said. "It's been an interesting two days."

If he only knew, Travis thought. His hyperventilation was under control, and now he was almost afraid to breathe. He felt one little move or the slightest sound would alert everyone to his presence upstairs.

"Would you like a drink, Marcus?" Conrad asked. "I was about to pour myself a Scotch, and well, Geoff and Flannery here don't appear to have any desire for spirits tonight. I hate to drink alone."

"It's been a very long day, so no thanks," Marcus said. "I think I'll go upstairs and turn in. But before I do ... Flannery, may I have a word with you? In private?"

"Sure, let's go down the hallway," Travis heard her tell him. *Oh God! What if she attacks him and takes his blood when they go in the other room? Holy shit, what am I going to do about this? What can I do?*

Travis heard the clicks and taps of their shoes on the hard marble floor below as they left the living room, walked across the foyer, and went down the adjacent hallway. They were apparently heading to the study, or one of the other rooms down the corridor. After a few seconds he could no longer hear them.

206

But he could still hear the conversation in the living room.

"Marcus is *mine*," he heard Conrad tell Geoffrey. "I'm adding that condition to our agreement. I want him to marry me."

Geoffrey scoffed. "First, I had no idea you were *that way*. Second, you can't legally marry another man in this state. Don't you keep up with the news? Third, you're not even human anyway. God, one day you're fucking my wife, then announcing you're married to my sister, and the next you're trying to have at my brother. Who's *next* for you in this family?"

Conrad's voice turned stern and icy. "Listen, you son of a bitch, just because I've killed you once tonight doesn't mean I still can't destroy you and fuck your shell of a body after I'm done," he said, low but authoritatively. "So maybe *you're* next."

Travis was afraid he was going to piss his pants. It was all getting to be too much for him to take in.

"Okay, okay," Geoff said, backing down. "You know I don't approve of Marcus and his lifestyle. Never have. That's just the way I am."

"Oh? Afraid *he* won't get into heaven?" Conrad said sarcastically. "You've forfeited all your claims on family values. Shall I remind you how badly you betrayed one member of your family before all the events of the last two days?"

What is Conrad talking about? Who did Geoff betray? Travis thought, as he stayed against the wall at the top of the stairs.

Geoffrey was in full backstroke mode. "Please, just accept my apology. I can try to be more supportive of you and Marcus. It will just take a little time for me to get used to it is all."

"Why did Marcus want to speak with Flannery in private?" Conrad demanded. "If you know, you better tell me. Look into my eyes. You better not lie to me. If I find out you knew and held back I promise I'll drive a stake through your heart while you sleep tomorrow."

"I don't know anything, I swear," he said. "I have no idea why he called her in there. And what is so special about my brother? You barely know him. Why are you so obsessed with having him?"

"Don't worry about it," Conrad said. "He was out with Zeke Colson just now?"

"Yes, apparently they took off on some kind of weird date after Reverend Washer got on their case," Geoffrey said.

"I want Ezekiel Colson eliminated from the equation," Conrad said. "And you'll help me do it."

Travis felt chills. Were they going to kill Doctor Colson?

"I think I already know what you need me to do," Geoffrey said. "I am getting hungry."

"Then go to the good animal doctor's house, and do what must be done," Conrad ordered him. "And don't you dare feed him from yourself afterward. I want him dead as a fucking doornail. Don't stop until you've fed on every last drop of him, and I repeat, do *not* reanimate him in any way, shape, or form. I want him gone from this Earth."

"Oh holy shit, I have to stop them from hurting Doctor Colson. Oh fuck, I have to figure out a way to warn him," Travis said to himself at the top of the stairs.

"Ooooh! You said a bad word! I'm going to go tell on you."

Travis nearly jumped at the unexpected sound of Maxine's voice. He turned to find the chubby little girl standing there, holding a doll. Her brown hair was down, and she was dressed in pink pajamas, but she still had pulled on the familiar thick, red-framed eyeglasses before she climbed out of bed and sneaked up on him.

"Shhh!" he said, trying to shush her once his senses returned. "Go to bed," he whispered. "You shouldn't be here."

"I'm going downstairs, and I'm telling Mama and Daddy on you," she said, walking to the foot of the stairs.

"No, please, Maxine, come back," Travis said. "What if I let you ... What if I take you to my room and let you play with Harry?"

"Yuck, he's a big, giant spider. Why would I want to hold him? Gross. No way," she said, wrinkling up her nose.

He remembered the crickets he had caught from the yard earlier and put into a glass jar. "Okay, you don't have to hold him," he said. "but what if I let you feed him?"

"I never saw a tarantula eat a cricket before," she said, suddenly fascinated.

Travis had never seen it either. He just dropped the crickets into the aquarium and always noticed they were gone later. She didn't have to know that though. "Well, wouldn't it be cool to see it happen?" he asked, trying to calm himself and coax her out of the hallway.

"Why are you shaking?" Maxine asked, staring at him strangely. "You look like you're scared."

He realized he was still trembling from the conversation on which he had been eavesdropping and quickly tried to control himself for his little sister's benefit. "I was afraid you were going to tell on me," he lied.

"Well, don't worry. If you let me feed Harry the crickets, I guess I won't say nothin'."

"Okay, they're in a jar in my room, on my desk. Drop them one at a time into the aquarium. Don't let any hop away. And go back to bed after you're finished," he told her quietly.

"Aren't you comin' with me?" she asked.

"I can't," Travis said. "I have something to do first."

He was trying to come up with a way to sneak out of the house without anyone downstairs seeing or hearing him leave. He watched as Maxine walked down the hallway to his room and disappeared from view. He peeked around the corner down the winding stairway again.

He could still hear Conrad's and Geoffrey's voices in the living room.

"Aren't you coming with me?" he heard Geoffrey ask Conrad.

"I don't know. I feel like I should stay here and keep an eye on things," Conrad said. "Tilda can always provide you with an alibi if the police get involved. You know what you must do."

"And I *will*," Geoffrey assured him.

There was no possible way to get down the stairs and out the front door without being detected by Conrad. Travis thought about the wooden trellis that reached the second floor of the house. It was right outside the window of one of the spare bedrooms on the east end.

It would have to do.

THE INCUBUS AND THE OTHERS

26

Flannery did a quick visual survey of the study to make sure there was no evidence of the two murders that had taken place there in the past two nights before she led Marcus inside and closed the door behind them. The room was neat and orderly, and everything was arranged back in its place on the desk—the same desk where she had attacked and killed Tilda. The same desk where Conrad had strangled the life out of Geoffrey not even two hours earlier.

There was still a spot on the wall from the Tilda attack the night before, but unless someone knew what to look for they would likely never see it. The dark splash of blood almost seemed to blend in with the rich mahogany hue.

Marcus wasn't inspecting the walls anyway. As Flannery closed the door and turned to him, his eyes were pointed directly at her.

"What did you want to talk about?" she asked him, trying to manage a smile, though she felt uncertain. She assumed it wouldn't be a pleasant conversation if he had called her away from the others.

"I want to talk about you," he said, his hazel eyes locked on her.

"What about me?" she asked. "I know we've barely had a chance to catch up since we've both been back."

"Yeah, you're never around during the daytime," Marcus said. "Why is that?"

"Well, you know how it is here," she said, turning and starting to pace around the room. "Too many bad memories. I mean, don't you remember what happened the last time we were both in *here?*"

"How can I forget," he said, glancing over at the desk where Maximilian had sat and announced to them they were both pariahs, before removing them from the family. "But it's what I remember afterward that came back to me just a little while ago."

She finally managed a shaky smile. "What would that be?"

"After you left out of the room that day five years ago. I was upset. Dad actually made me cry. I came out the front door of the house just a little while after you. I was so upset and out of it I must have blocked it out, or never fully comprehended what I saw. And then, I went back. I went all over that evening in my head again ..."

"Why?" she asked, stopping the pacing and standing before him. "It was a terrible time. It's best to forget it ever happened. He's dead now. He can't hurt us anymore."

"That's not what I'm talking about. I'm not talking about Dad. I'm talking about you. When I went out to the front porch ... I saw you off in the distance, across the yard. You transformed into this big black cape-looking thing and flew away."

Flannery shook her head. "You can't be serious. You were upset and must have seen things. I was in a rental car that night. I flew in and out on an express flight. The only flying I did was by plane."

"No, Flannery," Marcus said. "It was dark outside, but there was enough moonlight that I know what I saw. You turned into something else and flew off into the night."

"Well, I guess I've figured out a magical way to save on airfare," she said, with a more confident smile. A smile that was superficial. In her mind she was hitting the panic button and trying to figure out how to guide him elsewhere and better convince him that he had imagined all of it.

"I know what you're doing, and it won't work," he said, seeming to read her mind. "The more I've gone back over it, I know what I saw, and you can't tell me anything differently."

"Marcus, what you say is incredible and impossible," she replied. "How on earth would I be able to fly? What you're talking about sounds like the ramblings of a crazy person. I think you've been watching too much of the SyFy Channel."

"Izzy," Marcus said. "She came to the house tonight. She told me something was going on here. She even alluded to the fact you and Geoff are in some kind of trouble."

Oh my God, stop Marcus. Stop! she thought to herself. She gave him another smile instead. "Izzy?" she asked. "I'm afraid I don't follow you. Who the hell is Izzy?"

"This woman who used to work here. At least that's how she made it sound. She tried to sneak into the house after the funeral. She was here last night, too, but left before I could speak with her. She was back tonight, and she tried to warn me about evil inside the house."

"Okay, I'm really starting to worry about you, Marcus—"

"It all makes sense. What's up with dead animals popping up the last two days? And this strange influence Conrad seems to have over everybody?"

"Let's see. There's evil in the house. And I can fly. And somehow it's causing animals to die. What else? Oh, I know. Maybe there will be crop circles out in the yard tomorrow?" He's getting warm. *Too warm*, she thought. He had always been the perceptive one.

"You look so pale. Those circles under your eyes. I was worried you were on drugs, or in some kind of trouble. But now I think you really *are* in trouble, but not the kind of trouble I suspected. Not the kind most people get into."

"Oh? That's what your little imaginary friend Izzy told you?"

"Was it something related to Senator Castille? Did he do something to you to cause all of this? Is it all related to his disappearance somehow?"

"We are *not* going to talk about Frank," she replied brusquely. He was moving from warm to hot, and she was wondering who this Izzy person was—and how she seemed to know so much. Now she was becoming irritated. "I am *done* with that topic. It's followed me around way too long."

"Then let's go back to Conrad and this odd power he seems to weild," Marcus said. "You said you didn't know who he was when I asked you last night, yet you couldn't stop staring at him."

"Why are we talking about him? He stays really tight with Geoff and Ruffin, and I'm curious what is going on between the three of them. Aren't you?"

"Yes, but my question isn't about that. It's about how well you really know him," Marcus continued. "Izzy acted like her heart almost stopped when I mentioned his name. I think his presence in this house has a lot more behind it than just a grievance call to a friend. He's practically moved in."

"So I've noticed," Flannery said, keeping coy. "What do you think that's all about?"

"I'm wondering if you have better knowledge about that situation than I do," he said. "Why are you and Geoff in danger? Izzy even said it was too late—"

"Who the *fuck* is this crazy woman you keep talking about?" Flannery shouted, now angry. Damn it, why couldn't he leave all of this alone? His reporter's nose was about to put him in the middle of something he might not be able to get away from—or survive—if he didn't stop digging.

"I've already told you all I know about her. She gave me her phone number and address before she left."

"Oh really?" Flannery asked. "Are you planning to go visit her anytime soon?" She realized she would have to try to get into his phone later and look at his contacts.

"I don't know," Marcus said. "Maybe she can give me more answers than you seem to be."

"What do you want me to tell you, Marcus? You come in here and start babbling about how you saw me fly, and then go on about some strange woman, and evil supposedly being in this house. How am I supposed to respond to all of that?"

"The truth would be a good start," he said. "Why are you so pale? You don't look well. Has somebody done something to you? Why can't you trust me? There was a time in our lives when we were close."

"Maybe I'm just tired," she said. "Just like I'm tired of this interrogation. Can we go back to the others now? I really don't feel like anymore of this."

"You're hiding something," he said.

"Marcus, *please...*"

"Okay, so you won't tell me," he said. "I'll have to find out on my own." He turned to leave.

"Marcus," Flannery grabbed his arm. Her touch was ice cold. "Don't rile Conrad. He's dangerous. Don't mess with him."

"Flannery, oh my God, *your hand*. It's freezing. *Why?*"

"Like I told you yesterday. I don't feel well. I'm coming down with something, I think."

"Bullshit!" Marcus exclaimed. "I want the truth. *Now!*"

Flannery backed away with a frightened and vulnerable look he hadn't seen from her since they had returned to Ten Points. She buried her face in her hands and quickly turned away. "You're right. There is something. Marcus, you have to stay away from him. He's—He's ..."

Marcus walked over to her and pulled her around to face him. "He's *what?* Tell me, goddamn it!"

A text message alert interrupted him. He unlocked his phone. *Uncle Marcus it's me Travis! Dr. Colson is going to be hurt. I'm going over there. Don't think I can stop it. Hurry come fast!!!*

"What the hell is this?" he asked, reading the text again in confusion.

"What is it?" Flannery asked.

"I have to go," Marcus said, going for the door. "We'll talk later."

"No, you can't go!" she said, following him out of the study and down the hallway. "You have to stay here. You have to let me explain ..."

"I just got a strange text from Travis. I have to go check something out. Will you still be awake when I get back? Can we talk then?"

"Travis? Isn't he upstairs?" she asked, as they arrived in the foyer.

"No, I don't think he is," Marcus said, turning toward the front door. "I think he went somewhere else."

"Where did he go?" Flannery asked.

"What's going on in here?" Conrad asked, walking into the foyer from the living room. Geoffrey appeared to be nowhere around.

Flannery looked over to Conrad and then turned her eyes away.

Conrad grew suspicious. "What are you two discussing? Going somewhere, Marcus?"

"Mind your own goddamn business for once," Marcus said, turning to him. "I don't know who you are, or even *what* you are, but I've had about all I can fucking take of watching you weasel your way into this house and this family."

"He *knows*," Flannery said, refusing to look in Conrad's direction.

"You told him?" Conrad asked angrily, grabbing Flannery by the arm. *"Everything?"*

"Let go of my sister, you son of a bitch!" Marcus ordered, shoving Conrad off of her. "Don't you put your hands on anybody in my family ever again, or I swear to God I'll kill you."

Conrad backhanded Marcus across the face so hard he flew over into one of the walls, hitting the back of his head with a thud, and then falling over on to the floor, half-conscious as he landed. Blood began trickling from his nose as his eyes slightly opened and fluttered. A large bruise was forming across his cheek, which looked as if it were already starting to swell.

Conrad and Flannery looked blurry over in the middle of the room, as Marcus struggled to focus his eyes. His head felt heavy, as he tried to process what had just happened. His other senses were dulled, and he suddenly felt tired and as if he might go to sleep.

"Oh no no no!" Conrad cried, looking at his offending hand as if it were detached from him. "I didn't mean to do it! Oh Marcus," he rushed over and cradled Marcus in his arms and gave him kisses on top of his head and forehead. "You're *mine*. I didn't mean it. I would never hurt you on purpose, I promise."

You belong to me.

Conrad's voice was a foggy echo.

"Conrad, what the hell! You could have killed him!" Flannery stood stunned, looking at him with wide eyes. "Is he okay? Why did you do that?"

"You made me do it," Conrad growled, looking up at her as he held Marcus close to him. "I'll deal with you in just a moment."

"What? What's going on?" Marcus felt Conrad's arms around him. One minute the other man had struck him down, and the next he was treating him with affection. It was too overwhelming.

"I didn't make you do anything, you bastard. You brought all of this on yourself. On all of us," she said, staring down at him despicably. "I swear to God, if there is a way to send you back to Hell and have you out of all our lives, then I will find it. That is a promise!"

"Need I remind you if it weren't for me, you would still be trying to claw your way out of a grave right now," he said, his eyes on her venomously as he stroked Marcus' hair and held the other man's head to his chest. "You should have spent every day of the last five years on your knees thanking me for all I did to rescue you."

"I paid my debt to you a long time ago, and if he dies, then it's your fault," she said. "If you hadn't been manhandling me like you enjoy doing so much, he wouldn't have interfered and gotten hit by you."

"Just wait until my hands are free. I'll show you the true definition of manhandling."

"Conrad, please," Marcus whispered. His head throbbed, and he found a strange comfort in the way Conrad held him. It felt almost peaceful. *You belong to me.* It reverberated through him again. "Please don't hurt anybody else. I'll do whatever you want."

Conrad pulled him closer and used a tissue to dab the blood from his nose. "Let me walk you upstairs so you can lie down."

"He probably needs a doctor," Flannery said. "He may have a concussion, thanks to you."

"He only needs rest," Conrad insisted, standing and helping Marcus to his feet. Marcus' iPhone fell out on to the floor. Conrad reached down and picked it up, staring at the open screen. "You stay here," he said to Flannery. "After I take him upstairs I'll come back and deal with you."

He set the phone down on the side table beside a lamp and started to help a disoriented Marcus up the staircase. After they were out of sight, Flannery went over and picked up the phone, which was still unlocked. She scrolled through the contacts, found what she needed, and then set the phone back down before she quietly slipped out of the front door.

27

Travis ran through the woods, dodging limbs and nearly falling several times as he had little but the moonlight to guide him. He didn't take his car to Zeke Colson's house out of fear of being heard pulling away from Ten Points, so he decided to take the two miles by foot and avoid the driveway and nearby roads. He navigated the way as best he could, and nearly took a tumble when he came quickly down a hill and realized at the last moment he was in a creek bed. Luckily, the ground was mostly dry, and he was able to hurdle over the small waterway and keep going.

He was in a pair of tight black jeans, a black T-shirt, and sneakers he had changed into after the funeral. Thankfully, his color of choice obscured him in the dark woods. The jeans, however, made running more difficult.

As he picked up speed, a tree branch came out of nowhere, struck him across the face, and knocked him to the ground. It hurt like hell, but he quickly regained his senses, pulled himself off the forest floor, and took off again. He was determined to get to Zeke's house before Geoffrey, and time was not on his side. His stepfather had several cars at his disposal, and all Travis had were his feet, a fair sense of direction, and an uncharted path ahead of him. He ran on faith, not knowing for sure what was even twenty feet ahead of him.

After a few minutes, he reached a clearing and could see Zeke's house off in the distance. The brick house was dotted with lights, which meant Doctor Colson was there. Travis prayed he was still there alone. He was tired, his lungs burning as he gasped for air. He hadn't run this far since his year on the cross country team in ninth grade. That was back before he decided changing his style and being a nonconformist was much more cool than trying to be any kind of jock.

Travis took off across the field, determined to reach the one-story house. It appeared so much more comfortable and homey to him than the icy exterior of Ten Points. The mansion's castle-like architecture and grand columns weren't as inviting as the simple brick dwelling of Zeke's. He only wished he could get closer because it still looked so small from where he was as he charged across the empty clearing as fast as he could. What would he do if Geoffrey was already there? He couldn't think about that now. He just had to get there. He had texted his Uncle Marcus. Maybe *he* was there. Maybe he had already warned Zeke.

As he came closer to the brick house, he heard a vehicle coming up the driveway. Travis hid behind a large pecan tree over at the corner of Zeke's front yard and kept watch.

"Oh no," Travis said to himself, as he saw Tilda's white Range Rover pull up near the house. Geoffrey got out and looked around, as he stealthily made his way to the front door and knocked.

Travis' mind was all over the place, and he didn't know what to do. He watched from behind the tree as Zeke answered the door. "Geoff, what brings you here at this hour?" Travis heard him ask Geoffrey.

"I needed to have a talk with you. It's about Marcus," Travis heard Geoffrey reply.

"I don't feel like any kind of argument or debate tonight, Geoff," Zeke said. "I was actually just about to turn in."

"It's nothing like that. This won't take long," Geoffrey said. Travis could see the salesman grin from over where he was hidden in the shadows of the tree.

"Okay, come on in," Zeke said, stepping aside and letting Geoff enter.

Once the door was shut, Travis darted as fast as he could from the tree to one of the front windows. One of the living room curtains was parted and the blinds were up, so he was able to see inside.

"Would you like a beer or a drink?" Zeke offered.

"No thanks," Geoffrey said, walking over closer to him. "So since we've mentioned my brother, it appears to me that you two have gotten very close in a very short amount of time. Or *reunited*, I guess is a better word."

"Yes, it's true," Zeke said. "I told him some things I should have said a long time ago. And you may not agree with me on this, but I also tried to get him to stay permanently instead of going back to California."

"Well, Marcus is a grown man. I'll support whatever decision he makes," Geoffrey said.

"That's good to know. I'm glad you're supporting him. I know things haven't been easy for you two in the last few years, given all that's happened."

"There's no reason to go into all of that. And, despite what I said, Marcus isn't the real reason I came here to see you," Geoffrey said.

He used the mention of Uncle Marcus to get himself into the house, Travis thought, as he gripped the window ledge tightly. He was unsure of what to do. Should he go in? He pulled his iPhone out of his pocket. Marcus hadn't responded to his text. Why hadn't he answered back? He sent another:

Uncle Marcus please! I'm at Zeke's house & don't know what to do!

He made sure the phone was on vibrate and held it in his hand.

"Oh, then what brings you by?" Zeke asked.

"Angel's Glory," Geoffrey said. "I hope you won't report the horse to the authorities the way you did the ducks and the raccoon."

"I thought about it, but Wes Washer told me at the funeral that the matter with the ducks and the raccoon had been handled. He didn't go into any details. I didn't mention the horse, but I must say the whole thing is very suspicious. What's going on, Geoff? *How* was it handled?"

"The official story we are going with is that Travis did it," Geoffrey smiled at him. "The boy dresses and acts like a Satan worshipper. It's believable."

What the fuck?! Travis thought. *Geoffrey, you son of a bitch.*

Zeke wasn't amused either. "If you know it isn't true, then why are you letting the blame fall on your son that way? It almost sounds like you're blaming Travis to protect the person who really did it."

"He's *not* my son by blood. And what if I am protecting somebody else?" Geoffrey said, stepping closer. "Would you like to know who really did it?" he asked, feeling his cuspids start to sprout.

"I think I would," Zeke said, looking at him strangely. "You look a little pale, Geoff. Are you feeling okay?"

Geoffrey could no longer open his mouth without revealing why he was really there. He felt his canine teeth along the edge of his tongue and realized they were longer and sharper. He was about to move in for

Zeke's throat when there was a loud banging sound near one of the windows.

"What the hell is that?" Zeke said, walking away from Geoffrey and over to the door. "It sounds like somebody's out there."

Geoffrey's eyes widened and he grew fearful someone could be outside watching. This had to be quick and clean. Conrad had assured him that he was now unable to leave DNA evidence at the scene of a crime. But Geoffrey planned to fix it so the living room wasn't the scene of any so-called crime. He had other plans of how to dispose of the veterinarian's body.

Zeke came back into the house from outside. "I didn't see anybody out there," he said. "I don't have a clue what that could have been."

"How odd," Geoffrey said, his head turned away from Zeke so his teeth couldn't be seen. "Maybe it was the wind or something."

"It's not even breezy out there," Zeke said, walking back over to him.

Outside, Travis was back at the window. He had run back behind the tree before Zeke came outside. He knew if Zeke saw him he would say something, then they would both be vulnerable to Geoffrey. His only hope was to cause distractions until Marcus could get there. If only his uncle would text him back or give him some kind of indication he had gotten his message.

Travis watched Geoffrey walk closer to Zeke again. *What can I do to cause another interruption?* he thought to himself, looking around as best he could in the darkness. His only idea was to find a rock to throw through the window. He knelt down below the window frame and began running his hands along the ground to see if he could find anything larger than a pebble that could break the glass. As his hand felt around behind him he gasped aloud as it landed on another person's foot.

Someone's hand went over his mouth and dragged him away before he could make another sound to disturb Geoffrey's and Zeke's conversation.

"Now, back to what we were talking about. *Who* is responsible for the attacks on the animals?" Zeke asked Geoffrey inside the house. "You sounded as though you were about to tell me who it was."

"Yes," Geoffrey said, and suddenly lit into Zeke's neck, catching the other man off guard. Blood began gushing out, running down Geoff's mouth and chin and spilling on to Zeke's shoulder and soaking into his white T-shirt.

"Oh God, *wh—what?*" Zeke struggled and tried to fight him off, but even Geoff was amazed at his newfound strength. He pinned Zeke's strong arms down and continued sucking, deciding he would lick up the rest of what dripped away from him later. He went at the puncture wounds in Zeke's throat like a savage, starving beast, not letting up, even as the other man lost his power to stand and collapsed to the floor.

Geoffrey felt the life drain from Zeke's body and ecstatically continued feeding, climbing on top of him on the floor and ravaging him. The gratification of his blood lust was more intense than any sexual stimulation, orgasm, or line of cocaine had ever been. As he felt the warm blood go in him and down his throat, he came to the realization he loved and could easily embrace what he had become. He was no longer fearful about anyone being outside. From now on at Ten Points, he would allow Conrad to do whatever he wanted, control whatever he wanted, as long as he could enjoy this feeling again and again, night after night.

Geoffrey's loud slurps and moans went unheard, as unbeknownst to him, Travis Lanehart had been captured outside and dragged away into the night—a night of terror that was only just beginning for the teenager. It would be during this night the boy would learn that the dark existence he had invented for himself was only a fallacy, for there were the true forces of darkness about to prey upon and reveal themselves to him.

28

The old wooden house where Izzy lived was in ramshackle condition. The white paint had faded, and Flannery's eyesight was better than that of humans. But even a mortal would have been able to see under the moonlight that the house was in need of work and restoration. It was obvious Izzy likely didn't have the means to keep up her home.

Flannery parked the silver Bentley she had taken from Ten Points outside the house, behind an older model Oldsmobile Cutlass she assumed belonged to this woman, Izzy, who Marcus spoke so much about earlier. No other cars were parked anywhere around, and a bit of dim light shined through one of the windows in the front of the small house.

Flannery walked up to the front porch and searched for a doorbell but saw none. She reached up to knock, when the door opened without warning and a fiftysomething black woman with black-and-gray mixed hair and wearing a blue nightgown and robe appeared before her.

"Oh my God," she gasped, then looked away sadly and walked back into the house. "You've come to kill me."

"Kill you?" Flannery said, following her into the house. "I've come here to get answers. You said all those strange things to my brother. Now he's asking questions."

Izzy kept her back to her and refused to look at her. "Oh my Holy Father in Heaven, if only he could save you from this. If only *I* could have done somethin' to stop it." She shook her head. "Oh, why why why." She began to sob and continued shaking her head back and forth, refusing to face Flannery.

"What do you think you know about me?" Flannery said, walking closer. "And I guess my next question would be *how* do you know?"

"Don't come any closer," she said, sensing Flannery's approach when she heard the creak of the old hardwood floor of her small parlor. Izzy sniffled and wiped away tears. "You are not as you were in life. I can't trust you now that you are what you are."

"*What* am I? Will you please answer my questions?"

Izzy finally turned to face her. "You're one of the livin' dead. The senator's wife, she was one—*she* did this to you. You joined with the demon, and he helped you get rid of the evil woman. Oh, but he had you even before then. The horrible man. Didn't you know what he was?" Izzy shook her head more and paced around the room.

"Were you there? I don't understand—"

"I *just* know!" Izzy exclaimed, walking back over to her. "I know the demon was never out to help the senator. He used to the senator to get to *you.*"

"No, no," Flannery said, looking away. "Frank became acquainted with Conrad. I'm still not sure how they met, but Conrad promised to help Frank with money and his political ambitions, all in exchange for something."

"That was only what he *told* the senator," Izzy insisted. "The senator had already been fooled by that horrible woman, when she promised him great things. He was an easy target because he was greedy. You expect the Devil's disciple to tell the truth?"

"One might argue that I'm the Devil's disciple as well," Flannery said, turning her eyes back to her.

"Yes, one might," Izzy said, wiping away the last tear and giving her a strong stare. "So if you've come to kill me then you best get it over with."

"I wasn't lying about that," Flannery said. "I'm not going to harm you. Conrad might. You should be careful of him."

"If you didn't come here to kill me, then why are you so interested in some poor, vulnerable old woman like me?" Izzy asked.

"You don't appear to be *that* old," Flannery said. "Marcus told me you used to work at Ten Points?"

She nodded and looked away. "Long ago."

"How long ago?" Flannery asked her. "When did you work there?"

"Before you were born," Izzy said. "Didn't your brother tell you these things?"

"He tried to tell me some of what you told him, but he didn't get a chance to finish," Flannery said, thinking about Conrad striking her brother.

"The demon has already put a spell on him. He's asleep right now. That's when the demon can control him best."

"I still think I should call a doctor or take him to the hospital," Flannery said.

"A mild concussion," Izzy said. "He will be physically okay. His injury ain't what's causin' him to sleep. It's the demon. He's under the spell. I tried to warn him. Oh ..." She shook her head yet again, and her chin trembled.

"Yes, Conrad told us earlier he couldn't get into Marcus' head unless he's asleep. But enough about that. How do you know these things?" Flannery asked. "Are you some kind of psychic? I don't understand how you know what's going on."

"I've always been like this," she said. "I don't have a word for it. It's what got me into trouble with—" She cut herself off and turned away from Flannery.

"Got you into trouble with *whom?*" Flannery questioned. "Does it have something to do with why you weren't working at Ten Points anymore later on? I don't remember you at all."

"I used to see things in the house. Mr. Ogden Senior still lives in one of the upstairs bedrooms. Sometimes he's downstairs. The three children. The ones who died in the 1870's. They still play in the basement."

"That is just foolish," Flannery said. "I lived in that house my whole life growing up, and I never saw any of those things."

"You kept your mind closed. You weren't treated as your brothers were as a child. You dreamed of a happier day and better things," Izzy began to cry again and went over to grab a tissue from a box.

"You don't even know me," Flannery told her. "Why is all this making you so upset?"

"That terrible woman and her men. What they did to you. Oh, if only you could have been saved. Now you're ... you're ... *dead.*"

Flannery glanced around the room. Old, worn-out furniture and other meager belongings decorated the parlor. Over on a shelf there were several framed photos. A slightly faded one was obviously Izzy when she was younger, with another black man, and holding a small boy that appeared to be their son. There was another framed photo of a young black man that looked more modern and no more than fifteen to twenty years old.

"My son, Roy," Izzy said, looking up and seeing where Flannery's eyes had gone. "My husband Tom was killed in a trucking accident about seventeen years ago and never came home. They said he fell asleep at the wheel. I don't know for sure."

"Not even with your gift?" Flannery asked.

Izzy shook her head. "Sometimes it's sharply tuned in. Other times it's just static," she said. "With Tom it's just static."

"Well, I guess it's good you have your son," Flannery said.

Izzy shook her head again. "No. Roy died of leukemia about ten years ago. He was only twenty. It's just me now."

"He was your only child?"

Izzy started to sob. "Oh, I can't do this. I've spent so many years puttin' it out of my mind, and tryin' to forget. I can't do this again."

"You can't do *what* again?" Flannery asked, walking over to her. "What is so difficult?"

"I thought when he was dead it would be easy to go back to that house. I sensed I had to. Your brother. He would listen to me, I thought. I went to the wake, but I had to leave because it became too much to be back inside there."

"I'm afraid I don't know where you're going with this."

"That house," Izzy continued. "It had been more than thirty years. Almost thirty-five years. I never went back after they made me leave."

"After *who* made you leave?"

"Your father and his men."

"His *men?* Why did they make you leave?"

"Yes, his men. Business associates, I reckon."

"They forced you to leave Ten Points? I mean, usually if Dad let anybody go, he just gave them a final paycheck and sent them on their way."

"My case was a little bit different than most others," Izzy said, growing uncomfortable. She stepped to the other side of the room and turned away from Flannery again. "Jessica Lanehart wanted me gone as well."

"My *mother*," Flannery said, holding her hand to her chest. "She died when I was eight. Did you know her? Tell me about her."

"She wasn't anyone I remember with fondness," Izzy said, turning back and facing Flannery. She walked over. "But that's nothin' I should trouble you with."

"Was she unpleasant to work for? Please, you must tell me more about her. I can sense some hostility on your part. Is it true?" Flannery implored.

"The circumstances of her death," Izzy said. "They were always questionable."

"She died in a riding accident," Flannery said. "Her horse got spooked and threw her. Broke her neck. I wasn't there. I just remember when the ambulance came. But they said it was too late by then."

"Yes, yes, that's what they told you," Izzy said.

"Is there something more? Please tell me."

"I wasn't there either. But I know she liked to argue with your father. And they argued that day. They argued very much."

"How do you know that?" Flannery asked.

"How do I know anything?" Izzy said. "I just do."

"Did he cause—well, you know. Was Maximilian...?"

"Yes, he fired off a gun to spook the horse and teach your mother a lesson when she rode away. Only he didn't expect the worst to happen. He only wanted her to have a rough ride and maybe land on her behind if she did fall," Izzy said, not taking her eyes on Flannery.

"Why were they arguing?" Flannery asked, her face falling. She wasn't sure why she was surprised by any of this, but she was.

Izzy looked deeply into Flannery's eyes. "My child, if you only knew."

"Knew *what*? You keep going in circles! Please. Just tell me what happened."

"They argued about you, dear. About how you were different from their other children," Izzy finally said.

"How was I different? Because I was a girl? Trust me, Maximilian spent my entire life reminding me. He acted like he hated me, and I may have given him reason to later, but early on he acted that way. I *tried* to please him the best I could in the beginning. It never worked."

"It was out of your control," Izzy said. "And *if* he bore any hatred for you it wasn't because you were a girl."

226

"Then *why?*" Flannery demanded to know.

Izzy shook her head violently and then spit it out. "Because you weren't the son he lost. *That's* why."

"The son he lost? I really don't understand what you're talking about," Flannery replied, as Izzy began to cry yet again.

"I was young when I came to work at Ten Points. Only eighteen," Izzy began, wiping away tears and pacing around the room. "Maximilian Lanehart was a cruel man. He called me a nigger and said awful things about civil rights and the movement. He treated all of us like we were beneath him and the family. Even D'Lynn was dirt on the bottom of his shoe in those days. But at least she was white. She ended up becomin' like a family member there. That would've never happened for me. And Jessica Lanehart made damned sure I always knew my place. Please forgive my language, but the thought of Maximilian and Jessica Lanehart really gets me riled up."

"I can identify with people getting under your skin," Flannery said, putting a cold hand on Izzy's arm. The older woman bristled at her touch, and Flannery quickly took her hand away.

Izzy took Flannery's hand back and held it in hers. "You're so cold," she said, her chin trembling with emotion. "You're dead, but you're here talkin' to me."

"Please, Izzy," Flannery said. "Please finish your story."

"Your father was a terrible, controllin' man," Izzy said.

"Tell me something I *don't* know," Flannery said.

"I was at Ten Points for nearly four years. After the second year, he started tryin' to get at me," she continued, anguish on her face as she traveled back in time in her mind. "Puttin' his hands on me, tryin' to do things. I would find ways to avoid him, but after a while it'd start up again."

"That sounds about right," Flannery said, looking away.

Izzy tugged at the sleeve of Flannery's black funeral dress to make her look back toward her. "It didn't stop there. One night I was cleanin' up after a party. All the guests had left. He dragged me into the study. He had his way with me."

That damned study, Flannery thought to herself. So many detestable things had happened in that room, including one of her own transgressions. She was her father's daughter in that moment, she

227

thought to herself.

The study should be boarded up and never entered again. Perhaps she could make the suggestion to Conrad later, if he wasn't planning to destroy her when they met again.

"I'm so sorry," Flannery said, uncertain of what else could be said about the horrendous matter.

"I realized after a couple of months I was with child," Izzy said, looking as if the crying was about to start. "Jessica Lanehart was also expecting a baby."

"She was expecting *me?*"

"I hid it as best I could. I had no husband yet, and I had nobody I could turn to. I was so ashamed. Then there was the night of the tornado."

"The tornado?"

"Yes, we were trapped at Ten Points," Izzy said. "Jessica Lanehart went into labor, but the ambulance couldn't come. And nobody could leave. The storm was terrible ... trees were fallin' across roads everywhere and the power was out. She was yellin' and screamin' at all of us. She kicked me and made me fall on the floor when I tried to help her into her bed upstairs. That was when my pains started. I walked down the stairs as best as I could, but my water broke. D'Lynn saw what happened."

"Oh my God," Flannery said. "I'm sorry that happened to you."

"D'Lynn saw how scared I was. She took me down to the basement. The pain was horrible. I started moanin' too much. D'Lynn put me in a storage closet and tried to keep me from bein' heard in there..."

"The same closet—" Flannery began.

"Yeah, the one you been sleepin' in," Izzy finished, and the two women stared deeply into one another's eyes in silence. "You had white skin. The black hair was the only thing that looked like me," Izzy finally said. "When you wouldn't stop cryin', that's when they found us. Jessica Lanehart's baby boy was born dead. Stillborn. She passed out from losin' too much blood. They took the dead baby away and replaced him with you. They took you away no matter how much I cried and begged. The ghosts of the three Ogden children were in the basement that night. They started to cry when they saw the agony I was in.

Jessica Lanehart woke up with you in her arms and never knew the difference at first. Or if she already did, she stayed in denial about it."

"Oh my God, I can't believe this," Flannery felt as if she wanted to cry but wasn't sure she still knew how—or if she could. So many emotions went through her. She felt human again for the first time in five years. *You're* my mother?" she whispered, looking back at Izzy.

"Yeah," Izzy started to cry. "And now both my children are dead."

"But I'm here," Flannery said. "And *you're my mother* ... We can still be a family ..."

Izzy looked at her sadly. "How? You're not even a human anymore."

"So my mom figured this out, and confronted my Dad about it? Is that what happened?"

"Jessica figured it out before then. She spent a while holdin' it over Maximilian's head, threatenin to divorce him and expose the truth if he didn't do his duties as a husband."

"You saw all of this?"

"No, I only *knew.* Your father and his men forced me off the property after you were born and told me to never return. You came out lookin' like your white side. They said nobody would ever believe me and would think I was crazy if I tried to tell the truth. My word versus the Laneharts? Those three little ghosts couldn't talk. So I didn't tell nobody either. Not till now."

"But D'Lynn *knew!* She knew all this time and never told me the truth. *Why* ... Oh, I'll make that old woman pay for this ..."

"Don't harm her," Izzy urged Flannery. "She had no education and no other job skills. She was scared of your father and his influence back in those days. There was nothin' else for her out there if she didn't go along with what they wanted and make herself forget."

"She still owes me answers," Flannery said, frowning and angry. "All those years she spent trying to be our mother after our real one—well, the woman *I* thought was *my* real one—died. She had plenty of opportunities to tell me then. She wasn't scared of Dad anymore in his later years. He treated her like family by then. She could have told me the truth."

"D'Lynn helped give you life. She helped me deliver you. If it hadn't been for her the two of us might've died in that closet. Don't judge her too harshly for this," Izzy said. "She knew no better at the time."

"I need to leave," Flannery said, uncertain how to process this news.

"Can I come back tomorrow?"

Izzy paused for a moment before answering. "Okay. But isn't there something else you want to know before you leave?"

Flannery shook her head and narrowed the green eyes. "You just told me something that changes the whole course of who I am. What more could there be?"

"What Geoffrey has promised Conrad in return for his help. I know the answer to the question you keep askin' him. He won't tell you, but I will ... because I also know what the answer is."

Then Izzy pulled her daughter closer to her for the revelation.

29

"You've been a very, very bad boy, Travis!" Conrad barked, dragging the teenager up the stairs at Ten Points. "Sneaking off to warn Ezekiel Colson that Geoff was coming for him. I thought you were going to be a good servant to me."

Travis was petrified he was about to die. Conrad had somehow followed him through the woods to Zeke's house, or that was how it appeared, since it was through the same woods he had forced the boy back to the house. He had threatened several times on the way back to kill him if he made a sound or tried to call for help.

The fact he made it to the house alive gave Travis hope that Conrad would spare him. He still wasn't sure why Marcus had never replied to his text or if Geoff had followed through with his deadly plan back at Zeke's house.

"Please, Conrad, you're hurting my arm," Travis cried, trying to pull free.

"Shut up, you little bastard," Conrad hissed, once they were at the top of the stairs. "If you wake up anybody in this house I will have to kill them while you watch, and I know you don't want that."

Who's left in the house that isn't dead? Travis thought. His Uncle Marcus, D'Lynn, the twins. He *assumed* they were all still alive. "Where is everybody?" he asked. "Where's my Mom?"

"She's probably still out in the woods somewhere sucking every last drop of blood off the bones of James Ruffin," Conrad said, with a sneer. "Doesn't that make her a super cool Mom for a little Goth punk like you?"

Travis started to cry. "Please, this can't be real," he said with a sob.

"This has to all be some fucked-up nightmare. Oh God, let me wake up ..."

"Shut up before somebody hears you," Conrad ordered, dragging him down toward the end of the hallway. "Let's go to your room and have a little chat about your future and whether you have one, Travis."

"I'm sorry. It's just that I like Doctor Colson. I didn't want something bad to happen to him," Travis said, as Conrad shoved him into his bedroom and closed the door behind them.

"Your job is to please me, not Doctor Colson," Conrad said to him. "Do you not remember what I told you earlier today?"

"I'm confused," Travis said. He sniffled and tried to stop crying as he sat on the edge of his bed. "I'm starting to remember you doing something and snapping your fingers in my face."

"Yes, your parents are both aware I've enslaved you, so I'm letting the hypnosis wear off. We no longer have to keep this between us anymore," Conrad smiled. He went over to a desk where Travis kept a stash of comic books and studied macabre posters on the wall along the way. "My, you really get off on dark stuff, don't you?"

"What will Uncle Marcus say?" Travis asked.

"What will *Uncle Marcus say* about what?"

"When he finds out what you're doing to me and other people in this house," Travis said warily, knowing he was walking a tightrope.

"Your Uncle Marcus is indisposed at the moment and may be for a while," Conrad said. He set down a comic book he had been flipping through and walked back over to Travis.

"Oh no, did you kill him?" Travis asked, starting to cry again.

"Don't be ridiculous. Of course not. He's just going to need his rest for a while."

"Why?" Travis asked, looking fearful. "What did you do to him?"

"He had an accident," Conrad said. "Your Aunt Flannery ran her mouth and told him too much. He has to sleep until I can figure out how to get these bad thoughts he has about me out of his head."

"Oh no," Travis said hopelessly. "I don't have anybody now."

"You have *me*," Conrad smiled. "I'm your new father, Travis."

"*Wh—what?*"

"You always wanted a real Dad. You treat me the way I feel I deserve, and I can give you a happy life, Travis. I'll make you much happier than

Geoffrey ever did. Everybody knows he never saw you as anything more than annoying baggage that came with your mother when he married her."

"You're *not* my father and never will be!"

Conrad wasn't moved. "I think the sooner you learn to accept this, the better. Now I have a task for you. If you're successful, then this little matter of you running away and trying to help Zeke Colson will be forgiven and forgotten."

"What do you want me to do?" he asked, anxious and starting to tremble.

"I need you to help me find and destroy your Aunt Flannery. I've given her way too many chances, and she keeps disappointing me. She's stubborn and disobedient and never learns from her mistakes. It's time to get rid of her once and for all. She's a bloodsucker who preys on humans anyway. You and Bobby and Maxine will never be safe as long as she's around."

"So are my Mom and Dad," Travis said. "Will you want them gone next?"

"Not if they learn from the example I set by destroying that insubordinate bitch of an aunt of yours," Conrad said angrily, and then shook his head and smiled. "Are you going to be a good son and help me or not?"

"I'm *not* your son!" Travis protested, shaking and sobbing again. "This is too fucked up! I can't be what you want me to be!" He suddenly stared at the Civil War replica sword hanging in its sheath on the wall.

Conrad saw where his eyes went. "Don't even think about it," he said. "Do you really think some fake sword Grandpa gave you is going to kill me?"

"That's not what—"

"Don't lie to me," Conrad said. "Don't tell me you weren't thinking about grabbing the sword and taking your chances with me. I can see inside you, foolish boy."

"You're scaring me. I don't know what to do," Travis said, increasingly unnerved and looking away.

Conrad roughly took Travis' face in his hands and came in closer. "You *will* obey me and do what I say, *that's* what you'll do. Would you like to know what happens if you don't?"

Travis started trembling again and shook his head. Conrad was taking great delight in scaring the bejesus out of him. He laughed and was so close Travis could feel a warm, neutral, odorless breath hit him. "Please don't hurt me," he finally mustered.

"Good boy. Hey, Travis," Conrad said, with another grin forming. "You like this little dark side role-playing thing so much, don't you? The hair, your clothes, all the strange little piercings. Would you like to see what Hell is *really* like?"

"*Huh?*" Travis asked, confused and his eyes growing wide.

Conrad jerked the boy's head forward so that they were nose to nose and their eyes were only an inch apart. "Look into my eyes. Don't look away from me," he said, as Travis began to shake violently. "Look inside, Travis..."

"Oh God, *no!*" Travis screamed, as he saw inside. "Don't make me. Please! *Oh God, make it stop!*" He saw agony, torture, wailing, the gnashing of teeth, rivers of blood, death, and much more. All the dark things of the world magnified by a thousand. He cried out, and his head began to pound, but he couldn't take his eyes away from Conrad's no matter how badly he wanted to do so.

"Don't you fucking look away, you little bastard," Conrad whispered, smiling wide as he continued to subject the boy to a sadistic mental slide show. "We're almost done. Remember, this hurts Daddy much more than it hurts you."

"*Please! Oh God, I'll do anything! Make it stop!*" Travis was hyperventilating madly and felt himself become sick as Conrad finally shoved him away. He stumbled over to a small trash can in the room and vomited, with loud heaves that echoed across the room.

"That's what awaits you if you defy me again," Conrad said, standing and walking over behind him. "You'll experience it firsthand. Now, young man, does that give you incentive to behave?"

Travis was still hunched over the wastebasket, dry heaving and trying to process what he had just seen. He sat up and fell back against the wall, a glazed look in his eyes. The idea of sneaking downstairs, taking one of Geoffrey's guns and blowing his own brains out went through his mind, but he quickly tossed it away, mostly out of fear that Conrad could read his thoughts. Maybe there was a God, and God would have mercy on him if he ended his own life. It would be a better alternative than living in a house under Conrad's rule. But he couldn't think such things right now with Conrad only a few feet away.

"I'm going downstairs now," Conrad said. "Don't do anything foolish while I'm gone. You should stay right here and think about everything we've discussed. And also brainstorm some places we can look for your Aunt Flannery. There is that big problem that still needs tending to."

Travis stared over at him blankly.

Conrad laughed. "Hell and the dark stuff is *just* a little understated in all this bullshit pop culture you humans eat up, now isn't it?"

A strange sound came from Travis' throat, and as he struggled to close his mouth, it was then he realized he wasn't able to speak. At all. He opened his mouth and tried to say something but could not. He knew the words, but couldn't form them on his tongue.

Conrad nodded. "Insurance," he said. "We can't have you running your mouth and making your aunt's mistakes. I also knew showing you a glimpse of Hell would help. Oh, and I took your phone. You won't need that until I decide you can have it back." He walked out of the room and closed the door behind him.

Travis remained seated on the floor against the wall. A single tear rolled down his cheek. He had been made to feel like an outsider his entire life at Ten Points, but it was the first time in his young life he felt so utterly helpless and alone.

30

"Listen to me," Zeke said to Marcus. "When they find me, it was your brother who did it."

"What are you talking about?" Marcus asked. They were in a field somewhere he had never been before. The array of wildflowers and the sycamore trees off in the distance looked like Louisiana, but the arid climate felt like southern California.

"Just be careful with what you say and how you act," Zeke warned. "The dead are growing in number at Ten Points. Conrad orchestrated all of it. He's got more in store. I don't know what exactly he'll do next, but he won't stop until something even more horrible has happened."

"Did Geoff *kill* you? I'm confused," Marcus said, extending his hand but unable to reach Zeke.

"If you have to ask, then I think you already know the answer," Zeke said, sadness in his eyes.

"No!" Marcus cried. "Damn it, I'll kill him!"

"You can't kill him," Zeke said. "He must be destroyed."

"I don't understand," Marcus was confused and shaking his head. "What's the difference? What is it? Zeke, you have to tell me," he insisted, perplexed by all that was happening. The wind started to pick up, and Zeke seemed farther away. He was wearing a white suit, and he looked as if he were on his way somewhere more festive than he had been earlier at Maximilian Lanehart's funeral. "Where are you going? Come back!"

"I can't tell you everything about Geoff, and I can't come back," Zeke said. "The wind. It's picking up. It's about to take me away." He was being pushed farther back against his will, and there was now about one hundred feet of distance between them across the field.

"Taking you where?" Marcus asked, growing agitated. "Fight it, and come back here."

"I have to go," Zeke said. "There's no choice. I have to leave now."

"Don't leave me here!" Marcus shouted. The increasing intensity of the wind made it more difficult for them to hear one another.

"I can't stay right now, but I'll find you, Marcus!" Zeke shouted over the wind's howl. He fought back tears and continued as he was forced even farther away. "I don't care how. I'll find my way back...*however* I can—whatever it takes! I swear on everything I believe in I'll find my way back to you! We didn't come this far to get separated all over again, and I'll find you one day. I love you, Marcus! *I will come back to you!*" he called out loudly, as the wind picked up at an otherworldly pace and carried him out of sight.

"*Zeke, no!*" Marcus was startled awake. It felt as though he was in his bed upstairs, but it was pitch black around him. Unable to see anything, he tried to sit up in the bed, but his head began hurting, so he immediately fell back down to the pillow.

What had just happened? He suddenly knew. Zeke was dead. No one would have to break the news to him.

But someone would have to give Marcus answers. Zeke said *Geoffrey* did it. But why did he do it? Marcus felt a sudden fusion of anger and rage and sadness and wanting to kill Geoffrey. But his head began spinning and a fog came over him. One moment he was in a field, then back in his bed, and now he felt himself drifting off somewhere else.

"Zeke is right. Geoffrey must be destroyed," said a voice Marcus recognized. The darkness turned to blue, and Maximilian Lanehart appeared, wearing the same gray suit he had been buried in.

"Dad?" Marcus said. "You're in the ground. How are you here?" But even Marcus was unsure of where *here* was at the moment.

"Try not to ask a bunch of questions," Maximilian said disapprovingly as always. "This all falls on you now, Marcus. Your brother and your sister. They're not what you think. The house is out of order, and you have to put it back. Find Travis. You're the only two left in the family who can fix anything."

"*Travis?* What does he have to do with it?" Marcus asked. First it was Zeke, and now it was his father who was causing him distress and bemusement.

"Conrad," Maximilian said, keeping a neutral expression.

"You have to tell me—" But it was too late. Before Marcus could finish the sentence his father was gone.

"What is going on?" Marcus said to himself, as the blue around him faded and returned to black. He realized he wasn't in a black room but in the darkness. He felt the mattress of his bed underneath him again. He flinched as he felt something else again. The small hand of a child holding his in the darkness.

"Who's there?" he called. "Who are you?"

The small hand tugged at his, trying to coax him from the bed. He tried to pull away, but it refused to let go of him and kept pulling at him.

"No! I won't go anywhere until you tell me who you are!" he demanded. He was angry at not being able to rationally explain anything that was happening.

"But please," cried the voice of a child. It sounded like a small boy. "I'm scared. I need you to help me."

"What is your name? Tell me your name," Marcus insisted, feeling more anxious than frightened.

"I don't know my name," the little boy said, starting to whimper and cry. He was the one who sounded frightened. "Please."

"I'm turning on the light. I want to see you," Marcus said, reaching for the bedside lamp with his free hand.

"No, I'm scared of the light. Please leave it off," the child said, sniffling and lightly sobbing.

"Bobby, is it you?" Marcus asked, realizing he had never heard his nephew's voice and wouldn't recognize it if he did.

"I'm not Bobby," the child said. "I know who Bobby is, but it ain't me."

"I want to see you," Marcus said. "Let me see you." He reached over and turned on the light but whoever had been there was gone. His hand was empty. "Where are you?" he shouted. The bedroom was spacious. Nobody, especially a child, would have had time to run away and hide— not even scramble underneath the bed.

Marcus' head was still aching and felt heavy. He relaxed back on the pillow and felt a need to turn the lamp back off. The fact he had been visited by three ghosts no longer registered clearly with him. His thoughts were scattered and the fog returned. Then a thought of a red tricycle from when he was a small child randomly popped into his mind. He must have only still been a toddler but could suddenly remember it all. A young black woman pushed him along on it down the concrete walkway in front of the great house, causing him to laugh out loud as small children often do. The woman laughed along with him.

Izzy. Oh dear God, he hoped she was still alive. There had been Zeke, Maximilian, and the boy. Why was Izzy now entering into his mind? Was she somehow a part of all this?

He felt himself drifting off to sleep again, but he didn't want to go back to sleep. He felt like he needed to stay awake, but then he found himself back in the field where Zeke had been blown away by the wind.

Only this time, it was a gloomy, misty, and foggy day across the field. He was near a sycamore tree at the corner of the clearing. Did he go there to look for Zeke? He wasn't sure, but a dark shadow he decided was sleep cast itself over the field, blocking out what was left of the sun and closing over him by the tree. He tried to hide behind the tree, but the sleep crept closer and closer. He tried to turn away from it, and there she was.

About fifty feet away from where he stood, Marcus saw Flannery walking into the woods.

"Flannery, where are you going?" he called after her.

She turned back and stared at him. She was extremely pale, even underneath the gray sky. She kept looking at him for a moment before responding.

"I have to go find Tilda and tell her what I know," she said.

"Wait up, I'll go with you," Marcus shouted out. "What do you have to tell her?"

She shook her head and held her hand out to warn him to stay back. "I have to go alone," she said. Her voice was flat and without emotion. "I have to do this alone. She must know what I've learned."

"Let me help you," Marcus said, trying to follow after her. "You always want to do everything alone and never let anybody else help you."

Flannery walked behind a tree and was gone. Marcus went over but she wasn't there.

Maximilian was right. It was up to him. And Travis, too, he said. Only Travis was nowhere around. Where was he?

"Oh yeah, he sent me a text message," Marcus said to himself. "I didn't know what it meant at first. Now I do."

He had tried to warn Marcus about what was going to happen to Zeke. Then something about going over there. Dear God, was Travis okay? Marcus wondered where his phone was. Maybe he dropped it somewhere in the field on his way over to the tree.

Then it came to him that he wasn't really in a field. He was in his bed back at Ten Points, but for some reason he couldn't wake up. He thought he had once, when the little boy appeared at his bedside and grabbed his hand, but here he was obviously asleep again and in a dream. The fog lifted, and beneath the thick curtain of confusion lay the first time he could recall being asleep and in a dream and fully aware of it.

He walked back out of the forest where he had tried to follow Flannery and saw a bereaved Travis sitting by a pine tree with a gloomy look on his pale face. He looked up as Marcus approached.

"What happened? Did you go to Zeke's house? Is he really gone?" Marcus asked.

Travis looked up at him sadly and nodded.

"What's the matter? Can't you say anything?"

The teenager slowly shook his head.

"Why can't you speak? What's the matter with you? Did *he* do it?"

Travis' face went from despondent to distressed as his eyes moved to something unpleasant he saw behind Marcus. He looked as if he desperately wanted to speak but couldn't. Instead, he extended his arm and pointed.

Marcus turned around for a look and was stunned at the sight before him. In the sycamore tree, an impression of Conrad's face was forming in the bark, and as the features became more prominent, it appeared to come to life, and a pair of eyelids slowly slid open, revealing the dark brown eyes. The prominent chin and cleft were the last to form.

Conrad's familiar smile came from the tree, as an icier wind returned and began drawing Marcus and Travis closer. Against their will, they were pulled toward the tree, where the face of Conrad beckoned them with a magnetic grip.

"Come to me," it said. "I'm the master of the house, the way it was intended to be, and you'll both serve me as such. Now come to me. *You belong to me.*"

"Never!" Marcus said, suddenly wide awake and sitting up in the bed.

The bedside light was on again, and this time D'Lynn was there. He realized he was sweating profusely, and she was bent over him wearing a pink robe over a nightgown and using a cold washrag to dab at his forehead.

"Honey, you've been rollin' around and moanin' and talkin' in your sleep the last few minutes," she said. "I've been tryin' to shake you awake."

"Oh my God," he said. "Zeke's dead. Geoff killed Zeke! Something's wrong with Geoff and Flannery. And Conrad did something to Travis. Geoff brought that *thing* into this house, and he's trying to destroy us all."

"Who?" she asked. "I heard you fell and hit your head. You're hysterical and talkin' gibberish."

"I didn't fall. Conrad hit me and I banged my head hard on the wall downstairs. We have to call the police!" Marcus said, trying to climb out of bed. "Please, they need to get to Zeke's house. Where's my phone? I think it's downstairs. Please, we have to get help!"

"You stay put!" D'Lynn said, putting her hand on his shoulder and preventing him from stepping on to the floor. "You probably have a concussion. You need to rest."

"Please, D'Lynn, you have to believe me. I need to go check on Travis, too. Something's wrong with him! He and the twins. We must protect them!"

"Bobby and Maxine are asleep, and Travis is probably in his room listening to that God-awful music and drawin' horrible pictures of monsters. I clean in that room, and to heck with bein' an individual. That boy is disturbed."

"Just *please* call the police and go make sure Travis is okay—"

"Honey, you're havin' bad dreams and gettin' carried away. I got out of bed to check on you and make sure *you're* okay. I'll check on Travis in the mornin'. Now you get some rest." She reached over on the nightstand and picked up a ceramic mug. "Here, drink this. It'll help you go back to sleep and get some rest."

He took the mug and drank from it. It tasted like a warm herbal tea, maybe chamomile, he wasn't sure. There was a lemony aftertaste. "Okay, there. Now can I please have out of this room? I need to get to Zeke's house and meet the police there!"

"Marcus, you're imaginin' things—"

"D'Lynn, I'm not a child anymore. You can't make me stay in this room. Something is wrong, and I have to get out of here."

Marcus felt weak and dizzy but climbed out of the bed over her objections. He was still wearing a dress shirt and slacks from the funeral. He stumbled toward the door but nearly fell over, groggier and more off balance than when he first stood up.

"Get back into bed!" D'Lynn ordered. "You're hurt and need rest."

"What the hell did you give me to drink?" he asked, catching himself on the wall so he wouldn't fall over. "I feel ... funny. What was in the cup? Did you *poison* me?"

He turned back to face D'Lynn and let out a yell. Conrad was sitting on the edge of the bed, and D'Lynn was no longer there. "Come back to bed," he said to Marcus, motioning him forward with a hand.

"What the fuck is going on?" Marcus asked, wide eyed. The room was starting to spin, and it made no sense D'Lynn had vanished into thin air and Conrad had appeared out of nowhere. "Where is D'Lynn? What did you do to her?"

"She's fast asleep in her room. She was never here. You just thought she was," Conrad said. "I do one hell of an impression, don't I? Now come to me."

"Oh God, you were in a tree, and now you're here," Marcus said, stumbling around and holding his hands on each side of his head. "None of this makes any sense."

"It was the only way to get through to you. You never let me when you're awake."

"I don't want you around me," Marcus said, losing sense of where he was and starting to slur his words. "You killed Zeke, you son of a bitch."

"No, Marcus, I didn't do that. Your brother did that," Conrad said matter-of-factly. "I don't think it's a fair statement to say *I* did it."

"You were responsible, and you can't do this," Marcus said, starting to lose his balance again. The room grew darker before him. "I'll figure out a way to stop you...I'll—"

"No you won't," Conrad said. "You're stubborn, but the tea will make you sleep again until you can come around about our future together. You'll change your way of thinking soon. You'll be mine, and we will be happy and live here together. Forever."

"Like hell we—"

Everything went completely black mid-sentence, and Marcus felt the floor come up to meet him just as he went unconscious. Conrad continued to sit on the edge of the bed and stare at him for a few minutes before getting up, picking him up off the floor, and putting him back on to the bed.

31

Tilda returned to the house about twenty minutes after Geoffrey arrived home from killing Zeke Colson. She walked up the curved granite steps of the front porch of Ten Points armed with the information Flannery had given her in the woods. She was still processing what she had been told, and she had to figure out what to do about it. The last time she had seen her husband, he was sprawled out dead across the antique wooden desk in the study—the same desk where she had been killed by Flannery the night before.

She opened the front door of the house and walked into the foyer, not expecting to see her undead husband standing there to greet her, with a smile and glint in his baby blue eyes, which now had a coldness and a sobriety never there before. Without asking, and just by a new instinct she acquired during her own transformation, she immediately discerned what he had become.

"Well, hello my darling wife," Geoffrey said calmly, reaching out to take her hand.

She played along, uncertain about what to do with what she had learned in the woods. Flannery had given her a valuable bit of information but hadn't bothered telling her she had reanimated Geoffrey.

"I see you've recovered from that little chokehold Conrad had you in," Tilda said passively, staring into his eyes. She realized she was challenging herself to stay calm. She hoped he couldn't sense what she now knew.

"Isn't it glorious?" he said to her. "We never have to grow old."

"Isn't it," she said back to him. Only two nights ago she had stood with her glass of Scotch in one hand and a cigarette in the other contemplating plastic surgery and fearing the hands of time. After helping Rochelle devour Ruffin in the woods, she was starting to wonder if her old life had been such a bad thing after all.

"Why the serious look?" he asked. "It's time to celebrate. We have eternity ahead of us."

"I just helped a woman you cheated on me with decimate the family attorney in the woods and scatter whatever was left for wild animals to finish," she said. "Should I be in a light and happy mood right now?"

"The guilt afterward is just part of our leftover humanity," Geoffrey told her. "Conrad told me it would happen at first. I should know. I just did something bad, too," he said. He wore the expression of a mischievous boy with a naughty secret he wanted to share.

"What did you do?" Tilda asked, indulging him.

"I killed Zeke Colson," he said, with a devilish grin. "And I drank his blood. And I enjoyed it. It was like nothing I've ever experienced in my life."

"Why did you kill Zeke Colson?" she asked, not caring for the details of how it made him feel. The knowledge she now carried also outweighed any feelings she had over Zeke being dead.

"Why did you kill Ruffin?" Geoffrey asked, with a nonchalant shrug. "Because Conrad told us to. Isn't that reason enough?"

"It's nice to see you've come around about Conrad killing you and are now fine with doing his dirty work," she said, walking into the living room. "Forty-eight hours ago we were nowhere near this. He was in our lives, he was screwing me a couple of times a week. But we were nowhere near where we are right now."

Geoffrey followed after her. "Why is *where we are* right now such a bad thing? We'll never grow old. We will soon have enough money to live like royalty, and we don't have to worry about getting sick or dying. What could be better than that?"

"What will we tell people when we stay the same age and never get older? Our family? We will probably have to move away and live in seclusion. What will D'Lynn say when she never sees us in the daytime anymore. What will the kids—"

Tilda quickly cut herself off. She *knew*. But Geoffrey couldn't know that yet.

"What about the kids?" he asked. "We don't need them anymore."

"Is that really how you feel?" she asked, staring at him intently.

"Yes," he said. "We're not human anymore. They don't need us anymore. We can't be there for them in the same way. Conrad will be their father now."

She turned away from him and walked across the room. "So, you don't love the children anymore?" she asked, looking away so he couldn't see her face. "Tell me, Geoff. Is that what you're saying?"

Geoffrey gave a short laugh. "Let's be honest, Tilda. I never loved Travis at all. I only tolerated him. I never would have adopted him if it weren't for Dad breathing down my neck. He was all over me about how it would make us all look bad if I didn't claim him as my own. Oh my word, what a crock ..."

"And the twins?"

"Maxine is a sweet girl, yes, I *did* love her. But Bobby..."

"What about Bobby?" she said, turning to face him. "Tell me about Bobby, Geoff. Tell me all about your plans for Bobby."

"You still haven't told her about Bobby, Geoff?" Conrad said with a smile as he appeared in the living room. "She isn't stupid, and you'll have to explain everything sooner or later."

Tilda gave Conrad a smirk and then looked back to Geoffrey. "Yes, Geoff, you'll have to. *Sooner or later.*"

"I don't want to talk about it right now," he said.

Suddenly Geoffrey was the one to turn away from her. He went over and stared out a window into the dark. With his newly-enhanced vision, he spotted a fox over near one of the oak trees in the distance. He marveled at his scotopia, knowing he would have never been able to see such a thing as a human.

"Why not?" she asked.

The sardonic look on her face was enough for Conrad. "Something tells me you either know, or you think you've figured it out," he said.

Tilda turned to Conrad. "Well, I may no longer have to worry about looking older, but you surely do, don't you?"

He gave a condescending smile. "Please explain what you're talking about..."

"Oh come on, Conrad," she said. "Don't act like you don't know what I'm talking about. That body of yours isn't going to last forever. You'll need a new host soon, won't you? Say in about nine or ten years, when that body you currently possess starts to age. How old are you *supposed* to be anyway? Twenty-eight, twenty-nine? Part of your appeal when I first met you was that you were under thirty and wanted some of my forty-year-old ass," she scoffed.

"Well, it was more a control thing than an attraction thing," he said. "It was a bit of fun to make you think I actually wanted you, but it was more my way of humbling your loving husband over there."

Geoffrey turned and smiled at them. "It kind of worked," he said. "I also kind of enjoyed watching."

Tilda turned and gave Geoff a disgusted look. "We were married in a church, for Christ's sake. We're *Republicans!* It wasn't supposed to be like this."

Conrad laughed out loud. "Oh you two are a hoot, I must say."

Tilda looked back to Conrad. "You made a bargain with my husband to take my son's body when he came of age. Geoff is so reluctant to have a mentally challenged son he's willing to let you have Bobby to take control of when that body you have now isn't good enough anymore." She faced Geoffrey again. "I *finally* know the truth!" she screamed at him. "You son of a bitch!"

"He's a retard," Geoffrey said, with a curl of his lips and a shrug. "He's no good to us, sweetie. Conrad can take over, *become* Bobby, and it all makes sense when we take our—" he held up his fingers in quotation marks "—'retirement' and go away. Conrad acting as Bobby will take over all the family holdings while we go live off in our own Paradise for the rest of time. Nobody will know us; they won't suspect a thing when we never get old. We can keep going to new places every few years. We can roam the countryside at night and hunt together. Whatever Conrad decides to do with Bobby or Maxine *or* that queer brother of mine *or* that whore sister of mine *or* that ghoul of a son of yours is up to him. For the love of God, Tilda, *what is so fucking terrible about all of that?* It's all part of our grand plan, and so far it's working. I was going crazy and was full of anxiety because I knew Conrad was eventually going to kill me and force Flannery to turn me into what *we* now are. Now that it's done, I feel wonderful. I feel marvelous! The world is *ours*, Tilda."

She shook her head. "So, Conrad, you did this to *me* as part of the plan? You had Flannery attack and turn me—"

Conrad smiled and placed his hands on Tilda's shoulders. "Flannery was as much a pawn in all of this as you were, Tilda. I was smart enough to know she didn't care for me enough to be jealous when she walked in on us having sex. But knowing how the two of you disliked one another, I knew if I could pit you two against each other, well, then she would attack and we would have you as you are now."

"It killed me at the time to see that, and I decided to try and stop it at the last minute—I wanted it all to stop—first you, then seeing you go after Rochelle when outsiders weren't part of the plan. I knew my time was coming, and the anxiety over knowing it was all set in motion was driving me nuts. Conrad finally made me see in the long run it would be beneficial to us," Geoffrey said. He acted as if it had all been long ago instead of only the night before.

Tilda quickly knocked Conrad's hands off her shoulders and walked over to Geoff. "You knew I was going to be attacked and killed? *You* set me up?" She slapped her husband hard across the face, but he neither flinched nor felt it.

Geoffrey smiled gleefully at his immortality. "Oh God, do that again," he said to her. "I'm immune to pain. I love it."

Conrad nodded. "That may be so, Geoff, but not all of you are. Flannery felt the one I gave her the other night. Don't worry, Tilda, in a hundred years or so you'll attain more skills and tricks. Maybe Geoffrey will need a good slap then, and you'll be able to make him feel it one of these days."

"I don't care about that!" she exclaimed, going back over to Conrad. "You set me up? You decided I would be a part of this no matter what? What about Rochelle? What about Ruffin? They're just collateral damage in all of this?"

"Rochelle was a slut who was getting screwed by your husband, and Ruffin would be stuck to the back of ambulances if he hadn't lucked up and gotten into the employ of your family," Conrad told her. "Why do you care so much about what happened to either of them?"

"It isn't important anymore, Tilda. Look at the bigger picture," Geoffrey said, walking back over to her. "Soon none of this will matter anymore."

"Maybe there's still too much of my human side left to go along with this," she said, as she looked at them both. "I'm sorry I can't be so cold and devoid of emotion as the two of you are. The demon and the greedy bastard who brought him into our lives!"

"Let's put off the name calling," Conrad suggested. He glared at Tilda. "I gave young Travis a task, and Tilda I need your help as well. I assume Flannery is the one who told you the truth. She didn't know about all of this before, but she found out tonight, didn't she?"

"What does that have to do with anything?" Tilda asked. "I know, and that's what matters."

"I need you to help me find and destroy Flannery. You never liked her. Don't you want her gone for what she did to you last night?" Conrad said, in an effort to goad her.

"Flannery finally opened my eyes to the truth. You orchestrated the entire thing," Tilda said to Conrad. "If I wanted anyone destroyed, it would be *you*"

Conrad grabbed her by the arm. "If you don't play along, Tilda, you could go to sleep permanently at sunrise. Now tell me where I can find Flannery. I know she's around here somewhere."

"The last place I saw her was the woods. I don't know where she went after that. I didn't ask her where she was going," Tilda said calmly, not breaking eye contact with him. "Now let go of my arm."

"Where is Rochelle?" Conrad asked. "Why didn't she come back with you to the house?"

"She ran off into the night after we were done with Ruffin," Tilda said. "I don't know where she went. She said something about going to look for more blood. She went into a frenzy and couldn't seem to get enough."

Conrad shook his head and frowned. "I suppose we should've just left her dead last night," he said. "I can see her turning into a huge liability down the road. If she returns later, I'll make sure she's taken care of. Permanently."

"She's annoying anyway," Tilda said. "Do what you must."

"Now *that's* the Tilda I like," Conrad said, with an approving smile. "We will just have to get you on board about this thing with Bobby. I know it won't be easy for you at first, but it will be for the best for your continued existence in the future. You'll see."

"If you say so," she said, looking at Conrad and over to Geoff. "Now if you'll both excuse me, I need to go upstairs."

"Going to your slumber so early?" Conrad asked. "You still have a couple of more hours until sunrise. You could always help us by going out to look for that wayward sister-in-law of yours."

"I'm very tired," Tilda said. "It's been a long night. I'm sure Geoffrey can help you search for her. Excuse me."

She then walked out of the room. Once in the foyer, she gave a glance back at the two of them over her shoulder. When she saw they had begun talking amongst themselves and were paying her no attention, she slowly began climbing the stairs.

When she reached the top of the winding staircase she stared down the long second-floor hallway.

So many doors lined the corridor on each side. She took a glance at each one.

But there was only one that caught her eye and drew her forward.

32

"*Wake up, wake up!*" *the voice of the little boy cried, as he tugged on Marcus' hand. "Tilda knows. Now somethin' bad is about to happen.*"

Marcus slowly opened his eyes, but no one was there. No one was holding or tugging at his hand anymore. This time the little boy, whoever he was, had only appeared in the dream and wasn't there at this bedside any longer.

The inside of his mouth felt dry and parched, and his throat ached when he tried to speak. Marcus turned his head slowly toward the nightstand and hoped he would see a glass or a bottle of water. None was there, and he realized he had to try and get to the bathroom and stick his head underneath the faucet in the sink or bathtub. But he felt too weak to climb out of bed. His head felt like a cumbrous boulder weighing him down as he turned it back on the pillow so that his eyes faced the ceiling.

He swallowed and tried to moisten his lips with his tongue, but it felt like sandpaper rolling across them.

"Hey, little boy," he called out hoarsely. "Come back. *Please.* I need you."

The room was still swirling, and his head ached terribly. He closed his eyes and hoped it would make everything slow down or stop. He was curious about what time it was—or even what day it was—but he decided he had to try and focus on one thing at a time if he was going to make his way out of the room.

His eyes fluttered, and he realized he must have dozed off again, when another tug at his hand woke him up. He slowly turned his head and could see the silhouette of a child in the dark.

"You came back," Marcus said.

"Why can't you get up?" the little boy asked him.

"My head hurts really badly. I don't feel well," he said, barely able to speak above a whisper. "I need you to help me. Please help me."

"I know. That's why I came back," the little boy said, continuing to pull at his hand.

Marcus slowly pushed himself into a sitting position and groaned as he moved his legs around off the mattress and put his feet on the floor. "Thank you," he said to the little boy, who still had his hand. "Who are you? Where did you come from?"

"I don't know," the little boy said, sounding frightened. "I've always been here." He sounded as if he might start to cry.

"Don't be scared," Marcus said. "Why are you afraid?"

"They put me in the wall," he said, beginning to whimper as he had earlier. "I came out of the wall. Please help me and don't let them put me back in there!"

Marcus' head still throbbed, and what he heard made no sense. "The *wall*? No one's going to put you in any wall. What on earth?"

"Please. Don't let them put Bobby in the wall either."

"Why are you saying these things? I don't understand what you mean."

The boy stood there and said nothing.

"Listen to me," Marcus said. "You have to help me get downstairs. You have to help me find a phone so I can call the police."

"I can only go over there," the little boy said, pointing to the door. "I can't go where the light is. They can't see me. If they see me they'll put me back in the wall."

"I *promise* I won't let anybody hurt you or put you inside a wall. Now please, I need you to be a little man and help me down the stairs. I'm hurt and weak and don't know if I can make it by myself. Okay?"

Marcus still felt drunk or stoned from whatever was in the cup Conrad had given him to drink from. He also desperately needed water and couldn't decide whether to let it wait until he found a telephone. The closest remaining landlines he knew about inside the house were in the living room and downstairs in the hallway past the foyer.

"What if they see me? What will they do to me?"

The little boy's voice quivered terribly with fear, and Marcus couldn't understand why he was so jittery, who exactly had mistreated him so badly in the past to make him so skittish—or, when all was said and done, who the hell the child even was. His presence in the room had no logical explanation, and Marcus wondered if it was another dream or his drugged imagination. It was obvious the tea he had drunk had been laced with something. He put the thoughts away and focused on getting out of bed and standing steadily on his feet.

"Can you walk?" the little boy asked. "I learned how to walk when I watched Bobby. Do you need me to show you how?"

"Are you Bobby's friend?" Marcus asked, clutching his scratchy throat. "You keep talking about him. You also said Tilda *knew* something when you woke me up. *What* does Tilda know?"

The child stood there and said nothing but started tugging at Marcus' hand again. "Come on," he finally said, trying to pull him forward. He didn't seem as frightened anymore.

Marcus stood to his feet and almost fell over. He grabbed on to the edge of the bed to steady himself and then tried again, slowly putting one foot in front of the other. "What the hell did he do to me?" he said, mostly to himself.

He thought about Zeke, and then tried not to think about not having him anymore. He had to think about what he would do when he got out of the room and faced Geoffrey downstairs. Conrad would also likely be there. He would figure out a way to deal with both of them. Zeke had seemed almost peaceful in the field, before the wind took him away. Marcus hoped he hadn't suffered when Geoffrey killed him. He felt tears and sadness coming but willed them away. There wasn't time right now.

His thoughts also drifted to Landon. Was he dead, too? Marcus realized he would probably never get any form of satisfactory closure in that situation. For the first time since Landon's disappearance he suspected Maximilian, or even Geoffrey, of having something to do with it. Why else would someone never come home without any explanation? The two of them hadn't been having any major problems beforehand. The whole thing reeked of a Lanehart machination, Marcus decided to himself. What had they done with Landon? What had they done with

Zeke?

He would seek answers. He had the right to know, he decided, as he slowly made his way to the bedroom door.

"Are you still there?" he asked, not feeling the little boy's hand in his any longer.

"You're too close to the light. I'm over here," the small voice said. Marcus turned and saw the short silhouette back over near the bed.

"That's okay," he said as assuredly as he could despite his dry, aching throat. "I think I can make it the rest of the way on my own."

33

Marcus held the bannister tightly as he slowly walked down the winding stairs. He could see the glow of the marble foyer floor below him, and there was the sound of Geoffrey's and Conrad's voices coming from the living room. He almost stumbled and fell halfway down the staircase, but his grip on the sturdy wooden bannister kept him from further injuring himself—and warning the other two he was headed their way.

He reached the bottom of the stairs and thankfully was starting to feel a bit more poised and steady on his feet than when he had first climbed out of bed upstairs. He was able to walk with little effort across the foyer and toward the living room. He hoped his balance issues were a side effect of whatever he had drunk and not his head injury. He was able to think more clearly now and his head hurt less. Getting out of the bed and moving around again cleared some of the cobwebs.

Marcus had almost reached the doorway of the living room when Conrad turned and saw him. "Well, look who's out of bed," he greeted. "You should really be resting, Marcus. It's not even sunrise yet."

Marcus stared at him but didn't say anything. He slowly walked over to the bar in the living room.

"Where is he going? What's he doing?" Geoffrey asked, confused and watching him.

Marcus walked behind the bar and held on tightly as he bent down and pulled a bottle of water from the small refrigerator below. He stood and opened it and drank, the icy coldness quenching his thirst and helping invigorate him a little more. He felt better, but his mouth still felt a little dry. He tried not to drink too fast and finally set the bottle down. He walked back around to the other side of the bar, prepared for whatever was about to happen.

"You son of a bitch," he said, walking toward Geoffrey. "I know what you did." He looked over to Conrad. "And I know who told you to do it."

"I think you need more rest because you—" Conrad began.

"Shut the fuck up!" Marcus yelled at him, his voice strong again. "I'm nothing to you, you evil bastard, and you'll have to kill me before you ever think anything will be between us." He turned back to Geoffrey. "What the hell have you done?"

"It was for the best," Geoffrey said. "Zeke was—"

He couldn't finish getting the words out before Marcus punched him in the jaw again, hard enough to make his head swivel but clearly not inflicting any pain.

Geoffrey turned back around with a smile and a shrug. "Much more force than Tilda, but still, not a thing," he said, keeping a grin as he looked over to Conrad. "Maybe I should become a boxer now?"

"Where is Flannery? What did you do to her? Where is Travis? Who's left in this house you two haven't harmed?" Marcus' eyes went back to Conrad. "You transformed into D'Lynn when you were in my room drugging me with whatever that shit was you fed me. Did you hurt D'Lynn? *How* did you transform like that? What the hell *are* you?"

"Your sister is a nuisance, and we don't know where she is," Conrad said to him. "As far as that rebellious little nephew of yours, well, he's up in his room. He and I are playing *the quiet game* right now."

Marcus shook his head and squinted. "The quiet game? I swear to God, you better not have harmed him."

"Your God means nothing to me," Conrad smiled. "Haven't you figured that out yet?"

Geoffrey laughed out loud. "I just realized I don't have to go to church anymore. Hallelujah," he said mockingly.

"What are you talking about?" Marcus said to Geoffrey. "What is going on here?"

"You and I are going to be the joint masters of Ten Points. As husband and husband," Conrad said, walking over closer to Marcus.

"The hell we are," Marcus said, giving him a disgusted look. "Geoff, why are you giving control to this *thing*? What the hell are you up to?"

"I do wish you would stop referring to me that way, my *betrothed*," Conrad said to him.

"Go fuck yourself," Marcus told him and then turned back to his brother. "Explain to me what's going on here!"

"Well, I guess you might as well know," Geoffrey replied. "Tilda and I are leaving soon for new adventures. A new way of life that doesn't include this estate or our children. You're so fond of Travis, so now you and Conrad here can be his parents. And Bobby and Maxine can even have two Dads as well. I may not approve of you guys' lifestyle, but I have my own to be concerned about now."

"A Baptist hypocrite to the very end," Marcus muttered, shaking his head.

"Geoff and Conrad, you haven't told him everything," Tilda said. She appeared at the doorway and walked into the room. "You should tell him the entire story if you're going to try and convince him to go along with this."

"Entire story?" Marcus asked, looking around at all three of them. "Yes, please tell me what all is going on here."

"Just a technicality," Geoffrey said. "In order for Tilda and me to gain eternal life and wealth, we had to promise Conrad here a little something."

Marcus' head began throbbing again. Just as it had the evening of the wake, when the passenger door of the Bentley opened in the driveway and Conrad stepped out. He suddenly felt ill and dizzy but quickly caught himself on the edge of the green velvet sofa and willed the dreadful feeling away.

You belong to me, it said.

No, I fucking don't! he yelled back inside his mind.

Marcus looked up and caught Conrad staring at him with a disapproving head shake. "I can't even believe what I'm hearing," Marcus said to Geoff. "Eternal life and wealth? What is he, some kind of genie?"

"You're getting warm," Conrad smiled at him. "You look pale and like you might be sick again, Marcus. Can I get you something to drink?"

"After the last time?" Marcus said, with a fastidious laugh.

"Well, let one of us help you back into bed. You need more rest," Conrad suggested, walking toward him. "Maybe after you've *rested* you'll see things our way a little more."

"Stay the hell away from me," Marcus said. "You'll have to kill me before you expect me to go along with any of this."

"Don't try to shelter him from the truth," Tilda said, hand on her hip. "Go ahead and tell him everything. Let him form his own opinion."

"Tilda, you should stay out of this," Conrad said, turning to her with a faint smile. "Just remember you have to go to sleep soon, and what I told you might happen when *that* happens. Okay?"

"The truth, Marcus, is that Conrad is enamored with you, but his body won't be as enamored with him in a decade or so when he starts to age," Tilda began, her eyes on Conrad as she openly defied him.

"I'm warning you," he said, the smile completely gone.

"His evil spirit will have to leave that body and go possess someone else who's younger ... more vital ..." Tilda kept her eyes locked on Conrad.

"That's it, bitch," he hissed, moving toward her with rage and murder in his dark eyes.

"Mommy, why do I have to stand outside?" Bobby appeared in the doorway of the living room, staring at everyone with his large blue eyes and catching them all off guard. Everyone but Tilda.

"I've never heard him speak before," Marcus said, looking at the boy strangely. He stood there in dark blue pajamas clutching what appeared to a stuffed animal toy. For a child of ten years old, he looked and sounded much younger.

Conrad froze in his tracks before reaching out for Tilda's neck. "Why is he out of bed?" he demanded. "He's a growing boy. He should be asleep!"

"Conrad is right. Why is he out of bed?" Geoffrey asked, walking over. "He shouldn't be hearing any of this anyway."

Marcus went over for a closer look. "Oh my God," he said, the breath leaving his body. "What's wrong *with...?"*

As he got closer to Bobby, he could see four tiny holes in the left side of the child's neck, along with what appeared to be dried blood around the puncture wounds and on the boy's pajama collar. Bobby looked up at Marcus with a wide expression, and suddenly opened his mouth, revealing large white cuspids.

"I'm hungry," he said, looking back and forth at Marcus and Conrad. He was somehow able to sense they were the only two people in the room with mortal bodies. "Please feed me now."

"No!" Conrad cried, in great distress. He grabbed a silver fire poker from the edge of the fireplace, and in a flash stabbed Tilda through the

chest with the pointed end. He shoved it through as hard as he could in his rage, piercing her heart. She elicited a gasp as the poker came out her back on the other side.

Marcus tried to pull Conrad off Tilda as Geoffrey stood and watched in horror. Conrad knocked Marcus to the Persian rug on the floor and turned to him, his eyes glowing a bright orange-yellow hue and his voice deep and guttural, as part of his fist disappeared into the hole in Tilda's chest.

"*Back off!*" Conrad ordered, causing Marcus to quickly move back a few feet on the rug.

"What *are* you?" Marcus asked, then winced, as Tilda's body, poker and all, fell away from Conrad and began disintegrating before their eyes.

The flesh around her face and hands began to wither and quickly rot away, until her skull and bones were visible. Then she imploded and her remains fell to the floor with her clothes, into a pile of dust.

"What ... just happened?" Marcus asked, convinced he was back in his dream state. None of it could be real, he told himself. Tilda had just deteriorated into dust in a matter of fifteen seconds. It wasn't possible for a decaying human body to do such a thing.

Conrad walked toward him, the eyes losing their glow, and the voice returning to normal. "You will obey me! You are mine, Marcus. *You belong to me.* Together we will stay here. Forever."

"You're not even anything of this world," Marcus said, wanting to wake up if this was some kind of nightmare.

"I once was," he said. "I once was in charge here, and I will be again, damn it."

"What are you talking about?" Marcus asked.

Geoffrey appeared to be in some kind of shock and ignored them, as his eyes went back and forth between Bobby, who stood and stared at everyone, and Tilda's remains, which were a pile of dust beneath the funeral dress she had still been wearing.

Conrad gave Marcus a sardonic smile. "I call myself Conrad after a man whose body I stole decades ago, but in life I was Theodore Ogden, Junior," he said. "And I've come home, and you're going to stay here with me."

"That's not possible," Marcus said, even though *possible* was slowly becoming a word with less limitations during this long night.

"My bloodline was lost to the Laneharts," he said. "Influenza took all my children away from me. But no more."

"What in the hell," Marcus whispered, trying to process it all.

"A slave master isn't looked upon kindly in the afterlife," Conrad said, as he recalled the beginnings of Theodore Ogden, Junior's life after death. Or, *Teddy*. "But I had to find my own Master's favor somehow, and *he* allowed me to come back. And that's what I've done, his work on Earth, through different incarnations, of course."

"I don't understand how any of this can be," Marcus said, shaking his head.

"It was such a delight to find your sister through Frank Castille," Conrad continued, with a smile. "Destiny smiled on me, and I couldn't *not* take advantage. Now come, get up off the floor. Let's begin our life together in our home, Marcus. You're my great-grand-nephew a few times down, but we're *distant* relatives. Besides, we always kept marriage and family blood much closer in the old days."

"I won't begin anything with you," Marcus said, shaking his head. "You're completely insane, and none of this can be happening."

"You are a mirror image of my first cousin, Adam Ogden," Conrad continued his narrative, unfazed by the remarks. "The first time I saw you it was as if he had come back to me. I wanted to be with him so badly, *not* his sister, whom I was forced by my father to marry. In those days we couldn't talk about such forbidden things, much less act out on them. Adam and I were each other's true loves. I loved him so much. If only it had been a different time...but here you are, a new Adam, and we have *now*."

"This is all too twisted," Marcus said.

"Adam died of influenza before my very eyes," Conrad said, walking closer to Marcus. "Or so I *thought*. I ran away from the bedroom and went downstairs to the study. I put a pistol in my mouth and pulled the trigger. But Adam *didn't* die. Doctor Lewis called after me when I ran away to go kill myself. Adam opened his eyes and started to breathe again after being declared dead. He lived fifty more years and died when he was seventy-nine years old. *If only I had waited a few minutes ...*"

"I'm *not* some reincarnated, incestuous kissing cousin of yours from the 1800's, and you're rambling on like a crazy person," Marcus said, backing farther away from him.

"She's gone," Geoffrey said helplessly. He heard nothing Conrad was talking about and was over near the pile of dust Tilda had become. "Despite our problems, she's my wife. Conrad, you have to bring her back to me!"

"I can't," he said, looking away from Marcus over to Geoffrey. "She was what she was, and I have no power over that. She's destroyed, and she took away my chance to try and keep this family pure. Bobby may not be in my direct bloodline, but he's still a relative. It was my chance. *Damn her!*"

"What does that mean now?" Geoffrey asked, shaking his head. He looked over to his son. Bobby's canine teeth were still extended, and the boy appeared antsy and ready to attack something—or someone.

"Bobby is useless to me now," Conrad said. "I'll need someone else. Someone from *this* family. Travis isn't blood. Maybe we should send Maxine away to a fat camp. I don't really want to be a woman, but it may be the only—"

"*No!*" Marcus protested. "This has to stop. This is crazy!"

"No, it isn't," Conrad said, moving toward him. "Don't say that. You're a part of this now."

"I'm not a part of anything," Marcus said, standing. "I'm making sure you both pay for what you did to Zeke. I'm calling the police, and I'm having you both arrested."

"Like hell you will," Conrad said and grabbed him by the arms. "Don't make me hurt you," he said, moving his hands around Marcus' throat. "It will hurt me worse than it will hurt you if I have to—" He looked over to Bobby. "—but if I make you what Geoff is and what Tilda *was*, then I can have you to myself *forever*. Bobby did say he was hungry..."

"Conrad, please," Marcus gasped, as he was being choked. He tried to pull the stronger man's hands off his neck but was too weak. His head was hurting again. "Let go..."

"You will serve me any way I can make you do it," Conrad said. His hands gripped Marcus' neck more tightly, as their eyes locked. "I didn't want to have to do this, I tried the other way, but you leave me no choice, Marcus."

Marcus felt himself getting weaker and continued to try to gasp for air even though it was futile. The room started to go dark around him, as Conrad throttled his neck while giving him a sick, lustful leer.

Just then the tip of a sword plunged through Conrad's throat, spraying crimson red blood into Marcus' face and hair. The sword's tip came only an inch from piercing Marcus before it stopped.

Conrad's grip loosened, and he fell to his knees, coughing and making horrifying gagging sounds, as Travis pulled the sword out of his neck. More blood oozed from the open wound, leaving a stain down the front of his white dress shirt and starting a dark puddle on the green and blue Persian rug below. Marcus fell back to the floor and struggled to catch his breath. Then, instinctively and without hesitation, Travis took off Conrad's head with one swipe. His eyes grew wide and his mouth opened in amazement at his own actions, as the severed head rolled across the living room floor.

"Holy shit, I can't believe I just did that," Travis said. He held on tightly to the replica Civil War sword from his room and then looked over at Marcus on the floor. He clutched his own throat. "Oh, thank God, I can talk again."

"What the hell," Geoffrey cried. He stared at the dust of Tilda and then to Conrad's headless corpse. "All the things he promised me! What am I going to do now? Why? *Why?!*" His blue eyes radiated with intense loathing as he glared over at his stepson. "You bastard! I should kill you. I *will* kill you!"

"Stay the hell away from me, you dead motherfucker," Travis warned, holding up the sword. "I'll put you in the ground forever, asshole."

Geoffrey stayed back but still looked to be plotting a way to get at Travis and attack him. He walked backward and stealthily around the room, circling and trying to make his way toward Bobby, who was off near a corner. The little boy hissed like a cat and showed his fangs.

"Don't worry, son, I'm coming for you," Geoffrey assured the boy. "I won't let that evil brother of yours hurt either one of us."

"That's the pot calling the kettle black, asshole," Travis said, keeping the sword up and slowly moving toward Geoff.

D'Lynn suddenly appeared in the doorway, in a robe and house slippers. "What the tarnation is all the racket—" She stopped and screamed loudly when she saw a decapitated Conrad on the floor and Travis nearby with the sword. "Oh my God!" she cried. *"What happened?*

Oh God, Travis has the Devil in him and is gonna kill us all!"

When D'Lynn turned and saw Bobby with his fangs out and hissing at her, she screamed again and then fainted on to the floor. She appeared so still that Marcus worried she was dead from a heart attack.

"She thinks *I'm* the one who's the bad guy?" Travis asked, a combination of worry and offense written on his red face.

Marcus knelt down to check for a pulse. "She's alive," he said. "She just fainted."

"Let's get out of here," Geoffrey said, grabbing Bobby's hand. "Daddy will find us some blood later. We have to go rest now before the sun is up."

"No, you don't," Travis said to his stepfather, blocking the doorway and extending the sword. "You can't take him out of here. You can't have Bobby!"

"Watch me, you little punk bastard," Geoffrey said.

"I swear to God I'll stick this thing through your heart before I let you take Bobby out of this room," Travis said, catching a wary glance from Geoffrey.

"The sun is about to rise," Geoffrey said. "Let me by, Travis."

"But I'm hungry!" Bobby exclaimed. "I need it *now*, Daddy."

"Then go visit with your Uncle Marcus," Geoffrey said, throwing his brother a disdainful look, and shoving Bobby toward him. The little boy eagerly ran to Marcus, leaping up and lunging for his throat while grabbing at his shoulders.

"Bobby, *no!*" Marcus yelled, trying to hold off the eager, hungry, dead child. He grabbed Bobby around the torso and was doing his best to keep him at bay. The ten-year-old had developed incredible, otherworldly strength and had an iron grip on Marcus' shoulders as he tried to move in and take a bite out of his neck. His dead, blue eyes were bulging with blood lust, and he hissed wildly as he stared down his petrified uncle.

"*Sic him, Bobby!*" Geoffrey called out approvingly, starting to laugh wildly. He bore the wide grin of a proud father whose star athlete son was scoring a touchdown on a high school football field. "You can take him, son! *Do it!*"

"No, Bobby!" Travis ordered. "Get down and leave Uncle Marcus alone!" he said forcefully to his little brother.

The sound of Travis' voice caused Bobby to stop trying to attack Marcus and look over his shoulder.

Travis' eyes met the little boy's. "Get off of Uncle Marcus *now,*" he demanded.

Bobby slowly loosened his grip on Marcus' shoulders and hopped down. "But I'm hungry," he insisted, spying Conrad's headless body on the floor. He quickly ran over and began slurping blood from the stump of Conrad's neck. Travis and Marcus recoiled and couldn't watch the morbid and horrifying sight. They both looked away in Geoffrey's direction.

"What the hell was that?" Geoffrey spat at Travis. "Since when does my son take orders from a little freak like you?"

"You're never home, and you never paid him any attention," Travis said, continuing to point the sword at his stepfather. "Maybe he recognizes the sound of my voice better than he does yours, *Geoff.*"

"He doesn't take orders from you. Ever," Geoffrey said, starting to rub at his neck and looking uncomfortable.

"What's the matter?" Travis asked. "You look like you're not feelin' too good."

Geoffrey shook his head and looked over to where Bobby was hunched over Conrad's remains. "Bobby, come on," he called. "We must go upstairs now."

"Why upstairs?" Travis asked, not lowering the sword. "Is it time to go to sleep? Do you think I'm letting you stay in this house with us? It's not safe having you in here."

"This is *my* house, you little son of a bitch," Geoffrey said to him. He began rubbing more frantically and roughly at his neck. "If anybody gets the privilege of continuing to stay here, it will be *you.*"

"We can outvote you on this," Marcus said, walking over to Travis' side. "You killed Zeke. The only place you're going is jail."

"Uncle Marcus, jail won't hold him," Travis said, not taking his eyes off Geoffrey. "He's not human anymore."

"I don't understand," Marcus replied.

"You saw what Bobby tried to do to you," Travis said. "Geoff is like that, too. He'll be gone forever if the sunlight hits him."

"You are to call me *Dad!*" Geoffrey yelled at him. His nose was twitching, and his eyes were turning red and appeared on the surface to be excessively bloodshot. "I signed the goddamn papers claiming you as mine. My own Dad made me do it, but I still earned the right for a little more respect from you."

"Well, *Geoff,* Conrad said I had to call him Dad, too, and look where he is now," Travis replied. "So I don't really think you're in the position to give orders right now."

"You little bastard—" Geoffrey began, but then started twitching violently. "Oh my God. Bobby, upstairs. *Now!*" He moved as though he was on fire. "Bobby, we must go. Stop what you're doing and come with me!"

Bobby ran over to where Geoffrey stood. "Daddy, I want more!" he demanded. Blood and pieces of Conrad's flesh were stuck to his face and pajamas.

"There isn't time," Geoffrey said quickly, grabbing the boy and stepping around a passed-out D'Lynn as he headed out of the living room and toward the stairs.

Marcus moved past Geoffrey into the foyer to block the stairway, as Travis followed with the sword. "Oh no you don't," Marcus said to his brother. "You're going to face the sunrise for what you did to Zeke. I'll make damn sure of it."

"You stupid faggot," Geoffrey growled at him. "Get the fuck out of my way before I rip your head off."

"If you touch Uncle Marcus, then this sword is going right through you," Travis said from behind him.

Geoffrey started shaking more and sounded as if he were about to hyperventilate. "You two can't do this to me!" he snarled, through clenched teeth. "This is my house. I say what happens here, not you. Now let me go upstairs, goddamn it."

"Bobby, go upstairs," Travis said to the boy and then looked back over at his stepfather. "Geoff stays here."

"No, no, no," Geoffrey said, clutching the boy closer to him. "He goes nowhere without me."

Marcus reached out toward Bobby, but Geoffrey stepped back closer to the front door. "If I have to face the sunrise, then I won't do it alone," he said. "Those are the terms. You better think long and hard before you destroy a poor, defenseless little boy."

"He's not a little boy anymore," Travis said. "He's already dead."

Without warning the front door swung open, and Deputy Wes Washer burst in, his service firearm drawn. "Put down the sword!" Wes ordered Travis half-convincingly, in the most authoritative voice he could muster.

Geoffrey turned toward Wes, fangs out, and hissed at him.

"Oh dear God," Wes cried out, backing out of the open door.

Bobby lunged for Wes as he made his way on to the front porch, but when the rays of the rising sun hit him he screamed out.

"Daddy!" Bobby yelled. Smoke rippled from his body and the top of his head.

Wes ran down the span of the front porch, and Bobby followed after him, despite the burning. "Daddy! Make the police man stop! *It burns!*" he screamed, as he continued chasing Wes down the curved, granite steps and into the grass of the front yard.

"Bobby, *no!*" Travis commanded, as Geoffrey ran for the door after his son. "He's confused! He doesn't know what he's doing!"

"Bobby, *don't!*" Geoffrey yelled after him as he stepped onto the porch, flinching as the smoke began to emanate from his own body.

Geoffrey barely made it to the end of the porch when he exploded, body parts flying and then disintegrating into dust when they landed on the ground.

Travis shook his head, dropped the sword, and began to cry when he reached the edge of the porch and looked out into the yard.

Wes was sprawled out across the grass panting heavily, as he tried to regain his composure and stand.

About five feet away from Wes, the sun's dawn rays shined down on a small pair of dark blue pajamas mixed into a pile of sandy dust in the St. Augustine grass.

34

In the months that followed, the missing persons case involving Geoff Lanehart, his wife Tilda, and their young son Bobby grew increasingly cold. Only three people knew for certain what had happened, and none of them said a word.

A frightened Maxine was the one who had called Wes to Ten Points that morning from upstairs, dialing 911 on her cell phone like Tilda taught her. She only heard the commotion downstairs but never knew what really happened.

As for those who *did* know, Wes Washer was a constant in his father's Baptist congregation as the doors of the church opened on Sunday mornings, Sunday evenings, and Wednesday nights. He prayed for forgiveness and protection from the forces of Satan. He was convinced the devil was present in whatever he had seen that early spring morning at Ten Points, when Geoff and Bobby exploded and then turned to dust before him.

Wes had never made it into the living room to see the remains of Conrad or Tilda, something Marcus and Travis were thankful for.

But soon, it never mattered that Wes had seen what became of Geoffrey and Bobby. In an effort to protect her brother and nephew, Flannery managed to erase Wes' memory of the events—as she drank from him.

The green and blue Persian rug from the living room went missing shortly after the events of the night of the funeral. Marcus told D'Lynn someone spilled wine on it, and the rug was sent away to be cleaned. When a new, similar rug appeared in the living room a few days later, he explained that the old rug couldn't be salvaged. Thankfully it disappeared before detectives inventoried the living room.

When D'Lynn awoke from her fainting spell the night of the funeral, she was quickly ushered by Marcus and Travis back to her room before she could see Conrad's decapitated corpse again. She never asked about Geoffrey and Bobby and later couldn't seem to remember anything she had seen in the living room before passing out. She bought the story of Geoffrey's, Tilda's, and Bobby's disappearances, and Marcus was thankful she had seemingly blocked out all the bad things. She carried on in her duties as head housekeeper at Ten Points.

While the disappearances of the three Laneharts gave the media and the north Monroe gossip mill plenty to talk about, the vanishing of the family attorney, James Ruffin, III was kept more hushed. A search of his home turned up child pornography on one of his computer's hard drives, and his bank records showed suspicious deposits during the last months before his disappearance. Investigators first wondered if he was involved in the disappearances of the other three Laneharts, and the conjecture was finally that he had run away when everything became too much for him. The embarrassment and humiliation of the child porn discovery led his family to quietly pretend as if he were dead. Little did they know that no pretending was necessary, and the porn had been planted on the computer by Conrad as insurance long before Ruffin was killed by Tilda and Rochelle.

Marcus had his things moved to Ten Points from his apartment in San Diego, including the maroon, modest Toyota Corolla he preferred over the flashier cars there. He assumed guardianship of Travis and Maxine and helped D'Lynn run the household while he took over the various Lanehart business holdings. Since no one else in the family was left to give him guidance, familiarizing himself with that took up most of his free time. It also kept him from dwelling on Zeke and Landon and gave him an outlet to keep his grief at bay.

Marcus began to dream of Zeke, but unlike their goodbye in the field, the dreams were fleeting and nonsensical and only his imagination seeking something impossible. Zeke told him in the field he would find his way back, but Marcus couldn't put any faith in it. At the end of the day, as he sat out on the front porch of Ten Points beneath a starry sky, he would look up and wonder if there was any truth to what Zeke told him. The two days they had together again were all he could hold on to and know was real.

Travis returned to school a few days after the funeral and pretended as if nothing had happened. He sometimes wondered how cool it would be if the other kids knew he had cut off a demon's head, but that was a secret he couldn't share—especially after Marcus reminded him the body Conrad inhabited had belonged to some other poor soul. Like other of life's mysteries, the teenager and his uncle realized they would probably never know to whom the body had belonged. Another of Conrad's victims was all they could assume. They made a pact to never tell anyone how they had disposed of the stranger's body.

Travis continued to date Regan and now had only her disapproving mother to deal with. Geoffrey and Tilda were no longer there to frown upon the relationship between the two of them. The two teenagers still had one more year of high school ahead of them, and Marcus urged the boy to think more about college and less about romance. Travis brushed off the suggestion, knowing not everyone was as unlucky in love as his Uncle Marcus had been.

"There are rats in the wall downstairs," D'Lynn said to Marcus one day in the dining room as they were having breakfast and coffee. "I hear rumblin' in the basement walls. I put out traps, but there ain't nothin' gettin' caught."

"That's strange," he replied, not thinking much of it at the time.

A few weeks later, the sounds persisted, and both a contractor and exterminator came to the house. Both yelled out in terror at the sight before them when the contractor tore out part of the wall.

"What's the matter?" Marcus asked, running downstairs after hearing the commotion from upstairs.

All color had left both the men's faces, and one of them looked as if he were about to start weeping. The other looked at Marcus and quietly and shakily pointed to the hole in the wall.

Marcus walked over and was taken aback when he saw what had them so upset.

The skeletal remains of what appeared to be an infant were inside the cramped space.

The coroner later determined the remains had been there at least thirty years.

"More like thirty-four-and-a-half years," Flannery said disgustedly, refusing to elaborate, when Marcus later told her about the grisly discovery.

Marcus knew not to prod Flannery on how she knew the answer to that mystery. He added it to the list of other things he wouldn't ask her, like why she was only around at night. Deep down he knew the answer, but if he didn't hear her actually say it then maybe there was still a chance his suspicions weren't true.

He thought about the little boy who was scared to be put inside the wall. He had told Marcus he had always been in the house and learned to walk by watching Bobby.

Marcus never again awoke to a small child holding his hand in the blackness of night after the ordeal with Conrad ended.

FLANNERY

"He was an extremely handsome wannabe actor and sometime model who friends say was willing to do whatever it took to become famous."

The blonde cable TV news channel commentator wore a smirk on her heavily made-up face as she gave the story to viewers across America, with dramatic enunciations and pauses in just the right places, as she read from the teleprompter. Her voice blared across the large-screen TV that had been left on in the study at Ten Points.

The large swivel chair at the desk was turned toward the wall where the TV was mounted, as the one who was seated attentively watched.

"It's a story with the makings of a Hollywood mystery written all over it ... Jimmy Van Buren was only twenty-nine years old when he was last seen at a well-known gay bar in West Hollywood seven years ago. People who know him say he had fallen on hard times and resorted to prostitution after his acting career failed. Sadly, his only claim to fame was a, err hmmm, large supporting role in a late-night cable soft core adult movie titled Lays of our Lives. *Hey, America, what can I say, that was the name of it. You really can't make this stuff up. Anyway, on a more serious note, Jimmy Van Buren's identical twin brother, Doctor Remy Van Buren, a successful general practitioner in Chicago, has renewed the search for his missing brother after reported sightings in Louisiana. Doctor Remy Van Buren held a news conference today. Here's what he had to say."*

An extremely handsome man with a well-sculpted face, a chin with a familiar cleft, and thick wavy brown hair appeared at a podium, wearing a gray designer suit and a solemn expression as he read from a prepared statement.

"For more than seven years my family has sought answers and hoped beyond hope that we would have some closure in the disappearance of my twin brother, Jimmy," Remy Van Buren said, occasionally glancing down

at a piece of paper in his right hand at the bottom of the screen. *"In the early days after he went missing, we had great faith he would be found alive and with a simple explanation of where he had been. As time went on, we began to accept the fact it wasn't likely to happen. But now, we have new hope. Numerous sources have reported sightings of my brother in Louisiana, in both the New Orleans metropolitan area, as well as near the city of Monroe in north Louisiana. Investigators in both areas have been contacted, and I plan to travel there myself to seek answers and hopefully bring my brother home. Let this be known: I will leave no stone unturned and will help follow every lead there is until I know where my brother is and have satisfactory answers as to what happened to him."*

The swivel chair creaked a bit as the person sitting in it leaned in closer to the big-screen TV on the wall above.

Without warning the overhead light came on, as Flannery appeared in the doorway. "Who's in here?" she demanded, walking into the room. "Show yourself!"

The chair spun around, as the face from the past greeted her with a smile, and the woman used an index finger to twirl her long blonde hair.

"Hello, *whore,*" she said to Flannery.

MARCUS

"I got the last box of my things from San Diego today. It looks like I'm back in Louisiana to stay," Marcus said into his iPhone, as he unpacked the said box in his bedroom upstairs at Ten Points.

"Oh damn it, please come back," Jane Waldenson said, on the other end. "What am I going to do without my Marky Mark?"

"I guess you'll have to come up with somebody new to bestow the nickname of a Calvin Klein model-turned-rapper-turned movie star on to," Marcus laughed. "I miss you, too, Jane. Peter was a tool, and you don't have to worry. Nobody at the *Sun-Times,* or anywhere for that matter, will ever know you were my source."

"I know you'll never tell," Jane said. "So you're sure you can't come back?"

"Not even if I wanted to," he said. "I suddenly have two kids and five businesses to look after." *And other things to keep covered up until they nail the final nail in my coffin one day,* he thought.

The bones of the infant found inside the wall were processed and in a box at the coroner's office. Investigators had decided after a fruitless and emotional interrogation of D'Lynn that no answers would ever come, since Maximilian and Jessica Lanehart were both dead. D'Lynn had kept mum about dropping Izzy's name as she was badgered with questions by detectives. Finally, a lawyer hired by Marcus showed up and pulled her away from the questioning.

Since there was no DNA of Maximilian or Jessica on file anywhere, and the fact Marcus refused to provide a sample, the case of the mysterious infant in the wall would grow cold over time.

"I *cannot* imagine you as a father," she said jokingly. "I hope you're not the one cooking for those poor kids."

"Nope," he said. "We have a couple of other people here for that."

"I can't imagine you as a businessman either. Even though I'm sure you'll be great at it," Jane said to Marcus.

"It wasn't by choice," he told her. "It all just worked out that way." His thoughts went to Zeke. He tried to quickly will it all away and remain in his pleasant mood.

"Will you ever tell me what happened?" she asked him. "You seemed so sad and lost the last time I talked to you. Right after your brother and his wife and kid disappeared. But you seemed sad about something else."

"I was, and I still am," he said, recalling Zeke's final words to him.

I'll find my way back ... however I can—whatever it takes! I swear on everything I believe in I'll find my way back to you!

Marcus started to cry before he could stop himself. "Oh Jane," he said, tears burning his eyes. "I found him but then I lost him again."

"Who?" she said. "Landon? Oh my God, did you find out what happened to him?"

"No, it wasn't Landon," he said, sniffling and getting control of himself. "Geez, I need to man up."

"It's okay to cry sometimes! Just don't start chewing tobacco or wearing boots, Marcus. No matter where you are, just be you."

"I will," he said. "I need to go. You take care, Jane."

"Oh don't worry," she said. "I will. My guy is gonna be here any minute to take me out. We're going to this little place up the coast for dinner. And maybe a movie after. *Or maybe...*" She began to giggle.

Marcus laughed along with her. "Well, you will have to tell me about him sometime. Have a good time, and I'll talk to you soon."

Jane set down her own iPhone, just as the doorbell rang at her small apartment in San Diego's Little Italy district. She opened the door to a large bouquet of red roses greeting her. There was more than a dozen of the roses, enough to obscure the face of the man holding them.

"Oh my gosh!" she exclaimed brightly. "You are just too much."

The dark blond, blue-eyed man finally looked around the bouquet, and stared at her with the dazzling handsome smile that had mesmerized Jane the first time she had seen it across the room at a coffee shop a month earlier.

"I hope you like them," he said to her, leaning in and giving her a kiss on the lips. "I know it's not Valentine's Day or anything, but I couldn't resist getting them for you."

"They're beautiful," she said, taking them from him and closing the door as he walked inside the apartment. "Let me go put them in some water really fast, and then we can go."

"So you really like them?" he asked, not losing the smile.

"Of course!" she insisted, affectionately touching his arm. "Red roses are my favorite."

"Look in my eyes and say it," he said, keeping his tone affectionate but maintaining strong eye contact. "Don't lie to me. I'll *know* if you're lying to me."

"Oh Conrad!" she said to him, with a laugh. "You know I wouldn't do that."

View other Black Rose Writing titles at www.blackrosewriting.com/books
and use promo code PRINT to receive a 20% discount when purchasing.

BLACK ROSE
writing™

53992825R00167

Made in the USA
Lexington, KY
28 July 2016